ALPHAS POSSESSION

JESSICA HALL

Format Design by CED

Editing by Kylie Hammel @Reedsy

Proofread by Arden Black

Cover by MCDamon

Art Design GNIN https://www.facebook.com/max.gnin

PACK OF HOWLING READERS

Hello, Pack of howling Readers,

This tale is not for the faint of heart or those who shy away from a bit of fur and fang. The four dashing and delightfully savage wolfish gents in this story aren't exactly gentlemen with our leading lady. Yes, you heard right: four. This is a reverse harem romance, so our heroine is romanced by multiple enticing men who all hold a piece of her heart – and no, there's no need to pick a favourite! This book might just tug at some triggers, though, including domination, aggression, blood play, dubcon, and a hearty amount of snarling and biting. If you aren't familiar with reverse harem or dark romance, it may be time to take a walk on the wild side – or consult your friend Google. If you're okay with a dark, thrilling journey through the moonlit world of werewolves, then buckle up – this is going to be a howling good ride! See you in the den.

TO THE LANGUAGE BUFFS

Greetings, Language Buffs (and Grammar Police)

Fun fact: I'm an Aussie who decided to tango with American English. So, if a 'centre' instead of a 'center' or a 'favour' instead of a 'favor' slips through, don't throw a boomerang at me. We're here for the twists, turns, and tantalizing text, not to play Grammar Sheriff. If that's too much, maybe try wrestling a crocodile—it might be easier. Now let's loosen up, let the language rules slide, and leap into this howling saga. Onwards and upwards, my literary adventurers!

CHAPTER
ONE

~**H**arlow~

My Omega test results have just been released, and over a hundred bidders have joined the online auction. As my sister, Zara, and I watch the screen, I feel sick to my stomach. How did my life become this? All because my gene test proved potent—the perfect match for an all-Alpha Pack.

We can't see who the bidders are, but we recognize some of the pack names, and I pray they don't win. My heart races, and I can't watch anymore. I stare down at my pink cotton pajama shorts, picking at the lint to distract myself from my unraveling life. I can't believe Mr. Black is selling me off to a future I never wanted.

Zara and I have been stuck in the Omega facility since our parents died. The facility owners groomed us to become the perfect Omegas, and now they're auctioning me off to the highest bidder. This isn't the life I imagined or wanted. Not one I would choose for myself.

My twin, Zara, loves being Omega: the attention, the never-ending praise, and the adoration. I wish I shared even half of her enthusiasm or confidence.

1

For twins, we couldn't be more opposite. We look identical, except for the scar that runs across the bridge of Zara's nose, under her eyes, and to her ear. Despite that, her beauty is undeniable. But a lot of her beauty comes from the way she carries herself. She's confident, tough, yet sweet—the perfect Omega. Qualities all Alphas want in their Omega.

While I'm standoffish and quiet, Zara thrives in the spotlight.

As yesterday's events come to mind, I'm once again plunged into that abyss of fear and helplessness. The auction is taking place, and I'm terrified of the outcome. What if the notorious Obsidian Pack—the so-called Omega Killers—wins the bid for me? How will I survive?

~THE DAY BEFORE, OMEGA TEST ANNOUNCEMENT~

Zara grips my fingers and gives them a squeeze as we wait for my Omega gene score to come back. I had hoped we would both bloom at the same time, but fate always has other plans for me. Fate really likes to test me, and testing is literally what the Omega Sanctuary does. Now, I am worried I will be separated from my sister, doomed to a fate I don't want and doomed to it alone.

"They said we would stay together, Low. They won't separate us. Omega twins are rare. You'll see; everything will work out," Zara whispers, nudging me with her elbow. I smile sadly at her and nod, praying she is right.

We sit in the lobby of the auction house, waiting before I'll be put up for auction, depending on how high my gene tests come back. The door to a nearby office bursts open, revealing an overjoyed Mrs. Yates. I've never seen a woman so ecstatic as she squeals excitedly, waving the papers above her head.

Zara and I jump at the startling sound, while the auctioneer, Mr. Black, looks up at her from where he sits in his expensive suit. "What's made you so excited, Yates?" he asks.

Her eyes are wide as she stares at me. "She broke the record," Mrs. Yates whispers, her eyes still glued to my shocked expression.

Zara glances at me, and I at her, both of us confused out of our minds.

"What? Impossible! No Omega's pheromones sit above fifty-five. The score hasn't changed for years," he says as he gets up from his seat and reaches for the paper in Mrs. Yates's hands.

The awed look on her face doesn't fade while Mr. Black snatches the results and looks them over.

"Eighty-seven percent pure Omega," Mrs. Yates beams. I gasp at her words.

"This can't be real. Test her again," Mr. Black huffs, forcing the papers back in her hands in disbelief. I agree with him. Test me again. I think. This is not something I want in my records.

"They tested four times," she murmurs. The grin on her lips nearly splits her face in half. Her graying hair almost looks white under the bright fluorescent lights, and I feel the blood drain from my face.

Then, out of nowhere, Mr. Black howls and breaks out in laughter. "We just hit fucking bank, baby. Do you have any idea how much we can get for her?" He all but jumps with joy.

"Wait, you said we would be auctioned together," Zara intervenes, glancing at me nervously. As always, Zara is ready to jump to my defense, while all I can do is stare at everyone in horror. This can't be happening!

Eighty-seven percent is an Alpha Pack status level, meaning an all-Alpha Pack. Panic envelopes me, spreading through my body like wildfire, taking over every muscle and all my senses.

"Things change; she's worth too much. She'll be auctioned tomorrow. Fuck, she will bring in some money. Hopefully, enough to save this place," Mr. Black announces.

I watch him flick his dark hair from his face. The paperwork miraculously appears in his hands again, and he stares down at the score. I can almost see the dollar signs cha-chinging in his eyes.

"Wait! Stop! We're twins; you can't separate us," Zara fights back, still keeping her voice despite knowing it is pointless.

Mr. Black sneers as his eyes flick to her and narrow slightly. "You're owned by the state. You live under my care, and raising Omegas costs a lot of money. She goes to auction tomorrow, without you. But you never know, once you bloom, maybe whoever buys her will want a spare." He cackles, sounding as evil as ever, and wanders off while Mrs. Yates flashes us a smile full of pity.

"It's alright, girls. You'll fetch a high price, Harlow. That means your buyer will take good care of you," Mrs. Yates tries to comfort us.

Tears burn my eyes as Zara's grip on my hand tightens. Sure, as if I don't know what she means by saying someone would take good care of me. As good as they can after buying me at auction to make a damn breeder out of me. And to top it off, they'll separate me from my twin.

Zara's gasp pulls me out of my thoughts, and I instantly look up at the computer screen. My heart sinks: five hundred thousand dollars.

I stare at my sister. Her mouth hangs open, just as shocked as I am. We keep waiting for the pack name to appear. We have to see who had offered the highest bid and won me.

Yet the moment the name pops up, dread pools in my stomach, a pit forming so deep I forget how to breathe.

Obsidian Pack.

It is a pack I've heard of, but not for good reasons. It is also an all-Alpha Pack, that much I know. I shake my head as tears brim and spill from my eyes, slipping down my cheeks and dripping off my chin. Zara's lips quiver.

"No!" she gasps, horrified. That pack is notorious for losing Omegas, and I will likely be no different.

The Obsidian Pack bought six girls from the sanctuary while we lived here, and not one survived. None could take the Alpha's knot. Not even with the serum. The other girls in the facility called that pack the Omega Killers!

4

I swallow the bile.

"Maybe we can tell them no," Zara suggests in a whisper, but it offers no hope. We are the state's property and have no choice in the government's eyes. We owe the state for caring for us, so we have no say at all. Omegas are property because Omegas are the only ones who can provide an heir to continue Alpha's bloodline. We are revered and special, and apparently, we fetch a high price.

All Omegas end up in packs eventually, but I didn't think I would be sold off to one so cruel and feared. I never imagined I would end up with the Omega Killers.

Zara wraps her arms around me, her own tears wetting my shoulder. "I won't let them take you," she promises me fiercely. "We'll figure this out, I promise. I won't let you become another victim of the Obsidian Pack."

LATER THAT AFTERNOON, I RECEIVE THE OBSIDIAN PACK ALPHA'S SERUM. It's supposed to help Omegas acclimate to our Alpha. It also ensures the Alpha DNA is passed on to its potential heir because once an Alpha marks his other pack members, the DNA changes.

Mrs. Yates sits with me while I rub my ass, sore from where the doctor jabbed me with his needle. Mrs. Yates squeezes my fingers. "I'm sorry, Harlow, I tried to talk Mr. Black out of it."

"That pack ... They killed six girls. Six, Mrs. Yates, six girls!" I whisper, aware that I will be the next to die at their hands.

Or claws.

Or teeth.

Or knots!

"You're stronger than the others," she offers, but I shake my head. "I'm sorry, but ..." she sighs. Nothing she says would make me feel better.

"Promise once I die, you won't send Zara to them. I know she will test just as high; we're twins," I beg her.

Mrs. Yates nods. "I'll do my best. Promise." She nudges me and escorts me back to my room.

A FEW DAYS PASS BEFORE THE PACK COMES TO COLLECT ME. ZARA DOES MY hair and make-up. She does hers too, but I can't figure out why. Despite her being the more girly of the two of us, she hates make-up just as much as I do.

Today, I'll meet my pack. A pack I want no part of. Watching the clock only makes me more nervous, while Zara sniffles as she fixes my hair to look precisely like hers. We're pulling on our matching dresses when I hear the buzz of the pager, telling me they have arrived.

My skin prickles as fear seeps into every cell of my body, but I feel cold when I get up to leave the room. The moment I reach for the door, I feel something sprayed on the side of my face. I swat at it and turn to see Zara holding a spray can in her hands. Tears fill her eyes, and my vision blurs when she sprays it again.

"Why are you spraying me with a de-scenter?" I ask, choking and coughing when some gets in my mouth. During my coughing fit, she jabs me in the arm with a needle. Before I realize what is happening, my legs turn wobbly, and I reach out for her.

Zara drags me back and tucks me into bed, but I fight to remain conscious.

"Zara!" I murmur in panic.

"I won't let you die. Just know I love you," she whispers, kissing my cheek.

What did she jab me with, and where did she get it? I can't move as I watch her scoop up my bag and ID in horror.

6

This explains why she used make-up. She needs to cover the scar on her face. It is the only thing that sets us apart. Just before she walks out, she comes over to me.

"When you wake, pretend to be me; I won't let the Obsidian Pack kill you. I know you hate this Omega stuff, and I can't let you go through it. Escape and keep using the de-scenter until you do." her words become softer as my vision blurs. My surroundings slowly vanish as my sight is stolen by whatever she used to drug me.

"I love you, Low. Now be a good Omega," are the last words I hear before the door shuts behind her.

She's taking my place. Zara's taking my place and sacrificing herself for me. I'm killing her, killing my own sister, my twin. A lone tear slips down my cheek at that thought as my paralyzed body gets sucked into the oblivion of darkness.

CHAPTER
TWO

~H arlow~

FOUR DAYS LATER

So far, there has been no news, not a single word from my sister. I'm out of the de-scenter she left, having used the last of it last night.

Mrs. Yates is nervous when she picks me up from my room. Today is the day Zara is supposed to be tested, but I'm getting retested in her place. Mrs. Yates hardly speaks to me and is tense as we walk to the auction house. I did my make-up the same way my sister occasionally did hers, keeping up the appearance that I am Zara.

"You never know; your test scores could be as high as your sister's," she chimes happily as we reach the doors leading in.

Oh, they will be high, alright, because the tests have already been run, I think dryly.

"Have you heard anything from Harlow?" I ask, curiosity lacing my voice.

Mrs. Yates becomes even more nervous, but she remains silent and gives a swift shake of her head.

8

After they run their tests and take my blood, I wait in the same lobby at the auction house, sitting in the same hard, blue chair as before, only this time, Zara isn't with me holding my hand. This time I am completely alone.

Yet when Mrs. Yates comes back, overly excited and bubbly, confusion crosses my features. Surely, I didn't test higher than before. I try to be upbeat, to act how I know Zara would.

"What's the verdict?" I ask, pretending to be excited.

"Perfect, eighty-seven percent, just like Harlow," she announces, though I don't miss the way her lip quivers at the mention of my name.

A tear slides down my cheek, and my heart starts pounding against my ribcage.

"Mrs. Yates?" I whisper when Mr. Black strolls into the lobby.

He snatches the paper from her hands; his greedy eyes take in the numbers printed on the page before a sly smirk spreads across his lips.

"Splendid! Marvelous! Unbelievable! The luck, Mrs. Yates, two in a row! Oh, those Obsidians will jump on this one too. I'll launch the auction," he cheers and rushes away before either of us can utter a word or objection.

I just sit and stare after him. Mr. Black's shiny, black shoes click on the sterile floor as he rushes off in his flashy suit. It looks new, and I bet he got it with all the money they got from my previous auction. The money that might have cost my sister her life.

"Mrs. Y-Yates?" I stammer as I stare after him.

"Harlow didn't make it, Zara. I'm so sorry. She couldn't take his knot, and he tried to force it. Harlow bled out," Mrs. Yates admits, staring down at her feet. I hope she feels ashamed of herself, of how they keep selling off girls, knowing they'll end up dead.

I blink back tears. My eyes sting, and I suddenly can't breathe. Something deep inside me shatters into a million sharp pieces, slicing through me like a razor's edge.

A deep, guttural scream leaves my lips as I collapse to the floor.

For days, I wondered, yet had heard nothing. I figured no news is good news.

A wave of pain tears through me and steals the air from my lungs. I killed her; I killed my twin. She died because of me.

I remember little besides the wailing howls I make before a pinch in my neck causes everything to shut off. Everything goes black, and I welcome the darkness. Anything to stop the pain, I am sure will tear me apart and leave nothing behind but fractured pieces.

I am in an omega facility hospital room when I come to. Mrs. Yates hovers over me. I try to sit up, but the handcuffs on my wrist prevent me from moving.

"Seven hundred and fifty thousand! We need to celebrate," Mr. Black hollers.

My head rolls to the side, and I instinctively look for Zara before I remember, with ice-cold tendrils piercing my soul all over again. I start to hyperventilate, and Mrs. Yates clutches my face in her hands.

"It's alright, honey; the Obsidian Pack didn't win this time. Nightbane did. See?" She points to the screen over on the doctor's desk as if that would somehow make me feel better.

That's what she thinks I care about? My sister is dead, and that is what she thinks I'm worried about? Tears stream down my cheeks, and I shake my head.

"I know, honey, I'm sorry, I'm sorry about Harlow," she whispers, wiping tears from my cheeks.

She barely lived. We aren't even eighteen yet; we still have two weeks. I bloomed bloody early while still under the facility's care. Two more weeks, and we could've signed ourselves out, paid off the debts, and found our own packs! Zara always intended to stay, but I knew I could talk her into leaving. Instead, I did this to her.

I killed her!

Sobs wrack my body, and days slip by. Mr. Black keeps me sedated and out of it.

I'm staring at the ceiling when I feel a jab in my ass that causes my gaze to pull away from its standoff with the spider in the corner, spinning its web.

I glance down to see the doctor pull my pants over my hip when the door bursts open.

"Don't jab her; she isn't Zara!" Mr. Black screams, bursting through the doors.

"What?" The doctor's voice trembles.

Mr. Black grabs him by his shoulders and starts shaking the poor man, snarling like a maniac, "Tell me you didn't jab her already!"

The confused doctor frantically looks between the raging man holding him and me. I glance at Mr. Black, wondering if I have ever seen him so furious.

He growls, and I try to sit up, but my wrists are still bound to the bed, so my body is jerked back. The moment my back hits the mattress, his hand connects with my cheek.

My head twists to the side and collides with the wall; my teeth gnash together, and the copper taste of blood fills my mouth as I bite my tongue.

"She isn't Zara; she's fucking Harlow. Autopsy reports just came back; there is a scar on her face," Mr. Black snarls, walking over to the sink basin and wetting a cloth.

He strides back, and I flinch away from him, but he grabs my hair and viciously wipes my face. Once he's done and my face is make-up free, he growls even louder.

"You have no idea what you did! Now I have to try to clean up this mess!" he screams at the top of his lungs before slapping me again. A yelp escapes me as I try to bring my hands up to protect my face, yet he doesn't stop assaulting me.

I pull my knees up, tuck my face between them, and wait for Mr. Black to stop. When he finally does, my scalp aches from him yanking my hair out, my body is bruised, and my lip is bleeding.

The doctor runs out of the room, escaping Mr. Black's wrath. My assailant hits the intercom and dials two sets of numbers into it.

"Mr. Black, you better tell me you have the girl I bought," a deep baritone voice comes through the speaker.

"Who the fuck is that?" Another voice joins the conversation, but this one is even more profound and much more angry.

The men argue until Mr. Black finally breaks his silence. "Gentlemen, there has been a mix-up."

"Where is my Omega? That skank hadn't even bloomed. How the fuck is it even possible for such a fuck up to happen?" the first man roars.

THREE

~*H*arlow~

"Mr. Bowman, she is here, but we have an issue. Mr. Keller also purchased this girl tonight before you called about the mix up," Mr. Black admits. A growl comes from the intercom, and I swear it shakes the windows and I feel his threatening aura through the phone.

"Doesn't matter; I bought her originally. I have a claim, so give him his money back!" the first man growls, sounding equally as pissed off as his opponent.

"See, that's the issue. If it were only the money, I could simply fix it, Mr. Bowman."

"Then what is it?" the annoyed man snaps.

Mr. Black shoots me a glare over his shoulder, his lips pulling back over his teeth in a snarl, and I drop my gaze to my lap.

"I already injected her with Mr. Keller's serum," Mr. Black answers.

"You what?" Mr. Keller roars through the phone, making Mr. Black jump.

"So, wait, what does that mean? Fucking reverse his serum," Mr. Bowman argues.

I can't understand why these men are still trying to negotiate since both of them seem equally unhappy about the serum already being injected.

"Like fuck you will; that was the last of my serum!" Mr. Keller snarls.

Okay, at that point, I take back my previous observation. The injection isn't the issue; the lack of serum is.

"Not my fucking problem, Keller," Mr. Bowman snarls as I take the risk of peeking at Mr. Black. He's rubbing his temples as if he has a headache.

"Mr. Bowman, you know it can't be reversed. If you can't share, I'm sorry, but I have to hand her over to Mr. Keller. He marked his pack last night. His DNA is no longer pure, and that was the last of his serum," Mr. Black explains. I gasp. Mr. Keller, whoever he is, will now have to rely solely on me to produce an heir!

"I don't see how that is my issue; it's not my fault he didn't take more samples before marking his pack mates!"

Mr. Black sighs, clearly done with the pointless arguing back and forth. "I have five other girls that rank in the high forties. You can take your pick or try them all, but I am sorry, Mr. Bowman. You have eighteen samples left, and this is Mr. Keller's last sample."

"Whatever you paid him, I will cover it," Mr. Keller interrupts.

Mr. Bowman remains quiet, waiting for Mr Black's rulings.

"And you can have the other girls," Mr. Black adds.

I glare at him, equally shocked and disgusted with the man.

"Fine, fine, we have a deal," Mr. Bowman gives in, and Mr. Black sighs before he pins me with his glare.

"I will wire the money to you, Bowman, and Black?" Mr Keller adds.

"Yes, Alpha Keller."

"I will send my mother to pick up the girl; she will remain with her until she turns eighteen."

"Very well. I will personally remain with her to ensure no more blunders."

"Make sure you do because your life now depends on it," Mr. Keller warns Mr. Black before hanging up.

Tears stream down my cheeks. My sister is gone, and I've been sold, again. Fate is beyond cruel.

The very next day, a woman in a flashy-looking sports car comes to retrieve me. Her clothes scream money, and her dark hair and equally dark eyes are vibrant. She wears an elegant suit and stilettos, her smile is soft, and her tone of voice is kind. I find her energy soothing as she escorts me to the car. The moment I climb in with my satchel full of Zara's stuff, she turns on me.

I jump in fright, tugging the shoulder strap higher and getting ready to use it as a shield. "Who marked up your face? Did that prick Black do that?" she asks, her hand reaching to cup my cheek.

Her touch is feather-light, her thumb brushing over my swollen eyelid. She clicks her tongue, glaring at the place I called home for far too many years.

"Very well, my son will deal with him," she says, starting the car with a growl.

We drive in silence. Doesn't it bother her that her son literally bought a breeder? Maybe she was acquired the same way. Most Omegas enjoy this lifestyle, yet I see the bitter truths of the control the Alphas have.

"Are you hungry, Harlow?" she asks as we go around a sharp bend, heading into town.

"A little," I admit. She nods.

"I saw a nice little restaurant on the way here. We will stop and grab a bite to eat," she says, reaching for my hand. She gives it a gentle squeeze before gripping the steering wheel again.

We arrive at the diner and eat, sharing very little in conversation as I am still very uncertain about her son and his mates. I don't want to end up with the life of a breeder, being mounted solely for heirs. Hana, as she introduced herself, attempts to reassure me of her son's intentions. She says they want more than heirs. They want a mate to love and grow old with. Upon getting back in the car, Hana begins talking again about Mr. Keller as she merges onto the highway.

"No need to be frightened. My son is a good man, and so are his pack mates. You'll like them," she says, smiling at me.

I am about to ask her their names when suddenly, we're hit. A truck slams into the side of our car and tosses the little vehicle into the barrier. She screams, blood gushing from her head where she banged it on the steering wheel when the truck starts to back up.

It stops before accelerating and hitting us again. When the door crashes into my side, glass rains down all over the place, and the car begins to roll down the hill. The creak and groan of metal is loud, but not as loud as our screams. The car finally stops and lands on its roof. I stupidly unplug my seatbelt and fall to the roof, the glass tearing my hands apart.

Mrs. Keller is slumped and dangling from her seat. I hear men shouting from the road.

"Down here, quick. Grab the bitch, and let's go!"

I blink, blood tainting my vision from the gash on my head, and I shake the woman. She groans, peering around as the voices grow closer. She turns, and I will never forget the look she gives me. One of pure fear before she screams at me.

"Run! Run, Harlow. They are coming for you!" she screams.

I don't need to be told twice.

Snatching my satchel off the roof, I clamber out, my back tearing open on a jagged piece of metal, and I hear her fall out of her seat behind me. I start running like she told me, expecting her to catch up. I have no idea what is going on, but I do as she asked, trusting this woman blindly. Only, she never catches up, and I stumble blindly into the woods.

CHAPTER
FOUR

~H arlow~

TWO YEARS LATER

My landlord's voice in the stairwell makes my stomach drop as she speaks to the handyman about the damn light fixtures that don't work. I cringe, tugging my blazer higher to cover my neck and part of my face, praying she doesn't notice me. My rent is four months late. I try to sneak past Martha by holding my ratty-looking handbag higher to cover my face, but I don't go unmissed when I am forced to squeeze past her as I hastily try to escape.

"Zara!" she shrieks, as I try to escape her wrath. I pause and slowly turn to face her. Her reddish, graying hair is pulled into a bun on the top of her head, with two snake-shaped hair picks stuck through it. Martha steps around the handyman standing on a ladder pulling apart the old light fixture high up on the wall.

"Where is my rent money? You promised to have it last week!" she screeches, and I internally groan. Martha is a tough old woman, and she looks the part with her denim jacket, black boots, and dark-blue, skinny-leg jeans on. No one messes with Martha here.

She would kick your ass and toss you to the curb if you tried. I had seen her beat a group of vandals that once got past the crumbling lobby. Martha whipped their asses real good and broke a skateboard over one of their heads. Safe to say, they didn't return. It secretly makes me wonder if she isn't human. She strikes fear in everyone, but she is also quite understanding and lovely, too. As long as you're not four months behind in rent like I am.

"I will have it. I just need a little—" I try to tell her.

"No, it has been four months. You have until the end of the day, 6 p.m., missy," she says, clicking her fingers at me before pointing her index finger at me.

"6 p.m.," I nod my head and gulp.

Martha is usually nice. I, however, have surpassed the tipping point of her generosity. Sure, the place is a dump, but it is cheap, but I can't even afford cheap at this point. I can't even sell anything because the place I rent comes fully furnished, and I have little in the way of possessions.

"I have a job interview today. Soon, I will have it," I plead my case to her.

"Soon isn't good enough. I have bills to pay."

I rummage through my pockets and pull out my last hundred dollars, besides some loose change floating around in the bottom of my handbag. Brianna, my only friend in the city, recently introduced me to her boss at the local strip club she works at. Talon lets me wash dishes occasionally, so I have enough money to buy some groceries and money to get around the city while I hunt for a job. Martha snatches it, shaking it in the air at me.

"I am sick of the crumbs. I mean it, Zara. 6 p.m. or I will have Mike change the locks," she says, pointing to Mike. He hangs his head and smiles sadly. The dude is creepy as fuck and mute, but he always comes running when something needs to be fixed.

"I'll have something for you this afternoon," I tell her.

"No, you will have all of it. You owe me nearly four thousand in rent plus utilities. I was nice enough to let you stay here with your fake ID and your shitty backstory, which I don't for one second believe," she snaps, turning away from me and dismissing me.

Shit! Martha figured me out. I wonder about how long she's known and if she saw straight through my fake ID from the start, giving me the benefit of the doubt. God, I hope the company I am interviewing at doesn't look too closely at me. They may question why I don't have the scar from Zara's ID photo. Or why I am using a dead girl's ID in the first place. Though I always explain away the scar as my expert skills in contouring. Ha! I can't contour to save my life. They don't need to know that, though.

Technically, she is my twin. We just aren't 100% identical. Similar, but not identical. Twins are one and the same, so it's not like it is exactly a fake. It is my dead sister's. Not like she is going to use it. And I can't risk the Omega facility finding me. No one is looking for a dead girl! But I will worry about that later. I have a job interview and need to get to the city center in twenty minutes or I will be late.

I race across town for the interview and just make it, with only three minutes to spare. The skyscraper is intimidating as I gaze up at the massive building. I was shocked when I got a call back to be interviewed here. They must be desperate, because just stepping into the lobby makes me feel way out of my element. It's some tech company, and I am interviewing for a receptionist position.

Walking in, I follow the signs to the elevator and find the correct floor. A woman approaches me the instant I step out through the elevator doors. Her little black dress is tight, showing her curves and ample cleavage. Her blonde, wavy hair is tied in a ponytail, high on her head. She has porcelain-perfect skin and bright red lipstick on. She is beautiful. Her heels click on the marble floors as she makes her way over to me. She sniffs the air as she stops in front of me.

"You must be Zara. I'm Leila. We talked on the phone," she says, holding out her hand to me.

I gulp, noticing the blood-red ring around her eyes. This woman is a vampire. I take her icy hand, and she squeezes mine gently.

"Yes, I am. Have you been waiting long?" I ask her. That doesn't look good, if she was waiting in the foyer for me. Am I late? I glance at the huge, gold clock above the elevator doors that are so shiny I can see my reflection in them.

"No. I am conducting the interview, if you'll follow me," she says, turning and briskly walking away toward a set of double doors.

I stumble after the woman. Leila is definitely a vampire. Although, I am confused as I catch up to her, and she starts talking about the position.

"Thane wanted to conduct the interview himself, but he and his mates had to leave on short notice for a meeting downstairs, so I am tasked with the interview. I am sorry about the short notice, but you can meet them tomorrow when you start. The other two girls... Well, let's just say they will not do. You know how Betas are. They don't take orders well, and all those two could talk about was Thane and Rhen—" she says, shaking her head, and I stop walking.

"Wait, I thought this was for a receptionist's job? The ad said lobby receptionist," I ask.

"Thane didn't want the media knowing he killed another personal assistant."

My eyes go wide, and I mouth *what the fuck* to myself. Thane? I'm assuming he is the boss. Why did she keep saying that name? And wait, did she say he *killed* his last assistant?

Leila keeps talking, not noticing that I'm on the verge of having a panic attack. "Yet, when I saw you are of Omega blood, I knew you would be perfect and controllable," she says. By Omega blood, I know she means easily commanded and submissive by nature. *What the fuck did I apply for?* She takes me to the top floor and shows me around.

"Don't you want to interview me? I have references." I rummage through my handbag, but her hand falls on my arm.

"No need. I have a strange feeling you are exactly what they are looking for... and what they need," she says with a soft giggle, while her eyes roam over me from head to toe and she licks her lips. I fight the urge to step away from her hungry gaze.

20

It is near impossible to find a job in this city, especially one that doesn't risk your life. The last company I worked at went broke after some vamps killed their manager and set the place ablaze, and I have been up Struggle Street ever since. There are hardly any jobs, and the jobs available require tossing any scrap of dignity out the window and being prepared to do things I am not sure I am comfortable doing.

The 'interview' goes for an hour, and by the time I leave, Leila assures me the position is definitely mine. I'm not sure how I feel about that. The last thing I want is to be trapped with four Alphas. *They could literally destroy me, command anything of me.* I shake that thought away. I can't be picky. A job is a job, and this is the largest tech company in the city, so if I can survive here, even for just a year, it will look great on my resume.

But now I have something else to worry about. I can't go back to my apartment empty-handed, and I am starving. So, I do something I thought I would never do. I ring Brianna in the elevator.

In addition to being my only friend, she is the only one I know here on a personal level, and that is only because I helped her when she was locked out of her apartment one day, which just happened to be next door to mine. She has since moved, but we keep in contact. I am seriously thinking about asking her if they need someone on the floor for tonight. I shudder at the thought of being half-naked with leering horny gazes, but I also have no choice with Martha breathing down my neck about the rent.

Briana says the floor is where the money is. In fact, so does her boss. Martha left me no choice, and my new salary is paid monthly, so I need money to tide me over until then. The pocket change jiggling around in the bottom of my handbag will not pay the rent or feed me.

Yet selling my body doesn't sound that appealing either, considering I am still a virgin, which is rare for an Omega. Usually, packs claim us quickly, or we claim them, but I had been using suppressants for years. My scent is faint, though my ID clearly states what I am, and there is no way I am going to go screaming it from the rooftops. I don't want to be some Alpha's bitch.

I laugh bitterly because now I am literally the coffee bitch to four Alphas. I already dread this job, and it hasn't even started yet. Leila said they are all mates, which is odd. Usually, a pack is comprised of one Alpha, not four, and an Omega. Yet she said it is just the four men.

I plan on walking over to the club. It will take me a good half an hour to walk there. I hope Tal will just let me work behind the bar for the night because I sure as hell don't want to get on stage with Brianna.

I am lost in my thoughts when the elevator opens, and I step out, thinking it is the ground floor, only to smack into a hard chest. Burning hot liquid tips all over me and I hiss as I bounce off the person and fall on my ass.

A thunderous growl rings loudly through the air, and I yelp when hands reach down and grip my arms tightly. Sparks and warmth slip up my arms, yet the pressure of his tight grip is bone-crushing as the man pulls me to my feet and shakes me.

"Fucking whore, you ruined my fucking suit," the man snarls. I tremble under his rage-filled, silver gaze and he shoves me backward. My back hits the closed elevator doors, and I realize I have run directly into an Alpha's path. His tailored suit is drenched in hot coffee, and instinctively I reach out to try to help clean up the mess.

"Fucking useless, Omega," he sneers as I rush to get tissues from the nearby reception desk. I try to pat his shirt dry when his hands lock around my wrists and the crushing pain steals the air from my lungs, his fingers bruising me instantly.

"I'm sorry, so sorry, I didn't see you," I stammer as heat crawls through me, and I curse at myself. His aura is potent and powerful, and despite taking my morning suppressants, slick wet forms between my thighs. *Stupid fucking Omega genes!* I curse to myself, curse being an Omega.

"Don't fucking touch me," he sneers, shoving me backward. His jaw clicks as he clenches it tight. The look he gives sears through me. My neck prickles and my cheeks flame as people stare, and I drop my gaze. Tears burn my eyes at the embarrassment of being scolded.

"Now get out of my face," he growls, shoving me toward the elevator. I do, gladly, anything to get away from the intimidating Alpha.

I wonder who the man is and hope I never run into him again. I leave the place shaken to my core, but after leaving the giant building, I feel myself relax, the tension slowly leaving with every step I take, putting distance between myself and the massive skyrise building.

~ R hen~

"I'm starving," Leon groans as we step into the strip club. His blue eyes look hungrily at the barely clad, half-naked girls on stage. The red ring around his irises glows brightly, confirming his hunger more than words ever could. His bloodlust is insatiable, since he is the only hybrid among the four of us. Thane likes bringing him here. Sure, he could feed from us, but like Leon says, eating the same thing every day gets boring, so we don't mind if he indulges. Hell, we all do. We may be mates, but we still have urges and don't mind sharing a woman now and then.

The strip club is one of a few local businesses that owes Thane money, and Talon is really starting to push the limits of Thane's generosity. As we step into the dimly lit place, Brianna, one of the girls that works here, rushes over as soon as she spots us, glancing nervously to the office upstairs.

Talon knows Raidon likes her. Raidon is a sucker for big boobs, and she is not lacking in that department. The beaded bra she is currently wearing barely covers her nipples, and Raidon grabs her the moment she comes over to bury his face in her chest with a growl. Thane, however, has one goal in mind, so he pushes past her, heading for the office.

"He isn't in!" Brianna shrieks, escaping Raidon and chasing after Thane. I move to follow them up the spiraling staircase to the VIP section. Thane turns once he reaches the top and storms toward Talon's office, kicking the door in. Talon would be dead by now if he wasn't Leon's cousin. I sigh and lean on the banister overlooking the bottom floor, listening to the grunts from the beating Talon receives from Thane. Brianna chews one of her nails nervously, glancing at the door every once in a while, petrified for her sleazy boss, while my eyes roam the floor. Something smells exceptionally sweet here tonight.

The pheromones that pump through this place always make the air sickly sweet, but this is different. This smell is pure. And suddenly my eyes lock on the girl behind the bar pouring drinks.

"New girl?" I ask Brianna, and she glances over the banister to where I'm pointing.

"Um... no, she sometimes works here," Brianna says before her eyes dart back to the office where we hear a loud bang and the frosted glass windows rattle behind us, followed by a garbled grunt.

Sniffing the air, I can't sense what the girl is. The mask covering her eyes covers most of her face, except for her plump lips and little nose, but her scent instantly awakes my senses. I can even smell it above all the pungent scents in this vile place. I glance around the room below to find Raidon and Leon sitting in a booth, their eyes locked on the girl as she serves someone. She flinches when the man tries to grab her wrist, the girl pulling away just in time.

"She's a virgin?" I ask, finally picking up why she smells so sweet.

"She isn't one of the working girls," Brianna answers before rubbing her face where the mask itches. The door opens behind me before Thane comes out and drops a hand on my shoulder. He has a wad of cash that he must have grabbed from Talon's safe.

Gargled grunts sound behind me, and I look at my mate as he

25

peers over the banister to see what captured my attention. No doubt he can feel Leon's hunger through the bond, and Raidon's suddenly piqued interest. Thane rolls his sleeves to his elbows and leans on the banister while observing the floor below.

"New girl?" he asks, and Brianna quickly recites the same thing she told me.

"Leon and Raidon want her," Thane says, nodding toward the booth they are in.

"Oh, she doesn't work the floor. She sometimes cleans dishes," Brianna butts in quickly.

"Werewolf?" Thane asks her, and Brianna nods.

"She smells odd," Thane muses.

"It's just the pheromones," Brianna blurts, and I pull away from the banister to stare at her. Her eyes are locked on the girl with what appears to be worry.

"Is she one of your friends? You don't seem very keen on us going near her," I ask, raising an eyebrow at her. Brianna presses her lips together.

"What's her name?" Thane asks.

"Z. You know we don't give out real names here. Defeats the purpose of the masks," Brianna says, and I raise an eyebrow at her. I know her real name.

"I'm different," Brianna defends quickly. Yeah, she is; Brianna has her side tricks. She is one of Leon's favorites to feed on, and they are friendly, but it still irks me that she refuses to tell us the girl's name.

"She is a sweet girl. Z isn't like the rest of us here."

Sweet? She didn't look sweet. In her little hot-shorts, her soft curves and large bust look like sin. Turning back to the railing, I watch her. There is something else about her. I try to put my finger on what it might be, when Talon walks out of his office. He leans over the railing, fixing his suit jacket, dabbing his bleeding nose with a tissue before using a fresh handkerchief to wipe the blood from his face.

"That girl," Thane says, pointing at the woman.

"Z, and she is not working the floor," Talon says in a shaky voice.

"Leon wants her," Thane replies, but I'm curious if he does too. He has never shown any interest in the girls here before. He mainly likes watching us destroy them, and he's never asked for a specific one.

"She doesn't work the floor," Talon repeats.

"She does tonight. Make it happen," Thane says, leaving no room for argument and heading toward the VIP section.

Brianna makes a strangled noise, and Talon moves to stop Thane with a hand on his arm.

"That girl has never worked the floor. Brianna will be happy to assist you," Talon tries to tell Thane.

"They don't want Brianna. Get the girl, Talon," Thane says, dismissing him.

Brianna glances down to the bar where the girl is still serving drinks, and I turn to look at Raidon and Leon, who are watching her with such focus that they struggle to remain in their seats.

I nod toward the VIP section when they notice me, and they instantly get out of their seats and head upstairs while I follow Thane. We step into a curtained-off booth, and Thane takes a seat with a sigh. The others come in moments later.

"Leon," Thane says, his eyes lifting to our youngest mate. Leon smiles seductively and saunters over to him before Thane grips his wrist and jerks Leon onto his lap. Thane grips his face between his huge hands, and the tiny points of Leon's fangs slip past his upper lip. Thane observes him briefly, searching his eyes and tugging on the bond. It makes me curious, and Thane's next words make me wonder if I'm right about his interest in the girl downstairs.

"You won't kill her," Thane growls, his tone cold and commanding. Raidon falls into the booth beside Thane and chucks his arm over the back of the seat behind him.

"He'll behave," Raidon says, leaning into Thane and whispering to him. Thane growls but raises an eyebrow at Leon, wanting to hear it from him. Leon groans and pouts.

"Fine—" his words stop as the curtain is drawn back, and the girl from downstairs steps inside the booth. Leon's entire body tenses, and the girl freezes like a deer in headlights. She swallows and looks like she's about to run back out. Her plump lips part as if she is about to say something before swiftly turning.

I catch the movement as she starts to second-guess coming in here, and I am behind her instantly, blocking her exit. Her petite body hits my chest before she stumbles backward, only to bump into Leon, who has just jumped off Thane's lap. The girl freezes, stunned, as he trails his nose across her shoulder and up her neck before his hand moves to her hip and he purrs.

Her eyes flutter shut, and I tilt my head, observing her reaction. Most women would run at that sound, yet it seems to subdue her, before her eyes fly open, almost as if she realizes the strange reaction she's having to Leon. Only Omegas have that reaction to Alphas, yet Leon isn't a full werewolf. He is a hybrid.

My eyes flick to Thane and Raidon behind them, both watching her almost as if hypnotized. I have never seen Thane interested in any of the girls here, yet the obviously straining in his pants as he moves tells me he wants to fuck her at the very least.

Leon purrs and runs his tongue up her neck and behind her ear before pressing his fangs against her neck. The girl shudders and whines. Still, she reacts by turning to putty in his hands. I sniff the air. Besides her sweet virginal scent, she smells like a regular wolf. The moment his fangs prick her skin, she jolts, shoving him away. Her heart rate picks up as she looks around us, trying to find an escape, but Raidon moves to catch her wrist and yanks her onto his lap.

"Please, I changed my mind. I want to leave," she whispers, and Raidon lifts his hand to her face, brushing his thumb over her jaw while Thane watches him toy with her. Her pulse thumps in her neck, and Leon groans, sweeping her light brown hair over her shoulder.

"He won't hurt you. Leon just wants to have a little taste," Raidon purrs, and this time, Thane observes the same reaction I saw the first time. He watches her with avid curiosity as her breathing hitches and she turns languidly in Raidon's arms, melting backward against Leon, while he sinks his fangs into her neck from behind.

She gasps, trying to pull off Raidon's lap. She is caged in, and Raidon palms her breast through the thin crop top she wears. His thumb circles around her nipple while Leon's arm snakes around her torso, tugging her closer as he feeds on her. Arousal smashes into me through the bond when he pulls his fangs from her neck and groans loudly.

"Omega!" he purrs, licking his lips, and my lips part, my eyes darting to Thane, who snarls and shoves her off Raidon's lap. The snarl that leaves his lips makes my stomach drop as he abruptly stands. Raidon growls at the girl who clutches her neck, trying to stem the bleeding. No wonder she is such a fucking whore! Just like the rest of the fucking gold-digging Omegas.

All Omegas are. Despite her being a virgin, we all know why she came in here. The last Omega nearly tore our business out from under us and destroyed our bond, yet it explains our allure toward her. Thane snarls, storming out of the room. The girl sits on the floor, still clutching her bleeding throat. She looks like she is on the verge of tears.

We won't fall for her little Omega tricks. We see through them. Gripping Leon's shirt, I rip him out of the room and follow my mates.

CHAPTER
SIX

~ H arlow~
Something is going on upstairs, after four terrify-
ing-looking men in suits come in. I watch two of them
go straight to the VIP level while the other two sit in a booth by
the door. Alphas, all of them, yet one of them smells a little odd.
Almost as if he is more than a werewolf. I can feel their hungry,
leering gazes watching me as I pour a drink for a customer. I kind of
wish I could be washing the dishes right now. Their staring has me
on edge.

It isn't worth the wedgie these tiny little shorts are giving me,
and I fight the need to tug the skin-tight shorts from my butt. How
Brianna wears skimpy stuff like this on the daily is beyond me. I am
freezing, my nipples poke through the thin crop top I have on, my
midriff exposed. I might as well be naked for the coverage it
gives me.

Brianna, I notice, is talking animatedly with one of the men
upstairs, trying to draw his attention. He leans on the railing,
watching everyone below. His black suit looks like it is a part of him.
The four of them are intimidating. The way they walked in like they

owned the place and the loud banging from upstairs behind Talon's office door tells me they are dangerous. I can't place them, yet there is something familiar about the one that went into the office in a blur of pure Alpha fury. This city talks, and I can tell whoever they are, they instill fear in the customers who keep nervously glancing at them.

I stare at the one talking to Brianna. She appears nervous all of a sudden, and he turns to speak to her. The man is enormous, and I lose sight of her as he turns his body, blocking my view of my friend. The aura radiating off him is potent and I can feel it from here, making me shudder as I turn to serve the next customer. Pouring the drink, I glance back up to check if Brianna is alright when his glowing, silver eyes lock on mine. I quickly glance away, returning to clean glasses, when the other two in the far booth suddenly get up and head upstairs.

I watch them slip into the VIP section before I hear arguing break out between Brianna and Talon and she storms off. Talon grips the banister and makes eye contact with me. He lifts his finger in a come here motion and my brows furrow, but I set the glass down on the bar before walking out from behind it. I climb the staircase and move toward him.

"Everything okay?" I ask the huge, burly-looking man. His hair is shaved short, and he looks more like a thug than a businessman. Talon sighs and glances down the hall where Brianna disappeared.

"You need to make money, right, to cover your rent?" he says, and I instantly become wary.

"I will give you $1,000 dollars," he grips my shoulders and turns me toward the VIP section, pointing to a closed-off room, "if you go in there and entertain the four men waiting in there."

"What?" I choke out, glancing over my shoulder at him. His eyes darken, an angry look gracing his face.

"How bad do you need the money?" he retorts.

Badly, but not badly enough to fuck four men!

"What do I have to do?" I ask.

"Whatever they ask."

"Well, that is not an answer. I am not fucking them, Tal."

"I think the youngest one just wants to play with you a bit."

What the fuck is that supposed to mean? Play with me? There are plenty of definitions of play, sordid and not sordid, like play cards, or... I shudder at the other thoughts that come to mind.

"I... I think I will pass. Maybe one of the other girls," I start to say as I step away, but he grips both my arms, leading me toward the curtained-off area.

"You don't have to fuck them, just see what they want," he says.

"I don't have to sleep with them?" I ask, my heart beating in my chest like a drum.

"Not unless you want to. Better tip," he chuckles, and I scoff. I am not about to sell off my virginity for a shitty thousand dollars.

"Who are they?" I ask him.

"That doesn't concern you, but they asked for you, so," he shrugs.

Well, it isn't like they would recognize me. I have a mask on. Maybe they just want me to dance or something. That wouldn't be so bad, and maybe the money would be enough to tide Martha over until I get my first paycheck.

"They won't hurt you. One of them is my cousin, okay? And you don't have to do anything you don't want to. Just go in there, and when you come out, I will give you the money," Talon says, and I chew my lip.

Martha will kill me if I come home empty-handed, and I only have two hours before I need to have something for her. *Fine, let's get this over with*, I think. I nod, wondering if I am making a mistake. I am definitely making a mistake, but bills, rent... I need to do this.

"Good girl," Tal says, slapping my butt and making me jump. He nudges me toward the curtain. I open it, stepping inside and instantly regretting it as I soon recognize one of the men. It's the man I ran into earlier. What are the chances of having another run-in with him today? I want to flee, but I am soon overwhelmed with Alpha scent!

Not even my suppressants, which are starting to wear off, could save me from the Alphas' dominant auras and the scent that threatened to overwhelm my mind and control. Their scents wash over me, my pheromones going haywire, and I want to retreat as I run my eyes over the four men that are way more intimidating in person than from afar. I gulp, turning to leave, only to smack into the chest of another that stood off to the side. Only he moves so quickly, cutting off my exit, that I stumble backward.

Only to bump into another one. His breath on my neck sends a shiver up my spine as his scent envelopes me. He runs his nose across my shoulder and up my neck, stopping below my ear. A deep, rumbling purr awakes senses I usually try to keep locked away. I lean back against him, when I feel sharp points press against my skin, and my eyes fly open, a gasp leaving my lips. I shove him back, looking for an escape, when I'm yanked onto the lap of one man, his hands grabbing and holding me in place.

"Please, I changed my mind. I want to leave," I murmur in panic. Too many scents, and I feel out of control. *I should have doubled my suppressants this morning,* I think when the man's voice purrs below my ear and gentle fingers sweep my hair over one shoulder.

"He won't hurt you. He just wants to have a taste," he purrs at me, and I feel fangs pierce my neck. A moan escapes me as his saliva fills me with endorphins, and my body turns to putty in his hands. His tongue laps at my neck as he tugs me closer, his grip like iron, when he rips his teeth from my neck and growls.

CHAPTER
SEVEN

~H arlow~

"Omega," he groans lewdly, when I find myself abruptly tossed onto the floor. My backside hits hard. It takes everything not to cry out. He just shoved me, as if he thinks I'm diseased and contagious. My Omega instincts take over, wanting to please the Alphas and beg for forgiveness, but I squash it down quickly. The sting of rejection is like a slap in the face. Stupid Omega instincts and Alpha pheromones are messing with my head.

I touch my fingers to my neck when I feel the trickle of warm blood run down it. *Hybrid?* I think to myself. I glance at the men to find them glaring at me, and two of them growl, making me flinch. *What did I do?*

I swallow when the largest of them stands. If looks could kill, I would be dust. His murderous growl is thunderous and I come face to face with the man I spilled coffee on earlier. I'm glad for the mask obscuring half my face, so he can't recognize me, yet he doesn't even give me a backward glance as he storms out, making tears brim in confusion. I hate that instinct makes me helpless against Alphas. I should have taken extra suppressants, but I needed maximum tips tonight, and nothing drives Alphas crazier than natural Omega pheromones.

Now all I want to do is crawl back into my little Den, in my shitty apartment, and curl into a ball. It's stupid that strangers, people I do not know, can reject and toss me away so easily, and it has this effect on me all because I was born with genes I despise.

I gather myself, wiping the tears of humiliation and rejection off my face, when Brianna walks in. She notices me and is quick to rush over to me. She grips my arms.

"I'm okay, just stupid instincts," I tell her, and she nods sadly. She is Beta blood, and she uses it to her advantage. She doesn't crumble and fall at the feet of Alphas. Brianna isn't the lowest on the food chain. I wish I had the confidence she has, how she can easily slip into the stereotypical Omega stuff, despite her not being one. Yet here I am, an Omega, and I fail miserably at it.

Yet I hate being Omega, hate that Alphas hold such control over us just because we are made for Alphas. Omegas are the only ones who can take their knots. I must be an oddity. I despise what I am. Brianna would kill to be an Omega, while I'd kill to be Beta. At least then, I wouldn't have to reform or put up with baser instincts I hate.

"Come on, let's get you cleaned up."

I shake my head. I want to go home, and I am about to tell her as much when Tal races into the room.

He sighs. "You didn't take your suppressants, did you?" he says, and I shake my head.

"I didn't take my nighttime ones," I admit. He curses under his breath.

"That explains... the allure you held for them, without knowing." He sniffs me, and I fight the urge to cringe.

"They called on you?" he murmurs, and I shake my head.

"Your scent is ridiculously strong. I could barely notice it before, but now," he pauses, "you smell ..." He groans. "Fuck, you smell good." His words come out in a snarl as his eyes flicker. He shakes himself, and Brianna puts herself between us. He blinks a couple of times before snapping himself out of it.

"Yeah, your scent is a little too strong, but a promise is a promise," he says, handing over some cash.

"Who are they?" I ask him, taking the cash.

"You know we don't speak of our clients, just like you girls. We don't give them your real names, and you keep your masks on. It's for everyone's safety."

Brianna quickly takes the cash from me, counting it.

"Brianna gives them her name," I tell him.

"Yes, but she does the behind curtain entertainment," Tal says, and Brianna glares at him.

"You should have told them no, Tal," Brianna growls at him, and Tal sighs.

Since I barely did anything, I would have given most of it back if I didn't owe Martha so much, but I am kind of desperate for the cash right now. Hopefully, it will be enough until I start this new job tomorrow and hopefully start bringing in a paycheck each month.

"Well, with your scent as intoxicating as it is right now, Zara, I suggest you head home before you scent all over this place, since you aren't into the extra services," Tal says, and he is right. I need to get home before my scent becomes dangerously strong. An unmated Omega does not want to be caught on the streets late at night while smelling like a drug to damn Alphas.

I quickly get changed and grab my handbag, pulling my hoodie over my head. Just as I'm about to leave, Tal calls out from behind the bar. "Good luck tomorrow, Z," he says, nodding to me, and I smile, slipping out of the club.

Getting home, I am exhausted as I trudge up the steps, only to stop when I see Mike changing the locks to my doors. Martha leans on the wall next to him but pushes off it when she notices me.

"You got my money?" she demands, and I dig through my pockets, staring at Mike's back. I hand it to her and she counts it.

"There is only $1,000 here, Zara! Where is the rest of it?"

"I just need more time," I plead, looking at my apartment door.

"No, you have had enough. You were warned, Zara. I'm sorry. I am not running a charity," Martha says, and I almost choke on fear.

"I will get you more. I start a new job tomorrow," I tell her, rummaging through my bag to show her my employee card. Martha shakes her head.

"Martha, please, it is the middle of winter."

"Lock it up, Mike," Martha says, glancing over her shoulder.

"Martha!" I beg. Martha looks at me sadly but shakes her head. I look at the door desperately.

"Please, just tonight," I beg, but once again, she shakes her head.

"Well... I... can I at least get my suppressants and some clothes? It's freezing out there, and I can't go to work like this."

"The answer is no, Zara. I won't be taken advantage of."

"Taken advantage of is what I will be if I don't get my suppressants. Please, Martha," I tell her, throwing myself at her. She wrinkles her nose and pushes me back.

"Fuck, Zara. You almost smell like you're in damn heat," she snarls, but that just proves she isn't human, something I had suspected in the past.

"Please, I will leave. Just let me grab a few things and shower first. I can't go out there like this," I beg her, and she looks at Mike. Martha sighs and nods to Mike to unlock the door.

"You have an hour, or I am sending Mike up to drag you out. Don't be here when he returns," Martha warns, and I swallow but nod.

I race inside my apartment, closing the door before falling apart. Now, what will I do? I can't stay with Brianna. She lives with Tal, and, well, Tal would expect me to earn my keep in ways that involved my body, something I am not giving up, especially to no damn Alpha.

CHAPTER
EIGHT

~H arlow~

Walking into my room, I briefly glance at my bed where I made my burrow. I want nothing more than to bury myself in my blankets, but I only have an hour. An hour to figure out somewhere to go. An hour before I am tossed out in the cold of night.

Grabbing a backpack, I stuff some clothes in it that will be suitable for work tomorrow and a pair of heels. I can't take all my shoes, so I have to choose wisely and add a pair of heels and black flats. I set my boots next to the bag, intending to wear them after a shower.

I grab my gray parka and as many warm clothes as I can find and fold them carefully, stuffing as much in the bag as I can without breaking the zipper. Afterward, I grab my handbag, squeezing any paperwork I need into it. I set some warm clothes on the bed before rushing to shower and scrub the Omega scent off my skin. I would be an instant target out there smelling like this. Tears burn my eyes as I scrub my skin raw with my loofa.

When finished, I dress in leggings and pull a pair of jeans over them, a cami, a long-sleeved shirt, a sweater, and the parka, knowing

38

it gets so cold here at night I could freeze, and I am pretty sure we are supposed to get a dusting of snow overnight. I grab my beanie and woolen gloves, slip them on, and jam a small makeup bag into my handbag before retrieving every can of de-scenter. I don't know how I am supposed to fit in, but I have no choice.

I also retrieve my suppressants. I have three empty bottles, yet there is one that is still almost full.

However, I know it won't last long. I will have to take extra if I don't want to fall to my knees tomorrow at the damn office. Had I known I would be working for four Alphas as a personal assistant, I can honestly say I would not have applied. However, it is my only option now, so doubling up on my suppressants is the only chance I have, hoping I can pull a few nights at the club for Tal.

A shiver runs up my spine, remembering the men tonight, and dread makes my stomach sink and tears prick the corner of my eyes as the humiliation returns.

Shaking that thought away, I have to focus. I am about to step outside and be exposed, not only to the elements, but everything that goes bump in the night. Undoing the cap on my suppressants, I take three instead of my usual one nightly tablet.

Nerves are kicking in at the thought of heading out into the night. I always make sure to be home before 8:30 p.m.. That is when the nasty shit happens in this city. And now I need to find somewhere to stay. I won't make it back to the club this late without falling victim to someone, or something, so I rummage for the change in the bottom of my bag and groan.

$4.50. Yep, that will help. Not. Why was I stupid enough to hand Martha every cent? I would have given her half had I known she would really kick me out. With a sigh, I walk into the kitchen and open the cupboards. I find some cans of spaghetti and moldy bread. Looking in the fridge, I down the leftover milk straight from the carton, which is all of two mouthfuls, and put the cans of spaghetti in my bag along with a fork.

Grabbing my scarf and a throw blanket that's light enough and small enough I can just squeeze it into my bag, I head for the door. The moment I toss it open, I find Mike standing outside, about to knock.

He looks over his shoulder before jamming a twenty into my hands. Mike gives me a wink and smiles sadly before briskly turning away. I pocket it and take one last wistful glance at my shitty apartment when he motions for me to step past.

Swallowing the bile that threatens to bubble up and spill out past my lips, I nod and head down the stairs, hearing Mike locking it up. When I reach the bottom, Martha is waiting with her arms folded.

"I'm sorry, Zara, but I gave you plenty of time," she says, and I bite the inside of my cheek. I know she did. She has let me off the hook so many times, but it doesn't make going out those doors any less intimidating.

She nods toward the doors before whistling. "Keys for the main door," she says, clicking her fingers.

I was hoping I could sneak back in and sleep in the front entrance, but that option is gone now.

I pull the keys off my keychain before shaking my head and giving her the entire damn thing. I only had the keys to this place on it, anyway. I hand them to her.

"Good luck," Martha says, opening the door for me. I step into the icy-cold, crisp night and shudder then look in both directions of the street. *Now what?*

Martha locks the doors behind me as I ponder my next move.

There aren't that many options, and after a few minutes of walking, I decide it is best to stay as close to work as possible, seeing as I have no money to pay the fare for the bus to get there. The walk takes me an hour and a half before I am about a block away.

There is a small mall nearby, with a little outside area that leads into an alleyway. With a sigh, my bones aching from the cold, I hesitantly step into the alley, listening for any noises of someone being up the alley. I stumble over some garbage before finding a set of stairs that leads down to a storage area.

Glancing back up the alley, I see no one, so I sling my bag off my shoulder and descend the stairs, taking a seat beside the small roller door. It isn't the first time I've lived on the streets, and knowing my luck, this probably won't be the last time. This is what happens when you live a life on the run.

Yet, as I made myself comfortable, I couldn't help but think if my twin was still with me, I would never be in this situation. Zara was resourceful. She always found a way, just like she found a way to save my life. She took my place, gave her life for mine, and here I am wasting it.

Zara would have been better off. It should have been me who died and not her. At least she wouldn't be wasting her life. No, she would live her best one, while I sit here, trying to warm my fingers enough to swipe my phone screen to set the alarm so I won't be late on my first day.

I try to remember what time the mall opens so I can slip into the bathroom in the morning to get dressed and put a face on. I am pretty sure it opens around 8 a.m., which would give me an hour to sneak in and quickly change before making the walk around the block to the skyrise and my new place of employment.

"I can do this!" I whisper to myself while resting my head back on the roller door. At least the stairs offered a wall to be protected from the ghastly, icy breeze.

CHAPTER
NINE

~ Thane~

~   "I bloody told you we don't need a new personal assistant," I snap at my sister-in-law, Leila, as we step into the elevator. She ignores me, as she usually does. She is so much like Leon in that way. I swear she enjoys driving me to the edge of my sanity just so she can claim to have brought me back from the brink.

"Where is my brother, anyway?" she asks while batting her lashes at me and feigning innocence, pursing her lips as she glances between Rhen, Raidon, and me. Ignoring her, I press the button for our floor.

"So, who is she?" Rhen asks Leila while leaning against the elevator wall. Leila shrugs and I know she is up to something.

"Her name is Zara. She worked for some firm that burned down, and—" the doors open, and I get a whiff of de-scenter. The growl that leaves me is thunderous, making the girl jump as she rearranges the files in her hands. The manila folders fall from her grip and land on the table.

"Oh, you have to be fucking kidding me, Leila! You hired an

Omega, and her, of all fucking people?" I snap, instantly recognizing the woman as the one who spilled coffee on me yesterday.

She's wearing black slacks and a white blouse with a black blazer over the top. Her long hair is tied back in a ponytail, high on her head. She stares in horror at me, and she should, because I will be her worst goddamn nightmare. What was Leila thinking, hiring a damn Omega?

Leila, however, strolls forward excitedly. She needs to get all this Omega business out of her head. We are content with just our pack, and it's not like I can produce an heir since the last of my serum was wasted on that stupid Omega who killed my mother when she escaped us.

I glare at the girl, who is staring back at the three of us. Her hazel eyes are wide as she takes us in. I growl, shaking my head when Rhen's hand falls on my shoulder, making me look at him.

He steps past me, holding his hand out to the girl, who quickly takes it, while he shoots a look at me over his shoulder, telling me to remain calm. I press my lips in a line, but I know what he means.

If we fire her and she runs to the media, they will have a goddamn field day over this. We are already in hot water from claims of discriminating against Omegas. God knows why, when hardly any pack allows their Omega to work. I glare at Leila, who smirks. Bloody brat. Her brother will have to deal with her because she won't like it if I have to.

"Zara, isn't it?" Rhen asks her, and I see the way his eyes run the length of her quickly as she shakes his hand and nods.

"You seem familiar for some reason," he mutters, his eyes narrowing on her lips and face.

"Yes, she is the bimbo who spilled coffee on me yesterday," I retort, glaring at her. She drops her head, her cheeks heating and causing an adorable blush to cover her face.

I shake my head at my thoughts. *Adorable. Where the fuck did that thought come from?* The girl swallows, sucking her bottom lip between her teeth before introducing herself.

"Yes, I'm Zara. It's nice to meet you—" she looks at Leila, who introduces us, motioning to each of us.

"This is Rhen, Raidon, and Thane Keller."

The girl jerks her hand away from Rhen almost instantly, taking a startled step back.

"Keller!" she exclaims, shaking her head and taking another step back until her ass hits the desk and she jumps with a squeak leaving her lips.

"Yes, Nightbane Pack. I'm sure you've heard of them. Though I wouldn't believe everything you hear in the media," Leila says,. Zara looks between us nervously.

"Right, sorry. Just, when I applied here, I thought the job was as a lobby receptionist downstairs, not working for four Alphas," she stammers nervously, and I roll my eyes at her fake apprehension.

"This is going to be a fucking nightmare. I swear if you go into heat in my damn office, you're fired. You step through those damn doors without your de-scenter or off your suppressants you're fired! I will not have my mates go into rut because you can't contain yourself. Am I understood?" I snap at her.

She swiftly nods her head, and I actually feel bad when it looks like she might be on the verge of tears. She quickly shakes her head and clears her throat.

Well, at least she has enough control to suppress her instincts. Most Omegas would have fallen at my feet by now, begging for forgiveness. At least she has some self-preservation instincts.

"Understood, sir," she says, and I curse under my breath.

"And stay the fuck out of my office, unless called on," I tell her, storming away from her when I hear Raidon ask her a question.

"Why don't you have a pack?" he asks.

"I never found one I was interested in and have no interest in joining one either," she answers, yet there's a tremble in her voice, almost as if she fears Raidon. She doesn't have to worry about us claiming her. We all fucking hate Omegas after the shitstorm Harlow caused us. Leaving them, I slip inside my office and close the door.

CHAPTER
TEN

~ H arlow~
I'm cursed. It is the only thing that makes any possible sense. Of all the places to land a job, it has to be working for the very people I have been running from for years, and the jerk I spilled coffee on just has to be the damn Alpha and my new boss.

Great, the first chance I get, I am buying a sage stick and cleansing the heck out of myself. A bad omen must be clinging to me. Surely my luck isn't this shitty?

After Thane stalks off toward his office, the other two follow quickly to their own as they part ways, leaving me with Leila.

"I think that went rather well; don't you think?" she asks while side-eyeing me. I raise an eyebrow at her. Well? More like a disaster. It's clear they hate me already. I have been here minutes and am seriously considering telling her to jam her job offer up her tiny ass.

Leila shows me around the floor. I discover it has a small kitchenette, which has Chinese takeout containers piled in the sink, the bin is overflowing, and there are coffee stains on the counter.

If this is their place of work, I would hate to see the state of their home. Leila then writes a list of how they like their coffees before showing me the bathroom, which is surprisingly clean, or cleaner than the kitchenette anyway, and then she shows me to the filing room. That is a total nightmare.

The door won't even open completely from the stacks of files piled behind it. Every countertop is covered, and there is a little path from the door to the printer and a small fax machine. It also stinks heavily of dust.

"I'm assuming you know how to use the fax machine and the printer?"

I nod my head, gawking at the room in horror, yet I love cleaning. It must be an Omega thing. My mother loved it too. There's nothing better than seeing the before and after of hard work, so at least I know my tasks for today.

"Great, well, here is your login. This is the key to the fire exit, you know, just in case, though I doubt you will need it," she shrugs, handing me folders and a tablet.

Leila follows me to my desk and watches me log in before nodding. "All set then, lunch is at one, finishes at 1:40, the day is over at 6 p.m.," she says, about to walk to the elevator.

"Ah, Leila?" I call. I have to ask, praying my assumptions are wrong, yet I need to know.

"Yes?" she asks, moving back toward me. She stops at the edge of the desk, and I lean over, keeping my voice low.

"Um, Thane, his dislike for Omegas—"

She waves a dismissive hand in the air. "They'll get over it." She rolls her eyes.

"They once had an Omega, and she ran from them, taking Thane's last serum with her," she says.

"That's why they hate Omegas? Because she ran from them?" I ask. Leila nods and sighs.

"That, and the fact that Harlow killed Mrs. Keller. They were barely able to hold the pack together. Thane hunted Harlow after what she did, but he couldn't find her. She just vanished. She must be dead. No way anyone could survive in those woods, especially an Omega, in full-blown rogue territory," she says, staring off vacantly.

"Their Omega killed Thane's mother?" I ask, outraged. I did no such thing.

"Yep, they found her body next to some restaurant, her throat was cut, and her car was gone, though we found it in a gully, along with the poor man she ran off the road and killed. Tragic, really; Thane and the pack wanted her as a mate, not a breeder.

"She nearly destroyed them. Thane's fathers killed themselves after his mother died. Leon went crazed with bloodlust. Thane— well, that's another story," she says, and I swallow.

"So, you have worked here for a while, I guess," I tell her, sitting back in my chair. Whoever attacked us that day covered it up and framed me.

"Of course, I started here when they first took over. I'm Leon's sister," she says with a flick of her hair. So, won't be confiding to her then, I note quickly.

"I should probably get to work," I tell her. She laughs and nods.

"Me too. It wouldn't be the first time Thane has fired me for slacking, so make sure you're always doing something. Don't let them catch you twiddling your thumbs," she says, giving me a wink before strolling to the elevator.

Surprisingly, the job is straightforward, or maybe they just aren't as demanding since it is my first day. After cleaning the kitchenette, I sort my desk. Those are simple tasks. However, after cleaning, I spend most of the day in the filing room, or should I say paper room, because not a thing is actually filed in the cabinets, just tossed on the counters.

I spend all day scanning everything into an electronic system, which I think is odd being that it is a tech company, and yet nothing is filed electronically. They certainly have not put a file away in months, maybe years, in the cabinets.

Lost in the task at hand, I don't realize one of them is looking for me until his rage-filled, booming voice reverberates to me, making me stiffen.

"Omega!" Thane bellows. I press my lips in a line. Surely, he will not address me like that all the time?

"Maybe you scared her off already," Raidon chuckles, and I listen as the footsteps draw closer.

"Can only fucking hope. Now where the fuck is she? Useless, bloody woman thinking—" his words stop as he enters the filing room just as I am about to get up off the floor where I was sorting the last stack of documents.

Thane's mouth opens and closes as he glances around the room that was piled almost to the roof in some places with files, now, tidy as can be. He scratches the back of his neck awkwardly before his eyes fall on me, his gaze turning to a glare.

"If you threw the files out—"

I open the drawer beside me, and he shuts up instantly.

"Do you need something? Everything is filed by the year, date, and in Alphabetical order. I also added the electronic filing system to each of your desktops," I tell him. Raidon whistles low and laughs, rocking on his heels and placing one hand in his pocket.

"Well, guess we aren't firing her," Raidon chuckles, patting Thane's shoulder.

"Get me a coffee and then go to lunch," Thane says, walking out. Raidon quickly follows, and I sigh. Okay then!

As I'm making coffee for Thane, Rhen comes into the kitchenette and leans on the doorframe. His scent alerts me to his presence behind me and I try to breathe through my mouth.

His gaze bores into the back of my head, making me nervous, and I clutch the spoon tighter when I feel the telltale signs that my pills are wearing off. Slick dampens my panties, and I press my thighs together, only to realize he is purring, which induced it.

They are either trying to make me quit or give Thane a reason to fire me. I continue to breathe through my mouth, refusing to inhale his scent. I briefly wonder, however, if my pills aren't working because I am, in fact, their Omega.

The serum acclimates us to our Alphas, for our bodies to recognize them as our mates. Could that be why, since coming in contact with them, they suddenly appear to be hardly working at all?

Or am I looking too far into it? All I know is if I go into heat, it could be dangerous.

Thane may recognize me as his Omega. My pheromones would make him insane. I wonder if the serum had a use-by date; would it wear off one day if it is never activated and the bond is not completed? I'll have to remind myself to look that up when I can.

"Breathe, little Omega, I don't bite. Not Omegas anyway," Rhen laughs before doing that stupid purring again.

"Can you stop purring? I know you are doing it deliberately," I say through gritted teeth as I fight the instinct to crawl into the damn man's lap and scent him. Rhen laughs, and I feel the heat of his body radiate up my back before feeling his breath on my hair as he moves behind me.

"Why? Does it make you want to beg for my knot? Does it bother you that you are too weak to deny me if I ordered you on your knees? You're nothing but a lowly Omega. Must truly suck holding no power," he growls behind me.

"For a lowly Omega, Mr. Keller, I seem to have a great effect on your ability to restrain yourself," I tell him, pressing my ass against his legs and bumping the erection I feel digging into my back.

"You claim to hate Omegas, but you are fantasizing about me on my knees, fantasizing about me begging at your feet, because you wouldn't use your purr on a lowly Omega if you weren't," I retort.

Fire me, see if I care. I am not putting up with sexual harassment. If I want that, I can take Tal up on his offer to work the floor. Rhen growls, the noise sending a jolt through me.

"Watch your tongue, Omega."

I shrug in response.

"Must suck having no one to take your knot. Is that why you are fascinated with tormenting me, Mr. Keller? Are you hoping I will beg for you to take me, since your mates can't?" I tread dangerously.

We both know he can order me to my knees if he wanted, and just like he said, I would be powerless against it. Yet, he also knows I'm right. I've been fighting my instincts for years, but has he? Around an Omega, his urges and baser instincts could destroy him just as easily as me.

"Rhen!" Thane's deep voice echoes through the room, and Rhen startles behind me, moving away. I glance over my shoulder to find Thane standing in the doorway.

"Go pick up Leon for me and bring him back here," Thane says to him, yet his angry black eyes are on me. He clenches his teeth, making the muscle in his jaw pop. Rhen saunters over to him and I think it's the end of his little game, when he stops beside Thane.

Thane, clearly angered by whatever the heck Rhen is doing, looks at his mate. Rhen smirks, gripping the front of Thane's shirt and grabbing Thane's crotch, squeezing him as he presses his lips to Thane's. Thane growls, and Rhen steps back. The scene causes some strange sensation to ripple through me; one I have never felt before, and it only takes me a few moments to recognize it.

Pack urges. The urge to live within a pack, to be protected and cherished: something all Omegas crave, and I am no different. It makes me think of my parents and the love they shared, and then it makes me think of my little Den back in the shitty apartment I was kicked out of. The safety I feel within my Den, my little pack of one. How I crave what they have, that sense of belonging. I swallow and turn my gaze back to making coffee. I hear Rhen chuckle before hearing his footsteps as he leaves.

Thane, however, doesn't leave. Pouring the steamed milk in, I hand him his cup, trying to breathe around the lump that has suddenly formed in my throat.

You hate everything about being an Omega, I remind myself. Yet, that has changed over the last year or so. Werewolves are pack creatures and being alone is lonely. With my sister, I was never alone.

Until I was. Since since then, I crave companionship. Someone who understands me just as well as she did.

"Don't let me catch you teasing my mates again," Thane says, as I turn to hand him his mug.

The words slip from my lips before I fully register them. "Yes, Alpha," I say before internally cringing at myself and cursing at my stupidity. Yet, it doesn't make his following words sting any less, though they shouldn't have hurt at all. How is it possible to be upset over someone you despise? I hate Alphas, hate the control they have while I hold none.

"I am not your Alpha!" he growls, snatching the mug from my grip and stalking off, his words more painful than if he had slapped me. Omegas crave praise from their Alpha and want to please their Alphas. I hate that part, yet still, his words break a tiny splinter in me that I swallow down.

You will not break! Especially in front of that asshole, I scold myself.

CHAPTER
ELEVEN

arlow~

~H I make sure to keep my distance from the Alphas until the day ends, and am quick to leave the moment Rhen comes out and tells me I can. I know something is going on with them because when Rhen returned with Leon, I heard Thane cursing him out about something he was caught doing. So, I am relieved to get out of here; all the testosterone-filled anger is starting to affect my baser instincts.

Once out of the building and away from their threatening auras filled with Alpha dominance, I feel myself relax. I don't realize how badly they affected me until I am away from them. Yet, now what? I still have no place to stay, no money, and my belly chose that moment to rumble.

Digging through my bag, I pull out some change and walk to the nearest payphone. I call Brianna, dreading the conversation already. I haven't spoken to her since last night, after my run-in with the four Alphas who just so happen to be my new bosses. The phone almost goes to voicemail when she answers.

"Hello?" she asks warily.

"Hey, Bree. It's me, Zara." I hear her sigh.

"Ah, I thought you were a debt collector or telemarketer," she chuckles.

"Nope, just me. I um... do you think Tal will let me work behind the bar tonight? I could kinda use some cash," I admit.

"Sure, yes, I will let him know. Head over and I'll find you a uniform," she says, and I let out a sigh of relief.

Finally, something is going right for me. We bid our goodbyes, and I quickly hang up before rushing to the other side of town, to a seedier area. I come in the back entrance and find the teeny, skin-tight little uniform hanging up, waiting for me. Rushing to the staff bathrooms, I change quickly, making sure my mask is secure.

Tal greets me as I enter the bar and nods to me; I feel a little awkward around him now that I know he is related to one of my bosses, yet I have to work. Luckily, the cook I like is on tonight, and he sneaks me some dinner before I handle the 7 p.m. rush.

I hardly make any tips. A measly $7, and it's a slow night since it is a weekday. But once it nears 7:30 p.m., I know I have to leave soon If I want to find somewhere to crash. I briefly consider asking Tal if I can sleep here, but dismiss it since this place runs 24/7 and I don't want to find myself in a vulnerable position by sleeping in one of the VIP Booths.

I am getting ready to clock out and take a shower in the amenities here when Tal whistles from the landing above. He nods toward the entrance, and my heart stalls in my chest when I turn and see Leon waltz in. I quickly rush toward the back staff area when I hear my name called.

"Z!" Leon calls out, and I cringe. Fuck! If he finds out who I truly am, I am so screwed. I make a beeline for the rear doors when Tal suddenly steps into my path, having rushed down the steps.

"He spent most of the day here, hoping you would be in," Tal whispers, and I glance over my shoulder to see Leon chatting with Brianna. I wonder if that is what Thane and he argued about earlier.

"You didn't tell him who I am, did you?" I whisper.

"Of course not. If I had known you would be working for them directly, I would have taken the beating instead of sending you in there with them, but Leon... he is..."

"A Hybrid!" I offer, and Tal sighs.

"He's my cousin. He has an addictive personality."

It makes me wonder how big Leon's family is.

"What's that got to do with me?" I all but shriek.

"Blood addiction or blood craze, and you are an Omega," Tal states, like that is supposed to make any sense to me.

"So?"

"You're forbidden fruit. Thane has one rule with him: no Omegas. It caused quite a stir when Rhen hunted him down earlier and found him here, looking for you."

A shocked gasp leaves me.

"Wait, he waited here all day, wanting to feed on me?"

"Yes, so maybe use that to your advantage, Z. You need the money, and tonight was a slow night for you," he says. I chew my lip when he grips my wrist and drops $50 in my hand. $57, wow.

"Did you call him and let him know I was in?" I ask.

"I don't remember," Tal says, feigning innocence. I shake my head, knowing he did. Why would he do that? I fold my arms across my chest and pin him with my glare.

"Look, I owe Thane money. Leon said if I let him know when you're in next, he would pay a chunk of the debt."

So that is why he was eager for me to stick around past my normal leaving time.

"You sold me?" I ask incredulously.

"It's just blood. Virgin, Omega blood! It's addictive to a hybrid, and since he fed on you last night, he has been bombarding me with messages. But I know he will pay you well, if you let him."

"Let him feed on me!" I hiss at him. Tal shrugs, and waves to Leon over my head. I cringe when I feel him coming up behind me.

"Tal!"

"Z! Advantage, use it," he says, and I swallow when I feel arms

54

wrap around my waist. Thank god he didn't scent me before I resprayed myself with de-scenter at work.

"Omega," Leon purrs, burying his face in my neck.

My heart beats erratically, thumping against my ribs painfully. Turning in his arms I push him off me. He chuckles.

"I'll give you a hundred dollars, just to let me bite you," Leon says waving it in front of my face. I raise an eyebrow at him and fold my arms.

"Two hundred?" he offers.

"Three! And I am not fucking you," I snap at him. This feels so degrading, but at three hundred I can book two nights in that shitty motel near work and buy some food and phone credit while I hunt for an extra job. One thing is clear: I need options. I can't live off fresh air and sunshine, plus I need more cans of de-scenter. I just pray I won't run out of suppressants, because those are expensive; nearly $700 for a month's supply. I am running dangerously low, already having to double up, and tomorrow I'm going to triple the pills. Two pills did hardly anything today at work, so three pills a day morning and night won't last me long.

"Deal," he says, gripping my wrist and pulling me into the closest booth.

TWELVE

~H arlow~

    Leon doesn't bother to give me a chance to sit down and calm my nerves. No, he has one intention, and that is to take what he wants with no regard for who he is taking it from.

To Leon, I am just some whore; an Omega who works in a seedy strip club and would do anything for money. Disposable. And damn, do I feel used. The moment the curtain closes, blocking any light from invading the gloomy looking booth, his teeth sink into my neck.

As his tongue laps at the surface of my skin, I release a startled, broken gasp from my lips. The pain intensifies as he pulls my body tight against his, eliminating any space between us.

A loud growl leaves Leon's lips as I try to thrash against his grip, desperate to escape him, to escape the pain and the room. It wasn't this painful the last time he fed off me. The pain this time is almost unbearable, until the endorphins flood my system and overwhelm me.

I begin to lose track of time, and my surroundings blur slightly.

Yet, the longer Leon feeds on me, the more the pain dissipates, and ecstasy starts to vibrate through me. A feeling of euphoria washes over me as my body tingles, which only scares me more because I have to fight against this feeling, too.

His hand moves to my hair, and Leon tilts my head to the side a little more, exposing my neck to him and giving him a more beneficial angle. Leon's grip rips hair from my scalp, leaving a painful, tingling sensation behind, and my eyes prick with tears at the discomfort of his grip.

A whimper escapes me when he bites another spot on my neck, this one slightly lower but close enough to the previous one, and I hiss at the new stinging sensation while feeling my blood slip down my shoulder and onto my chest.

As his sharp teeth puncture my skin, I can feel the blood draining from me, gushing out of my neck as his lips latch on to suck harder.

Pure, raw, and wild panic sets deep in my bones when Leon doesn't stop. His grip on my hair becomes nearly unbearable, and fight-or-flight kicks in.

I pivot enough to force my knee right in between Leon's legs. He still has a tight grip on my hair though, so the action tugs on my scalp, sending waves of pain through me. I ignore it—all that matters is getting away from him.

The dangerous fangs keep sinking into my flesh, slowly draining me of life, and Leon doesn't seem to care about the damage he is causing. Maybe he doesn't see value in my life, but I do. I want to live. Led by pure fear and adrenaline, I bring my knee up with all the force I have left.

Leon's lips instantly unlatch from me as he tears his teeth out of my neck and grunts loudly. He lets go of me, and I stagger back on instinct, desperate to increase the distance between the blood sponge he is being and myself. The asshole was absorbing all the life from me.

I slap my hand over my neck, hoping it will stem the bleeding. Leon glares at me, as if I'm the one at fault. I kneed him in the nuts, yes, but it was self-defense. How else am I supposed to stop him from killing me?

I force down the lump that somehow forms in my throat. Leon's blood-red eyes blaze as a crazed gleam makes them glaze over. A deep, thrumming growl resonates from him, making my legs wobble. If he commands me, I am fucked.

Leon steps toward me, and I can't help but yelp in fear as he stalks closer. Didn't he have enough? I'm pretty sure he took more of my blood than he needs, so it can't be that he wants more. Or can it?

The backs of my knees hit the small table behind me, and I know there is nowhere I can run, no way to escape him. But then, Leon shakes his head, and I nearly fall backward, unsure if it's a sign that Leon won't touch me anymore or if it's because he's not in the mood to chase me around and is disappointed at my attempt to get away from him.

"Sorry, I got a little carried away. Happens," Leon mutters as if it's something usual and I shouldn't feel violated by his doings.

Which I do. I do feel violated and taken advantage of. This man just leeched on my blood to the point I had to fight him off to survive. What's he want, a fucking pat on the back? A thumbs up and reassurance he did no wrong? 'Yeah, no biggie, we're good.'

I watch him dig through his pocket, stalk closer, and toss some money on the little table beside me. I stare at him, petrified at what he will do next, when Leon wordlessly turns on his heel and swiftly walks out of the room, leaving me alone in the darkness of the VIP booth.

I don't dare move an inch as my hand still clutches my neck. I'm so scared. Frightened to the core, I fear any movement might cause a tear in the deep indents left by Leon's teeth, which would result in a slow and agonizing death. The Omega who bled out after a vampire played around with her sounds like some horror movie title, not real life.

I feel disgusted with myself. I feel like a cheap whore who sold something of herself to get another dose of whatever drugs those people use. I wonder if this is how Brianna feels when she does unspeakable things like this. Does she feel as violated and disgusted as I do now? Can she get up and leave this place without a single pang of guilt or hurt to her heart, or does she need time to rid herself of the thoughts before she carries on with her life?

The more I think, the more I doubt my thoughts. Perhaps at first, she struggled with conflicted emotions the same way I do now, but in time, she got used to how her life is. It's a funny phenomenon but true—eventually, everyone gets used to their life and suffers comfortably in their own misery.

However, even though I know how getting used to your circumstances comes along with the journey, I don't see myself ever getting used to doing such things or getting used to the feeling currently tearing me apart inside.

I glance at the table where Leon tossed his money. I must look like a fool while I stare at the cash, until I gather enough courage to scoop it up and check how valuable my life is in the eyes of a vampire. After all, that's what he paid for—my blood. Blood he took too much of and nearly killed me for.

A few dollars. A few dirty dollars are all Leon believes my life is worth. Disgusting, impossible, blood-sucking leech!

I sigh in defeat and focus on counting the money to make sure all of it is there. But the curtain is ripped open and Tal rushes in, so I don't get a chance to properly count it.

A heavy sigh leaves his lips as Tal's wary gaze takes me in. Was he worried that Leon might have killed me?

"Thank god," Tal groans, walking closer to me. "Leon told me to check on you. He said he lost control, so I..." Tal shakes his head and stops himself mid-sentence, looking somewhat guilty about the entire situation.

I nod as Tal steps in front of me and pries my hand from my neck. I watch him bring his wrist to his lips, bite it, and then offer it to me as my eyes widen in disbelief. Did he just...?

"Drink it. It will heal you," Tal explains.

I gape at Tal, appalled, but he just thrusts his wrist toward me, and only then do I realize he is a hybrid. How had I not noticed that before? Then again, I never really paid much attention to Tal.

"You're a hybrid?" I gasp, and stare at him as if Tal is a unicorn, despite just being fed on by Leon, who is also a Hybrid. Yet I never pictured Tal being one.

"I told you, Leon is my cousin," He mutters and rolls his eyes at me.

"Yeah, but I just thought you were a werewolf."

He shakes his head. "Easier this way. No one really likes vamps now, do they? Would you even think of working here if you knew I'm a hybrid?"

CHAPTER
THIRTEEN

~ **H**arlow~

When Tal puts it like that and directs me closer to his perspective, I have to admit that he has a point. A good one, at that. Vampires are far more dangerous than werewolves. While wolf shifters are angry and capable of ripping anyone to shreds, which is scary, vampires are unpredictable—no one knows how or when they will lose control, so the aspect of surprise makes them much more dangerous than shifters.

"Now, hurry, unless you want your bosses to see those marks on your neck and start asking questions," Tal mutters and offers me his wrist again.

I sigh and give in. Tal is right. The last thing I need is for my bosses to think I'm a feeder on top of everything else they already hate me for. It's bad enough they already think so little of me. There's no need to add extra fuel to the flames of their disgust. I don't want them to think they hired someone who's an addicted feeder. I'm not, and I won't let them belittle me like that.

"I called a cab for you, so you can get home. And don't worry, the fare is covered already," Tal speaks as his eyes inspect my neck, probably to ensure it is completely healed. Once he's content enough, Tal nods, turns on his heel, and walks away.

I wait for another minute before heading downstairs to the staff area and quickly changing back to my clothes. Tapping the pockets, I check that the money is there and rush outside to meet the cab.

The cab driver is an older, pleasant gentleman who looks like someone who has experienced some hardships in life, so I don't feel ashamed when I ask him to take me to the seedy motel near where I work.

I can't go to a nice motel or hotel, not only because I can't afford one, but mainly because I can't provide an ID since I don't have one. Okay, maybe I do, but it's not mine—it's just a shitty old ID of my sisters that I paid the firm I used to work for to 'fix up' for me.

They added a questionable last name, too, which is as much a blessing as it is a curse.

It's truly fascinating how many jobs one can find that don't require the bosses to actually know who you are, simply because they don't want you to know who they are either.

Vampires owned the company I used to work for, and I truly believe it was a cover for something more sinister they did behind the scenes. I didn't want to know what it was because I didn't want to be a part of their shady business or find myself caught up in it. Though with the amount of foot traffic that went through the place, I knew something was up, I just knew better than to ask.

Hence why I never questioned anyone; I was just relieved that they let me work there with no previous experience nor any proper, legal proof of my identity.

I'm still beyond shocked that Leila didn't bother to check my ID properly or run a background check on me. If she had done that, she would have noticed that the social security number isn't correct, because it doesn't exist; it is a row of random, made-up numbers, but so far, it hasn't gotten me into trouble. So, I should be grateful for that much.

Sometimes I worry because of that small, laminated piece of

paper. It's my only ID, yet it's so terribly fake that even a fool would notice it's nowhere near the real thing.

It's clear that Martha knows it is a fake. She just didn't seem to care about it at the time. Either that or she knew I am no danger to her. Most of them really don't care about such things, but from what I gathered from Leila, she doesn't care about who I am or where I came from. She's more interested in the fact that I am an Omega. Yet, she never questioned me about being packless.

I shake my head to get rid of the thought before I start another round of vicious overthinking and walk into the shady motel. The place stinks. No, it reeks of something disgusting and a mix of everything I hate, but I ignore the pit in my stomach and walk toward the reception.

I hand over half my money to the girl behind the counter wearing heavy eye makeup and a shade of foundation far too light for her skin tone. She watches me as she checks every bill, holding each of them up to the light, inspecting it as if she thinks it is counterfeit, and then tosses me a key attached to a wooden block.

The girl chews her chewing gum and blows a bubble. She still stares at me with suspicion, as the bubble pops, and I try to understand which number is written on the wooden block attached to the key to my new home, at least for the next few days.

She rolls her eyes at me and groans, obviously annoyed. "Upstairs, third door on the right," she mutters out the directions with another roll of her eyes.

The woman probably thinks I'm incompetent or stupid, but that's not the case. It's the shitty, faded, handwritten number that I can't figure out, not the directions.

To avoid an unnecessary confrontation, I press my lips in a thin line, nod swiftly, and give a quick thanks. Without the small talk the clerk obviously doesn't want, I leave to find my room.

At this point, anything, literally anything, is better than the streets. Besides, it's not only a bed I get here; I also have enough money to buy some decent food. For once in a long time, I don't have to settle on dry pot foods and noodles.

Although I followed the directions the clerk so kindly provided, it took five minutes to find the door to the room I am renting for the next three nights since the receptionist took pity on me and gave me the third night cheaper.

Hopefully, I can go back to Tal's in a couple of days and try to earn some more cash to afford a few more nights here.

Once I thrust the key in the lock, twist it and pull down the knob, the room door squeaks loudly, like no one has used it in a couple of years. The first thing that stops me is the intense stench.

The motel room stinks heavily of mildew and god knows what else on top of a horrific, rotten stench that smells like rotting flesh. I suck in a deep breath and remind myself that I'm lucky to have a roof over my head, so complaining would be the same as spitting in the face of someone who tries to help me.

Besides, a little stench can't be too bad. After all, I don't need to hide behind massive trash containers or in dirty stairwells behind the old plaza.

I didn't expect a penthouse, luxury suite in a shitty motel, but I didn't expect my skin to feel this itchy the moment I step inside, either. Maybe it's more about the dirty vibe around here than the dirt itself...

No, I can't give up like this. Anything is better than the streets.

Holding my breath, I walk to the relatively inviting-looking bed and rip off the blanket covering it. An icy shiver runs down my spine and makes me shudder as my eyes take in the stains on the white sheet. I know better than to dig deeper by pulling off the sheet to inspect the state of the mattress beneath the covers.

The room appears grimy, as if no one bothered to clean it. No, more like all of the staff members refused to enter the filth and deal with it for the money they got for their services.

Besides, I'm pretty sure there are some bloodstains on the dated, floral curtains, so who knows what might have happened in the room? Maybe no one entered it because it is haunted; it sure gives off that vibe.

Cringing, I make my way into the tiny bathroom and groan. It's worse than the public toilets at the plaza. Beggars can't be choosers, though, so I strip off and ignore the surrounding filth, desperate for a shower.

FOURTEEN

~ R aidon~

"Where is Leon?" Thane asks when I sit down and place my plate on the massive hardwood table. He hasn't calmed down since we left work. Not even giving me a chance to greet him, he's already up and running a whole interrogation at the dinner table.

I shrug, even though I might know where he is. Alright, I'm pretty sure I know where he is, but I don't want to rat on him. "Where is Rhen?" I ask, trying to distract Thane from the issue with Leon.

We usually eat dinner together every night. No matter how busy each of us is, dinner together is a must. Dinner time is compulsory, so when I look around and see only the two of us, I frown. It's surprising to see the table so unusually empty.

Is Leon really that stupid to skip the one thing Thane ensures we do together every night? I glance at Thane, who sits across from me and drums his fingers on the edge of his whiskey glass. The muscles in his jaw tense, and if I don't come up with a way to distract him, the dinner will turn into a disaster before it even begins. I can feel his anger festering. Though looking at him, he is a picture of calm, besides the tight set of his jaw.

Thane clears his throat and focuses on the glass as he explains. "Rhen should be back soon. He called earlier, while I was cooking dinner. He went to pick up some files for me on the new girl."

Thane doesn't move to eat, and I know he won't; he won't until Rhen and Leon arrive. As big and intimidating as Thane is, there are a few things he values and holds close to his heart. One of them is pack dinner. For outsiders, it might seem silly, but I understand why he's so adamant about this tradition—it's the only time of the day we can sit down, talk, and spend quality time together.

He tips the glass to his lips and swallows some caramel-colored liquid. By the looks of it, I'm almost certain that Thane will kill Leon if he arrives late or misses dinner.

Thane chewed him out good in the office earlier today. He had a reason, though—Leon lied to his face. Technically, Leon tried to lie, but Thane saw right through his bullshit act. Leon refused to tell Thane where he had been. Thane refuses to command us around unless we disobey him outright, which Leon had done, yet Thane wouldn't embarrass Leon at our place of work like that. We have to remain a united front at the office, but Leon is so in for it when he gets home. That much I know, without a doubt.

"Where do you think Leon went today?" Thane suddenly asks, pulling me from my tumultuous thoughts.

I turn my attention to see him watching me over the rim of his glass. His eyes nearly burn my skin. His gaze digs deep enough for him to see my soul, pull it out of me, and toss it wherever he wants.

I gulp loudly. Thane may be my mate, but that doesn't make him any less terrifying in my eyes. Not that he would ever hurt us, but sometimes, his words are enough to inflict more pain than anything he might do to us physically.

It's the words that bring the most pain and damage to a relation-ship. We are fortunate; not all mates are as understanding as Thane is, in certain aspects at least. Any other dominant man would have dragged Leon in front of us and humiliated him for lying.

With those thoughts in mind, I open my mouth, glance at Thane, and instantly snap it shut. This doesn't seem like the best moment for me to speak up, so perhaps it's better that I avoid the question. At least for now.

However, my hesitation is not missed by Thane. "Choose your words wisely, Raidon. You know I detest liars, and Leon is in enough trouble when he returns. So, unless you want to be punished along with him, I suggest you speak truthfully," he warns, in a low, threatening tone.

I sure as shit don't want to be Leon when he gets home.

The thing is, all of us are Alphas. We are destined to clash, but Thane is the most dominant of us. So, he's the one we chose to lead us, and with that comes a power none of us could withstand once we submitted to Thane.

"May I answer a little later?" I ask as I lean back in my chair. Instead of responding with words, Thane nods—one tense, sharp nod.

But then the silence draws on and he decides to speak. "You may if you promise the answer will be truthful. I understand that you don't want to betray Leon, Raidon. However, it would be best if you keep in mind that I'm asking only because I already know the answer," Thane states. I just nod my head in return; there isn't anything I could say at this point.

"What do you think of Zara? That Omega," Thane suddenly asks, bringing up a much-needed change in topic.

"She is quiet. Why?" A simple answer, though a truthful one. Or at least it is for now.

I can tell she has a defiant streak and I'm curious—no, eager—to see the moment she snaps.

An angry Omega is so entertaining. Like an angry beaver swinging around a tiny tree it just bit off. I internally chuckle at the mental image of her pitching a fit at our feet. I can picture how Thane would drag her over his lap to put her back in her place.

Blinking, I shake my head to get rid of the mental images built up by my mind.

"Good. So, I can assume you're not rattled by the Omega, then?" Thane asks and raises an eyebrow. His question, however, makes me wonder if perhaps he is rattled.

We haven't had an Omega work for us in years. Thane can't stand to be in their presence, so I know Leila will have some answering to do.

Zara is the only Omega in the building that works for us, and we have our reasons for that, reasons Leila plainly ignored when she hired her.

"Not really," I answer with a shrug, a little too excited to see where this conversation might bring us.

Thane isn't a person who discusses anything just for the sake of discussion. He always has a reason for why he brings up specific topics, and the Omega seems so irrelevant to our current conversation that I can't help but wonder why Thane would mention her in the first place.

"Good. In that case, you can help me get her to quit or find a good reason to fire her," he announces and brings the glass back to his lips.

"Wait, you want to fire her?" I ask, a little too shocked for my own good. The office really needed an assistant, and none of us are good at keeping up with the place the way she had on her first day.

I know Thane can be cruel to the employees. Shit, I've lost track of the number of times we had to cover up their deaths when Thane let his temper get the best of him. But I worry he might go too far this time, simply because she is an Omega.

He wants me to make her quit, or find a reason to fire her, but what if I can't do that? What if Zara turns out to be more challenging than Thane thinks? What if she can take any humiliation Thane dishes out and still keep working with a straight face, like a true professional?

Or what if she's so good at what she does that there won't be any actual reason to fire her? It's not like I can pull a reason out of my ass. I'm not a magician.

Thane chuckles and shakes his head as if I amuse him. "They always break. She will be no different."

FIFTEEN

~R aidon~

Thane lets out a breath and places his glass back on the table. "Rhen is on board; I already spoke to him. Leon, though, I don't trust him with this job. You know how he gets whenever he's around Omegas," he explains.

I nod at his observation, fully aware of the truth behind his words. We all know why Leon went back to that strip club—he was looking for that Omega.

The door to the dining room opens, and I sigh in relief the moment I get a whiff of Leon's and Rhen's scents. However, I can't say I missed the smell of Leon's fear mixed with his arousal.

Leon knows precisely what is coming his way. The moment we catch his scent, Thane is already getting out of his seat.

Rhen walks in first and Leon is right behind him, nervously glancing around Rhen as if he can use him as a shield. As soon as Leon spots me, a cheeky grin spreads across his lips. I do my best to stifle a chuckle when I hear Thane slide his chair across the floor and tuck it back in place at the table.

The sound of his movements don't go unnoticed by Leon. His

eyes widen in horror. Just as I thought. Yep, he knows exactly what is coming his way now. He shouldn't have lied to Thane's face. Maybe then, we wouldn't end up in this mess together. But what did I expect? We always end up pulled into Leon's dramas, even when we have nothing to do with it.

Leon is our youngest mate and a cheeky little shit who loves pressing Thane's buttons and testing his patience. I swear, sometimes it seems like Leon enjoys Thane's punishments more than he fears them.

My eyes follow Rhen as he quickly abandons Leon, stepping to the side right as Leon shrieks. He darts back through the living room and heads toward the stairs.

"That's right, Leon, now you want to fucking run from me, huh?" Thane yells after Leon while he casually stalks after his prey. He forces his hands into his pockets and meanders up the stairs, looking like the most relaxed guy I've ever seen.

Thane could easily be mistaken as someone who's just mindlessly striding around the place, not an Alpha leader who's about to discipline the fuck out of someone.

Rhen lets out a heavy breath and shakes his head as we listen to Thane hunt down Leon. The commotion going on upstairs is loud, but as usual, we ignore the sounds. It's not like this is our first time witnessing something like this happen under the roof of this madhouse.

"I suppose I should reheat dinner; it has to be cold by now," Rhen groans, and I get up from my seat to help him when we hear Leon squeal from what I suppose is Thane finding him wherever he was hiding.

"Where did you find him?" I ask Rhen as I follow him out to the kitchen with a baking tray in my hands. Rhen opens the oven door and pulls out the first rung as I slide the tray inside.

"Where do you think I found him?" Rhen answers as if it is obvious, and it is. I just kind of hoped I was wrong.

I sigh and lean against the counter. I cringe the moment I hear the thunderous smack of Thane disciplining Leon. Rhen stands aside and grits his teeth.

"That sounded painful. However, knowing Leon as well as we do, he's probably wriggling his ass and begging for more," Rhen says right as we hear another sound of a slap echoing off the walls. Damn, that one had to be painful. Thane's getting down with hardcore discipline tonight. Leon pressed his buttons today.

"But Thane is pretty pissed, so we shouldn't be surprised," I say while we listen to Thane go to town on Leon's ass.

"I think I will try to speak to Thane later. Maybe he will allow it if one of us goes with him," Rhen says, looking everywhere but at me.

Either way, we need to figure something out, or this will become a daily thing. I have no idea how long any of us could roll with it, or how much Leon's ass could take, if this became an everyday thing.

There is a reason we refuse to allow Leon to feed on Omegas. Their blood is intoxicating to vampires, even the most powerful ones. It's sweet and addictive. I don't want to see Leon in rehab again for his addiction.

Leon wouldn't struggle like this if our Omega hadn't escaped. Leon would have a constant source of blood, yet, without her, we can't monitor him. Above that, it's nearly impossible to stop Leon from killing Omegas—he has done it in the past and will do it again. Not because Leon is heartless or a psycho; it's his addiction. He does not know when to stop, and it is too late by the time he realizes he should.

After about twenty minutes, Leon falls quiet upstairs and Rhen grabs the tray from the oven, knowing they will be down soon. I take the rest of the plates and set them on the dinner table.

Rhen portions the food on our plates and just as I take my seat, Leon comes downstairs, buck naked and pale as a ghost. I suppose he didn't enjoy Thane's punishment this time. Thane's punishment isn't over until he allows Leon his clothes. I chew my lip nervously as I quickly assess Leon, double-checking he is okay.

Evidence of how brutal Thane was in his punishment is left clear across Leon's reddened ass cheeks. Leon stops beside the table and stares, which is unusual for him. Not a word leaves his lips, and I go to reach for him when I hear footsteps and stop myself. A moment later, Thane enters the dining room, tugging off his tie as he walks closer in a blaze of fury.

"Sit!" Thane snarls at Leon, who whimpers and instantly complies.

I don't blame him, though. The dark cherry color of his ass looks painful, and I can tell that Thane didn't just use his belt but also took his hand to Leon's ass.

I watch as Leon shifts in his seat and hisses in pain while Rhen sucks his lips into his mouth, trying his hardest to stifle his muffled laughter.

Rhen carefully sets the food in front of Leon, but Thane grabs the plate, adds more food, and sets it down, tossing a napkin over Leon's lap.

"Eat!" Thane orders him, sounding all sorts of pissed off and challenging him to disobey. Thane is looking for a fight and Leon recognizes that, so he doesn't push him. Leon knows he would be on the losing side of any fight if it escalated.

Rhen takes his seat beside me and we both try to ignore the sounds that escape Leon. We can tell he is pretty uncomfortable, but Rhen and I know better than to comfort him. Not until Thane gives his approval, and after seeing his mood today, I sure as shit won't risk getting my ass spanked by Thane.

When Leon finally brings a forkful of food to his lips, Thane turns his gaze toward us, focusing on Rhen. "So, did you find her files?" he asks, but Rhen keeps his gaze down, staring at his plate, stuffing his mouth and shaking his head.

As silence creates a heavy tension in the dining room, Rhen gulps down his food and speaks up. "Nope," he says, popping the 'P' at the end.

Thane growls, knowing damn well Leila didn't bother to do any background checks on our new assistant. I know the woman well enough, so I'm confident that Leila probably just saw Omega on her resume, did a sniff test to ensure she wasn't lying about it, and hired her on the spot.

For the past year, Leila has been doing everything in her power to force us to accept another Omega. She needs to stop trying to force it on Thane. It won't end well, and by the angry look on Thane's face, Leila will be his first victim tomorrow.

CHAPTER
SIXTEEN

~H arlow~

The alarm blares so loudly, it reminds me of an air horn. I'm tempted to smash my fist against it as soon as I wake up, or even better, toss it out the damn window that doesn't even lock.

At least this morning, I could sleep in a little, even though I can hardly describe my sleep as anything close to restful. My skin feels like it isn't a part of me anymore, as if it's crawling and the bed beneath me is alive.

Sitting up, I shudder with disgust, as violent as ever. Yep, it's clear that I need to take another shower to get rid of the bedbugs. I'm sure the dirty stairwell behind the plaza would have been a cleaner choice to spend the night instead of the bug-infested bed in the shitty motel room I had to pay money for. So much for thinking anything would be better than the streets. The streets would definitely be better than this.

After rummaging through the small number of toiletries I own, I hop in the shower and scrub my skin so hard with my loofah that I'm surprised I didn't scrub off a dozen layers of my skin. With the strength I have to use, I might as well just scrape all of my skin off. If only that would help eliminate the awful feeling those bed bugs left on me.

As I finally focus on scrubbing the shampoo into my hair, which I'm sure is now infested with the critters from the seedy bed I slept in, I hear my phone ring on the nightstand next to the bed of nightmares and despair.

I let it ring out, fully aware that I don't have to be at work for an hour. Instead of running around the motel room like a lunatic to pick up the phone, I close my eyes and rinse the shampoo from my hair. Then, I turn the taps off and step out of the shower.

My hand reaches out to retrieve a towel, but once I notice the state of it, I drop the idea and opt for my clothes from yesterday and use them to dry myself.

The phone on the nightstand starts ringing again while I struggle to dry myself, figuring out that clothes aren't the most effective way to reach my goal.

Cursing under my breath, I race out of the shitty bathroom and snatch my phone. Dread pools in my stomach, and my heart nearly stops when I see Thane's name on the phone screen.

Hesitantly, I answer it, bringing the phone to my ear with a wildly shaking hand.

"What part of being a personal assistant did you fail to understand when you read the job description?" he growls through the phone, sending a cold shiver down my spine.

Thane is scary, and if he can scare me like this during a phone call, I fear what he could do if we were to stand face-to-face right now.

But, as I focus back on his words, I have to resist the urge to roll my eyes because the bastard may somehow notice that. As for his question, I didn't understand the personal assistant part because I applied for a damn receptionist position, not to become an Alpha's personal, perfect little coffee-bitch.

"My apologies, sir, I was taking a shower and didn't hear the phone ringing," I answer as politely as possible, while in reality, I wish I could kindly invite Thane to suck on my imaginary dick, or even better, to fucking choke on it and die.

"Fucking useless Omega! I need you to wait for the mailman out front," Thane snarls at me, sounding far more pissed off than he was a moment ago. There goes the give and get principle—I give him kindness, he gives me shit. Fucking prick!

"Around what time does he arrive?" I ask and slowly lower the phone from my ear to check the time. Well, that's not the only reason. I also do it to avoid the high risk of this Alpha asshole screaming so loud I go deaf.

"6:30 a.m.. The package I'm waiting for has to be signed for. If I have to collect it from the post office—you're fired!" Thane snaps and hangs up on me.

I stare at the phone screen in disbelief until the numbers finally make sense and dread fills my gut. Fuck! I have barely ten minutes until Thane's stupid mail carrier arrives.

I guess it's a good thing I chose this crappy motel because the office building is only a street away. I race around the room, grab my clothes, and dismiss the ironing board I set up. If Thane wants me in at such an ungodly hour, he has to take what he gets.

I hurry to rip my clothes on, the fabric sticking to my wet skin, and I barely manage one clasp on my bra before I snatch my de-scenter and suppressants.

Hurriedly, I tip the bottle of pills to my lips and down three tablets right before spraying the de-scenter over every inch of me. I toss the can in my bag, throw the bag over my shoulder, snatch the keys, and pick up my heels by the door.

I have no time to fiddle with the damn heels, so I rush out the door and quickly lock it behind me. It's not like I have any valuables anyone could steal, but it's better to be safe than sorry. I check the knob, ensure the door is locked correctly, and race for the stairs. Halfway down the steps, I jump the rest to be faster.

"Not today, you fucker. You won't be firing me today!" I hiss under my breath as I run like someone set my ass on fire, and honestly, I'm pretty sure Thane would gladly do that if I'm late. Well, that and fire me, whichever that heartless asshole prefers.

I'm sure he would get the word 'fired' branded on my ass just to prove his stupid point. That's how petty the scary motherfucker appears.

By the time I finally reach the huge skyrise building and nearly vomit up my lungs—just in case anyone is wondering—my hair is dry, and I'm sure it looks as messy as a bird's nest.

The postal delivery officer stands next to his car, about to get in, and I push myself harder, almost tackling the poor elderly man before he can close the back of his van.

"Keller documents!" I pant out, clutching my sides, wondering if he even understood the gibberish words I just blurted out. I must look like a madwoman to him.

"Miss? Are you okay? Do you need help? Can I call someone for you? An ambulance, or maybe the police?" the kind man offers as I clutch his arm, still struggling to regulate my breathing back to somewhat normal.

"My boss, Mr. Keller, he's expecting a package, and I'm here to sign it for him," I gasp out, grabbing my sides with more force as I feel a sharp stitch in one of them. Body, don't you fucking dare to fail me now!

CHAPTER
SEVENTEEN

~H arlow~

"Zara Maverick?" the mailman asks, looking a little shocked. Okay, who am I kidding? The poor man looks so shocked he could jump out of his own skin.

I nod and smile at him as politely as I can, while the only thought in my mind is to not close my eyes and faint right in front of him. I will drop dead before I let Thane humiliate me like this or fire me for a stupid joke he's pulling.

I mean, who, in their right mind, sends their employee for an important package ten minutes before the supposed arrival of the mailman? That prick is more slippery than a sea cucumber.

I try to focus on deep breaths as I dig through my bag and present the mailman with my work ID. The old man sighs but still digs through the back of his van and hands me a huge envelope of what I suppose has to be some important documents.

I sign for the package, thank the man, and walk to the stairs in front of the building. Once I reach them, I collapse on the steps. My breathing is as heavy and rapid as it was when I caught the mailman. And yet, even now, I don't care that I might look homeless—I just ran down an entire street, all the way here in panic. They could give me a damn break.

Once I'm sure I can stand up without fainting or throwing up, I move toward the doors I saw the security staff unlock a couple of minutes ago.

As I enter the building, I show the security guard my employee ID and he lets me through. I ignore the odd look he gives me and hurry toward the elevators.

When I get to my floor, I walk around, turning on all the lights. Then, I turn toward my desk and power up my computer. Setting the envelope of documents on the edge of my desk, I dig through my bag for a hairbrush and the small set of makeup I carry around for emergencies. Such as this.

Hastily, I do a rush job of my makeup in the bathroom. Taming my wild hair, I pull it into a bun on top of my head. Satisfied with my appearance, I move to the kitchenette where I get five mugs ready and prepare them for the bosses' morning coffee, while making one for myself too. I dump two teaspoons of instant coffee in my mug and grin—this much I've earned after the awful morning I had. Fuck, I hate running more than I hate morning-people.

I swear, once the coffee is ready and I can gulp down a few mouthfuls of the warm juice of gods, I can feel the caffeinated beverage warm my soul. There's nothing better than the first coffee of the day.

I take my cup back to my desk and focus on checking all the work emails. I send the important ones to their tablets and desktops. Once I'm done with emails, I check their meeting schedules and equip the conference room down the hall.

As I walk back to the kitchenette, I'm about to make their coffees when a childish, evil thought creeps into my mind.

Thane wants to speak to me like shit and treat me as such. Fine, freaking fine by me! I dump his coffee in the trash and take his mug to the toilet, giving it a rise inside the toilet bowl. Snickering to myself, I flip off the cameras in the hallway. God, I hope they don't check those.

Then I walk back to the kitchenette and use a paper towel to dry his mug before I wash my hands in the sink.

Retrieving his mug, I set about to make the coffee when I gasp. Fuck! It's the wrong mug! The golden lettering I mistook for T is actually an L.

How the fuck did I miss that detail and mess up so spectacularly?

I'm about to quickly wash the mug and fix my stupid mistake, but I stop in my tracks when I hear footsteps coming from the elevator lobby. God damn it, they arrived already!

Rhen walks in first and retrieves his mug as my heart hammers against my ribcage. I quickly make Leon's coffee, fully aware that if I wash the mug in front of Rhen, he might suspect my doings. What's done is done; I can't take away the stupid mistake I made.

The men file in one by one, retrieving their coffees, and Leon plucks his mug from my hand just as Thane walks in, as grumpy as ever.

"The files," he demands. Oh, that means there will be no 'good morning, sunshine' now? I'll show him! One day he will regret ever thinking about messing with me!

"On my desk," I stutter out, and he looks at Raidon.

"Don't you live on the other side of town?" Thane asks as he brings his hand to his face and pinches the bridge of his nose. What got him so worked up?

I nod my head, unsure if I should say anything at all. I was here to sign for the documents. Isn't that what he wanted from me?

"How did you get here so fast?" Rhen asks, and I blink at him as this shitstorm clicks together. They are looking for a reason to fire me. *How dare they?* I've been an outstanding employee. Do they not remember the state of that damn filing room and the clusterfuck they left the kitchenette in!

"I always arrive early to work," I lie, shrugging my shoulders to make my words more believable. "Early bird catches the worm," I grit out, infuriated by the thought that these four men are trying to sabotage me.

"Good. You can get the mail every morning," Thane growls at me and snatches his cup. As Thane brings the mug to his lips, my eyes dart to Leon's right as he sips his coffee.

My heart does a double, no triple, backflip as I restrain myself from showing off the devious smile that tugs on the corners of my lips. I grab my mug and walk out of the kitchenette, suppressing my laughter. Maybe I didn't get to hit my actual target, but Leon deserves this after what he did yesterday anyway, so it's not all bad.

"I think our dishwasher needs deep cleaning again. My coffee has a funny taste," I hear Leon whine behind me.

I don't bother to turn around and observe my small victory, but I can't help but smile as I walk back to my desk. I reach for the envelope that turned my entire morning into a catastrophe and turn around to find the devil himself standing directly behind me. By the devil, I mean Thane, because if the devil actually walks the face of the earth, there is no more precise representation of the source of evil himself than one of my bosses.

Thane snatches the envelope from my hand, turns on his heel, and storms off toward his office. *Well, good morning to you too, asshole!* I think as he slams his door, making the windows rattle.

CHAPTER
EIGHTEEN

~Harlow~

It seems like the following week flies by in a blur. All four of the asshole Alpha-gang keep dumping ridiculous tasks on my shoulders, but the one I'm stuck on now is definitely the icing on the goddamn cake.

Apparently, there is another package coming in tonight for Thane that is so damn important, and I'm the one who has to deliver it to their packhouse before the clock hits 7 p.m.. Those morons never promised to pay me for overtime hours, yet gladly use every chance to make my work experience as miserable as possible.

"Here is the key you can use to lock up when you leave. The delivery will be at the loading docks behind the building," Rhen says with a chuckle as he passes me the key. This is so unfair! I have to stay behind for an hour after the workday ends.

I watch him leave with the others before I make my way down to said loading docks. The place looks like what one would expect to find—down here, it's a dimly lit area, but I still manage to find a few staff areas, a cleaning supplies closet, and some kind of storage area packed with packs of printer paper of various sizes and broken computer parts.

This week, the four men have done everything and sought any—even the stupidest—reason to fire me. Too bad for them, because they've actually taught me a valuable lesson about myself—I'm damn amazing at working under pressure, and each time I complete one of their ridiculous tasks successfully, I swear, Thane looks like he is about to blow up or murder me. Ah, the sweet, silent taste of little victories.

As I wait by the loading dock, I glance at the key in my hand and the security password. I'm back to sleeping in the plaza stairwell, and the last few nights I had barely any sleep. I have also reached a dangerously low amount of my suppressants, which only makes matters worse.

I dread running out of them because Thane and Raidon have me running ragged all day long; I'm too tired to even walk to the strip club and beg Tal for some work.

Oddly enough, Leon was AWOL today and yesterday. The rest of them are tense and acting out of character, making me wonder what is going on with the fourth asshole.

Nevertheless, this is not the time for me to dwell on something that is not even remotely related to the task at hand nor any of my business. So instead, I watch the time tick by and grow annoyingly impatient. Where the hell is this delivery person?

My eyes are once again drawn to my phone as I glance at the time. I have fifteen minutes until the delivery arrives. Honestly, I still don't understand why Thane didn't let me leave work and return around the time I am supposed to pick up his delivery. And what really confuses me is why he couldn't get it delivered to his pack-house if he needed it there, not at the office.

A chuckle leaves my lips as I shake my head at the silly thoughts. Of course, I know why Thane is doing this. He wants to break me and have a reason to fire me or push me out of the company by driving me to quit. I guess that's the reason why he and the rest of the assholes have been doing nothing but killing me with one impossible task after another for the past week. God, do I hate them. I hate them with passion.

My eyes dart in the direction of the storage locker behind me. I have a master key to the building. For a brief moment, I contemplate skipping across the street to the smoke store where I know they have a key cutter. I pass by the building so many times that it's impossible to miss the sign. Besides, the store is only open for a few more minutes, so technically, I have enough time to run there and back before the delivery person arrives.

In spite of my better judgment, I succumb to the temptation as I chew on my bottom lip. At least it sounds a little better than spending my nights on the stairwell at the plaza.

Taking the risk before I can hesitate or overthink, I run across the road, and my stomach instantly drops when the man behind the counter announces that cutting a copy of the key would cost me fifteen dollars.

I hand him the money and the key, cursing to myself as now I'm left with twenty-five dollars to cover food and other necessary items.

I tell the man I will return to pick up the key once it's done and rush back to work to wait by the loading dock. I tap my foot against the concrete impatiently when I notice a smoke store worker pull the roller shutters down; I shriek and rush back across the road. I wave my hands at the man from the smoke store, only to see the delivery van pull into the loading docks. Fuck, damn it, shit!

"The key!" I extend my palm toward him as I ask the vampire who works there to return what I paid for, along with the original. Leaving such an important key in the hands of someone as shady as this guy is absolutely not an option for me. My career, and probably my life, would be at stake if I make a mistake like that.

As the man groans, he pushes up the roller shutter and darts inside, cursing and groaning. A few minutes later, he comes out again and hands me an envelope with both keys inside. When I see the delivery driver get out of the vehicle, I gush a quick, "Thank you!" and I sprint back to the loading docks as a woman steps out of the delivery van.

CHAPTER
NINETEEN

~**H**arlow~

A low, angry row of curse words leaves me when I realize what this important delivery is. A fucking load of dry cleaning! Is Thane for real right now? I had to stay behind, after work hours, to pick up his dry cleaning and bring it to his house? That man must be delusional, because there is no other excuse I can think of to explain his unreasonable requests and the insane lack of brain cells. The van even has a sign on it stating it delivers city-wide! No reason he couldn't get it delivered to his damn house.

I stomp to the back of the van, boiling in anger, barely holding myself together. The small woman jumps as she turns around and faces me. I don't mean to startle her, but I'm too pissed off to care. I assume she is scared because I am panting like a heifer from dashing back and forth across the road.

Once the woman piles up Thane's clothes, I sign the paperwork for his stupid dry cleaning and watch as the woman drives away while I'm stuck in the shittiest situation of my life.

Well, not quite the shittiest of them all, but I'm so damn close to a mental breakdown. I'm sure Thane would be delighted to see that because he would be rid of me and probably land me in the loony bin because of his antics.

Glancing at my phone, I see I have twenty minutes to get to the packhouse, and I head for the bus stop. I barely get to the front of the building when I see the bus drive past me. I chase after it, waving frantically in an effort to get it to stop.

The bus driver either ignores my waving arms and screaming or doesn't see me. I am seriously on the verge of a nervous breakdown. I will never make it in time, and I need this job. I didn't put up with their fucking bullshit only to get fired because of a fucking dry cleaning service being bloody late!

I rummage in my bag when I notice the man from the smoke shop getting in his car, having finished locking all the roller shutters in place and securing the building. Walking over to him, I stop beside his flashy silver car.

"Excuse me, do you know where the closest taxi stand is?" I ask him, knowing I would have to use my last twenty-five dollars to get to the packhouse on time. As he looks over at me, he scratches the back of his neck. He isn't bad looking, but it is clear he is as sleazy as most vamps.

"Down near the subway," he answers, and I groan, stomping my foot in annoyance. Great! That is a ten-minute walk alone. "Where are you headed?" he asks, and I rummage through my bag and hand him the paper with the address.

"I am headed that way. How much money you got?" he asks while pulling on a leather jacket, and I roll my eyes. No one could do a good deed around here. He just said he is headed that way!

I pull my scrunched-up money from the bottom of my bag. "That's it?" he asks, flicking his dark hair from his red eyes and licking his plump lips. His fangs protrude slightly from his upper lip, glinting under the streetlights, and I fight the urge to take a step back from him.

"Do I look rich to you? Yes, that is all I got," I snap, annoyed and about to snatch my money back. He glances me up and down and purses his lips before sniffing the air. "Ah, definitely not, buddy. You are not feeding on me," I tell him before he suggests such a thing.

"Depends, how badly you want to get to Mr. Keller's place?" he taunts. My face falls. Of course, this asshole knew my boss. "I will make you a deal. Let me take one little bite, and—"

I hold up a hand, stopping him.

"No freaking way. I know Omega blood is addictive," I tell him with a wave of my hand. He lets out a breath, eyeing me.

"And I am not fucking you either. Just give me my money back," I tell him, trying to snatch it back, but he pulls it away.

"Then give me something else," he purrs, licking his lips.

"And I am not sucking your dick. Just give me my damn money. Fuck, all you men are the same!" I growl at him.

"Fine, fine, show me your tits. I won't tell him you just had his master key cut in my store and I will drop you off at his place," he says slyly. I feel all the blood leave my body at his words. He knew what the key was for? He laughs while I'm on the verge of throwing up. I glance at my phone and curse. I don't really have a choice. If I'm late, Thane said he would fire me, and this asshole now knows he has me.

"Fine, but I have to be there in twelve minutes. Think you can manage that?" I ask. He whistles and rocks back on his heels and sighs.

"Yeah, I can get you there in time. We have a deal?" he asks, his eyes sparkling mischievously, and I nervously glance around. Man, anyone would think the man had never seen a pair of breasts before with how eager he is. Yet, the street is pretty empty.

"Hurry, hurry, or we won't get there in time," the vampire says.

I grit my teeth and put the dry cleaning on the hood of his car. Closing my eyes, I cringe. It's just skin. I remind myself that I need my job. I lift my shirt, wishing the ground would swallow me whole. He huffs before he grabs one. I growl when I hear the click of his phone camera and I rip my shirt down and growl at him.

90

"You'd better not have taken a photo," I snarl at him, knowing he did. He quickly pockets his phone.

"Need something to have a jerk-off to later, so thanks," he purrs, and I glare at him.

The man laughs and rolls his eyes. "Come on then. What's your name, anyway?"

I contemplate lying, but it's clear he knows my bosses. How? I don't know, but if I lie, he might snitch on me about the key.

"Zara, and yours?" I ask, slightly nervous about getting in the car with a vampire, but what choice do I have? He seems friendly enough, if not a little sleazy. Besides, if I go missing, there are plenty of cameras to witness me getting in his car.

"Vadum," he answers, climbing in as I do. I clip my seat belt while holding the dry cleaning on my lap. He drives me to the pack-house, and I grip the leather seats the entire way, cringing at every corner we slide around. Yet, he gets me there with two minutes to spare.

"Thanks," I tell him, shutting the door before he revs the engine and takes off down the street.

The packhouse is a fancy, over-the-top mansion just on the outskirts of the city. I learned from Vadum that the Kellers not only own the business where I work, but the entire damn block. So that explained how Vadum knew them. He rents the store from them. Looking around after Vadum drops me at the white iron gates out the front, I walk over to the intercom. I press the button and wait for one of them to answer, hoping it won't take too long because it is getting cold, and I know it is supposed to snow tonight. I do not feel like making the trek back and being caught in a damn snowstorm.

CHAPTER
TWENTY

~T hane~

"I'm guessing she wasn't there again?" I ask Raidon as he walks in, finally getting home. All week, Raidon has taken Leon to the strip club looking for the Omega. I fucking knew this would become an issue from the first night he fed on her.

"Yep, we waited until we spotted the manager. She didn't know who we were talking about, so she must be the new night manager to fill in for Bree. I haven't seen her before," Raidon answers as Leon shoves past him. I try to grab him, but he slaps my hand away.

Leon storms past and goes down to our Den, no doubt to go looking through the blood bags, though he won't find what he is looking for. Most of them are either our blood or donated blood from the blood banks, which do not stock Omega blood, given its addictive qualities.

I could probably source some, however, by making a few calls. It is fucking pricey, though, which is half the reason we searched for an Omega, not wanting to chuck him into rehab in the first place. Though another stint looks to be in the cards at this rate. Great, the media will have a fucking field day, just what we need.

Tal and Bree can't help us. They are both out of the country, visiting Tal's parents.

Leon refuses to feed on us, and I am on the verge of ordering him to. He is ravenous, and I had to keep him home from work for the past two days. One sip of Omega blood and he has relapsed entirely.

"Leon, now!" I order. I hate ordering them, hate taking their free will, but even Rhen suggested it on the way home.

"What are we going to do? He can't keep going on like this," Raidon asks worriedly. I hear stomping up the steps as he comes back from our basement Den. The last time I had been down there was when we built the Den for Harlow, and I haven't been back there since.

I usually send the others down there. I can't stand seeing what could have been. Our pack would have been complete with Harlow, but she had to go kill my mother and get herself killed in those damn woods. There is no way she would have survived out there; though we searched, and still continue to, holding onto hope but knowing the chances are slim.

It is rogue territory; unsafe even to pack wolves due to the high numbers of rogues in the area. Even if we had found her, I probably would have killed her for what she did to my mother. My mother didn't deserve that. She was so excited when she learned we found an Omega, and so were both my fathers.

Leon comes up from the basement, his clothes all wrinkled, and he is a mess. His eyes are bloodshot, showing no white left. His fangs haven't retracted in two days, and he is turning crazed—another reason I couldn't let him be at work. With Zara there, it is too risky. If he fed on her, she could sue us. Or, even worse, I'd have to cover up her death when he overfed on her.

Thinking of her, I curse, remembering the most recent impossible task I gave her. I even called the dry cleaners to make sure they would arrive with only twenty minutes spare, knowing a bus or taxi would take her at least thirty-five minutes to get here. Well, at least now I have reason to fire her. I smile at the thought before waving at Leon to join me where I'm sitting on the sofa.

"You need to feed," I tell him as he steps closer. Raidon moves behind him, blocking his exit. Rhen slips silently into the living room, taking up the exit to the foyer. Leon glances around and growls, not liking the way we cage him in. He almost appears rabid. I know he doesn't want our blood, but it is better than him starving because he has been craving Omega blood all week. He also stopped eating, which isn't good and only makes him worse.

I hate seeing him like this, hate the feelings of longing and despair I get from him through the bond, the starvation he feels. "Come here," I order and he tries to fight the command. I growl at him, throwing the total weight of my Alpha command behind it when I heard the intercom button for the front gate. Everyone freezes, and I drop the command, looking at Rhen.

I nod to him, and he wanders to the front door to see who is on the screen. "Who is it?" I call out while watching Leon.

"Uh, it is Zara," Rhen calls back to me, and I jump up. "Fucking impossible," I curse. There is no way she could get here in time.

"It is definitely her," Rhen says, poking his head around the corner of the entrance. I glance at my watch and curse. Fuck, how did she get here so fast? That second of distraction cost me as Leon bolts past me and out the door as soon as Rhen hits the button to let her in.

"Grab him!" I call to Rhen, only to hear him get knocked over and the sound of breaking glass as the vase hits the floor from its home on the hallway stand. Raidon growls, chasing after him. I give chase too, ripping Rhen to his feet as I pass him. He is on his back, on the floor where Leon had tackled him. But Leon, being a damn hybrid, is way faster than us, and by the time we reach the door, he is long gone.

"Fuck!" I scream, chasing after him, when I hear her voice.

"Leon?" she asks before I hear her blood-curdling scream.

CHAPTER
TWENTY-ONE

~Harlow~

I stand by the gate, and at this point, the waiting isn't just getting on my nerves. No, it's so much worse —I'm literally freezing my ass off, the brewing storm giving the wind a harsh bite.

The bag with Thane's dry cleaning hangs folded over my arm, and its weight is slowly getting to me, but thank god, I hear the buzz of the electronic gates. As the gates swing open, I can't wait any longer, so I quickly slide through the gap and walk up the long driveway toward the house.

It's actually not a house. It's a goddamn mansion—a little too fancy for someone like Thane if anyone asks me, but so be it. As I walk closer, the surrounding lights make the building look like some fairytale fantasy. Too bad the only fantasy I expect to be greeted by is the angry troll.

I'm about a quarter of the way up when I stop. Leon appears ahead of me. He stands on the concrete path, breathing so heavily that it makes him look like he's in pain.

"Leon?" I call out to him, a little confused about why he's outside, not inside the house with the rest of the assholes.

He tilts his head to the side and the moon reflects off his face, revealing his sharp, pointed fangs. I gasp at the view before me. One minute he stands at least twenty yards ahead of me, and the next, he appears right in front of me after a blur of motion. Leon grabs me so suddenly that I drop my bag and Thane's dry cleaning.

His fangs pierce my skin and sink into my neck as a feral snarl leaves his lips. The scream that escapes my mouth is so loud that it could deafen, but I can vaguely hear someone else screaming his name.

My attempts to struggle against him are futile as Leon's fingers press into the flesh on my arms with so much strength, I'm sure he will leave ugly bruises all over my skin. My scream dies out once I feel someone rip Leon off me, sending my body sprawling on the hard, concrete driveway.

An unbearable wave of pain shoots throughout my whole body as I land on the concrete, hip first. With a loud groan, I struggle to roll over and sit up, but more pain shoots through my body with every move I make. My elbow is badly grazed and my neck throbs as if it has a heartbeat of its own.

I look up, just as Rhen stalks toward me and Raidon walks over to help subdue Leon, who is currently fighting Thane, screaming at him to let him get to me.

I have never seen a crazed vampire before, let alone this danger-ously close to me. Leon is terrifying and acts like an absolute savage until Thane punches him. I cringe at the thud as I watch Raidon catch Leon before his body hits the concrete.

Fingers aggressively lock around my arm and pull me to my feet. I turn my head in a daze to face Rhen's furious expression. He glares at me as if it is my fault that his mate just attacked me out of the blue.

Oh, no, sir, it's all Leon; I didn't do a thing to get stuck in this mess. If they need someone to paint as a bad guy, they are welcome to blame Leon, who is the actual villain in this situation. Or, blame Thane, because that asshole had the brilliant idea of getting me this close to his stupid packhouse.

"Dare to report this to the media, and I will bury you alive! Do you understand me? You won't risk my mate!" Rhen snaps at me, shaking me.

Now it's absolutely clear that they blame me, but for what? For doing my job and fulfilling their stupid wishes? Wow, this is some twisted way to thank the employee of the month, which I should be, because who else has enough patience to put up with their mess?

"Leave her, Rhen. I will command her to keep quiet, just get her back to the packhouse and clean her up. We can't chuck her in a taxi like that," Thane snaps at Rhen.

A menacing growl leaves Rhen as he drags me toward the mansion. My heart thumps painfully in my chest as I glance behind me to see Thane toss Leon over his shoulder and follow us.

I stumble over my own feet as I try to keep up with Rhen, while he all but drags me closer to the massive building. He stops at the mansion's open door and glares down at me. "No snooping around, and don't fucking touch anything!" he screams and leads me down a corridor beside a set of double marble stairs.

My eyes burn with hot tears that I refuse to let out. My entire body trembles under Rhen's potent aura. He shoves me into a bathroom and looks at me like I'm a dirty animal. I stumble once he pushes me but manage to catch and steady myself by grabbing onto the edge of the huge clawfoot bathtub.

"Shower and meet us in the living room as soon as you're done here. I'll send Tania in. She will bring you some fucking clothes!" Rhen snarls at me as I swallow down the lump forming in my throat.

He slams the bathroom door shut with so much force that I wince. After sucking in a few deep breaths, I look around.

The bathroom is massive. It has double sink basins and a huge shower, and in the center stands the huge clawfoot tub that I'm using to hold my balance.

As much as the thought of a hot bath tempts me, and I would love to sink into the hot water to forget all my worries for a moment, I know that I can't. Even if I think back, I can't remember the last time I had a bath. Probably at the Omega facility, but it has been so long since then.

Despite the temptation, I'm able to pull my gaze away from the tub. It takes me a few seconds for my eyes to focus on the image in the mirror, and once they have settled on it, I gasp.

Blood has soaked into the fabric of my shirt and blazer; I am bleeding all over my clothes. I sniffle as I reach for the hand towel and wet it to dab it on my neck, which has thankfully stopped bleeding.

However, I can't help but cringe at the view—Leon's bite is as savage as he acted, and now, the bite marks look like someone pierced my skin with a rusty can opener. I can barely hold back tears as I clean off the remaining blood. The mental image of Leon's terrifying, animalistic facial expression overwhelms me. There's no way I will ever forget that sight.

While dabbing at my neck and checking that I don't miss even a spot of blood, an older woman slips into the bathroom. Silently, without glancing at me, she places some clothes on the bathtub. She is silent and keeps her gaze on the floor the entire time, slipping back out of the bathroom just the way she entered.

I try my best not to let that get to me, but the way she slips in and out like a thief in the night makes me feel as if I have, in fact, done something wrong. As a result, I perceive myself as an invader, unworthy of kind words. As I hear Thane, Rhen and Raidon argue somewhere in the distance, the tears well up in my eyes, and I try to hold them back, their cruel words not helping my situation either.

CHAPTER
TWENTY-TWO

~H~arlow~

There is nothing I want to hear from those men, and I have no desire to listen to what they have to say. All of them blame me for what happened, and they are angry about my presence as much as they blame me for what happened. It's not as if I ever asked to be dragged down here or inside their mansion.

Maybe if Thane and his gang of mates weren't such absolute assholes and didn't come up with all those stupid tasks for me to do, I would be happy and asleep in the storage closet. In that case, none of this would have happened, and they wouldn't have to deal with the current situation. And, of course, I wouldn't be trapped in their mansion, covered in blood, simply because Leon is too weak to hold himself together and not suck dry every person who walks up their stupid driveway.

My life is such a mess.

I turn on the shower and slowly slip off my ruined, blood-soaked clothes. Initially, I plan to have a hot shower, since that's as much as I deserve after what Leon did to me. But it's not enough, so I turn the faucet to boiling. My skin turns red and probably burns some places, but I don't care because once I step out of the shower, I feel clean as I haven't in ages.

By now, the loud arguments have stopped, and every movement I make in the bathroom sounds extra loud. I let out a shaky breath, reach for the clothes and carefully slip them on, doing my best to avoid ripping the fabric. I won't pay those assholes for clothes I wouldn't need if it weren't for their beloved mate. As I glance in the mirror, I almost smile at my reflection because these clothes aren't too big for me. It's hard to find clothes that fit, yet they do. Like a glove. Which I find quite impressive. I am not built like most girls of short stature. I have more junk in the trunk and am top heavy, usually buying stuff that is either too long or a few sizes too big so I can squeeze my assets in. Yet these fit as if they were made for me.

I can't help but wonder about the actual owner of the clothes they lent me, because I can't see the elderly maid wearing skinny-leg jeans and a low-cut top.

I slip on my shoes and then pull the hoodie over my head. Every article of clothing still has a tag on it, making me wonder if they have a girlfriend. That could explain the clothes and why they are so upset Leon had fed on me. The rest of them can't possibly allow Leon to feed on anyone but their girlfriend, right?

Oddly enough, those thoughts also make tears prick in the corners of my eyes.

I know that it has to be because of the serum—Thane's serum and my stupid Omega instincts kicking in. The realization makes me remember I'm due for my nighttime suppressants.

I grab my bag and rummage through it until I find the bottle, grip it and pull it out. As I open the lid, I tip the bottle up and frown at the six little pills left.

Since I have no other choice but to cut the dosage, I take two pills. I can't afford to take more, especially now. Soon, very darn soon, I need to find some time to get back to the strip club and make some money to buy more of these.

Honestly, I hate to think about what I would have to do there for the seven hundred dollars I need for another bottle of pills. Making that money in tips behind the bar would take ages, so I can't let myself assume it's possible.

I cup my hand under the running water until my palm fills up and bring it to my lips to swallow down some water with the pills. Once I finish with that, I stare back at my reflection in the mirror.

My eyes focus on the lady's clothes I am wearing. I pick at the hoodie and frown. It should have been me; I am supposed to be their Omega, but all of them hate me for crimes I never committed, for the doings of someone I don't even know. They're being so unfair, and it's pissing me off.

I return my attention back to my bag and pull out my de-scenter to spray myself. It's yet another reminder about another thing I am getting dangerously low on, and I don't want to think about the money I need for another one.

I shove my belongings back into my bag, take a deep breath, and move toward the door. My hand lands on the handle before I am ready to leave, but I remind myself it's too late to step back, so I suck in a few deeper breaths, grip the handle, and encourage myself to open the bathroom door.

Once I finally do, I stick my head into the hall and Thane's loud, angry voice echoes off the hallway walls before I step out of the bathroom.

"I'm in the living room, Omega. Get here, now!" A wave of sharp pain ripples through me at his order. I hate it when Alphas do this to Omegas—to show off their power over someone. Yeah, what better way to feed their stupid ego than picking on someone smaller.

But despite that, I have to admit that Thane's aura truly is magnificent and scary at the same time. It's so potent that I don't have to be in front of him to feel the power of his command.

My feet move on their own as I follow my nose toward a massive sitting room. An incredibly large TV sits on the wall above the stunning fireplace. The room has a huge L-shaped couch and a few armchairs scattered around it. The room is twice the size of my old, shitty apartment.

I spot Thane glaring at me from an armchair by the fireplace. The flames illuminate his face, making him look much more dangerous and menacing than he usually appears to be.

He sneers and motions with his fingers for me to come closer. I swallow down the bile that rises up my throat, and my feet obey him before I register how close I'm getting.

As I stop right in front of him, I feel the total weight of Thane's aura crush down on me. My knees go out from under me and hit the floor hard, instantly sending a painful ache through them.

I grit my teeth and feel a bead of sweat run down the back of my neck. My entire body trembles like a leaf in the middle of a storm, getting throttled by violent gusts of wind.

I cry out at the agonizing pain of it. The tears I had been trying to hold back brim and spill over. I bare my neck to him, catching the angry look on his face as Thane glares at me.

"You will not speak of this to anyone. Not a single fucking word. If you so much as utter one damn word about what happened here tonight, I will kill you. Do you understand me?" he roars, and I yelp as he crushes me further under the pressure of his aura. The pain crushes the air in my lungs, and my voice fails me.

Panicking, I nod my head as the tears stream down my cheeks. It does nothing but make Thane angrier than he was before. He growls.

"Words, Omega!" Thane screams at the top of his lungs.

CHAPTER
TWENTY-THREE

~ *Harlow~*

"Yes, yes, I understand, I swear, I understand," I choke and rasp out, and Thane finally releases me from his hold.

I am gasping for air as I attempt to figure out what I did to deserve such treatment. Leon attacked me. He is the one who should carry the burden of blame and guilt, but Thane is acting as if I was on my knees, begging for this to happen.

"A taxi is waiting for you by the main gate. Now get out of my house," Thane snarls, then gets up from where he was sitting this whole time and storms out of the room, leaving me on the floor.

The asshole doesn't have enough decency in him to check if I'm okay. To make sure I will survive the night. How can he be so careless after watching the attack happen before his eyes? What if Leon managed to steal enough blood to kill me? He cares for his and his mates reputation, not the lives that might be taken by the reckless psychopath, Leon.

I know that staying around for any longer will most likely get me killed, so I grab my belongings and ignore how violently my knees shake as I bolt out of the cursed mansion.

Once again, I freeze my ass off as I stand by the gate, waiting for the taxi to arrive. So much for claiming one was waiting for me here already. That Thane is a fucking soulless liar!

I keep stealing glances back at the brightly illuminated mansion. It's creepy to stand here out in the open where everyone can see me, but I can't spot any figures approaching me. The trees hold massive shadows that I find ominous the moment the fear starts creeping up on me. The place is dead silent; too darn silent for me to feel even slightly comfortable to stick around.

The chill of the air steals all the warmth from my body, even with the clothes they gave me. Honestly, I'm grateful they thought of getting a taxi for me because I have no money left, there isn't even a single dime in my pocket.

The lack of money worries me more than it should, so I turn my head to see if the taxi is approaching and notice car lights coming toward me just as the first flurries of snow fall onto my face.

I glance up at the sky as the car wooshes pass me. Well, at least now I know it isn't the taxi I'm expecting. A shiver runs through me as I rub my hands and try to stay at least relatively warm. Freezing to death before the taxi arrives is the last thing I want to happen.

Thane lied. The longer I wait, the more the realization sinks in that the taxi isn't coming. It has to be another of his cruel jokes. Fucking asshole.

I glance back at the now-closed gate, but I'm too scared to approach it, to press the buzzer and ask if Thane could call the cab company to check how much longer I need to wait for it.

After waiting for half an hour, I've had enough and start walking away from the mansion. I jump at every noise and hold onto the hope that the taxi will arrive every time I see a car light turn down the darkened street.

I nearly reach the end of the long street when a black Mercedes pulls up alongside me. I stop and glance at it right as the window rolls down. Relief floods me when I see it's Raidon sitting behind the steering wheel.

"Get in the car, Omega," he growls, and I bite my lip at the name.

Would it really be so hard to call me Zara, not Omega? Their endless taunting is demoralizing, and it makes me feel like I am nothing but a useless mutt to them. But then again, I suppose, in a way, I am nothing but that. It's not like any of them ever try to hide their dislike of me.

"Can you hear me, Omega? I said get in the fucking car. The cab company just called; the taxi that was supposed to pick you up broke down, so I am driving you home." Raidon growls again, freely showing off the displeasure he feels for being forced to deal with me.

I bet they had a whole argument about which of them would be the unlucky soul who has to spend another few minutes in my awful presence, and Raidon is pissed off because Thane decided for them.

Sighing, I glance ahead. I give in and move toward the car. Walking the entire distance to the city would be way worse, so a quick ride back won't kill me. And it won't kill him either, or so I hope.

Raidon leans over, shoves the door open, and I climb in. He doesn't even bother to give me a chance to put on the seatbelt as I am tossed back in my seat when Raidon floors the gas pedal.

As fast as I can, I place on the seatbelt and rub my hands together, attempting to warm them up a little. At this point, I can't feel the tips of my fingers anymore because they are freezing after spending so much time out in the cold today, my feet are sore from standing in the small heels I wore today, and even my toes are numb from the freezing temperatures.

The first half of the trip is filled with nothing but deafening silence, creating an awful tension in the air that I want to escape the first chance I get.

"Leon. He isn't like that. I swear he isn't. It's just that he lost control," Raidon speaks up out of the blue as we reach the city limit.

I stay quiet and stare out of the car window. Is there anything I can say at this point? It was Leon who attacked me. I did not provoke him in any way. All I am guilty of is trying to do my job.

Ultimately, I don't care what any of them think. It won't change the fact that Leon attacked me. He hurt me, so I'm hardly going to feel sorry for his lack of control.

Thane already managed to make me feel guilty for the mere fact of my existence, anyway.

I still can't shake off the thought of how he glared at me earlier. The image is burned in my mind, and I don't think it will leave until the day I die. At this moment, I feel so small, so darn unwanted. And I know I am unwanted, at least in his eyes, but to see those feelings out on display like that really stung.

Since I still refuse to speak up, Raidon sighs and continues, "It's not the wisest decision to go to the media and speak about what happened. I know Thane commanded you not to, but I also know that there are ways around every command, so I thought it is better if I warned you. Just in case." he says, and the car falls silent again.

I peer out of the window as I breathe out of my mouth so I don't have to inhale his heady scent. Raidon pulls his car into a nearby McDonald's and goes through the drive-thru. Great, everything that happened tonight isn't enough for him. Now, he has to torture me with the strong scent of food I can't afford. Fucking fantastic way to end a clusterfuck of a workday.

CHAPTER
TWENTY-FOUR

~H arlow~

"What do you want?" Raidon asks, startling me.

I bite my lip to keep the words from passing my lips and ignore Raidon. It isn't like I have any money left to buy anything to eat anymore. Because of those assholes and their stupid attempts to get me fired, I had to give my last few dollars to Vadum to drive me to their stupid mansion. I don't want to lose my only job, and all my attempts to go out of my way to keep it resulted in getting attacked by Leon.

Raidon growls at my silence and places an order at the window. He drives through to the next window. My stomach growls in hunger, and at this point, I'm thankful that Raidon decided to turn on the radio to kill the silence in the car, so he can't hear how hungry I am.

He retrieves the paper bag with food, pays the worker and tosses the bag onto my lap, making me jump in my seat.

"Eat your goddamn food and point me in the direction of that dump you live at," Raidon says pulling back onto the main road.

A little shaken up, I direct him to my old apartment building, since that is the address I put on my resume. I can't let any of them know that I am homeless. If Thane were to find out about my living situation, he would use it as an excuse to fire me and rid themselves of me for good. Despite the horror and misery I have to endure from my bosses, I can't afford to lose my job, so I have to suck it up.

I don't dare to touch the food he threw at me while I'm still in the car with him. I don't trust my hands, which are still trembling from the entire ordeal, the cold, and Raidon's aura so close to me.

He parks his car in front of the shitty apartment building and stares ahead at the road, as if the view around here disgusts him. "Get out and don't be late for work tomorrow," he says, dismissing me like a servant.

I retrieve my bag from the footwell of the car and the paper bag of now cold McDonalds he bought for me.

"And make sure you cover your neck. The last thing we want is rumors we have a feeder working for us," Raidon growls out before I shut the car door. He speeds off before I manage to blink, let alone snap back at him. Is it my fault now? How? Your stupid mate attacked me, and now I'm to blame for his lack of control? Those men, they're impossible! All of them!

Taking deep breaths to calm myself, I stand at the side of the street and stare after him, waiting for him to turn at the set of lights at the end of the road.

I feel unusually numb, and an odd calmness overtakes me as I walk back to the office building. The streets are also pretty quiet, providing me with a perfect atmosphere to think.

As I look around and notice a few darker alleys ahead of me, I quicken my step, a little scared to roam the streets alone in the middle of the night.

When I finally reach my workplace, I walk around the building to the hedges that run along the side of the loading dock. I try to remember which hedge I stuffed my backpack in earlier, and it takes me twenty agonizing minutes, but I finally locate it.

Once the backpack is in my hands, I glance around nervously to make sure no one saw me slip past the open gates of the loading dock.

I double—even triple—check my surroundings before I spot the smoke-mart store across the street, and I turn back to the door. Carefully, I place the key in, twist it, and shove the door open to race toward the alarm panel.

I know that I have only forty seconds to shut off the alarm before it alerts the security company that monitors this building at night. My hands shake as I punch in the code, and I let out a heavy breath of relief once I see the panel light turn green.

At first, I wander around a little before heading to the storage locker I plan to use as my secret bedroom. I unlock the door and slip inside, moving right to the back, which is mostly filing shelves.

There is a slim gap behind one which is filled with old, broken computers and some parts. I drag the shelf slightly forward to create a tiny space where I can have a makeshift mini-Den.

No one should be able to see me back here, behind all the broken parts, and I doubt many people come in here. The place is so overtaken with cobwebs that I could gather them quickly and stuff a whole pillow full of them.

I sit on the cold floor and rummage through my backpack. I rustle out my blanket and some extra layers of clothing before grabbing my dirty laundry and making a bed out of it. It's not much, but at the very least, I have somewhere dry to sleep.

I sit on my improvised bed and open the paper bag. I reach inside and pull out the cheeseburger and fries Raidon bought. I don't hold back and take a huge bite of the soggy cheeseburger.

The food is ice cold, but I let out a heavy sigh of contentment once I start chewing it. At the end of the day, as cold as it is, it's still food, which I couldn't afford. I must be grateful for whatever I can get, especially when it's free. Perhaps tossing the meal at me is Raidon's way of trying to pay me off, but I feel like that isn't the case. Maybe he showed me a little humanity and bought me the cheap meal because he felt a little guilty.

Besides, there is no way any of them knows about my financial troubles. I've been working my ass off to hide those, and so far, I've been doing a great job. They don't know, and they never will know.

As I swallow another chunk of cold meat, I can't even imagine the wild things I would do for one delicious, hot meal. As soon as I get my first paycheck, I'm going to go to the little pasta joint down the street from the office building.

It smells like heaven every time I walk past it, and I have been craving pasta for days. Well, anything really, as long as it can fill my stomach. But for now, I devour the burger and fries instead of the food of my dreams. It barely hits the spot, but it's far better than nothing at all. At least I'm not going to bed on an empty stomach.

Yet, as I lay on my pile of dirty laundry and stare at the darkened ceiling, I can't help but wonder if Leon is okay, back at the mansion. I have never seen him so out of control, so far away from his usual giddy persona, before.

Yes, Leon frightened and attacked me, but despite him almost killing me twice now, I don't fear his presence even half as much as I fear Thane's wrath.

CHAPTER
TWENTY-FIVE

~L~eon~

Warmth surrounds me, and I know I'm in bed. The heavy weight of the comforter covers me, and Thane's scent envelopes me as I wake, so I know we are in his room. We all have our own rooms, yet mostly we tend to sleep in here. We don't enjoy being apart unless Thane is in one of his moods.

My head is pounding to its own beat as I groan, sitting up. I rub my eyes and yawn sleepily, trying to remember how I got here. The last thing I remember is receiving a scolding from Thane in the living room and the gate alarm sounding. As I yawn, my eyes squint at the lamp on the bedside table, making my jaw ache, feeling like it had been dislocated.

"You're fine. Lay back down," Thane says, and I blink, peering over at him. His aura is potent, and I can instantly tell he is in a bad mood, which means I am in for yet another scolding when flash-backs of his fist swinging at my face return. Why was I outside?

Thane pats his chest, and I roll my eyes at him. "One!" he counts. My face is sore enough, I don't want my ass beat too, so I quickly lie back down.

"What are you reading?" I ask while stretching out and tugging the blanket up. He doesn't answer but sets the book down.

"Do you remember what happened?" he asks, sitting up and adjusting the pillow behind him. I lick my lips, which are overly dry, when the taste of blood reminds me that I fed on Z.

Z! That was not Z, yet there is no doubt in my mind, it... Could Zara be Z? That startling epiphany smashes me harder than Thane's fist did. Everything floods back to me. She was here. So, where is she now? I fed on her; that is why Thane attacked me.

"I am booking you back into the Parksville rehab," Thanes says, and I sit up, ripped from my pondering thoughts and smashed heavily into reality by his words. No, I can't go back. They can't make me go back there.

"Wait, no. I have it under control, Thane. It won't happen again," I panic. I am not going back there. I am not leaving my mates. I can't go through that again. I hate being away from them; it nearly drove me insane last time.

"You attacked Zara, Leon. A member of our staff. I had to command her to keep quiet," Thane snarls.

"No, I will behave. I will be more careful, I- I slipped up; it won't happen again."

"Thane is right, Leon. You have become too much of a risk," Rhen says, and my head turns to find him sitting by the fireplace in the room. Tears burn my eyes.

"And Raidon?" I ask hopefully, yet he isn't here, and I can't smell his scent as strongly, so it's clear he isn't home.

Thane growls, and I know Raidon would stick up for me. "He isn't Alpha. What I say goes, you are going, Leon, whether you like it or not," Thane says, leaving no room for argument. Yet an argument is what he will get. I am not going back.

"No!" I growl.

Thane's returning growl is thunderous, and his attack is faster than I can track. Thane's hand wraps around my throat, and before I can even register the change in positions, I find myself pinned to the bed beneath him. His towering, muscular body looms over me.

"Thane!" Rhen panics.

"No, he risked everything tonight. He needs to learn," Thane growls, and tears prick my eyes as I shake my head. His grip isn't tight enough to cut off my air but more a show of how easily he could put me in my place if he so chose it.

"Please, I don't want to go back there," I beg him, clutching his hand. Thane's eyes soften. He knows how much that place destroys me, how much it almost destroyed our bond.

"It's for your own good, Leon. I don't know how else to help you," he breathes, and I can feel it kills him as much as it kills me.

"I'll be good; I will control it, please, Thane," I beg him, and he sighs, climbing off me.

"Leon—"

I move, climbing onto his lap and straddling his waist. Leaning forward, I kiss him, cutting off whatever words he was about to speak. He may be big and grizzly on the outside, but I know he hates the thought of me leaving just as much as I don't want to go. Mates aren't supposed to be apart.

"I know what you're doing," Thane mumbles against the lips that are assaulting his. I hear Rhen chuckle behind us before feeling the bed dip as he climbs on it.

"Is it working?" I purr back at Thane. He growls, the noise turning to a purr as my lips travel down his neck and my fangs graze his mark. I may be blood-crazed, but I know how much Thane loves it when I feed on him. He loves the high of the bite as much as any feeder does. When my fangs pierce his neck, he groans, his hand cupping the back of my neck.

"You're still going," he growls as I feed on him. His taste is as potent as his scent to me, yet Z's—no Zara's—is so sickly sweet it makes my fangs ache, and I crave her. Yet, as I feed on Thane, for some reason the underlying taste of his blood reminds me of her sweet, addictive blood, something pure and just as addictive, yet I can't explain why.

I retract my fangs and run my tongue over his neck, licking up the last remnants; I will have to heal him in the morning. Thane won't go to work with my bites on his neck, even though I love the sight of them on him. He would never allow anyone to believe he is my feeder. Feeders are seen as addicts, addicted vamps and hybrids as much as we are addicted to their blood.

It occurs to me then that maybe I do have a source after all. Because one thing I do know; I am now the only thing preventing Zara from being fired. If Thane found out that she works at Tal's, he would fire her on the spot.

Now I just have to convince Thane not to send me away. "One more chance, please. If I slip up, I will sign myself back in," I tell him.

Thane growls and looks over my shoulder at Rhen. Rhen shuffles closer, wrapping his arms around my waist and tugging me off Thane just as Raidon walks in. The sigh of his relief is loud when his eyes meet mine.

"Zara?" I ask him since no one had mentioned her.

"You gave her a scare, but I think she will keep quiet. She is okay, Leon. You didn't kill her."

"She better keep quiet, or I will fucking end her," Thane growls, tearing my attention back to him.

"You drop her home?" Rhen asks him, and Raidon nods, falling heavily beside us on the bed. Thane's bed reminds me of the one in the Den. It is easily the size of two super kings. It needs to be to fit all of us in it.

By the looks of it, Thane wants us all close tonight because Raidon starts stripping his clothes off before climbing under the sheets. He pats his chest for me, but I wait for Thane, knowing he has the last say on whether I get to sleep in here with them or if he would send me to my room as punishment.

Thane sighs and nods to Raidon, who smiles wickedly as he beams with excitement. I know he has been waiting to get his hands on me all day. He loves that I am the smallest; it drives me nuts because I am just as fast, if not faster, yet still, their auras will always outweigh mine, seeing as they are pure-blood werewolves while I am the mutt of the lot, but I also love their affections.

"One chance, Leon, one!" Thane says as I slip under the sheets with Raidon, who is already tugging at his boxer briefs.

CHAPTER
TWENTY-SIX

~Harlow~

I set my alarm extra early, knowing the loading docks open half an hour earlier than the main doors, and I need to sneak out and come in through the main doors, so no one will notice I slept at the loading docks.

Yet, as I quickly get ready, I hear the huge roller doors open and promptly rush to spray on my de-scenter. After popping two of my pills, I cringe, realizing that there are only two pills left in the bottle, which means I will have to skip tonight's dose if I want any left for tomorrow. It occurs to me briefly that if I get off early enough, I will still be able to go to the club tonight. Although, I tried calling Bree last night and she didn't pick up the phone.

Spraying myself in extra spray, I hope it conceals my scent enough; I am falling into panic mode. Thane said if I went into heat, he would fire me, and at this rate, I'm going to risk that because once my pills run out; I am all but screwed.

They are the only thing preventing my heat. Going into heat is one of my greatest fears. I have heard horror stories of how desperately helpless Omegas get and how much pain is causes if she doesn't have mates to ease it.

I quickly hide all my belongings, jamming them in the corner and pushing the shelf back as I climb out of my hidey-hole. Leaving my heels off, I go to the door and pry it open a little, peering out the gap, but I don't see anyone and can't hear anyone around.

I open it a little more and stick my head out, ensuring the coast is clear before dashing to the roller doors. I rush out and get far enough from the loading entrance to not be suspicious.

I place my hand on the wall and slip my heels on before straightening out my blazer and using my hands to smooth down my blouse. Despite my best efforts, a few loose strands of hair still come free after I tie it up in a messy bun, but I don't bother to fix it since I don't want to be caught outside in the alley.

As a result, I speed up the side alley and rush to the front doors as fast as I can. I know security will be opening the main doors any minute. On reaching the top of the steps. I am greeted by the security guard, who checks my ID, and I make my way to the elevators across the other side of the lobby.

As soon as I reach the top floor, I start my usual routine of cleaning up and turning everything on. Once I finish, I rush to the bathroom to brush my teeth and fix the haystack that is messily sitting on top of my head. As a last-minute decision, I decide to put on more de-scenter, giving myself an extra spray. My anxiety about running out of my suppressants is making me sweat. What comes with sweat: damn pheromones.

When I finish, I make my way to the small kitchenette and start making their morning coffees. I hear the elevator doors open before hearing all their voices. Despite being slightly worried about running into Thane after last night, I calmly continue working on their coffees.

Nevertheless, his oppressive aura fills the tight space behind me as he approaches. It feels like the air in my lungs gets squeezed out of me as he comes up behind me.

"Get your damn neck covered up," he growls at me, and my brows furrow in confusion as I stare at him. Almost instinctively, I touch my fingertips to it and I feel the tiny puncture marks that Leon left behind last night. A gasp escapes me. I was frantically trying to escape the loading docks and more worried about brushing my teeth; I forgot to put makeup on.

"Did anyone see you?" Thane growls, making me cringe.

"Chill, I will heal her, Thane," Leon reassures him, walking up beside me, and I feel my stomach tighten as I swallow. Thane ignores his words, more focused on their image.

"Answer me, Zara. Did anyone see you? The last bloody thing I need is to explain why my damn secretary has bite marks on her neck," Thane bellows, and I whimper as his aura crushes me.

"Only the security guard!" I cry out, clutching the small sink with both hands as I answer. Fucking prick. Adding insult to injury, he has to scold me today, as if last night wasn't bad enough.

"Thane!" Leon growls at him as my eyes fill with tears. *Don't cry, don't cry*, I think to myself. It stings that he cares more for the image it presents than whether I am actually okay after last night. It stings painfully that I mean so little to him. His aura drops, releasing me from the pressure it built up, making the hair on the back of my neck prickle.

"Fucking clean yourself up," he says before storming off. I turn, watching him go when I notice Rhen glaring after him. Raidon stands in the hall, and for a second, I think I see his eyes soften when he goes to say something before abruptly closing his mouth and walking off to his own office.

Rhen, however, reaches out for his coffee and takes it, thanking me before he turns to leave as well. My stomach sinks, and I ready myself for whatever excuse Leon is going to give me about his behavior last night. Instead, he watches me as I make my coffee. My belly growls hungrily and my face heats, knowing he can hear it.

Leon leans against the counter, watching me. "Did you forget to eat breakfast?" he asks.

"Yeah, I was in a rush," I lie, taking a sip of my coffee and heading back to my desk. However, as I turn toward the door, Leon's hand grips my elbow and pulls me to a stop. I swallow the mouthful of hot liquid, wondering what he wants.

TWENTY-SEVEN

~H arlow~

"I skipped breakfast, too," he tells me, reaching up to tuck a stray hair behind my ear. I notice the sharp points of his fangs pushing passed his upper lip, and he runs his tongue across his lips.

"Good to know," I tell him, about to turn away again, but I stop when he speaks.

"However, you might be able to help me with that, Z," he purrs, and I freeze in my tracks.

"Pardon," I gasp when the heat of his chest presses against my back. My eyes dart to the hallway, wondering if the others heard what he called me.

"I know you work for Tal," Leon purrs, and I swallow as his nose runs up the side of my neck and inhales deeply.

"But I am willing to keep your little secret. If you keep mine. See, I need a feeder or Thane is going to send me away. Now, if you want to keep your job, you will play along, Zara, or I will tell Thane exactly the kind of whore you are. He doesn't take too kindly to being deceived," Leon purrs.

I grit my teeth and turn to glare at him. "No, I'm not going to be your damn feeder," I growl at him, and the redness in his eyes grows brighter as I glare at him.

"Fine then, I will tell Thane he has a stripper working for him," Leon says, walking toward the door. My breath lodges in my throat at his words. I need this job, need the money if I ever want to get my shitty apartment back from Martha. I grip his arm.

"Wait, please, Leon," I tell him. Leon stops and turns, looking at me. He smirks, knowing full well he has me.

"Please, I need this job."

"I know, and I need a feeder. It's a win-win situation. So, what will it be?" Leon asks me and my eyes turn glassy. "I haven't got all day Zara, or should I call you Z? Because that will be the only place you will ever get a job in this city if Thane finds out."

"You're a fucking asshole. You know that?"

"And you're a skank, one that is willing to do anything for the right price. Spraying yourself up with all that pheromone shit, appearing all innocent to pull men in. You are in no position to judge me, so choose, Zara," Leon says, and I gape at him.

Is he calling me a skank? He should be able to tell I'm a virgin. Then again, with the pheromones Tal pumps through that place's air-conditioning, it's not surprising that he thinks I am just that. Leon turns to walk out, heading toward Thane's office, and I set my mug down on the counter.

"Fine," I whisper, knowing he'll hear me with his extra-sensitive hearing.

Leon smiles, wandering over to me before gripping my wrist and sticking his head out the kitchenette door. My brows furrow when he suddenly yanks me down the hall to the bathroom and shoves me inside, kicking the door shut behind him. I try to take a step back from him, but he still has a hold of my wrist.

Leon growls, his aura spilling out, making me freeze. He steps closer, pressing me against the cold, porcelain sink. He dips his face to my neck, and tears burn my eyes when he growls before sinking his teeth in. Panic sets in, not knowing if he'll be able to stop. But having fed on me last night, he seems to have more control. My system floods with endorphins, and the pain dissipates as quickly as it comes. His tongue laps at my neck, and I feel a little lightheaded when he pulls away. He wipes his lips with his thumb before sucking on it and then pecks my lips.

"See, that wasn't so bad," he purrs, yet I feel used, disgusted that I am now reduced to a feeder, just to keep my job. Leon bites his wrist, offering it to me. I grab it wanting the holes on my neck gone as soon as possible. It will be like it never happened. Leon chuckles, mistaking my eagerness for addiction. I shove him back, feeling the holes on my neck close. He growls when I try to push against him. He got what he wanted. As if last night wasn't bad enough, I sure as shit don't want to get caught in here with him.

Yet my attempt at escape seems to anger him. I am shoved back against the basin as he steps closer, caging me against it. "Just remember that I am the only thing preventing you from getting fired," he growls at me. I bite the inside of my cheek and quickly nod. I feel degraded and humiliated, it is one thing for mates to feed on each other, but they have no idea I am technically their mate, so Leon treating me like a damn whore only makes the humiliation hurt more.

He steps aside, allowing me to pass, but speaks as I push open the door. "And Zara, if you go back to Tal's, I will tell Thane you work there. I will not risk giving my mates some disease because you want to whore yourself out," Leon snaps. My stomach sinks. What else am I supposed to do for cash for the next two and a half weeks?

"If either of us has any diseases, it's the leech in front of me," I growl, pushing out the doors and going to my desk. Though the more I walked, the more vertigo takes over. How much did he take? He only fed on me for a few minutes. I stop by the kitchenette and retrieve my lukewarm coffee, needing the sugar, before falling heavily into my chair. Only, when I do, I look up to see Raidon peering at the bathroom door before looking at me. Leon walks out a couple of seconds later. Also spotting Raidon, he stops and looks at me, or more like glares at me, before storming past Raidon when he opens his door and nods for Leon to get in his office.

CHAPTER
TWENTY-EIGHT

~R~ **aidon~**

Leon is taking too long. He knows we have a meeting, and something tells me he is up to something. So, I wait in the hall, only to see him emerge from the bathroom moments after Zara rushed out of there.

"Are you fucking nuts?" I growl at Leon as he steps into my office. I shut the door, turning on him while he strolls into the room.

"Calm down. We have come to an arrangement that is mutually beneficial," Leon says, turning to look at me.

"How does you feeding on her benefit her? If Thane finds out, he will kill you both!" I tell him angrily. This is asking for trouble, and lately Leon has been a beacon for trouble. I do not want to get caught up in this with him.

"He's not going to find out because you aren't going to tell him," Leon says, falling into the armchair next to my desk. I raise an eyebrow at him and fold my arms across my chest. Leon shrugs, and I glare at him when he leans forward, bracing his arms on his knees. He clearly does not care for the position he is putting me in right now. And the prick knows I won't rat him out to Thane because I hate seeing him punished.

"I can't go back there, Raidon. Thane threatened to send me back to Parksville, and he is the one with the stupid Omega rule. If he would just take another Omega, this wouldn't be an issue," Leon growls while shaking his head.

"Leon, you can't just feed on an employee. What if she becomes addicted and goes into withdrawal? Then what?" I ask him. Leon sighs; he knows I am right, yet I can feel his struggle, his fear of being sent away. I hate the thought of him leaving just as much as he does.

"We'll be careful," Leon says, chewing his lip nervously.

"You'll be careful? Leon, she looked on the damn verge of tears when she walked out. What if she tells someone?" I ask him.

"She won't unless she wants to get fired," Leon says, so sure of himself.

"What do you mean? What have you got over her? Spill, or I am marching next door and telling Thane," I growl at him.

Leon sighs and leans back in his chair. He looks at the wall above my head, and I have a funny feeling I won't like what he is about to tell me based on the disgust that briefly flitters through the bond. His eyes move back to mine, and he groans, scratching the back of his neck.

"Zara is Z. I knew it as soon as I came back to my senses last night. I knew I had tasted her essence before," Leon states.

"Z?" I ask, confused, wondering what he is talking about. Surely, he doesn't mean...

"The girl from the strip club, from Tal's, the new girl we met," Leon says with a shrug.

"What? You're feeding off a fucking whore?" I snarl, knowing the risks that poses, not just to Leon but all of us.

"Her blood is clean, I can taste it, and I told her not to work there anymore," Leon defends himself.

"Fuck, Leon! If Thane finds out about this," I groan, knowing exactly his reaction if he finds out. And now I am going to be caught up in it with him. Leon gets up and comes over to me.

"He won't," he growls, nipping at my neck. I sigh, cupping the back of his neck and gripping his hair.

"But if he does?" I ask.

"He won't, and he won't send me away. Please, Raidon, I have it under control. This will work, and he will be none the wiser," Leon purrs. Yet still, I worry. Not so much for Leon, but for Zara, in case he loses control. I press my lips in a line.

"Fine, but you feed on her in my office where I can keep an eye on both of you. If you kill her, you not only lose your source, but Thane will find out, and we will have to cover up another employee death. And you know the media doesn't take Omega deaths lightly; we will be crucified. They are so bloody rare these days," I tell him. The thought of anything happening to the little Omega sickens me. We have a natural instinct to protect them, savor and covet them. If only Thane would give in to those instincts. He may treat her better.

I hate the way he treats her, yet I understand. I understand how Omegas ultimately have control. Once they are mated and marked, we Alphas are helpless to their demands, which also makes them dangerous. They may never rule over Alphas, but they have an advantage and know how to use it. We are a slave to their pheromones as much as they are slaves to our command.

"Deal?" I ask him, and he purrs, stepping closer, smiling deviously.

"Deal," he growls. Leon pecks my lips and nips at my chin before he grabs my crotch, squeezing my cock through my slacks. He pushes me against the wall. I close my eyes for a moment, knowing that sex goes hand in hand with his bloodlust, yet I will be the one to reap the benefits of it. He wants me. He needs me, and I am not about to tell him no.

I want him just as badly. Leon doesn't care that we are at work, that our mates are in the room next door, or that someone could catch us at any second. Nothing matters to him more than getting his lips around my cock, and I find his passion contagious. I get swept up in it too.

His fingers fumble with my belt, his bloodlust gone, replaced with desire now, as he desperately seeks to remove my pants.

"Raidon," he whines, and I can never refuse him. His voice is low and quiet. There is a need in it, though, and I know I am the object of that need.

CHAPTER
TWENTY-NINE

~Raidon~

He grabs my hand and tugs me over to my desk, pushing me against it before kissing me. His tongue slips into my mouth as he tugs at my shirt.

"Leon, we aren't at home. I am not stripping down," I growl, reminding him we are at work, biting his lips. Yet, his hands still roam, uncaring for my words as he kisses me with a hunger that matches his bloodlust.

The way his tongue moves in my mouth, messy and passionate but also so skillful, makes my cock twitch in my slacks. It's already hard, very hard, and I can feel pre-cum leaking out the tip. The way that his hands move over me and his tongue tangles against mine promise pleasure, and his whole body trembles with the need to give it to me.

Falling to his knees, he looks up at me with a smile. I can see how excited he is, rubbing his hand over the bulge in my pants. The friction makes me shudder slightly. I am so hard that I feel more sensitive than usual.

Seeing him on his knees before me makes my cock twitch, and I don't think I will last very long once he starts.

With trembling fingers, he unbuttons my pants and pulls the zipper down, his fingers moving inside, and he pulls out my cock. Leon smiles when he finds his prize.

"See, some secrets are worth keeping, aren't they?" Leon purrs.

I look down at him as he takes my cock in his hand, stroking it up and down. I shake my head a little in response to his question, but I really don't think I am capable of speech. My whole body is tense and ready for the incredible release that I know is only moments away.

As he looks over my cock, rubbing his nose along it before swiping his tongue across my shaft, I can hear Thane and Rhen next door arguing, and I know we don't have long before both of us will be called in.

I bite my lip, wondering how long it will take for them to stop arguing and realize what we are doing in here.

No doubt they feel it through the bond. What if Zara walks in on us? Would she be disgusted by catching us, or would she watch and enjoy the show? Would she want to join us? She is Omega, so I know she would. What would happen if we got caught? My heart pounds as I think about it.

My attention snaps back into our moment when Leon takes the head of my cock in his mouth and sucks hard. I shudder, letting out a groan that I pray can't be heard outside.

As he starts to suck the head, making my eyes roll as my pleasure overwhelms me, I stop caring about the people around us and the chances of getting caught. There is only one thing that matters at that moment, and that is his warm mouth around my cock.

After sucking hard on my cock, he really starts to show off his skills. Slowly, he pushes my cock to the back of his throat. Inch by inch, he takes more and more of my length. Looking up at me, he maintains eye contact as he takes me as deep as he can. He hardly gags at all, not even when he takes me so deep that his nose is pressed into my pubic hair.

I watch him, shuddering with the pleasure it brings me, but also incredibly impressed with his skill. I always am. When he starts to move his head back and forth, I see him roll his eyes with pleasure.

He is clearly enjoying himself, getting pleasure from my cock stretching out his lips and pushing down his eager throat.

His enthusiasm is evident from the manic movements of his head and the hand on my hip as he urges me to thrust into his mouth. He keeps sucking as I push my cock to the back of his throat. Repeatedly. Back and forth. He seems to want more and more. To take it deeper, to do it harder.

I feel my knees become weak as my pleasure builds higher and higher. I reach out and grip my desk.

Leon sucks harder, his tongue tracing my shaft, and I thrust my cock to the back of his throat until I find myself close to my orgasm.

Looking down, I feel his fangs graze my aroused flesh as he draws blood. The sight of him enjoying my cock just as much as I enjoy him sucking it makes it sweeter. It makes my orgasm more powerful.

Gripping his hair, I shudder and start to cum. He works hard for his mouthful, and I give it to him. Grunting hard, I thrust my cock to the back of his throat and shoot my load into his mouth. Rolling my eyes, I push back and forth three more times and make sure that I gave him every drop of my cum. I wipe the tip on his outstretched tongue when I pull out, just to be sure.

Leon swallows it down before twirling his tongue around the tip and releasing it with a pop. He smiles deviously up at me and I tuck myself back into my pants, when Rhen clears his throat.

"I swear, the pair of you are asking for Thane to punish you. Now hurry, Leila is here, and I would prefer to prevent her death, if possible," Rhen tells me, and I sigh. My good mood is short lived, knowing I have to save Leon's sister from being murdered because she hired our Omega assistant without doing a background check on her first.

Following Rhen out, I zip up my pants and look to the foyer. Leon also looks at Zara, and I notice she is sweating profusely and looking sickly pale. She fans herself with a piece of paper, making Rhen growl when her sweet, addictive Omega scent wafts to us.

"How much did you take from her?" I mind-link Leon when I feel his worry bleed into me.

"Not much, I swear. Fuck. Why does she look so pale?" Leon asks when Thane bellows from the office.

CHAPTER
THIRTY

~T hane~

I am not an idiot; I know what Raidon and Leon are doing in Raidon's office while the rest of us are god damn working. Now they are all standing in the damn corridor.

"Now!" I call to my mates as they loiter in the office hallway.

They rush inside and I turn my attention back to Leila, who sits across from me. She knows she fucked up, and she glances nervously at my mates as they enter. They won't help her. One thing we are all in agreement on is that she fucked up. Rhen waits for them to enter before closing the door behind them.

"Where are Zara's files?" I ask Leila, and she blanches and stutters over an answer.

"Don't lie to me," I warn her, and she pinches the bridge of her nose and exhales. When she looks up, Rhen moves toward her, sitting on the edge of my desk. I know he does it deliberately, so I won't reach over and strangle the bloody woman.

"I have her resume and her ID," Leila offers nervously, and a growl escapes me. I hold my hand out for them, and she quickly rummages through her folders with shaky hands, spilling some on the floor in her haste to retrieve them. She produces the few documents she finds and hands them to me. I quickly glance at them, noting it is the same bloody information Raidon and Rhen gave to me the other day.

"Did you check her references?" I ask, knowing she bloody couldn't have because the owner of her previous work is dead. Leila bites her lip and I growl at her for her carelessness. Rhen plucks the papers from my fingertips, reading them over again and sighing.

"Not that you can, since her last place of employment burned down months ago," he mutters, just as annoyed as I am. He understands the risk Leila has put us in.

"Did you verify her ID, or did you just do a sniff test to ensure she is an Omega? An Omega you are trying to force on us!" I snap at her.

Leila flinches and cowers away from my rage. Leon drops his gaze to the floor as well. I know he is close to his sister and seeing her cower away from me is difficult for him. I know it bothers him. Yet he won't say a thing to me in her presence. He knows better than that.

I growl, looking down at the Omega's photocopied ID, and press my lips in a line. Even with the photocopy, I can tell her ID is an obvious fake, and her social security number is three numbers too short.

"Well, you really fucked up this time, Leila," I tell her as I sit back in my chair and curse.

"What do you want to do?" Raidon asks.

"First, I suppose we need to verify who she is with her landlord. Other than that, we have no idea who she is or where she came from. And chances are if she gave this ID to us, she probably gave the same one to her landlord. It's an obvious fake."

"Why would an Omega have a fake ID? She could have a pack looking after her instead of working and hiding under de-scenter and suppressants," Rhen asks thoughtfully. It baffles me also.

"Maybe she is running from her pack. You know how dodgy some of those Omega facilities are," Leon offers, as I try to think of a more plausible reason for her to hide her identity.

"Could she be a spy?" Raidon says. I growl at the mere thought, though it is unlikely.

"With a shitty fake ID like that, doubtful," I tell him, and he scratches his chin.

"I'll task you and Rhen with finding answers. This week," I say before pausing. I snarl at what I am about to suggest, but we need answers, and at the moment, she is a security risk.

"Maybe try to speak with her and see what you can find out," I say bitterly. I don't want her near my mates. I'm not stupid. I know they crave an Omega for our pack, someone to complete us, but I just can't after Harlow.

"Then what?" Leon asks, and I narrow my eyes at him. He seems almost panicked about what might happen to her. I have no answer for him. I still want her gone, yet I am curious as to what a little Omega is hiding and why. It makes no sense because she could easily give herself to a pack. She could have a life of luxury yet prefers to work.

"We can decide that once we figure out who she is. Until then, just watch what you say around her. For all we know, she could be paparazzi, looking for the next story to sell," Rhen says, dropping her documents on the desk in front of me.

"Or she could just be an Omega, who doesn't want to fit into the stereotypical Omega role," Leon offers.

"Either way, we'll find out, but until then, keep an eye on her," I tell them before my gaze turns to Leila. She fiddles with her fingers and remains quiet.

"You're on probation; I mean it, Leila. One more slip up, and you are fired. For good this time, Leila. I don't care that you're Leon's sister," I tell her. She gets up and bares her neck to me before rushing from my office.

"You know she means well. She just wants nieces and nephews, since she can't have kids of her own," Leon defends his sister, and I growl at him.

"That's not her choice to make," I tell him, and he sighs.

CHAPTER
THIRTY-ONE

~ **H**arlow~
   I watch as Leila frantically escapes Thane's office, yet I don't move to see if she's okay. I feel lethargic since Leon fed on me; I just want to crawl into my makeshift Den and sleep it off. Yet as Thane and the others step out of the office, I force myself upright, clicking on the keyboard in an effort to look busy. Rhen talks to Thane briefly before Thane goes back to his office. Leon and Raidon make their way to the elevators, and they wait for Rhen, who joins them moments later. Once they leave, however, Thane comes out and heads toward the kitchenette. He glances over at me and growls, shaking his head.

   "Omega!" Thane snaps at me, and I force my legs to move as I swivel in my seat. Thane heads back to his office, and I quickly follow, stopping at his door, knowing better than to fully enter.

   "Come here," he says, clicking the mouse on his laptop. I wipe a hand across my forehead, and Thane looks up at me.

   "Omega, now."

   I bite my lip, wondering if this is a trick. He said to never enter his office, yet he's calling me in. When I feel the command wash over me, my feet move, and I stop beside his desk.

"Are you wearing your fucking de-scenter?" he snarls at me.

I sniff myself. My scent is potent because of how clammy I am.

"Sorry," I say, and he growls.

"Bring it with you next time," he snaps, clicking on his mouse angrily.

I see him trying to get into the electronic filing app I added to all their computers. "You may need to clear the cache. Sometimes it glitches," I tell him, grabbing the mouse. He instantly leans away from me. He watches me fiddle with his laptop when I notice quite a few update notifications.

"Do you mind?" I ask him, pointing to the screen, and he waves me to continue. He rolls his seat away from me and I crouch behind his desk, fiddling with it when it suddenly shuts down, and he growls.

"You fucking broke it."

"No, I am updating and debugging it. How the heck do you work at a tech company and not know how to use a damn computer?" I ask him before clamping my lips together at how rude that comes out.

"I own a tech company. This is more Rhen's thing, not mine. I prefer hands on work, not this tech shit."

"Then why own it?" I ask curiously.

"It was my fathers' and it's profitable. Honestly, Rhen handles most of the tech crap. I just handle the business dealings," he tells me. The laptop turns back on after reloading, and I stand up, typing in some codes.

"You're good with computers?" Thane asks, watching me click away and type in different codes.

"Yes and no. I know enough to keep myself out of trouble with them," I answer honestly, when I notice him shift uncomfortably. I glance at him to see him cross his legs, realizing my scent is overwhelming him. He reaches for his phone, dialing a number while I get the electronic filing system to open up.

"Can someone buy some bloody de-scenter and send it up, please?" he asks, and I hear Leon answer on the other end.

"Yep, I will bring it up. Her scent getting to you?" Leon chuckles, and Thane growls, hanging up. I pretend not to hear and point to the screen.

"Good. Can you show me how to work the damn thing?" he asks, and I sigh.

"What file are you looking for?"

"Mr. Bowman and the Obsidian Pack. I have a meeting with him next week and I need to go over our previous contracts," he says, scrubbing a hand down his face. I swallow, recognizing the name of my sister's killer.

"Omega!"

I shake myself at his command.

"Sorry, Alp- Sorry, sir," I quickly correct myself.

My hands shake as I type in Mr. Bowman, yet nothing comes up, so I type Obsidian Pack and multiple files show.

"You seem nervous, your scent." Thane sniffs the air, and even I can smell the scent of my fear filling the small room.

"You've heard of Obsidian Pack?" he asks.

"Everyone has. They haven't got an excellent reputation with Omegas," I tell him.

"Well, you don't have to worry. He won't be near you," Thane says, shocking me. Yet I do have to worry because Mr. Bowman met my twin, and if he has a good memory, he will easily recognize me.

"You may go," he says, dismissing me. I quickly rush out, and my heart beats painfully as I try not to have a panic attack. I stagger back to my desk as the elevator doors open up. Leon steps out and walks over to me. He hands me a can of de-scenter before plopping a juice bottle and subway sandwich on the desk in front of me.

"Eat. You look on the verge of passing out."

"It's not my break yet."

"I said eat, and Thane won't care. You look like shit, and for god's sake, put on the de-scenter. I could smell you the moment I stepped out of the elevator," Leon says, walking off toward Thane's office.

I spray myself in de-scenter, relieved to have an extra can because mine is getting low. However, I only eat half of the sandwich, saving the other half for dinner since I can't go back to Tal's. No doubt Tal will tell Leon if I do. How I am going to survive another two weeks of this, I do not know.

CHAPTER
THIRTY-TWO

~ H arlow~

THREE DAYS LATER

Leon feeds from me daily. I have only been taking half a suppressant at a time, but I am now officially out of suppressants and de-scenter, having just used the last of it. I am antsy and am starting to feel withdrawal, big time. My heat will come soon if I don't get my hands on some more suppressants. I shake the last remnants from the can Leon gave me the other day as I sneak out of the storage room at the loading docks and to the front of the building. Passing security, the guard grabs my arm, and I jump as he inhales deeply. I rip my arm from his grip and glare at him.

"Girlie, you have a death wish going to work smelling like that," he purrs. He is only a Beta male, and my scent doesn't affect him as much. The fact it affects him at all makes me gulp, knowing I am about to step into an office with four brooding Alphas. I rush to the elevator and jab the button to my floor. When I reach the top, I open up the window and blast the air conditioning before spraying the air freshener all over me in an effort to mask my scent some more.

Yet, the moment they step out of the elevator, I grip my desk to remain in my seat. Their Alpha scent calls to me and their powerful auras make my knees weak. Lust slithers its way through me. I know what estrus does to an Omega, but I didn't realize how powerful it gets—especially having never gone through it before.

Luckily, though, they seem distracted, and the air freshener makes them cough and sputter.

"Fuck, open the damn window," Rhen chokes on the lavender and citrus spray.

It is bad. I sprayed enough that even my eyes burn, yet I can't move. Knowing if I do, I will drop to my knees before them. I wrangle myself under control as they walk off into the conference room, down by the end of the hall.

They spend most of the morning in a Skype meeting, which offers a little reprieve, when I start to feel ridiculously hot and uncomfortable. Sneaking down the hall, I rush to the bathroom, needing to wet my face and cool down. Is the serum and Thane's proximity making this worse? It comes on so fast that I am panting by the time I get a whiff of his lingering scent in the hall.

I freeze in place when the door opens and Thane and Rhen step into the hall. They freeze, and I clutch my stomach.

"You did not come to work during fucking estrus," Thane roars angrily, and I whimper, my knees going out from under me as he smashes me with his aura.

Thane stalks toward me, and Rhen races to catch him by the arm as he reaches for my hair. His growl is thunderous.

"One fucking rule, Omega. One, and you couldn't fucking obey it!" Thane bellows.

Tears prick my eyes, and a yelp escapes me as Rhen slams Thane against the wall when he tries to grab me again.

Raidon and Leon rush out a side office, and I hear them gasp before Raidon shoves Leon into the closest office, holding the door closed as he growls, beating on it.

"You send my mates into a rut, I will fucking kill you," Thane sneers at me.

"Get her fucking suppressants," Thane snaps and shoves Rhen. Rhen moves toward my handbag, and I whimper.

"I'm out!" I cry, and Rhen stops.

"What? Why wouldn't you get more?" Thane demands.

"Because a script is $700. Money that I don't have!" I growl back. Only it turns to a whimper when he hits me with his aura.

"Thane, you're hurting her," Raidon says, his voice almost sounding pained. Yet Thane is livid.

"I'll take her to get some more. Just calm down. Everyone needs to calm down," Rhen says, gripping my arms. Yet the moment he touches me, a whiny moan leaves me, and he lets me go, making me fall against the ground.

"Fuck!" Rhen growls, and I look up to see his eyes bleed black.

Thane storms off, enraged. "Call Leila and tell her to bring up some de-scenter. Then take her to get her the suppressants," Raidon says while I writhe on the floor in agony.

Thane walking away causes pain to ripple through every cell, as if it's an outright rejection. I try to stifle the whimper that leaves me, but it is pointless. Everyone remains frozen in place until Leila arrives, dousing me in so much de-scenter it burns my hypersensitive skin, and I choke on the fumes. Yet the tension lessens in Raidon and Rhen when my scent is muted. Leon, however, is still smashing on the door Raidon is barricading, wanting to be let out.

Rhen reaches down, gripping my arm tightly and yanking me to my feet. He shoves me toward the elevator and I stagger, barely catching myself with a hand on the wall. He jabs the button on the elevator while I try to breathe through the pain coursing through me. When the doors open, he shoves me inside and I move to the back of the elevator. His body is tense, and he growls as he tries to remain as far away from me as the small space will allow.

"There is a pharmacy two minutes away. Have you got a script?"

I shake my head. Usually, I have others get the scripts for me. Rhen growls, but I can't exactly tell him my ID is fake, now, can I?

"Great, Zara. You've put me in a fucking horrid position right now," he snarls as if I have any control over my body.

When the doors open, Rhen grabs my arm, pulling me through the foyer quickly and outside into the fresh air. The cool breeze only gives a brief reprieve as he hauls me down the street toward the pharmacy.

When I feel my toes curl and my pupils dilate, I know I am in serious trouble. My hands clutch Rhen's shirt. He stiffens and stops. His nostrils flare as he picks up my scent before his eyes dart around nervously. He curses, ripping off his jacket in the hopes it would cover my scent as he tucks me beside him, draping it over me. My fingers sneak into his untucked shirt and I moan. Even that small amount of contact causes slick to dampen my thighs and ruin my pants; as if this isn't embarrassing enough. Rhen growls but grips my hand, shoving it inside his shirt to try to let it lessen the effects of my heat.

Growls and auras suddenly fill the air, supercharging it and making me hyper aware of the heat raging through me. Goosebumps rise on my entire body at the charged air, and despite my best efforts to not react, it still affects me. It's a promise that will end my pain, no matter how much my rationality fights it. Rhen curses when we hear other Alphas picking up my scent and he shoves me down a small alleyway between two stores, hiding me behind a dumpster.

"I swear if Thane punishes me for this, you'll cop it," he snarls at me, and I wonder what he means. He starts yanking at my pants, and my eyes widen in horror. No!

"Stop!" I grit out.

"I'm trying to help you. Unless you want every fucking Alpha hunting you down?" Rhen snarls, but I panic at the thought of losing my virginity next to a smelly dumpster.

Rhen rips at the button on my pants, trying to undo them when my hand moves. The sound of my hand connecting with his face echoes in the small space. My palm stings and his head whips to the side, but he stops. The growl that leaves him is menacing as he turns his face back to look at me. I glare at him only to whimper at the murderous look he gives me, shocked that I just slapped him. I slapped my boss! And not just any boss, but a fucking Alpha!

CHAPTER
THIRTY-THREE

~Harlow~

Rhen snarls and slams his hands against my chest, knocking me into the brick wall behind me. His fingers lock around my throat and I watch in horror as his canines extend from his bottom and top gums. He snarls, pressing his face closer while I smash my fists against his chest and shoulders, trying to shove his weight off. Me slapping him challenged him, and I can tell he wants me to submit as he fights for control over his instincts.

I am beginning to see that control is something they don't really have much of. Howls ring out loudly in the distance as my heat-ravaged body floods the air with pheromones. Fear coils and writhes inside me, and his Alpha dominance is only fueling it, making my scent even more potent. My body wants to give in to the demands of the Alpha holding me, if only to ease the discomfort. Luckily, however, I'm not in full-blown heat yet, so I have some control over my own baser instincts before submitting to him.

I gasp, choking as his fingers dig in, his aura obliterating my self-preservation and what resistance I have left.

"I am trying to fucking help you," he growls, inches off my face, looking more like a monster than a man.

He doesn't understand. I'm drowning in so much de-scenter that he can't pick up the sickly sweet scent of my virginity. I sure as shit don't plan on losing it next to a stinking dumpster where homeless people sleep—where I had slept before. I know how much spit and god knows what else is on this ground. Rhen shoves me, letting me go. My legs buckle and I catch myself against the bin. My fingers grip it feebly as I fight to remain standing under the intensity of his aura. He growls, glaring down at me.

"I am not rejecting you or challenging you," I breathe out, trying to catch my breath. I'm not stupid. I know Omegas need Alphas just as much as they need us.

"Fucking looks like it," he snarls as I catch my breath. "I tried, but you're too far gone. You don't want my help. Fine. You're on your own. Good luck fighting them off," Rhen snaps, turning away from me.

Panic courses through me at his words. Would he really abandon me here, leave me for whoever may stumble across me? I can feel them getting closer, and the air feels hotter, thicker as I breathe the pheromones they project back at me as they seek out the source of my pheromones. Rhen takes a step away, and fear has me moving. I clutch his shirt.

"Don't leave me," I stammer, and he stops, prying my hands from his button-down shirt. He growls, walking off when I hear a thud further up the alleyway. My heart hammers in my chest and I twist my head, spotting fluorescent eyes gleaming back at me before hearing another thud. Another Alpha wolf jumped off the balcony above the shop and onto the dumpster below.

Rhen shakes his head, about to walk off and leave me to fend for myself. I cringe, knowing I have no way to escape this without him.

"I'm a virgin," I murmur, and he stops. He turns, looking back at me. "I am not rejecting you. I just don't want to lose my virginity against a dumpster," I tell him before whimpering as another Alpha aura reaches me from the way we came in. I am effectively blocked off, and now I am prey.

"Bullshit!" Rhen snarls. Tears burn my eyes and spill over when the two Alphas in their wolf forms start fighting each other over who will get me.

"I swear, Rhen. Please, you can't leave me here," I tell him, jumping when they smash into the dumpster I'm cowering behind. Rhen snarls, stalking toward me, and I shriek, thinking he is going to attack me when he grabs the front of my blouse, jerking me closer. He buries his face in my neck and snarls.

"All I can smell is your heat and de-scenter," he snaps.

"I'm not lying," I squeal as he goes to shove me away. I clutch his shirt in panic as the other Alpha joins the fray. How Rhen is able to hold himself together while remaining so close to me is shocking. Maybe because he has a pack, and packs generally share.

Rhen curses before jamming his hand inside my pants. I squeal as he forces his finger inside me, which slowly turns into a moan as tingles spread across my flesh. He jerks his hand back, making me look at him. I wonder if he felt the tingles too. He must have because he has to shake himself. He gives me a strange look before staring at his fingers.

"How did you do that? Only mates—" he shakes his head before he jams the finger he shoved inside me in his mouth. I feel all the blood rush to my face in mortification. Gross! Though he doesn't seem to think so.

Despite this, the effect is instantaneous. His pupils dilate, removing all color, and his nostrils flare. The lewd groan that leaves him makes my knees weak. Slick further drenches my thighs at his reaction when he is suddenly ripped away from me and thrown across the pavement.

My scream is deafening as the wolf shifts back to the man. A very naked man. His savage look makes me cower as he sucks in a deep breath. His chest rises and falls heavily with his harsh breaths. His canines protrude, and his eyes reflect my terrified face as I stare into the onyx gleam. I try to press behind the dumpster when one of the other wolves attacks him.

I see Rhen shake himself while I back up further, cornered in the tight spot I am trapped in. A brown wolf lunges at me when Rhen attacks it. He shifts instantly and starts ripping into him. Fur and blood spray everywhere, coating the concrete. I hear the other two wolves stop their fight before circling around Rhen, whose aura easily outweighs all of theirs. The wolf Rhen attacked shifts back, and the other two circle him before he speaks.

"Help me take this fucker out and I will share her," the Alpha says. Rhen snarls at him before his eyes flick to me and glaze over. I can tell he is mind-linking before the color returns.

"Stay down. Help is coming," Rhen tells me before all three lunge at him. I scream, dropping to the ground as they fight.

Blood drenches me, and I see one wolf drop. Yet, my pheromones are only growing stronger. More wolves stalk into the alley, joining the fight to take down Rhen. A loud snapping crack makes me look up to find Rhen encircled. Another wolf steps in where the other had fallen, his neck broken. I look to Rhen and I can tell he is too injured to shift.

Rhen, also noticing this, looks at me. "Run!" he says, and I take off, only to feel teeth wrap around my ankle as one of the Alphas pounces on me. My hands and face hit the ground painfully. I clench my eyes shut, feeling fur brush my back before it is replaced with skin. The fighting gets louder than ever behind me, while I am trapped under a brooding male who shreds my shirt and rips at the back of my pants. Fight-or-flight kicks in, and I thrash to escape him. I try to roll over, only for him to flip me back onto my stomach when he presses his knees onto the backs of my thighs.

I swallow, knowing I am about to witness Rhen's murder before getting raped, when a thunderous growl rings out loudly. It echoes off the brick walls and sends a chill straight up my spine. I look to the end of the alley to see a giant black wolf with a grey patch over half his face. Every hair on my body rises, and I sense his aura like a tidal wave.

It is clear this mammoth of a wolf is from an Alpha Pack; he oozes Alpha-of-Alpha male dominance. Just the sheer size of his paws on the ground are bigger than my head. This is why Alpha Packs are so feared; Alpha Packs are more dangerous. They trump all. Many Alphas can't live together, it takes strength and control for an Alpha to make other Alphas submit to him.

It's something most Alphas refuse to do, yet those who manage it, and come to terms with being able to live with each other, have an advantage; because the Alpha-of-Alphas grows substantially bigger than their brethren and is more potent, deadly. Impossibly powerful.

I watch as the monster snaps its jaws and growls menacingly. The man above me freezes when the beast snarls, charging straight at us. I have no doubt the monster will win, and I just pray he doesn't kill Rhen. Sparks brush across my exposed back, and I gasp before I am drenched in my attacker's blood.

The scent makes me heave, and the warm liquid coats me as the Alpha tears into the man's throat before flinging him off me. I shake beneath the beast, making sure to breathe through my mouth and not inhale his scent as it stands over me. I am too scared to move as the wolf bends down to sniff my face, only to sneeze from the descenter still cloying to me. He shakes his head. I am paralyzed by fear. When I hear the other wolves whimper, I turn my gaze back to the fight, praying Rhen is alright.

Three more wolves jump down from the rooftops and balconies that overlook the alley. I suck in a breath when I see Rhen get to his feet. He is coated in blood. Yet he still moves toward the Alpha above me. My eyes widened in horror when the beast moves, stepping over me, and I roll on my back to clutch his fur.

"Don't hurt him!" I shriek in panic before I get a whiff of his scent.

Thane!

148

THIRTY-FOUR

~T hane~

The mind-link opens abruptly when Rhen contacts me. Raidon is trying to calm Leon down, who is still crazed with bloodlust and rut.

'I need your help. We're trapped,' Rhen says.

'Excuse me?' I ask him.

'She went into heat. I fucking need you here now!'

'Fuck, just leave her ass there. It's what Omegas are for,' I tell him. Fuck, she would probably even enjoy it.

'Thane! I am not leaving her. Get here now!'

The mind-link cuts off abruptly. Nope, she deserves this for not telling us she needed more suppressants. Raidon glances at me from where he holds the door; I know he heard Rhen, too.

"Thane!" he spits at me through gritted teeth. "She is our assistant. And an Omega!"

"Not my problem," I snap at him. I lean against her desk and look down at her neat handwriting on the notepad. I chew my lip as guilt fills me.

"Rhen won't abandon her to fend for herself. What about him?" Raidon snarls at me, taking one hand off the door.

I stand. I do not feel like fighting Leon right now, and if Raidon lets go of that door, Leon will come running out.

"Think Thane, she is tiny, and in a city full of fucking Alphas. Not just one. Hundreds live here," Raidon says, and a wave of possessiveness washes through me at the thought of other Alphas touching her.

I shake my head. Her pheromones still linger in the air, though not as strong, since I sprayed air freshener everywhere. However, her sweet scent makes my mouth water, and my cock is still painfully hard in my pants. Glancing at Raidon, so is his. I swallow, wondering if she is okay or if the estrus has overridden her senses.

Yet when Rhen's fear courses through me, I know it isn't for himself but for her. Rhen fears nothing and loves a good fight. If he is scared that means he is struggling to keep her safe.

I curse under my breath and shake my head, tugging my blazer off and tossing it on the desk while unbuttoning my damn shirt. "Get Leila up here to contain her damn brother and grab the fucking car. You can drop Zara home," I tell him before my palms hit the fire escape doors. The lock smashes as it hits the wall to the stairwell, and I start running to reach them.

The moment I burst out the doors, I shift. I thought I would have to follow the bond to their location, but one whiff of the air lures me directly to them. I race through the streets to the alleyway. Passersby stand at the end, staring horrified down the small street. This is prime entertainment for them; not much like this ever happens in the city. Sure, you hear the horror stories from what happens in the dark of night, but in broad daylight? Most Omegas are careful not to be caught out in a state like this, and she is a shining beacon of lust and sin.

Stepping into the alley, people scatter to get away from me. My eyes go to Rhen, who is drenched in blood as he tries to keep three

Alphas from her. Another two are dead on the ground. I see her run, only to be pounced on by a brown and white wolf. The wolf shifts, ripping the back of her shirt open and snapping her bra while she thrashes beneath him. The fact she is fighting at all is odd—she should be rabid with heat, seeking the Alpha's knot, not fighting him.

My brows furrow in confusion, and I suck in a breath, knowing once I get close enough, I will be as rabid as others. I need to hold myself together, knowing that is the only thing holding Rhen back. Pack wolves won't mate without the Alpha's approval. It dampens the effects of heated wolves because they need approval. Yet these are lone Alphas, bound by no pack and no Alpha.

Zara screams, rolling over as she tries to shove him off, only for him to grab her hips and flip her back onto her belly as he rips at her pants. The sight snaps me out of my confusion.

A savage growl leaves me. My mind screams that she isn't his to touch. I want to kill him, and kill him, I do. My teeth lacerate his throat, and I shake my head, snapping his neck. He goes limp as my jaws wrap around his throat, and I chomp down again before flinging him away.

Zara freezes beneath me. I sniff her, making sure the blood that coats her isn't hers. I get a whiff of Alpha blood and de-scenter, making my nose wrinkle, and I sneeze when Rhen mind-links me.

'A *little help,*' he growls, and I rear forward on the next one, my teeth slicing through his shoulder. Yet I can't bring myself to move away from Zara. She is still frozen with fear, cowering beneath my hind legs. Rhen kicks off another, and I hear more coming when I glance down at her.

'*Get her out of here. Raidon should be here any minute with the car,*' I mind-link. He walks over to me and runs his fingers through my fur while I step over her.

I don't know what shocks me more: Zara's fisted grip on my belly or her panicked shout of "Don't hurt him."

We have given her hell for weeks, and she would still beg for him? Shaking my head, I look at Rhen. They will not touch her or my mate. I growl before launching myself at the newly arrived wolves, giving Rhen the chance to escape with her.

THIRTY-FIVE

~R hen~

Zara is almost limp in my arms when I scoop her up just as I hear Raidon's car skid to a stop at the end of the alleyway. I race toward it, leaving Thane behind as he keeps the other Alphas at bay. Raidon jumps out of the car and races to open the rear door, but I thrust her at him.

I force her into his arms because I have been around her too long; I am fighting a war inside my head. I can't take her. Thane would kill me. It is a disrespect to disobey your Alpha, and though I can feel his instinct to protect her, he hasn't given his express approval. Which, by werewolf law, gives him the right to punish us as he sees fit if we were to take her now.

Thane wouldn't kill us, and his aura and rule hold us back, but we are still Alphas, stuck in a confined space with the scent of a heat-ravaged Omega.

Raidon gasps when the heat of her body touches him. "You take her," he says, trying to hand her back to me, but I hold my hands up, backing away from them. He growls, his pupils blowing out as he gets a whiff of her sultry scent before holding his breath.

"Fine," he snarls, sliding across the back seat with her, and I slam the door, rushing to the driver's side. I climb in and blast the AC, hoping to get rid of some of her scent. We can't roll the windows down without alerting the entire city to our location.

"Where are we taking her?" Raidon growls as Zara moans. Her estrus is forcing her into the next stage. She's becoming rabid with her need to mate.

"Fuck! This isn't good, little Omega. Are you trying to get me killed?" Raidon purrs, his chest rumbling with his Calling as he tries to settle her. Instead of having the desired effect, she attacks him. Her lips maul his neck as she bites down and sucks on his flesh. I speed up, Raidon's arousal flooding me through the bond.

"To her apartment, which way?" I ask Raidon, and he moans lewdly.

"Raidon! Focus," I snarl at him.

"Bit fucking hard right now when she is grinding her pussy all over me," he snaps back, and I glance in the mirror at him. Her claws have slipped out and shredded his shirt. A savage moan escapes her as she begins licking his chest. I force my eyes away from them, trying to blink through the haze her pheromones are putting us under. I swallow, breathing through my mouth, when Raidon growls.

"So soft and warm," he murmurs, and I glance in the mirror to see him rubbing and squeezing her.

"Raidon, focus! What's her damn address?"

He shakes his head. "Right, yeah. We can't take her there," he says, and I slow down.

"Where else are we going to take her?" I growl at him. He shrugs, and Zara grinds herself against his crotch before kissing him. Raidon groans, turning his face away, giving her the opportunity to latch onto his neck. She bites him, but she can't mark him. Unless she marks Thane first, any mark she makes on us will never stick. Though, he'll be livid when he sees her bite on him. He is a possessive beast.

"No idea, but I have seen her apartment building, and no way that place is secure. She will be hunted down in minutes," he gasps, and I peer at him again, watching as he grips her hips, trying to hold her still. His canines slip out as he fights for control.

"Man, I don't give a fuck where we take her but figure it out fast before I bury my damn cock in her."

Zara whines, tugging at his pants, trying to undress him as her instincts take over. It makes me wonder how she survived previous heats.

Is this her first?

I try to think where she would be safe. Nowhere comes to mind, not while she is in full-blown heat. Cursing, I rip the handbrake up and turn the steering wheel sharply, spinning the car around and jumping the median. Raidon slides into the door and grunts as he clutches the back of my seat, and Zara falls into the footwell behind me.

"So, where are we taking her?" Raidon asks. I glance at him in the mirror.

"Home," I tell him. He nods before gaping at me.

"Are you fucking nuts? Thane will kill us," Raidon gasps as fear smashes into me through the bond. Clarity momentarily returns as fear for our Alpha kicks in. Yet, where else could I take her that she would be safe in this state?

"Have you got a better idea? Because if you do, let me know," I snap at him. He mutters something and curses before hissing.

"Uh, uh, you don't bite," he says, and I hear Zara growl, making my eyes flick to the mirror.

"Raidon!" I scold.

"Hey, she wants to suck it, I won't stop her. Unless she bites it again," Raidon declares, and I glare at him in the mirror, glancing over my shoulder quickly. She had crawled out of the footwell and between his legs.

"Raidon, stop her," I grit out.

"Why? I can't fuck her, but Thane never said anything about her sucking me off," he says, and I grit my teeth.

"Taste her slick, asshole," I spit at him.

"Huh?"

"She's a fucking virgin!" I tell him.

"Bullshit, you're just saying that" Raidon scoffs, and I growl at him.

"Taste her slick!" I repeat, and his eyes widen as he looks down at her. I smirk at him, watching him in the mirror.

"Whoops, no girlie. My mistake. That is not a lollipop," he purrs, grabbing her and sitting her back on his lap, "or a pogo stick, so let me get that out of the way."

Zara growls, fighting him as he tries to tuck his cock back into his pants.

"Damn, and she has such plump lips," Raidon pouts.

"I'm surprised you were able to stop," I tell him.

"Mouth breathing and Thane's burning anger are quick but effective ways to give yourself a limp dick," Raidon tells me, and I chuckle, pulling up to the gates. He is right about that. I pull the visor down, and the fob falls into my lap. I hit the button to open the gates.

"Rock, paper, scissors ya for who takes the blame for bringing her here?" I ask him.

"Nuh-uh. He's already gonna skin me alive for the marks she left on me. This is your idea. My ass ain't getting branded for it," Raidon says.

"Where is Leon when you need him?" I mutter.

"Since when do you blame Leon?" Raidon asks.

"Since I was about to fuck her in the alley to abate her heat. I know Thane felt that!" And damn, will I pay for it.

"Well, that explains why he was being a prick before he saved your ass."

I nod, knowing I am in for it. Yet, how could he leave her defense-less? Surely, he isn't that heartless.

"I'll suck your dick?" I offer Raidon.

"Nope, not worth it. Nothing will get me to agree to tell Thane this was my idea," Raidon tells me as I pull up out front.

THIRTY-SIX

~ T hane~

What a bloody nightmare today turned out to be! I make my way back to the office. I shift in the loading docks and take the fire escape back up to the top floor. I don't feel like strolling through the main lobby buck naked. I have already made a spectacle of myself.

I know the papers tomorrow will read that my pack went into a rut over a damn Omega, which is far from the truth. I was merely protecting my mate. Yet, if mine and Rhen's roles had been reversed, I couldn't have left her with those monsters either. I would have fought to keep her safe, and that thought irks me more than it should.

Cuts and scrapes litter most of my body, and the authorities are dealing with the two dead bodies in the alleyway. They will meet me back here to go over everything. The media will, of course, blame this entire thing on me. I am their favorite scapegoat.

When I reach the top floor and push the busted fire escape door open, I discover Leila has duct-taped her brother to a chair. She has a nasty bite on her neck. He really sank his teeth into her and bit out a chunk. Even with her healing powers, it is going to take a while for that to heal. It is no doubt from her brother. It is cannibalistic, and I can see Leila is furious at being treated like a chew toy.

"I told you I am sorry. What more do you want?" Leon pleads with his sister as he struggles to get out of the duct tape.

"My skin back, for one! You bit a bloody mouthful out of me! You're so gross. And you got your slobber on me!" she snarls back, baring her fangs at him.

"It was an accident and not that big of a deal. I went into a rut. I just bit you a little too hard. It'll heal; you know it will. Stop being so dramatic over one little nibble."

She puts her hand on her hips and glares daggers at him. "That only makes it more gross, you asshole! Being blood-crazed is one thing. You can't help yourself when you just need blood down your throat. But this is ten times worse!" Leila shrieks, pointing an accusing finger at him.

"You fang-raped me. I'm your fucking sister! Keep your horny, blood-crazed fangs away from me! You just wait until I tell Mom and Dad about this. It's not like you can hide it. You fucking asshole. Do you bite your mates like this? Just take a giant bite out of him like he's some snack for you?" She rubs her neck, which is healing.

It's still a bloody mess, but it is at least healing. "You little shit. I can't believe you put your cock-sucking lips on my neck." She shudders, and I shake my head at their bickering.

"You taste like shit, anyway; I've licked asses that taste better," Leon snaps back at her. He holds his tongue out and spits, as if trying to get the taste of her out of his mouth. "Stop being a drama queen and let me go."

"I would hope I taste like mother-fucking-ass. I'm your damn sister, you bloodsucking leech," she snarls. She grabs a red and black stapler the size of my fist and throws it at the center of his chest. It hits him with a meaty thump and he growls, thrashing from side to side to get revenge.

"Bitch!" he roars.

For the love of god, please, someone strike me down so I don't have to listen to this shit. I am not in the mood for this crap. I rub my temples, praying that these two will magically find peace and shut the fuck up.

"Huh, you make no sense," Leila snaps, and I growl. Their argument sends me through every level of hell, some multiple times. My eye can't twitch anymore, and the pounding headache threatens to be the background music for the rest of my life.

How bad would it be for me if I toss them both out the window? Though, I like Leon. The man knows how to suck cock. Would he forgive me if I kill his sister and spare him? Would it really be that wrong? Anyone locked in a room with them for five minutes would empathize and class it as self-defense. These two would surely cause even the sanest people to go mad with their bitching.

I am, however, glad that Leon is under control, but I wish I had a mute button for these two. Besides, the office looks like a tornado just blew through. Crap is everywhere and torn to shreds. It will take time to set it all right, and I have no interest in doing any of it.

Maybe I should take them to the ground floor before I kick them off the side of the building and watch them go splat on the concrete.

I growl as their bickering reaches a new level. Muzzles for both of them and a leash for Leon. Leon can just be quiet and pretty for me, and Leila can just be fucking quiet. She jumps out of her seat and slowly turns to see what's going on.

She freezes, body tensing and eyes widening as she stares at my body before the blood rushes into her cheeks, and she jerks her head to the side, staring at the ground. "Sorry," she grumbles.

"Keep your whorish eyes off my damn mate!" Leon screeches.

When I feel better, I will take my frustrations out on Leon's ass for all of this nonsense.

"What are you going to say to Mom when I tell her you were eye-fucking my mate?" Leon screeches at her. I shake my head at him.

"I was not, Leech!" She sneers while Leon growls at her before looking back at me.

"What happened?" Leon asks, almost in a panic. It took him long enough to notice anything is wrong.

"Zara is fine. Raidon and Rhen are taking her to her apartment," I tell him as I move to the desk where I dumped my clothes. I start tugging them on just as the elevator doors open and two officers enter the foyer.

"Mr. Keller, I just need you to sign these statements and we are good to go. Witnesses verified that you were protecting your mate, Rhen?" I nod my head.

"Yes, he mind-linked me," I tell them while zipping my pants, and they nod. I already gave my statement, but the crowd became too big and I asked them to finish it here; I don't feel like having more of my nudes leaked on the internet. The media are vultures; they love displaying everything my pack does, seeing as we are only one of three Alpha Packs in the state. The Obsidian Pack is one, the other is Black Mountain Pack, also to the north of the city.

The officer takes a seat at the desk, pulls the paperwork out, and writes a few things down.

"The Omega woman, we can't find any record for her. Do you know how long she has resided in the city?" the female officer asks. I can tell she is an Alpha female, and the way she sneers at the word 'Omega' irritates me.

"She never registered her address. We have no such name in our system. She hasn't reported herself to the city yet, or anything about her pack links. You said she is an employee?" the officer continues. I feel the mind-link open up, and Leon's voice flits through my head.

'Thane, I know you want to get rid of her, but—' He doesn't finish, and I glare at him, knowing full well he had been feeding on her; I'm not stupid, and I may have turned a blind eye to it, but he has a point, and I know what will become of her.

If she can't afford her suppressants, I doubt she can afford the fines for failing to report herself to the city council. And if she can't pay those, then she goes into rotation to settle the debt. The thought of her being forced into rotation almost makes me growl.

"Mr. Keller? We need her employee reports," the female officer says. Catching Leon's eye and looking at Leila, she drops her head while Leon looks at me pleadingly. Fuck!

"She isn't an employee. Yes, she works here, but that isn't her purpose," I lie.

"Oh, so your pack is looking for an Omega, and she's here on a trial basis?" the woman asks, and I grit my teeth.

"Yes, we posted an ad looking for an Omega. Leila here posted it herself, Zara answered it, and we brought her to the city," I lie. Leila nods, confirming what I said.

"Oh, this is wonderful news!" the officer exclaims, and I fight back a curse. Just what we need, this shit getting out.

"It isn't public news yet, so if you don't mind keeping that to yourself for now," I tell them, and they nod.

"Of course, Mr. Keller, we have everything we need, and I am sure you'll want to get home to your Omega. Please just remember, if you don't choose to mark and keep her, remind her to register at the council. We can't keep her safe if we don't know her location and whereabouts," the male officer tells me. I press my lips in a line and give a quick nod.

I wait for them to leave and let out a breath once the doors close, before turning to glare at my mate and his sister.

"You lied for her?" Leila says, clearly shocked.

Yes, because she didn't leave me much choice.

"No, I lied because I had to. If you had done your job properly, she would never have been here in the first place," I tell her, and she looks away.

Turning to Leon, he uses his feet to scoot forward on his chair, his arms and legs still duct-taped. I can feel his burning hunger and his need to go home. With a shake of my head, I move to him, stripping the tape and making him hiss. I am not at all gentle about it, and I will deal with him further when we get home.

RHEN AND RAIDON DON'T ANSWER THEIR PHONES OR THE MIND-LINK ON THE way home. They're even ignoring Leon, which bothers me. Raidon would have to get suppressants from somewhere, so they are probably holed up somewhere while they wait. Or maybe they are ensuring she is tucked away safely in her apartment.

I'm full of tension on the drive home, yet it recedes when I spot Raidon's car parked in the garage. However, that relief quickly turns to rage when I step out of the vehicle and all I can smell is Zara.

Surely, they wouldn't be this stupid, but I am proven correct in my first assumption when Leon gets out of the car and goes stiff as a board. I glance at him before he lurches forward. I reach out to grab him, but he slips through my arms before I can catch him. I curse with a shake of my head before storming into the house.

CHAPTER
THIRTY-SEVEN

~ R hen~
My cock throbs painfully in my pants as I stare at the door to the basement. Chewing my fingernails, I begin to pace. Thane has been trying to mind-link us, and Raidon and I have been ignoring him.

He will be furious when he returns home, and I dread the punishment we will receive. The basement door creaks open loudly and my eyes go to it. Her scent perfuming the room becomes more robust and almost impossible to resist.

Raidon emerges, closing the door behind him, looking every bit as frazzled as I feel. His clothes are torn to shreds. He is sweating profusely, fighting his urges to mark and mate her. We sent Tania to get suppressants.

Not even Tania could handle her sweet scent. Tania had dropped them off before all but running from the place. But now we have to figure out a way to give them to her without her mauling us, or us mauling her. Zara's scent permeates the air even with the door closed. Sickly sweet and so addictive. I force myself to focus as I rush to the kitchen. I rip open the cupboards beneath the kitchen sink, searching each one.

Finding what I'm looking for, I grab a can of de-scenter and clench it tight as I hold my finger down on the trigger, spraying the entire ground floor, trying to get rid of the scent that assaults my nose and to awaken my senses. It only mutes her scent, but it's better than the full force and toxicity that comes with it.

"Fuck! I can't take this! She can't stay here. My dick feels like it's going to burst," Raidon says, adjusting his pants while he grips the kitchen counter. He lets out a lewd groan and I glance at him to find him squeezing his cock through his slacks.

I press my lips in a line, knowing the agony he's in. I nod, feeling the same way, yet something is off with Zara's scent. Something is gnawing at my insides and tickling my mind as I try to place whatever it is my instincts are telling me. Omegas usually smell sickly sweet, but we never struggled like this the few times we came across an Omega in heat.

"Her scent, do you—" I don't finish what I'm going to say, not knowing what the heck I'm asking him.

"She smells familiar," Raidon offers, and my eyes dart to him because I thought exactly the same thing. It's like Déjà vu had washed over me the moment I got a whiff of her.

I just have no idea why I feel that way, and I can tell through the bond that Raidon can't explain his odd feeling either. Her scent, for some reason, feels familiar, which should be impossible.

"Thane is going to kill us," Raidon groans when we hear things breaking in the basement. We both glance at the basement door before I reach over and grab the bag Tania dropped off. I rummage through the paper bag and slide the suppressants to Raidon across the counter.

"Nope, now way. I can't go back down there. It was hard enough forcing myself to leave her once," Raidon tells me. I growl, knowing I will have to. I'm not sure I'm strong enough to handle it either, but we need to before Thane gets home. He's going to kill us. No, he's going to skin me alive, boil my damn organs, and feed them to Raidon for our stupidity.

The possibilities are terrifying. I don't have time to ponder, however, because I hear the garage door: Thane's home.

Raidon looks at me in panic. I swallow nervously, and my heart thumps erratically in my chest so hard it feels like it is creeping up my throat. Her scent has muted a little, yet it is still potent, and there is no way he will miss it.

The sound of the door smashing against the wall makes me jump. Leon growls, rushing through the place and bolting straight toward Raidon, who moves to grab him but misses. I tackle Leon, pressing him against the wall before he can grab the door handle, only to stiffen when Thane's command rolls over me. His aura makes my back straighten. Raidon whimpers while Leon fights and pushes against me to get free.

"Let him go," Thane snarls, tossing his keys on the counter.

"Thane!" I panic, knowing Leon would feed on her.

"He's a glutton. He will be passed out and blood drunk long before he kills her," Thane snarls. I let him go when I can no longer fight against his command. Leon disappears, and Raidon whimpers as he busts through the basement door before Thane glares at him.

Raidon, the behemoth, buckles under the pressure of his aura first, dropping to his knees. My knees bite painfully into the tile floor when he turns his anger on me seconds later.

"Who thought it was a good idea to bring her here?" Thane asks, his voice deadly calm and ice cold.

"Mine," I grit out through clenched teeth. The noise that leaves him is a roar as his aura forces me completely onto my hands and knees before him, when Raidon speaks.

"Her apartment isn't secure. We couldn't have taken her there, even if we tried," Raidon growls, and I turn my head. The effort to do so is painful as I look at him.

"So, you thought bringing her here and putting her in our Den was the better option?" Thane bellows, when suddenly, Zara whimpers. Thane's aura falters, and we all stare at the basement door, knowing Leon got his fangs in her. Yet her whimper turns to a moan from the endorphins of his bite and her heat.

I sigh.

CHAPTER
THIRTY-EIGHT

~R~hen~

~ I look up at Thane, who sniffs the air, and his brows furrow in confusion. I watch him swallow. The same strange feeling Raidon and I had about her scent rolls through the bond from him, too. At least I'm not the only one imagining it.

"The suppressants?" Thane asked as he gathers himself and forces his gaze from the open basement door.

"We can't get close enough to her, not while she is like this," I admit, and he looks down at me. When she cries out in pain again, I can only assume that Leon has passed out.

"Fix it. Fix her, and get her out of my house," he says, reaching for the suppressants and dropping them on the ground in front of my face. I stare at his shoes, unable to look up and meet the furious gaze that I can feel bearing down on me.

"Thane, I can't go down there," I plead with him, and he growls.

"Use protection," he spits, and my stomach drops before he walks out, slamming the door to the garage as he goes. His aura drops, and I face-plant onto the floor before pushing up on my hands into a crouched position. Seconds after getting up, I fall on my ass as

168

I hear his car tear out of the driveway. I lean against the counter and stare at Raidon, who is also trying to catch his breath.

"Did he just give us permission?" Raidon asks, just as shocked as I am. I nod, but I can't help but wonder what Zara would have to say on the matter.

No doubt, in this phase of estrus, she wouldn't care if we fucked her. Hell, she would probably beg us to. Yet it feels wrong without Thane and without her being coherent. Looking at Raidon, I can tell through the bond that he feels the same.

Snatching the suppressants off the floor, I stagger to the basement door and descend the stairs to find Leon passed out, drunk on her pheromone-fueled blood with Zara snuggled up beside him amongst the cushions. I let out a sigh and hear Raidon come down the stairs behind me.

"I'll help you," he growls, staring worriedly at Leon. The moment I step onto the cushioned floor, Zara shifts her weight. Her breathing changes. She is as delirious as Leon is drunk. She rubs her face across his chest like a cat marking its territory.

I grip her ankle, and she freezes, turning to look at my hand before her eyes go to mine. I can see she is completely crazed with heat, yet seeing her like this, I know I can't take advantage of her state. No matter how good she smells. It would make me no better than the other Alphas in that alley. Zara purrs, crawling over to me before she pounces, tackling me and shoving me on my back. The air leaves my lungs in a short wheeze.

"Raidon!" I wheeze out before he stomps down the steps and drops into the cushioned space. He hauls her away and starts purring, clutching her squirming body to his chest.

"How do you want to do this?" Raidon asks while she licks any exposed skin she can get her tongue on. A heat builds inside of me that I know I can't give in to, not while she's like this.

"Hold her while I try to feed them to her," I tell him, popping them from the flimsy container.

"How many?" I ask. Raidon blinks at me.

"Three?" he says. I look at her, having no clue, and also wondering how long before they take effect. Raidon pins her while I pry her mouth open, only for her to chomp down on my finger. I jerk my hand back, thankful that it wasn't my dick. My finger is bleeding, and Raidon snickers before pinching her nose.

"Hurry up," he growls as she thrashes in his arms.

"Fuck no, you do it," I tell him, and he glares at me.

"She is a tiny Omega; it can't have hurt that bad."

Easy for him to say. She didn't bite his finger nearly clean off.

"Give them here," Thane snaps, making me jump. I look up to find him standing on the ledge around the Den.

He kicks his shoes off before dropping down onto the blue and black cushioned bed; he holds his hand out for the pill packet before squatting beside me. His aura is powerful as he purrs, Calling her to him, and Raidon lets her go. Zara launches herself at him, crashing into Thane's chest.

He catches her effortlessly before popping the suppressants into his mouth; Zara, crazed, claws and licks his chest, ripping his clothes to shreds as she tries to scent him. Raidon and I stand frozen, waiting for him to tear her apart. He hates Omegas, he hates Zara, yet looking at him, he's caressing her, being gentle and patient with her as she claws at him.

"Shh, Zara," he purrs as she tries to get to his neck, her instincts pushing her to claim him. Thane drops his neck, pulling her onto his lap before gripping her chin and kissing her. His fingers grip the back of her neck, forcing the pills down her throat. His eyes flash to mine as he glares at me. He is livid, but I am relieved he came back.

His aura alone is enough to settle the urges rolling through me. Zara moans as Thane feeds her the pills in his kiss. I look away, unable to watch the two of them kissing.

When he is finished, he starts purring, his potent Calling sucking her into a blissful sleep. Her breathing evens out as he scoops her up. I watch as he walks across the enormous space and lays her next to Leon before he tucks her in.

"Keep her hydrated and warm," Thane says before leaving us again.

So maybe his instincts toward Omegas aren't dead after all.

"She needs your skin contact!" he growls from the top of the stairs before leaving us alone with her. I glance at Raidon, who is already crawling over to her and Leon, his own Calling slipping out and keeping her sedated.

CHAPTER
THIRTY-NINE

~Thane~

Something about her scent bothers me as I leave my mates with her. I want to go back in there with them; to wrap my body around hers with my mates, even though I hate her. There is just something about the little Omega that calls to me. I can't go back in there.

If I did, there would be no escaping the feelings she's causing. Feelings I tried to deny before running as fast as I could. It has been years since I set foot in that Den. Yet seeing her heat-ravaged body... it kills me to leave her there.

The way my blood burned as her hands moved over my chest, ripping at my clothes, trying to pull them from my body so she could reach my skin. Her fingers had scrabbled at my shoulders, gripping me tight like I am a drug that she desperately needs.

I try to forget how her tongue felt, licking up the side of my neck before moving lower to the hard ridges of my chest and abdomen. The thick scent of her arousal bloomed in the air, making my mouth water. To taste her. To tease her. To ease the burning haze the Omega feels.

It had been too much for me, testing my control more than I liked. I want to take Zara in our Den. I want to bind her hands so I can pull the pleasure from her until she cries out for me; begging me for more of what I alone can give her.

The way her body had felt in my lap, the heat of her pussy seeping through the fabric of my pants, nearly sent me insane. Her slick heat coating my erection... Fuck...

I want to unzip my slacks to slip into that heat. To bury myself deep into her pussy and feel her body clamp down around my cock.

Her skin had been so soft beneath my palms. So soft and so markable, her ass would have looked perfect with my handprint staining her flesh red, with my fingerprints littering her body, showing the world that she is mine—that she is ours and no one else's.

I want to fuck her, want her to claim me. But not like this. I want her to be there with me, not lost in this haze. Therefore, I had to leave and get out of here before I give myself over to instinct. Because I know I don't really want this. It is her heat making me feel this way. I despise Omegas.

Snatching my keys, I head to my car. I need a distraction, and work seems like the best place for it. Away from her, and from my mates, who I know are fighting the same baser instincts I am. If I lose control, I know they will too.

Driving to work, I white-knuckle the steering wheel and roll the window down. The fresh air helps, relieving the assault her scent had left on me. Yet the longer I drive, the less sense things make. The urge to keep and claim her makes no sense. She isn't ours. Harlow is, and she is not our Harlow. Harlow was our light in the darkest tunnel, and she betrayed us. And for that reason, taking another Omega will never be safe. My hatred for them burns hotter than any bond ever could.

Harlow is dead, of that we are certain, yet why do I feel the urge to claim Zara? Why does her scent feel so familiar, yet not?

We hardly know anything about Zara, yet seeing my mates

struggle the way they did makes me certain of one thing: I have been denying both them and myself. Alphas need Omegas. I thought our little pack could survive without one, but now I wonder if maybe claiming another Omega wouldn't be the downfall I expect. Yet, I'm not sure if I can trust another Omega after Harlow.

So, I find myself at a crossroads. Can I keep denying my mates something they clearly need? I hate Omegas, yet I crave Zara. My mind is at war with the urge to claim her for my pack and my hatred for her kind.

The parking garage is dark as I pull in. I sit in the car for a bit, unable to pull myself out from behind the steering wheel and head inside. It isn't until the security guard taps on my back window that I realize I am still sitting in my car.

"Sorry, Marco," I tell him, shaking my thoughts away.

"Are you alright, boss?" he asks, and I sigh.

"Yeah. You may head out, if you want. I'll be here anyway," I tell him, and he gives me a strange look. He glances in the back of my car before looking around the garage for my mates or their cars.

"Are you sure you're alright?" he asks again. I usually have at least one or two of my mates with me. They are extensions of myself; I hate being away from them, and they feel the same.

"Go home," I tell him while opening my door and heading for the elevator. I get to my floor and spend a good few hours tidying up the place before sitting behind my desk. It's only then that I notice Zara's file sitting there. I pick it up, flick through pages that hold little to no information, until I find her address. I dial the landlord's number, but no one answers. Drumming my fingers on the desk, I sigh before growling. That little Omega is still playing on my damn mind.

With a growl, I rise from behind my desk, snatching the first page of her file and grabbing my keys. I catch the elevator to the garage before hopping in my car and punching the address into my GPS.

CHAPTER
FORTY

~Thane~

In all my years of living in this city, I have never passed by this rundown apartment building. After I pull up to the front of the apartment building, I double-check the address. Surely, this is not the correct place? It looks as if it is one busted window from being declared condemned.

What Omega would live here? They are territorial creatures and know the value of their Dens. Yet, when I peer around the place, I can only describe it as a dump, and I find it hard to believe she lives here.

Even so, the address is correct. Climbing out of my car, I lock it before walking over to the door and scanning the different buzzers. I'm looking for the Omega's name when I see one listed as management. I press the buzzer, and a woman's voice screeches back at me before I can react.

"Who is it?" she snaps before coughing.

"I'm looking for the owner or manager," I answer.

"For fuck's sake," she says in a snarling tone before hitting the buzzer to let me inside. As I yank the door open and step inside the room, my nose wrinkles in disgust at the foul stench emanating from the place.

The wallpaper is peeling and the lights flicker. I hear a door creak. A woman emerges from the shadows with a bat in her hand and a scowl on her face. She walks toward me, not looking impressed about having a late-night visitor.

"And what the fuck are you looking for me for?" she snarls before she stops. She glances me over before propping her bat on her shoulder.

"I think you're on the wrong side of the city, Alpha," she says.

"I'm looking for someone, actually. Her name is Zara. Her address is listed here," the woman groans.

"She isn't here," she snaps, clearly annoyed I pulled her from bed to ask about her.

"I know that. She works for me, and I am trying to find any information I can on her. I'm wondering if I could look through her apartment?"

"She doesn't live here anymore. I evicted her a few weeks ago, but all her crap is up there still; I haven't found a new tenant yet," the woman tells me, and my brows furrow.

"Do you know where she moved to, then?" I ask her, and the woman rolls her eyes.

"Last I heard is one of my other tenants saw her sleeping behind the old plaza at Central," she shrugs before stomping up the steps.

"You tossed an Omega out when she had nowhere else to go? In the middle of winter? In a city full of Alphas," I ask, outraged. It is dangerous being homeless here, more so if you're an Omega. I don't believe this place is safe enough for an Omega, let alone living on the streets.

"Hey, don't be judging me. I got bills to pay, and Zara owed me over four thousand dollars in rent and utilities," she snaps, stopping by a door that looks as busted as the rest of this god-awful place.

"Besides, I'm sure she could have stayed with that Tal. He's always offering her work. The girl is just too shy to take him up on it," the woman curses, and I wonder if she is talking about the same Tal. I know only one person who goes by that name, Leon's cousin.

"Tal?" I asked curiously.

"You know, that stripper joint? She worked there on and off. Went by the name Z."

I blink at that. Zara is Z? She worked for Tal! I try to wrap my mind around that information. I don't know if I'm more furious at Zara or Tal. Or the fact I have a whore working for me.

I still remember the cloying scent from the night I met Z, and it makes me gasp. I know Z is a virgin and if Z is Zara? Well, that would explain the allure she has to us. Now it makes sense why we all went into a rut over her. She's a virgin. That has to be it.

"I thought that's where she would have gone. Zara and Bree were pretty close. Bree lived next door to her for a bit. They must have had a falling out," the woman tells me, pushing the door open. As I step into the room, I see nothing but a shabby couch in the room's corner.

"This is it?" I ask, walking through the place. I glance over my shoulder at the woman, who looks bored. She shrugs, and I move into a small bedroom that is next to the living room. It is just as empty. This is where she lived?

Walking out, I stop in front of the woman. "What is your name?"

"Martha," she tells me, and I nod, glancing around one last time. I can't picture anyone living here, let alone an Omega; it makes me itchy just standing in this dilapidated place.

"How long have you known Zara?" I question her. She watches me for a second, as if debating whether or not to answer. Finally, she sighs and rubs her eyes as if tired. It is pretty late, and I know I likely woke her because she is wearing blue pinstripe pajamas, a gray, fluffy robe, and socks. That and the hair rollers are a dead giveaway. She doesn't look like the sort of woman that parades around with rollers in her hair.

"Couple years. I found her out front, asleep on my doorstep. She was barefoot, drenched in blood, and starving. I felt bad for her. She looked as if she was running from something. The girl was scared of her own shadow. I gave her a place to stay until she got a job. She was quiet, stuck herself, a good tenant, but once she lost her job, I couldn't keep her here. As I said, I have bills to pay, and she wasn't helping with them. I'm not heartless. I tried to help, but you can only help so much," she tells me, and I nod. She's given me much to think about.

As I leave, I stop at the door when Martha calls out to me. I turn around to face the woman.

"Is Zara in some sort of trouble?" she asks.

"What makes you think that?" I ask her.

"Well, for one, no one has ever come looking for her here, besides Bree and Tal. And if you are her employer, why didn't you just ask her?" Martha questions.

"Because she lied, her ID is fake, and her last place of employment burned to the ground."

Martha nods her head, looking at the wall above my head. "Yeah, I don't know where she got that shitty ID, but I hope she didn't pay for it," she chuckles.

"You knew it was fake?" I ask her, and the older woman nods her head.

"Blind Freddy could see it was fake, but yes, I knew. That and the fact she gave me a different last name."

"What do you mean?" I ask, turning and giving her my full attention.

"She told me a different first name than the one that is on it: Harley or Harlette. I can't remember the name exactly. I just remember it was different. A couple of weeks later, I saw the name on her ID, and it didn't match."

"Did she ever tell you where she came from?"

"Nope, and I never asked. Zara needed help; I helped. Even helped her get the job at the firm she worked at. I try not to get to know my tenants. Most never stay long," she says before turning down the corridor and walking off.

FORTY-ONE

~*H*arlow~

Every fiber of my being burns and aches with heat, yet the lust-filled haze gradually lifts and I am finally able to take in my surroundings. The last thing I remember was seeing Thane standing over me. Stretching out like a cat, I yawn. My body aches and the fever is still there. My scent is potent; I am still in the throes of heat.

That, however, isn't what makes me stiffen. It is the warm bodies pressed against my front and back as I move. Their heat makes my eyes fly open and I sit up, startled. Glancing around my surroundings, I find Raidon crammed against my back and Leon tugging me closer as he sleeps. Horror washes over me as I look down at my bosses.

Oh, please tell me I didn't fuck them. My eyes trail over their clothed bodies before noticing how very damn naked I am. I am as naked as the day I was born. Reaching over, I snatch a pillow, trying to cover up some of my nudity. I'm near tempted to strip Leon out of his shirt, just to cover up, yet the thought of waking him also makes me cringe.

I swallow—my throat feels scratchy and raw. I look around, trying to figure out where I am. I'm not back at the shitty apartment I was evicted from, and I'm not behind the dumpster at the plaza where I'd been sleeping. Or the loading docks at work. Based on the overwhelming smell of my bosses, I have to be at their mansion. However, I don't remember noticing a room like this last time I was here.

When I manage to move from between the two bodies that are pressed against me, pain washes over me, and I fight the urge to drop back between them so I can keep their skin pressed against mine. I'm not naïve. I know Omegas need Alphas to lessen their heat, yet I'm not about to snuggle with my bosses for it. Especially these assholes, who despise me and all Omegas. They treat me like I actually did kill Thane's mother, and his pet guinea pig when he was a boy. His hate for Omegas is unwarranted and unfathomable to me.

As I glance down at Leon, he instantly rolls toward his mate. I step over Raidon, avoiding Leon's rolling body, only to step on someone else. They grunt and quickly move, making me lose my footing, and I stumble backward before landing on them.

"Fuck," Rhen wheezes, as I crash on top of him.

I quickly scramble off, backing away. I wait for his attack, only to realize he is clutching his family jewels, which I must have stepped on.

He glares at me, and I yelp, scrambling for cushions to cover my nakedness.

"Kind of pointless, don't you think? I've seen you naked already," he groans, rubbing his crotch and sitting up. He looks over at his sleeping mates and I glance around, wondering where Thane is. Usually, where one is, they all are. Yet I couldn't see him anywhere in the vast room.

"Where am I?" I stammer, moving closer to the outer edge of what appears to be an enormous bed, set into the floor.

"Our Den," Rhen says before lifting a hand over his head and tugging his shirt off. He tosses it to me, and I quickly pull it on, turning as I do, giving him only a slight view of my ass.

This is embarrassing, damn embarrassing; I reek of them and them me. "What happened... We didn't... um..." My eyes dart to Raidon, who is in his briefs, and Leon is still fully dressed.

"No, and you would feel if we did," Rhen answers my question.

I let out a breath of relief. That would have made the workplace awkward. And Thane would definitely fire me if I had fucked one of his mates. Well, technically *our* mates. They just aren't aware of who I really am, especially to them. Turning, I move to the ledge and start to climb out, when Rhen speaks again.

"Where are you going?"

"Home," I answer. Though I would hardly call the loading docks home. My makeshift little Den behind the shelves isn't nearly as comfy as this place. I would think, however, that me climbing out of the sunken bed would be pretty self-explanatory as an attempt to escape from them.

"Get back in bed. You're still in heat," he growls.

"I'm good. I feel okay," I tell him. I climb out, having to dig my feet into the walls to haul myself up. Every instinct tells me to go back to them, tells me I need them. Yet, I can't have them; they aren't mine. Thane has made that abundantly clear. Besides, I need my job more than I need an Alpha, so I won't risk being fired by giving into temptation.

"Get back in the Den!" Rhen commands. My body feels the jolt of his aura instantly, making me freeze.

"The moment you step out those doors, you will have a target on your back. Until your heat abates, you will remain here," Rhen snarls.

I try to fight his command, when I suddenly feel his hand grip the back of his shirt I'm wearing. The air leaves my lungs in a whoosh as I'm ripped backward, falling onto the soft, cushioned bed with a soft thump.

"Thane said you are to stay here until your heat is over. Therefore, you remain here," Rhen snaps, glaring down at me.

I swallow. So, Thane knows I'm here. I'm sure he's plotting my murder already. That's probably where he is: digging my grave.

Rhen rolls away from me, and I look at Raidon. He's stirring, and I know he will wake soon. I can't stay here. It's one thing to tolerate them at work, but I don't want to spend any more time around them than I have to. That comes with far too many risks. Like them figuring out who I am; them commanding me; me becoming Leon's personal juice box, or dead. Yeah, the alternatives sound really fucking appealing.

"Where is Thane?" I ask nervously, and Rhen growls.

"He left because you're here," he tells me, climbing out of the Den. His words make me feel like an intruder, and the harsh tone makes my stomach sink.

"Wait here," he says, storming up the stairs. His feet sound loud in the quiet room. When the door opens, I welcome the draft. Goosebumps raise on my flesh and the cloud of their scents eases a little, although not much, because another wave of heat rushes through me.

CHAPTER
FORTY-TWO

~R hen~

As I go to fetch her some water, I'm not sure what bothers me more: the fact she stomped on my balls or that she tried to sneak off while we were sleeping; like this was a one-night stand, and she was trying to avoid the awkward morning after. Walking into the kitchen, I grab some bottles of water, knowing I should have probably restocked the bar fridge down there earlier, before making my way to the linen cupboard and grabbing some fresh towels. Tania also brought some de-scenting soap. It won't abate her heat, but it might help me think a little more clearly if she doesn't smell like my own lust-filled, personal sin.

I grab the bag with all the supplies Tania bought from the counter when I feel the mind-link, and Thane's voice flits through my head.

'You're awake?' he asks.

I roll my eyes. Of course, he felt me wake up. He always does. Nothing escapes that man when it comes to us.

'Where is Zara?' he asks.

'In the Den,' I answer warily. He isn't going to make me kick her

183

out, is he? The thought bothers me more than it should. She won't be safe out there. Her heat may have abated for now, but it will return. We gave her suppressants, but they won't stop a heat that has already started. They will just give her some reprieve until her cycle ends, which could take days.

We intend to keep pumping her full of suppressants through the end of her cycle. The only alternative is to fuck and knot her, and neither Raidon nor I are comfortable with that, even with Thane's permission. It feels wrong. Mates are a pack, which she isn't part of, and Thane has no intention of making her part of ours. Therefore, we will fight the urge to mate her.

'Good, keep her there. Let me know when her heat finishes and I'll come home,' he tells me, and my brows furrow.

'You're not returning?'

'No, I am looking into something. See what you can find out about her while she's lucid,' Thane tells me, cutting the link before I can question him further.

Thane is acting strange. I try to search the bond before realizing he's blocking it, making me wonder what it is he is up to. Or is he just trying to block how badly it affects him, knowing we are here with her? He should know us better than to believe we would be unfaithful. Sure, we all play around from time to time, but never behind each other's backs. We are always together when we do so. Sharing has never been an issue with any of us. So, it kind of stings that he thinks we would go behind his back, even with his permission.

Grabbing some towels, I rummage through the storage boxes at the bottom, pulling out some pajamas that we originally bought for Harlow. Not like she can use them. I don't even know why Thane kept them. It isn't like she's coming back. I shake my head before turning back to the basement door. As I walk down the stairs, the door swings shut behind me, and I notice Zara sitting on the ledge of the Den pit.

Zara is shivering, rubbing arms that are covered in goosebumps.

She's also drenched in sweat as another violent wave of heat courses through her. Yet she isn't crazed; the suppressants are keeping her lucid, though I can tell she is uncomfortable. My shirt is drenched with sweat as she fights her instinct to go to my mates.

Zara looks over her shoulder at me, and I notice her face is flushed, her cheeks a deep rouge.

"Are you okay?"

Her brows furrow at my question, and she nods. Her eyes go to the bottled water in my arms. Walking over to her, I pass her one, and she takes it before struggling with the cap. Her hands shake that badly.

Setting everything down beside her, I twist the cap before helping her hold it to her lips. She chokes and sputters on it as she gulps it down thirstily.

"Slow, or you'll make yourself sick," I warn her.

She gasps, sucking in a breath when I pull it back, realizing she is going to choke herself. She's gulping it that fast, having drained half the bottle already.

"Go lay between them. Their skin contact will help."

"I'm fine," she lies, and I shake my head before taking the rest of the water bottles to the mini-fridge and setting them inside. When I'm done, I move toward the paneled wall, feeling her eyes follow me. I push on one panel, which is actually a door, to reveal the bathroom.

"Zara," I call over my shoulder before looking at her. "Come," I tell her, and she hesitantly gets up.

She wanders over to me, curious, yet also wary. I notice how she stiffens when she stops beside me and sways on her feet as she gets a whiff of my scent.

"Do you want a shower? Or there's a spa bath in here, too," I tell her, nudging her in so she can look around. She steps in and quickly glances around. I hold the towels and soap out to her.

"There are more toiletries under the sink," I tell her, and she glances at it.

"Thank you," she murmurs. She looks on the verge of passing out. I touch her face. She flinches before leaning into my touch when she realizes it offers some relief. Her skin is burning hot, yet she's shivering, as if she has a fever.

"Try to be quick. You really should be in the Den."

Her eyes dart over my shoulder, and I catch my first glimpse of her animalistic side since she woke. Her hazel eyes burn brighter, almost turning a deep green. They briefly turn fluorescent before she shakes her head, regaining her senses. She nods before shutting the door.

CHAPTER
FORTY-THREE

~T**hane~**

I wait for hours at the strip club for Talon to return. He's pissing me off. He knows I'm waiting, and he's deliberately dawdling, wasting my damn time. I see Brianna walk in, and I know he won't be too far behind her. Brianna spots me instantly and runs. They spent the last few days out of the country, but I called as soon as his plane landed this morning and told him to come to see me. When he didn't show up, I came looking for him.

The moment he steps into the seedy place, he sighs. "If you're here about the money, can we do this in my office? My patrons don't need to witness this," he groans. I wave him to go, and he trudges toward the steps. I follow and climb the steps behind him to his office. He immediately walks to the safe and opens it.

"I'm not here about that," I growl.

He seems taken aback and stands, kicking the safe door shut and spinning the handle.

"You're not here about the debt?" he asks warily as he makes his way to his desk.

I fall onto the couch, watching him. Scrubbing a hand down my face, I rub my eyes. I need sleep. I didn't sleep a wink the night before. It was impossible; I'm used to being curled up with one, or all, of my mates. The couch at work did not offer that.

"No, I'm here about Z, or Zara, whatever you want to call her," I tell him, and he swallows and leans back in his chair, folding his arms across his chest.

"What about her? You know if the girls request their identity to be kept secret, we abide by their wishes," he states. I raise my hand, and he quiets immediately. I should beat him senseless for giving me the runaround. He knows better than to push me.

"I know the rules you set for this place. I don't care about those. Do you have any idea how bad it could damage my company's reputation if it gets out that I hired a hooker?"

"Zara isn't a hooker. She mainly cleans dishes. The first time she took on clients was you lot, and only after you demanded her," Tal defends. I click my tongue, finding it hard to believe she had no intention of whoring herself out. But then again, she is a virgin.

"What do you know about her?" I ask, giving him my full attention. Tal gets up and moves toward the bar area he keeps in his office. He pours two generous drinks before handing me a glass. I sip mine, waiting for him to answer my question, but he only shrugs.

"Not much. She's quiet, and I am pretty sure Bree is her only friend."

"She never mentioned family? Or anyone?" Tal shakes his head, and I groan. I'm no closer to figuring out who she is.

"So, you didn't know she's homeless, I gather?"

Tal shakes his head. "No, I've been to her apartment; Bree lived next door to her. That's how they met," Tal quickly adds. I shake my head.

"I spoke with her former landlady. She kicked her out a couple of weeks ago. The owner thought she was staying with a friend until one of her other tenants told her she was on the streets, sleeping behind an old plaza," I tell him.

"A homeless Omega?" Talon laughs. Yeah, it's almost unheard of. We certainly don't get many homeless Omegas in the city. Most are cherished possessions of their Alphas. Or they make good money doing rotations, which is basically just being a breeder, jumping from pack to pack, spitting out a kid or two before moving on to the next.

"Wait, you're serious?" Tal asks. I click my tongue, annoyed he didn't realize one of his workers was in such dire straits. Then again, she pulled the wool over my eyes too. A homeless Omega in this city is dangerous.

"Fuck, I had no idea. Had I known, I would have organized something or told the council," he exclaims.

"That's another thing I wanted to see you about. Zara never registered, and her ID is fake," I tell him, and his brows furrow.

"They're forcing her into rotation?" he asks. I glare at him with a growl.

"No. I covered it up by telling the council my pack is claiming her," I snarl at him.

"Oh well, that's great news! No harm done then," he shrugs.

"You know I won't have an Omega in my pack. That is why I'm here. I need to find out who she really is because it's clear to me that Zara is running from someone," I snap at him.

"She's Bree's friend. I did her a favor. Honestly, Thane, if she is hiding something, I have no idea what it is. Besides giving her shifts, I don't have much to do with her outside this place."

"So, what do you suggest I do with her? I can't keep her," I tell him.

"Why not? Because of Harlow?" he snaps. "Do you know why Leon comes here so often? It's not because he wants to feed on my workers, but because he's hoping you fucking find one you like. Your pack needs an Omega."

"We don't need an Omega. She would be useless to us," I retort.

"She wouldn't be useless. Sure, she can't take your knot, but does that matter? There's more to Omegas than just being a piece of ass," Talon says.

I know he's right, but it still irks me; we were so close to having an Omega, a family, yet Harlow blew that right out the window.

CHAPTER
FORTY-FOUR

~ **T**hane~

I can never fully claim an Omega. It's why Alpha Packs give them serum. A normal pack doesn't need it, though most still give their Omega serum anyway, to forge a stronger bond. Alpha Packs, however, need the serum.

Only the Alpha of a pack can claim an Omega and make her pack, yet being an Alpha-of-Alphas makes things more complicated. There are many benefits to Alpha Packs, the primary Alpha becomes larger and stronger, our auras more potent, and our wolves two to three times the size of the average Alpha.

But with that, our knots are also bigger, and most end up killing the Omega. Hence the serum. It gives some of our blood and DNA to the Omega. It strengthens them and acclimates them to us, kind of like a tailored suit, but even that is no guarantee. And giving an Omega serum made after a pack has already bonded means they would have the same rank as the Alpha-of-Alphas. That would cause disorder and trample any form of control within the ranks.

"Would it be such a bad thing, Thane? Zara is a good girl. She's quiet, submissive, not to mention gorgeous. Would it be so bad that she can't give you an heir or take your knot? It's not like you knot your mates, anyway? What difference would it make?" Tal asks.

"Submissive? She is a pain in my ass," I snarl.

"But your mates like her, don't they? Or you wouldn't be here whining to me. You'd be at home with them. And her," Talon says.

"We don't know her. Zara might not even be her real name. God knows who she truly is," I snarl at him.

"Maybe earn some trust and she'll tell you. Just something to think about," Tal says, and I sigh. I can't trust her. There's something she's hiding, and I plan to get to the bottom of it.

Talon has to get to work and check on his employees, so I wave him off. For a while, I sit there pondering. Tal's words have me worried. Does my pack really feel we are lacking without an Omega? Lost in thought, Raidon opens the mind-link.

'Can you please come home?' he whines. I blink and sit up.

'What's wrong?' I ask while stretching. My back is killing me. Tal really needs to get a comfier couch.

'Nothing, but her heat is getting worse. Leon is struggling, and her scent ...' He groans, and I can feel the discomfort from all of them.

'I told you to go ahead and do as you please,' I growl.

'As if we would do that without you here. Plus, she's not exactly compliant. She even slapped Leon for trying to touch her and kicked me in the damn balls,' he snarls.

'She attacked both of you?'

'Yes. We've been feeding her suppressants like they're Tic-Tac's, but she's still fighting her instincts. And Rhen looks like he's been moments away from strangling her all morning.'

I growl, appalled that she would reject my mates. It irritates me. Why would she reject them? Nothing is wrong with my mates. It pisses me off. Does she think she is too good for them?

'I'm on my way home,' I growl, cutting the link. Getting up, I walk out of the office, furious with her. I gave her my damn mates, for fuck's sake, and she throws them back in my face.

I don't remember the drive home or even getting out of my car. I only return to my senses when I climb out and her intoxicating scent hits me like a slap in the face. Slamming my car door, I can hear them arguing with her.

"Raidon, just grab her. We need to get her into the damn bath before she overheats," Rhen snaps. I hear her growl before Raidon hisses.

"Command her, damn it," Raidon growls.

"She's in enough pain, asshole. Just grab her," Rhen replies.

Having heard enough, I storm through the house, heading for the Den. The room falls silent as soon as I open the door. I trudge down the stairs, my footsteps deafening as I stomp down. When they come into view, I find Zara huddled in a ball, her knees pressed to her chest, and she's panting hard. She's completely naked, and I can see claw marks down her body, as if she clawed herself to try to abate the excruciating heat rolling through her in waves. Her face is flushed and bright red. Her skin glistens with her sweat, and her pheromones have me instantly hard.

Noticing me, she looks up and looks almost relieved. "Finally! Can you please tell them to let me leave?" she pleads, her voice coming out breathless.

Raidon glares at her while Rhen scratches the back of his neck awkwardly. He moves toward her, and her eyes track him like he's her prey.

Glancing around, I spot Leon chained to a chair. Blood drenches his front and I can tell it's fresh, so I know he bit her recently. He awkwardly wiggles his fingers at me. I pin him with my glare until he whimpers and looks at the ground.

"I will deal with you later," I growl at him. Turning back to the sunken Den, I focus my attention on Zara. She shrinks under my gaze. I know she can feel my aura, and I force it on her, pressing harder against her. In heat, most Omegas would be throwing themselves at any Alpha's feet, but here she is, fighting instinct and rejecting my mates as if there's something wrong with them.

"You, I will deal with now," I tell her, toeing off my shoes and shrugging off my jacket. I kick my shoes aside and toss my jacket on Leon's lap before dropping into the Den. Her eyes widen as I stalk toward her.

Fuck, she smells divine. My eyes flicker, and she shrieks, scrambling backward. Stalking toward her naked, retreating form, I bend down and wrap my arms around her waist, ripping her from the mattress. Zara squeals and thrashes, but I ignore her and walk to the cushioned corner.

"I didn't touch them, I swear," she panics as I sit down. "I didn't, I fucking didn't, you have to believe me!"

I pull her into my lap. She thrashes, but one growl is all it takes for her still. Her breathing is harsh, and I can feel her body trembling.

"Stay," I command, loosening my tight grip on her. She doesn't move, stuck under my command. I unbutton my shirt, tug it off over my head and set it aside. Placing my hand on her stomach, I force her back until her spine is flush against my chest. Zara moans in relief, yet I am more shocked by the tingling sensation moving over my skin.

"I swear, Thane, I never did anything with your mates," she pleads.

"That is not what I am fucking angry about, Zara. Or should I call you Z?" I snarl, and I feel every muscle in her body tense.

CHAPTER
FORTY-FIVE

~Harlow~

"That is not what I am fucking angry about, Zara. Or should I call you Z?" Thane snarls, and my blood runs cold. He knows I'm the girl from Tal's club. His aura presses down on me with his anger. What else does he know?

"Z?" Rhen asks as he looks at Raidon, who looks away guiltily. I know Leon and Raidon knew, but they promised they wouldn't tell Thane.

"Hmm, Zara here is Z, but we will talk about that later. For now, we will take care of her heat," Thane says. He moves his legs under mine before lifting his knees and hooking my legs over them. I try to climb off as soon as I realize what he's doing. No fucking way! Thane presses his hand on my stomach, and his teeth nip at my shoulder in warning.

"I gave you my mates, Zara. You will use them to abate your heat, or I will hand you over to the council, whom I know you never registered with," Thane snarls, and I swallow. No way I can pay those fines, and I sure as hell refuse to be a breeder. My heart races in my chest, and I shake my head vigorously. They will hurt me. They hate me, and I don't want to lose my virginity to men who would rather kill me than fuck me.

Raidon steps closer. I try to close my legs, but Thane pulls them wider apart. "Try it, Zara, and I will fold you like origami, tie you down, and let them run a train on you," Thane warns.

Tears burn my eyes. I shake my head as Raidon falls to his knees between our legs. Thane's hand moves to my scalp. His fingers brush the back of my neck, making me shiver. He sweeps my hair over one shoulder before bunching it in his fist. Thane tugs my head back, forcing me to meet his gaze, which is surprisingly softer than I expect. His nose skims across my cheek to my ear.

"This isn't a punishment. That will come later. But your heat won't stop until someone knots you," Thane purrs before nipping at my ear.

"My mates won't hurt you, Zara. We know you're a virgin," Thane growls. "We can smell your innocence," he groans as he flicks my ear with his tongue.

Hands run across my thighs, and I gasp at the tingling sensation that rushes straight to the apex of my legs. Thane lets my hair go, and I turn to see that the hands belong to Raidon. He moves them to my hips. My heart beats like a drum against my ribcage. Thane lowers his legs slightly, letting Raidon drag me closer to him.

Thane grips my chin, tilting my face back up to his. His lips capture mine, his tongue forcibly delving between my lips and stealing my breath. At the same time, Raidon's lips latch around my nipple.

Sparks move everywhere, and slick drenches my thighs while primal desire courses through my veins, setting me on fire. My heat awakens like a live wire, writhing through my body. Raidon growls, his teeth grazing over my hardened nipple before he bites it. A whiny moan leaves my lips, and Thane pulls away.

"Fuck!" Thane curses. I can feel his massive bulge beneath me, digging into the middle of my back. Raidon's lips travel south, nipping and sucking my heated flesh, each soft touch lessening the pain as I give in. I can't take much more of this incessant throb, and despite them hating me, they are being strangely gentle.

Raidon's eyes watch my face as he drops to his elbows between my legs. His hot mouth covers my pussy, and my eyes roll into the back of my head at the sensation. He sucks my lower lips into his mouth, his tongue delving between my folds as he licks every inch of me. My back arches at the intense feeling of his skillful tongue.

Another two sets of lips capture my nipples, licking at each breast. My eyes fly open to find Leon, who has been released from his restraints, with one nipple in his mouth and Rhen seizing the other.

"Shh, Leon won't hurt you. He just wants to taste," Thane purrs, his Calling slipping out and forcing my body to relax, despite the fear of Leon's fangs being so close to my neck. Their hot mouths are a sensory overload. As I take in the different sensations, every part of me buzzes.

Raidon growls, plunging his tongue inside me before flattening it and dragging it across my heated flesh, soliciting a moan from deep inside of me. I writhe, caught in the heavenly bliss of their hands, when Raidon's fingers brush against my entrance. He sits back on his knees, his fingers prod around my entrance, and slowly he forces a finger inside me.

I squirm at the intrusion, but Thane's hand presses harder on my stomach. His voice calms me as his breath dances across my ear.

"He'll go slow," Thane whispers, and my eyes dart to Raidon's. He winks at me and smiles deviously, his eyes going to his hand between my legs as he slowly withdraws his finger before adding another. I feel my inner walls stretch around them before clenching.

"Good girl," Raidon purrs while gripping my knee and pushing my leg out wider. Leon purrs, lifting his head from my breast to watch Raidon fuck me with his fingers. He curls them inside me before scissoring them and stretching me wider. He withdraws them slowly before plunging them inside me again and making me cry out at the pleasurable feel.

"So wet, so pretty," Leon purrs before leaning down and dipping his face between my thighs. He sucks my clit into his mouth. My walls clench around Raidon's fingers while Leon tastes me. My hips rock against his face as his tongue swirls around my clit. I explode on his tongue; my vision turns white, and my inner walls pulsate as I come undone.

Leon keeps up his pleasurable torture while Raidon continues to fuck me with his fingers. I ride out the waves of pleasure rolling through me. As the feeling recedes, I am left boneless and breathless. Leon laps at my juices before moving to Raidon's fingers. When Leon sits up, Rhen grips his face and tugs him across me. Rhen kisses him hard, and my walls clench at the sight of Rhen tasting me on his mate's lips.

CHAPTER
FORTY-SIX

~**H**arlow~

Raidon squeezes my thighs, pulling my attention away from the sight above me and making me focus on him. Raidon looks at Rhen who lets Leon go before licking his lips.

"You have more control than I do. I don't want to hurt her," Raidon tells him. I am momentarily distracted with how close Leon's lips are getting to my neck again, the sharp points of his fangs grazing my skin.

"Leon!" Thane warns as I squirm on his lap. "I won't let him drain you," Thane whispers behind me. Rhen leans over, gripping Leon's hair and tugging his head back.

"Gentle. If you act like a savage, I'll put you back in the chair," Rhen warns before letting him go. Leon's eyes go to mine before traveling down my body. My skin heats under his hungry gaze.

I sigh, turning my neck and offering it to him. I am far too exhausted to fight him. Besides, his bites aren't painful, more like a swim in ecstasy. Yet instead of sinking his teeth into me, he gently breaks the flesh, letting my blood flow down my chest. He plays with my blood, smearing it over a breast, then dips his head. His lips follow the trail as he licks at my flesh and ignites my heat again. God, this is torture.

Rhen stands and swaps places with Raidon. I watch as he steps in front of me. My eyes go to the huge bulge between his legs. His hard cock is straining against the fabric of his boxers. I know what to expect when he shoves them down his legs and his hard cock springs free. Yet, it still scares the hell out of me.

A pearl of pre-cum sits on the head. That huge thing is going to be inside of me soon. I wonder if it will hurt. Yet, with how gentle they have been with me, I can't imagine that monstrosity will bring me anything other than pure pleasure.

I watch him grip his cock and roll a condom on. He moves his fist up and down a few times, his eyes never leaving mine.

I can see a hint of something playful in his eye. My walls clench as I watch him stroke himself from base to tip.

Rhen kneels, looming over me and watching my face. His eyes move down my body to where his cock is just inches from my entrance. I feel my pussy clench with need for him. It is frightening to lose control of my body like this, but there is something very liberating about it too. Something primal and commanding that makes me yearn for him.

I hold my breath, aware of what is about to happen. Any moment now. But Rhen surprises me by leaning over and kissing my cheek.

"Relax, okay?" he whispers.

I nod, unable to form a reply.

"I'll go slowly... And you can ask me to go even slower if you need me to," Rhen says before looking to Thane behind me.

"She'll be fine; she's built for this," Thane says, and I feel his chin drop to my shoulder, watching as Rhen positions himself.

I nod, a little surprised at how gentle he is being. He positions himself at my entrance. When the tip of his cock first touches my opening, I feel a shudder move through my body, and I hold my breath.

"Breathe, Zara," Thane purrs just as Leon sucks a nipple into his mouth, making me moan softly. The tension eases slightly. Rhen starts to move forward. The tip of his cock pushes against my opening, wet with Raidon's saliva and my own juices. His cock stretches me open as it pushes its way inside.

Slowly, he pushes forward. And, slowly, I open up for him. I feel it, every single inch I stretch for him. There is a brief pain, and I still feel nervous as the tip of his cock slips inside, inch by inch, until he meets resistance and I tense. Every little movement he makes sends shudders of pleasure through me. My body has never felt so sensitive before, and it is overwhelming.

I try to relax, though, as I was told to; to let my body take the lead. I am doing something my body is designed for, something completely natural for Omegas. I am aware of my body the whole time. It knows what to do, even if I don't. That is something I need to trust, and when I feel a euphoria wash over me, I can feel the heat start to recede.

Rhen grips my hips. "This will sting," he says, and I bite my lip. His grip tightens before he thrusts the rest of the way. Our pelvises flush and I gasp, choking on my breath as the pain steals it.

"Breathe, Zara," Raidon purrs, gripping my chin and nibbling on my bottom lip. Thane licks at my neck, and his Calling thrums out, causing my muscles to go heavy as he forces me to relax.

I let myself focus on the feel of Rhen's cock deep inside me; the way my insides convulse around him; how good it feels being so full. I think he's waiting for me to get used to the sensation, to let him know if I am in any pain.

Rhen gently rocks his hips back and forth. He starts out so slowly, then eventually picks up the pace and thrusts a little harder. I moan loudly and cry out with pleasure. The sounds leaving me soon have him moving harder and faster. My back arches, my fingers dig into Thane's thighs, yet he doesn't complain. With every increase in pace, I feel my body tensing and quivering with pleasure. I want more. So much more.

I reach down between us and move my fingers over my clit. Rhen smiles, watching my fingers.

"Are you going to cum for me?" he asks. "That's it, Zara," Rhen purrs.

I rub at myself for a few moments; it doesn't take much. Before I know it, I cry out, shuddering in orgasmic pleasure. I see stars. I shudder and moan. Still, he keeps thrusting in and out of me, while Leon licks and nips at my neck, Raidon squeezes my breast, and Thane keeps me under his Calling. I come undone, hard. My fingers and his cock push me through wave after wave of pleasure.

I feel his knot expand, pressing against my entrance, and Rhen pumps his hips those last few times. He groans as my walls clench around him, pulsating with my orgasm. He plows into me with a loud moan, and my insides stretch to accommodate him. I squirm before feeling his cock twitch and pulsate inside me as we become entwined. He slows to a rocking motion, letting me recover before dropping his weight on top of me.

My body shudders and jolts with the aftershocks of my orgasm. My heat instantly dies down, and my body is alive in ways it has never been before. Yet, I am exhausted after the hours of heat and I feel my eyelids closing. Rhen slips his arms behind my back, pulling my chest flush against his as he rolls next to Thane, pulling me with him. He kisses my temple, positioning me on top of him. Rhen's chest heaves against mine as our breath slowly returns to normal.

"Sleep, Zara," Rhen murmurs in my ear, and I feel Thane move beside us. He sweeps my hair from my face.

"Yes, Zara, sleep. Because I have questions for you tomorrow. And you will answer them, one way or another," Thane says, brushing his lips against mine briefly.

FORTY-SEVEN

~ **T**hane~

I watch as Rhen runs his fingers up her spine, waiting for his knot to go down so he can pull out of her. "You wore a condom?" I ask him. He glares, which startles me.

"Yes, Thane," he says, looking down at her. The way he says my name is cold. I tilt my head, watching him, but he doesn't lift his eyes to meet my gaze. Instead, he buries his face in her neck.

Her scent grows weaker, the heat abated. I watch Raidon place a blanket over her when goosebumps prickle her exposed flesh, before lying beside her. Rhen rolls on his side, crushing her petite body between them to keep her warm. Leon moves away and sits on the edge of the pitted Den, his chin resting on his hand as he watches them.

"We can't keep her," I tell them, feeling their longing loud and clear. They want her; they want her to stay.

"Do you not feel the pull to her?" Raidon asks, but he's looking at Rhen, not me.

I swallow. I feel strange sparks when I touch her. The same ones I feel whenever I touch my mates. But she isn't our mate.

"It doesn't matter what I feel toward her. No Omegas," I tell them.

Rhen growls, and I can feel his sadness. It's natural for them to want an Omega, but I know it's only her heat and pheromones that are making us feel this way about her. Leon snarls, getting to his feet. I try to grab his arm as he passes by me, but he pulls away.

"You need to get over Harlow. She isn't here, yet you insist on punishing us," Leon snarls before stomping up the steps and leaving the Den. I sigh and turn back to my other two mates.

"She can stay until we find her a safe place to live, but that's it," I tell them.

"Leon's right, Thane. It's about time you got over Harlow. We want an Omega. I know you think it's because she was in heat and it's fucking with us, but packs need Omegas," Rhen says, sweeping her hair from her face.

"Not our pack," I growl.

"It's not just your decision," Raidon says, challenging me. I look to see if he truly wants to fight me on this. They never challenge my decisions, but I can tell they are willing to—for her.

"We don't even know her," I growl.

"She's an Omega, and they are rare. What does her past matter? I know we could convince her to stay," Rhen says.

"She hates us," I snap at him.

"Because you're a dick to her. She needs an Alpha, and she knows it. With us, she would have four. She would be safe and looked after. Who wouldn't want that?" Raidon asks.

"Harlow didn't," I snarl at him before leaving.

She isn't ours. After Harlow, we all agreed that no Omega would ever join our pack. How is it possible that only a few weeks around this one would make them change their minds? I head to my room, passing Leon's on the way. His door is open, so I pop my head in. I find him on the floor beside his bed with a blood bag in his hands.

"Get out," he snaps, lifting his gaze to mine.

"Leon, we have talked about this."

"No, you talked about it. We never agreed. You made the decision for us and we just accepted it," he growls at me.

He's wrong. We *had* all agreed, or so I thought. Am I in denial? Did I just assume they agreed with my decision? They definitely never spoke differently about the choice. Yet, acceptance and agreement are two different things.

"Leon, I—"

"I said get out," Leon growls. I raise my brows at his tone and press my lips in a line. Leon is the youngest of our pack and the most challenging when it comes to keeping him in line. He loves pressing my buttons, just so I will punish him.

Yet this isn't his playful, cheeky side. He's angry and doesn't want me near him. I swallow and nod, leaving him be. I close his door behind me and move toward my bedroom, which is next to his. Sitting in my room, it suddenly feels cold and lonely in here.

After a few minutes, the silence becomes deafening. The feelings of hurt coming through our bond is agonizing, so I get dressed and head to the office. Once again, I don't remember the drive and only become aware of my surroundings when I see the security car pass where I sit in my car in the underground lot. He's getting ready to close up the building.

I see him pull up behind my car and I climb out.

"What's up?" I ask, wondering what he wants.

"I was actually about to call you," he says, rolling down his window. "We found something while doing rounds at the loading dock."

My brows furrow in confusion.

"Hop in. I'll take you around back. We checked the security footage too, and there's something you might want to see," my security guard tells me. I sigh, retrieving my phone and keys before locking my car.

I climb into the security car with him. He drives slowly, checking the doors as we go and switching the elevators off, before driving out to the loading docks. He parks just inside the roller doors, and I see another of my security guards in the loft upstairs, looking behind shelving units with a flashlight.

"We found a can of de-scenter in the bin, which we thought was odd since no Omegas work here, except your assistant," he tells me.

"It might be hers. She was back here accepting a dry cleaning delivery for me a few days ago," I tell him.

"Well, we thought the same thing, but then we checked the cameras..." he pauses, and I look at him over the top of the car we just climbed out of.

"She's been sneaking in after closing. We also found a Den," he tells me. I follow him to the storage room.

"We've been looking around, but no sign of her tonight. According to the security footage, she hasn't snuck in for a couple of days. Do you want me to call the police?" he asks, and I shake my head, before heading into the storage room. It's faded, but I can still make out her scent. Most likely because I spent the night with her, so I'm accustomed to it.

"No, I will handle it," I tell him.

"Are you sure? I checked the logs. She didn't show up for work today or yesterday," he tells me, and I growl.

"Yes, because she's at my house," I tell him, stopping next to a shelf. I sniff the air and look behind it to find the makeshift Den he mentioned.

"Help me move this aside," I tell him. We drag it out far enough that we can both fit in the tight space. There's one blanket and a few clothes that she used to make her Den, also a backpack. I rummage through it, discovering her wallet and a diary. There's no cash in there, just some train and bus tickets. Her fake ID is in the wallet, along with 5 cents.

I chuck it back in the bag before rummaging through the blanket and clothes to find an empty noodle cup and an unopened can of baked beans. Sighing, I start stuffing everything into the bag when I pick up her diary. It is well worn.

My security officer clears his throat. "Boss, I think we need to notify someone. An Omega can't live on the streets," he says, and I glance at him over my shoulder. I watch his nostrils flare at her faint scent in the air. He picks up the blanket and sniffs it. I snatch it away from him, stuffing it in the bag with her diary.

"You do and I will fire you. No one is to know about this," I tell him.

"But what about her situation? I don't mind taking her in, my Alpha won't—"

I freeze, a threatening growl escapes me involuntarily, and he bumps into the shelving.

"I told you. She is at my house. You will not touch my fucking Omega!" I growl, rising to my feet. He holds his hands up in surrender.

"Sorry. I don't mean... I didn't realize you meant she's yours," he stammers, and I realize what I just said.

Fuck!

CHAPTER
FORTY-EIGHT

~Harlow~

I don't know how long I slept, but when I wake up, it's to Raidon and Rhen talking softly on either side of me. I am toasty warm pressed between their bodies and I don't want to move, knowing that my heat has now abated. I will be sent home; well, back to the storage lockers.

Yet, I can't stay here either. Dread pools in my belly as Thane's words come back to me. He knows I'm the girl from the strip club, and I know he will fire me. One thing I have come to learn after working for them for the last couple weeks is that image is everything. There's nothing Thane hates more than bad press.

"Wonder what time he'll be home," I hear Raidon murmur, and my eyes flutter open to see Rhen's tattooed chest. I want to trace my fingers over the patterns that are etched into his skin, but I hold back. Tingles spread across every inch of me that is touching them.

"No idea, but when he does, I'll try to talk to him again," Rhen answers.

"Talk, don't fight with him, Rhen. He'll say no just to prove he can," Raidon replies.

I want to keep listening to their conversation, but the urge to pee is too strong. Plus, I feel sticky from slick and cum, so I desperately want to shower.

Raidon's hand, currently resting on my hip, isn't helping the situation, especially with my stupid Omega hormones still running rampant. I want to press closer to him, and I know I need to escape when instinct starts to kick in. I know if I don't move soon, I'll end up crawling on top of him. Their scents are overwhelming me. Yawning, I stretch. My back arches, and Raidon's hand moves to my stomach.

"You're awake. We've been waiting for you to wake up," Raidon purrs, kissing my shoulder. I look up to find Rhen staring down at me.

I turn my gaze away, my face flaming with embarrassment. Now, what? Do I thank them for helping with my heat? Give him a pat on the back for taking my V-Card, or handshake as if this is some bizarre business transaction? I suddenly find myself unsure of what to do now. I feel awkward.

I am nothing more than their assistant and some strange Omega they fucked. Sitting up between them, I tuck the blanket around my naked body, and my eyes scan the room for Leon or Thane. It's just us down here, and I let out a breath. Turning back to look at them, I find them both watching me. I gulp suddenly, wanting to flee from their hungry gazes.

I rub my eyes and look toward the bathroom. I chew my lip, trying to decide what to say, yet I come up with nothing. Rhen sees where I'm looking and says, "You can use the bathroom. You don't have to ask."

I nod my head. "Thanks... um... you didn't have to stay. You could have left me alone down here," I tell them awkwardly. Man, why is this so awkward? I would have rather woken up alone. I don't like the idea, but at least I wouldn't feel so uncomfortable.

"I'll grab you a towel and some clothes," Raidon says, sitting up. He surprises me by pressing his lips to my cheek before getting up and using his arms to pull himself out of the Den. I stand up to follow. I'm about to climb out myself when I feel hands grip my hips and lift me over the ledge. Rhen jumps out behind me and follows me toward the bathroom. I suddenly feel extremely self-conscious. I can feel his eyes follow my every move.

Stopping at the door, I turn to Rhen, who seems amused about something. What, I have no idea, but it makes me feel even more awkward as his lips curve upwards.

"Am I... in trouble? I mean... is Thane going to fire me?" I ask.

I need this job to pay Martha what I owe her and get my shitty apartment back. If he fires me, I may be forced to take whatever job Talon can offer, but whoring myself out doesn't sound very appealing.

"I don't think so, but he is angry that you didn't tell him about working for Tal."

"He would have fired me if he knew," I tell him, looking at the floor.

"Maybe, maybe not—"

I raise an eyebrow at him, and he chuckles.

"Yeah, he would have fired you. Go shower, Zara. Raidon will bring you some clothes," he says, and I walk into the huge bathroom, making my way over to the shower. I hear him close the door before I call out.

"Rhen?"

He opens the door and looks at me.

"Thanks," I tell him, and he smirks.

"Anytime," he chuckles, closing it, and I shake my head. Well, I addressed the elephant in the room, so hopefully, it won't be so awkward when I hop out. I just really wish I could sneak out before Thane returns home.

The hot water is welcome as I use the de-scenting soap and scrub my skin raw. My whole body aches. The area between my legs is extra sensitive and uncomfortable, but not overly painful. While washing my hair, I hear the door creak open. I expect Raidon to walk in, but it's Thane.

He sets a towel and some clothes next to the sink. "Once you are finished, get dressed and meet us in the dining room," he says before turning and walking out.

CHAPTER
FORTY-NINE

~ **H**arlow~

I dress quickly in the clothes Thane left before making my way to the bathroom door. I peer out, finding the Den empty. There are no windows down here, and I know there is no escape from his wrath. Dread pools low in my stomach as I try to move silently across the floor, only for the first step of the basement stairs to creak as I set my weight on it. The sound is loud in the quiet room, and I suddenly don't want to leave the safety it offers, however slight it may be.

Yet I know if I don't go up there, chances are Thane will pull me from his Den and throw me out of his house by my hair. Sucking in a breath, I twist the handle and open the door to discover the smell of Chinese food filling the air. My belly growls hungrily, but I ignore it, gauging my chances of running to the door without them noticing, which means running past the dining room.

Recognizing how stupid that thought is, I close the door and move toward the dining room. Better to get this over with. Just rip off the Band-Aid, as they say. I wonder briefly how long it will take to walk back to the city, or to Tal's to see if I could maybe work there.

As I walk in, I find them sitting and talking at the dining table. Thane is watching them, and Leon is beaming happily about something. Thane's glare turns murderous when his gaze shifts to me.

"Sit, Zara," Thane says, pointing to the chair at the end of the table, furthest from everyone. That is fine by me. It means I am closer to the front door if I have to make a run for it. A quick escape.

His words cause the rest of them to turn their attention to me. I swallow, my heart pounding in my chest as I sit down. They all have plates in front of them, untouched. I'm surprised when Rhen gets up and places one in front of me before returning to his seat. They feel miles away. Instead of dinner, this reminds me of one of their conference meetings.

"Thank you," I tell Rhen, only for him to wink at me. My brows furrow, knowing Thane will see his strange gesture. I fiddle with my fingers under the table, wondering what's happening.

They all start to eat and resume chatting. Thane hardly speaks. He just sits at the other end of the table, observing his mates. I push the food around my plate, my appetite disappearing as I wait for the other shoe to drop, for his rage to be unleashed. The man is impenetrable. He's not usually able to hide his anger. Now, however, he just sits, staring at everyone while eating and listening, but not showing much interest.

His quiet, indifferent expression only makes me more nervous. The others are acting as if this is ordinary behavior for him. He isn't even using his aura and I still want to run. I find this version of him disconcerting because I don't know what to expect next. I expected his rage when I came upstairs. The silence is eerie and cold.

Leon goes to get a bottle of wine, pouring everyone a glass before sitting back down. I can't remember the last time I ate at an actual dinner table, maybe before my parents died. At the sanctuary, we lined up for our trays and took them back to our rooms, setting them outside our doors when we finished. Do they eat like this every night?

After they all finish eating, they remain at the table. I wonder how long they'll stay here. My ass is going numb, and one foot is asleep, yet still, they sit. My food is cold when finally, Thane speaks, and silence befalls the entire room.

"You'll remain here. You can have the Den and can carpool with us to work daily," Thane says before sipping his wine.

"No, my apartment is fine," I lie.

"The apartment you were evicted from?" Thane asks, and I chew on my lip, trying to find a way out of the lie I just told.

"Don't lie to me. I detest liars. I know you're homeless, Zara," Thane says, setting his wineglass down. He looks at my plate before looking up at me. "Eat."

"I'm not hungry, I..."

Raidon clears his throat loudly, and I glance at him, only for him to nod at my plate in some silent message I can't understand. Looking at Rhen, he appears to do the same.

"If you give me my handbag, I can just go, and I'll see you at work." I rise from my seat, but the look Thane gives me makes me drop back down. He presses his lips in a line.

"No one leaves the table until the last person is finished eating. So eat," he commands. I look around the table to see if he's joking. By the looks on their faces, this is the law in his household. My hands tremble as I pick up the fork, the metal rattling against the plate as I try to scoop up some rice. I feel like throwing up as they watch me.

Once I put the forkful in my mouth, Raidon's and Rhen's shoulders relax, and they turn their attention back to Thane. So do I, and I see him reach to grab something off the floor. I nearly drop my fork when he sets the bag I left in the storage room on the table in front of him.

"Now, as I was saying, Zara, you will remain here. It is not a question, or a request," Thane states.

CHAPTER
FIFTY

~H arlow~

    I swallow the bile that threatens to creep up my throat and spill onto the plate in front of me. My eyes are glued to the bag that contains every belonging I have left in this world as well as the diary where I keep the only photo I have of my twin sister. A diary filled with my darkest secrets, the only one I hadn't lost over the years.

"The key you had cut?" Thane says, and I blink at him. The key? Who gives a fuck about a key? He holds my entire world with that bag.

"Where did you get that?" I blurt, even though I already know. It's a dumb question, yet it's the only one my mind can conjure at this exact moment. My brain has turned to mush and threatens to melt out my damn ears as I try to come up with something, anything that will dig me out of the crater that has opened up at my feet, trying to suck me in. Thane growls, annoyed, and starts ripping stuff out of the bag. I shriek, lurching across the table to snatch the bag from him.

My heart thuds against my chest when Thane leans forward,

215

plucking the bag effortlessly from my grip. My fingers desperately cling to the fabric of the handle. I don't know if I will throw up or pass out. Either way, with how fast my heart is beating, I am dangerously at risk of a heart attack.

"What the fuck, Zara?" Thane bellows as he glares down at me. It's only then that I realize everyone is standing, and I notice the fork embedded in the webbing between my thumb and index finger. Staring down, the plates and cutlery are on the ground, the table is a mess, and my hand is bleeding as I try to figure out how I stabbed myself with a fork.

Still, I feel nothing except dread and panic. No pain. Nothing. I pull the fork out, drop it on the table, and look up. I'm an idiot. I should have remained calm, because now, Thane's looking at the bag he's holding as if it contains a bomb, or something equally dangerous.

I realize my mistake too late. He may have grabbed all of my stuff from the storage locker, but he didn't go through it. He rips everything out of the bag, and my eyes widen in horror when I see the diary fall onto the table. My hands snatch it before he does, and he growls. His aura washes over me with the weight of a damn elephant, and I am the peanut beneath its foot, about to be crushed to smithereens.

"Hand it over," Thane snarls. Yet, in my panic, I refuse and keep a death grip on the diary as he tries to pry it from my fingers. His command is excruciating, but I would rather his command kill me than hand it over. Either way: I'll be dead if he opens it, dead if he doesn't.

"Zara!" he bellows, yanking it out of my hands. He snarls, wiping it on his pants to clean my blood from the cover. The moment his aura drops, I lunge, trying to tackle him. Only he is quicker and swats me away.

Raidon grips my arm before I hit the ground. Thane is furious. Fuck him. Fuck my job. I couldn't care less. All I care about is that diary and the photo inside it. It is the only photo I have. Zara and I took it in one of those photo booths in a shopping center, the one time we were able to sneak out of that horrible place.

"We try to help you, and you carry on like this?" he snarls, his teeth turning to sharp points as his canines extend. Seeing his face half-morphed into a monster is terrifying. He looks demonic, his black eyes so dark they look like the bottomless pits of hell.

"Please," I beg, my eyes on the diary, and he looks at it in his hand.

"I didn't read it, but by your desperate attempt to keep it from me, I probably should," he snaps, gripping it in both hands, about to open it. I step forward, about to snatch it back, when Raidon yanks me away.

"Are you insane?" he growls at me as Thane opens it. The photo slips out from between the pages, falling to the floor. He moves to grab it, and I shake out of Raidon's grip. My knee lifts as Thane bends down to pick it up and connects with his face, hard.

I honestly didn't mean to do that, but the sickening crunch is loud. I hear them gasp before Thane clutches his face and roars. He drops the diary. I snatch it and the photo, bolting out of there while Rhen, Leon, and Raidon stand stunned.

I catch a glimpse of them as I slide on the tiles in the hall, before careening into the wall. My bare feet grab traction, and I run for the front doors. My hand twists on the handle. I yank it, but it's locked. I fumble with the locking system when I hear the table getting upended.

The loud bang makes the door rattle. I finally get it open and rip it wide, only for his hands to grip my hair and pull me back. My feet are yanked out from under me. I hit the ground hard, staring up at Thane, whose feet are now on either side of my head.

I blink up at him. He snatches the diary from my hands, only for it to be ripped out of his. Rhen backs away from him, holding the diary, until his back hits the open door.

"Calm down, Thane," Rhen murmurs.

"Give me the damn thing," Thane snarls, holding out his hand. Rhen's eyes dart to mine as I sit up.

"She has a right to privacy."

"Not in my house, she doesn't," Thane says, his voice ice cold.

Rhen swallows and looks down at me. I shake my head, pleading with him not to hand it over.

"Choose Rhen: her or me," Thane snarls. Rhen sighs, handing him the diary.

"Sorry, Zara, he's my mate," Rhen says. I see Raidon place a hand on Rhen's shoulder, as if he is about to pull him back, worried Thane will attack him. Leon stands in the doorway, looking at everyone, horrified.

"Thane, please. It isn't yours," I murmur as a last-ditch attempt. He growls.

"You attacked me over this!" he roars. I flinch and drop my gaze to the floor.

"We know nothing about you. Your landlord knew nothing about you! Talon and Bree, also nothing. What are you hiding? Are the answers in here?" he asks. I look up, only for him to crouch down beside me, shaking the diary in my face. I blink back tears, knowing if he opens it, my real identity will no longer be that of a presumed dead girl, but a real one. I was so stupid to put my thoughts where anyone can read them.

"Answer me. Give us something, Zara. If not, I will read it," he growls, gripping my chin. His fingers dig into my cheeks.

"What are you running from?" he asks.

"Everyone," I whisper. His brows furrow before going to the photo in my hands.

"What is that?" he asks, letting go of my face. I look down at the photo clutched in my hand, now crumpled.

"A photo," I answer. The Omega facility didn't take photos of us for their records. We were underage, and it wasn't allowed without either our permission or that of a parent. Omegas are rare, and the risk of any photos being leaked could result in our kidnapping. There are enough attacks on facilities. No way would they risk a photo circulating to the wrong types of people. It would put both the staff and the residents at risk.

It helps bring in more money at the auctions too. The bidders can't be too picky or judge us on our looks. Only our numbers matter. Still, a photo of me did leak: the grainy footage from the restaurant. So, technically Thane seeing this picture won't hurt, unless he knows the Omega he bought was a twin.

"Of whom?" Thane snatches it from me and turns it over. Zara and I are thirteen in the picture.

"You're a twin?" he asks, clearly shocked by that information. I nod when he hands the photo to Rhen. He looks down at the diary in his hand.

"Where is she now?"

"Dead," I tell him, and he bites the inside of his cheek.

"I'm sorry," Thane whispers. He holds his hand out for the photo. Rhen returns it to him, and he passes it back to me.

"And this?" Thane asks, holding the diary up.

"If I give this to you; then you need to give me something, Zara. Are you running from the authorities?"

I stare at him.

"Yes," I admit.

"For what? Robbery, murder, not registering? If I let you stay, I need assurances that you aren't a risk to my mates. Are you muddled up in that vamp business you used to work for?"

"No. I just didn't want to join a pack. I never have. So, I didn't register, and I don't have ID."

"And you can't afford the fines," he sighs, knowing full well what that means. Thane pinches the bridge of his nose and slowly exhales. I've given him enough information to stop his questions. I'm not going to add that I'm also running from him and the Obsidian Pack.

Thane hands me the diary, and I hesitantly take it back. "I'll fix your fines. Have you got a birth certificate?" I shake my head.

"Fine, we will order you one tomorrow at work, then we'll get you registered."

"You can't register me. I have no pack links," I tell him. Once registered, every Alpha in the city will be aware of my existence, and I will be hounded relentlessly. All because of my DNA. I'll be forced to hand it over to the council so they have my numbers.

Thane curses and looks over his shoulder before dropping his head, his shoulders slumping. He presses his lips in a line and rises to his feet.

"I'll register you with our pack," he sighs before turning on his heel and heading for the stairs. "And I want the master key you had cut!" he says, leaving no room for argument; not that I have one. I won't need the key when I go on the run.

I can't let Thane register me, with his pack or otherwise. My DNA is already in the system, and one cross reference is all it will take for them to find out who I really am. I have time though. He will have to wait for my birth certificate before getting me registered. I can give him a fake name and buy myself a few days to escape the city. Either way, by the end of the week, he will have figured out who I am, and I don't want to be around when he does.

I look up to see Leon practically bouncing on his heels. Raidon gives me a wink, a smirk on his lips.

"We get to keep her!" Leon nearly squeals with excitement.

"It appears so," Rhen says, smiling down at me. I gulp. They think Harlow destroyed them last time, and I'm about to do it all over again, as soon as they figure out that she and I are one and the same.

CHAPTER
FIFTY-ONE

~H arlow~
It feels awkward, cold, and lonely in the Den by myself. I'm pretty relieved when I wake to the sound of Rhen coming down the steps. I had stashed my diary in my pillowcase and tucked the photo inside my bra for safekeeping. It isn't like it can get any more crumpled.

"Zara," Rhen speaks softly. I blink up at the high ceiling before turning my head to see him place a mug of steaming coffee on the side of the small drop-off into the Den. He has clothes hanging over his arm, and he moves to drape them on the back of a chair.

"Get dressed. We're leaving soon. Thane ironed your clothes, so you just need to put them on. We have an important meeting this morning and can't be late," Rhen says before slipping out of the basement. I walk to the side of the sunken Den and haul myself out.

I can hear their voices upstairs as I change into the black slacks and a matching long-sleeve blouse. I try to pull the neckline of the top closed, but the zipper stops too low, creating a deep V when I can't pull it high enough.

I'm showing way too much cleavage in this top. It's hardly

respectable workplace attire. Yet Thane chose it, and I wonder if he realized that when he picked it. Groaning, I look at my other top, which is all wrinkled and creased, and it still smells heavily of my pheromones.

Clutching the neckline closed, I grab the coffee from where Rhen left it and almost groan at the taste. I swear I can feel it warm my bones and awaken my soul from its dormant, numb state. I'm about to walk up the steps when I remember my diary is still tucked inside the pillowcase.

Sighing, I rush back to retrieve it. I need to get rid of it, even if I dread doing so. I figure I can dispose of it at work. I'll tear out the pages, shred them and dump them in the loading dock bins. It's not worth the risk, and I recognize how foolish I was to keep it. Yet I like writing, and the small doodlings I have of people inside are the only way to remember their faces.

I despise time. It's amazing how the memories of the people you love remain vivid, yet their faces eventually leave us. Just like their touch and smell, their faces slowly slip away. First, it's small features that you can no longer picture, or if you can, there's something else about them that's missing. I draw them so I can keep their faces, so I never forget. But now I have to throw it away. This diary holds far too many secrets, far too many answers.

Tucking it under my arm, I climb the stairs with my coffee and wonder if Raidon has a hairbrush I can borrow. My hair looks like a bird's nest. I doubt Thane, Leon, or Rhen would have one. They have no need to brush their hair since they keep it cropped short. Raidon has long, thick locks I'm envious of, plus his equally beautiful eyelashes.

The door opens before I get the chance to grip the handle. Thane nearly plows into me as he goes to storm down the steps. He's in an obvious rush to leave. Clearly, I am taking more time than he believes necessary.

He stops and glances over me. He growls when his eyes go to my messy hair before moving to the top that I am practically spilling out of.

His eyes linger longer than necessary before he shakes his head. "You're not wearing that," he growls.

"Well, duh, but I'm not walking up there shirtless," I tell him.

"I wouldn't have minded," Leon purrs. He waves at me from the island, where he is eating toast. I roll my eyes at him as Thane walks off down the hall, muttering about my attitude under his breath. I look for Raidon, but he is nowhere to be seen.

"Where is Raidon?" I ask.

"Getting dressed upstairs," Rhen answers. I nod, and Rhen turns around, mug in hand. He sips his coffee, watching me over the mug's rim. He takes a mouthful before speaking.

"Last door on the right, upstairs," he says, pointing to the ceiling. I swallow nervously. Am I allowed up there?

"Hurry up. We can't be late, so finish getting ready," Rhen says. I nod, gulping the rest of my coffee and setting the mug in the sink before moving toward the stairs. I pass Thane rummaging in the linen cupboard.

"Where are you going?" Thane asks. I stop with one foot on the stairs.

"To see if Raidon has a hairbrush. The one in the bathroom downstairs is gone," I tell him, and he nods, waving me off and returning to whatever he's doing.

Walking upstairs, I find a hallway with doors lining both sides. Walking to the end, I find the door Rhen spoke of. It's the last door before another hallway, which opens up to the landing that over-looks the living room. I knock on the door, not wanting to walk in while he's getting dressed.

When I get no answer, I twist the handle and open the door to find Raidon sitting on the edge of a massive bed, pulling his black, leather shoes on. The enormous bed covers an entire wall, and I gape at it.

Do they all share a bed? I try picturing them all in it but can't. I know they are mates, but Thane appears to be the sort of person that likes his privacy.

Raidon looks up as he ties his laces. "Everything okay?" he asks, moving to do the other.

"Can I borrow your hairbrush?" I ask him, not wanting to step into the room. He points to a door, which I see is a bathroom. "Can I —?" I point to the door.

He nods. I quickly rush into the bathroom and find his hairbrush in the holder. I grab it and start ripping it through my hair.

"So, you all share a room?" I call out to him.

"No, this is Thane's room. We all have our own, but we mostly sleep in here," Raidon answers before I spot him in the mirror. He stands, walks toward the bathroom, and stares at me in the mirror.

"Thane's letting you go to work like that?" he asks, his eyes fixed on my breasts.

"No, of course not," Thane says, coming up behind him and answering before I can say anything.

"Try this one," Thane says, handing me another blouse. This one is made of a clingy, stretch fabric. I take it from him, waiting for them to step out, but they don't.

"What are you doing, Zara? Put it on," Thane growls, snapping me out of my head. Okay, then, clearly, they are going to watch me change. I quickly unzip the blouse and tug it off. Thane takes it while I pull the other one on. This one fits like a second skin, but at least I'm covered.

"Better. And fix your hair," Thane snaps, about to leave, but he stops, looking Raidon over. He clicks his tongue.

"Where is your tie?" he demands.

"Come on! I'm wearing the damn suit. I don't need a strangulation device, too," Raidon says. Thane shakes his head, moving toward the walk-in closet beside the bathroom. Thane presses his lips in a line before clicking his fingers at Raidon, but he just stands there.

"No," Raidon growls as Thane wraps the tie he grabbed around his neck before using it to jerk him closer.

"Behave. I am not in the mood," Thane growls, pecking his lips. Raidon rolls his eyes while Thane straightens the tie before walking out.

"Do your hair in the car. We're going to be late," Raidon says, grabbing my hand when he spots me watching them. He leads me downstairs and to the garage. I climb into the back seat, jammed tightly between Raidon and Leon.

"What time will he arrive?" Leon asks, glancing at his phone screen.

"At 10 a.m., and we still need to find the pack files," Thane says, navigating his way through the streets.

"You have a meeting today?" I ask them, wondering who it's with and if it's the reason Thane is so irritable.

"Yes, and you will behave. No throwing yourself at his feet, Zara, and keep your damn pheromones in check. I do not feel like fighting this asshole because of your Omega instincts." Thane states.

I blink, realizing I forgot to take my suppressants this morning. Thane's eyes go to mine in the mirror, just as Leon sniffs me and licks his lips.

"She didn't," Thane growls.

"Yep, she forgot," Leon declares, snitching on me.

"Fuck, we will be so damn late," Thane snarls about to rip the car around.

"I'll be fine. I've been around you lot for days. I should have some resistance, right?" I ask.

"Are you sure?"

I nod, and Rhen reminds him we have some de-scenter at the office.

"I mean it, Zara. If you act like a..."

"Omega?" Rhen cuts him off.

Sure, piece of cake. I'll just switch off my DNA, not an issue! *Asshole*, I think to myself.

"Not a problem. I hate Alphas," I say without thinking. I freeze. It's just an off-hand comment. Stupid word vomit. I declare I hate Alphas, while sitting in a car full of them. Smart move.

Leon chuckles and nudges me.

"You really are trying to earn those brownie points today, aren't you?" he taunts.

"I didn't mean..." I shake my head, but don't bother defending myself. It would be pointless.

"Is that your way of saying you like us?" Raidon asks. "Are we the exception?" he laughs.

"No, now you're putting words in my mouth. You four are tolerable, barely!" I tell him. "Besides, if I can control myself around Thane, I'll be fine. No Alpha in this city is as potent as he is," I say, rummaging through my handbag for my name tag.

"He's not from the city. He is from the Obsidian Pack, an Alpha-of-Alphas, so stick close and don't piss him off," Thane says. I almost throw up at his words.

"Obsidian Pack?" I squeak without meaning to.

"You'll be fine. We won't let him hurt you. Anyway, he's in our territory. He wouldn't dare," Thane growls, thinking my fear is for the Alpha's reputation. He can't possibly realize my fear stems from the fact that I have this Alpha's serum in my veins, along with Thane's.

Thane's serum should be stronger, since it was the second one I got, plus all the time I've spent around him. But how will I handle being between two Alphas-of-Alphas, both of whom my body has been wired to? Thane and his pack are hard enough.

But another thing dawns on me. This Alpha met my sister. My identical twin sister, minus the scarring. He'll know who I am!

CHAPTER
FIFTY-TWO

~Harlow~

Thane parks in the underground lot, and everyone hops out of the car while I try to come up with an excuse that will get me out of the building for however long the meeting will last. But I know there is no way out of it once Thane grips my elbow and tugs me toward the elevator.

"Maybe it would be best if I'm not here?" Thane glances at me. "You know, with me being an Omega. I wouldn't want to make anyone uncomfortable," I tell them as the elevator goes up.

"None of us have time to bring you home. It will be fine," Thane says while jamming the button a few extra times, as if it will make the metal box we're crammed in go any faster. I pray it gets stuck halfway up, and he'll have to cancel the meeting. But we all know my luck is non-existent, so of course, it goes directly to our floor without incident.

The doors open, and I see Leila leaning on my desk, frantically typing away on her phone. She looks up and tosses her arms in the air.

"Hell, not one of you can answer your phone?" she hisses. Thane growls at her. Leila narrows her eyes at him, holds a finger to her lips, and points to the conference room. Thane looks toward it before pulling his phone from his pocket. I glance at the clock. It's still a few minutes before ten.

"He got in early," Leila hisses.

I take a step back, only to bump into Rhen. He grunts when my heel connects with his toes, his hand gripping my elbow.

"Fuck, how long?" Thane hisses at her.

"He's been here half an hour already; said he has to head back earlier than expected," Leila says. Thane curses, turning to look at us. His eyes fall on me. My panic is making me sweat profusely and sweat means pheromones. Thane grips my arms.

"What is going on with you? Pull yourself together and go grab the Obsidian Pack files. He holds one of our largest contracts. We lose this deal, and we will lose other contracts too. You need to pull yourself together," he snarls, and I gulp.

"Rhen, Raidon, with me. Leon, watch over Zara," he says. Rhen and Raidon follow him down the corridor to the conference room, disappearing inside.

"Well, call if you need me, but I have to go let the technician in on level 2," Leila says, heading for the elevator just as Leon grabs my hand. He tugs me to my desk and pulls out my chair before dumping me in it.

Shaking myself, I breathe through my mouth, trying to ignore all the heady, dominant Alpha scents, hoping it will ease my discomfort. I switch my computer on and log in. I find the files and quickly send them to Thane's tablet, which I hear beep a few moments later. I move on to checking their emails, and Leon leans in closer, sniffing me.

"Fuck Zara, are you sick?" he asks, touching my forehead. All I can smell is my pheromones; if that Alpha walks out right now, I'm screwed. He'll know an Omega is here. I can hear them talking, yet I focus on my computer when Leon sweeps my hair over my shoulder.

"Damn, you smell good," he groans behind me. It suddenly occurs to me that Leon can probably dampen my scent.

"Feed on me," I tell him, grabbing his tie and jerking him closer. Leon shrieks, clearly not expecting the forceful invitation, but he can leech on me as much as he wants as long as it means killing my damn pheromones.

"What? You actually want me to?" he asks, shocked. I turn in my seat to glare at him.

"Fucking feed on me, now! I do not want to send that prick into a rut over my damn scent," I growl at him. Leon tilts his head to the side, observing my face.

"I'm not supposed to without Raidon or one of the others with me," Leon says, though his eyes darken, turning a deep crimson, and I can tell he wants to.

"Here, spray some de-scenter on," he says, opening the drawer in my desk and dousing me in it. He chokes and coughs on it, and so do I. Yet it only dampens my scent, it doesn't rid me of it. I'm gone, in full flight-or-fight mode, but I can do neither to escape the situation.

"Ah, Thane wants us to bring coffee in," Leon says, dropping the can into the drawer. I don't move as he walks down toward the kitchenette.

"Zara! I don't know how to work the coffee machine!" Leon hisses, waving me over. I nibble my lip, glancing at the door. To get to the kitchenette, I have to pass the glass-paneled conference room. Looking around my desk desperately, I grab a folder and use it as a shield to cover my face, pretending I'm reading it.

Yeah, real smooth, not at all obvious that I'm hiding. Leon passes the mugs to me while I get a tray and start the machine. I busily make the coffees and set them on the tray before giving it to him. Leon stares at me funnily before he laughs.

"Seriously, you're not scared of Thane, but that fool gets you all freaked out?" Leon chuckles and moves toward the conference room, slipping inside. I peek out the door, waiting for the Alpha to turn his head away as Leon enters the room. When he does, I dart for the elevator, but I don't escape Thane's gaze.

I know I'll get Thane's fury for this later. As I dart past, Thane looks up. My eyes widen when I hear him excuse himself. I run for the fire exit, knowing the elevator will take too long. My hands hit the door, and I'm almost free when Thane's hand wraps around my arm.

"Where do you think you're going?" he growls. "I knew you would run," he snarls, shoving me toward the conference room.

I turn, needing to leave, only to smack into his chest. He grips my arms. "Fucking settle down. You fuck this up, and there will be consequences."

"Please, I'll go sit with Leila. Just don't make me go in there. I don't want to be up here with that Alpha," I plead, as he looks down at me. When I hear his voice behind me, every muscle in my body tenses. His scent reaches me, and I hold my breath. Why, why do the stupid serums have to affect us like this?

"Thane, is everything alright?"

I cringe at his deep voice before I hear him sniff the air. I swallow.

"Everything is fine. Just having issues with the Omega. You know how they get," Thane answers, looking past me.

"I'm surprised you have one here after everything with Harlow," Mr. Bowman says as Thane turns me toward the conference room. I face the imposing figure standing by the door. I gulp, my eyes running over the monster responsible for killing my sister. He wears a gray, tailored suit. He's clean-shaven and bulky. He smiles before blinking. As soon as recognition hits, the smile slips off his face.

"Yeah, things change, I guess," Thane says, nudging me forward. The Alpha's eyes are locked on mine, and mine are on his.

"Zara, this is Alpha Jake Bowman from the Obsidian Pack. Jake, this is Zara, she's an assistant here."

He looks between Thane and me.

"You found her," Mr. Bowman whispers, sounding shocked. I only just catch his words, and my heart nearly stops.

230

"Pardon?" Thane asks, and the Alpha shakes his head.

"You found one. An Omega, I mean," he corrects himself. He holds his hand out to me. I take a step toward Thane and grip his wrist. The Alpha ignores my reaction and grabs my hand.

"Zara, such a pretty name. I knew someone by that name once," he says, his grip tightening on my hand. He jerks me toward him and out of Thane's grip.

"Fuck, you smell just like her too," he groans, burying his face in my neck before sweeping my hair over my shoulder. He groans lewdly, pulling me flush against him, and all I can do is hold my breath.

CHAPTER
FIFTY-THREE

~H arlow~

"Yes, I am sorry about that, Alpha. She forgot to take her suppressants this morning," Thane says, placing his hand on my shoulder and forcing his face away from my neck.

"Sorry, sorry. Where are my manners?" the Alpha says, staring at my unmarked neck as he takes a step back.

"Shall we continue the meeting?" he says. I wait for him to out me, but he never does. Thane leads me into the conference room.

"Such pretty little things, Omegas. I should know, I've gone through plenty of them," Alpha Jake states, watching me as Thane leads me to his side of the table.

I'm on autopilot. I can't think, speak, or do anything. I just stare in horror as my instincts tell me to flee or fall at their feet. They go about their business. However, the Alpha's eyes keep darting toward me. I barely pay attention to what they say, until I hear my name mentioned.

"I'm sure she won't mind, would you, Zara? And she is no good to you, Thane," Alpha Jake says, and I blink, wondering what I missed.

"No," Thane growls.

"You didn't even ask her, and I'll extend the contract's lengths by five years," Jake offers, and my eyes widen.

"Zara isn't for sale. Nor would I allow it, even if she agreed," Thane says.

"Everyone is for sale, Thane, for the right price. You know this," Jake says, staring at me.

Rhen's jaw clenches.

"What do you say, Zara? Want to help your boss out? You'll be rewarded," Jake says. The way he says my name is almost a taunt. He knows exactly who I am, and he knows that Thane is completely unaware. I gulp and shake my head.

"No, thank you. I already have an Alpha," I tell him, my voice coming out barely above a whisper. I look at Thane, begging him with my eyes to not contradict me.

"Now, don't be rash. I just want to see if you're compatible with my pack. I bet you are, and you don't bear a mark yet." Jake then turns his gaze to Thane. "How much for her?" he asks.

My heart beats like a drum in my chest, and I clutch Thane's leg under the table. He looks down at my hand on his thigh before looking at the Alpha.

"She's not for sale, Jake. She's ours," Thane states coldly.

"She bears no mark on her neck to stake your claim on her," Jake retorts.

Thane growls, jerking me out of my seat and onto his lap. My eyes widen when his hand grips the back of my neck. Horror washes through me. He wouldn't dare mark me in front of someone, would he? Not that I would mind wearing his mark, but that's something that's supposed to be private, not flaunted as an act of dominance.

Yet, instead of his teeth sinking into my neck, his lips cover mine. His tongue sweeps across my bottom lip, demanding access. His Calling thrums from his chest, and I immediately submit to it. My hands grip his shirt as his tongue delves between my lips, tasting every inch of my mouth, and I moan at his taste.

Thane deepens the kiss, and sparks flood everywhere. My skin tingles as he pulls away, leaving me breathless and biting my bottom lip. The moment he does, his Calling drops, and reality shatters around me. I blink, embarrassed. I'm about to climb off his lap when his hand grips my thigh. His other hand goes to my waist and tugs me closer to his chest.

"Do I need to make myself any clearer? Or do you want to watch me fuck her, Alpha, so you can hear her scream who she belongs to?" Thane challenges.

Alpha Jake presses his lips in a line and glances at the contracts on the table. My face heats at Thane's words.

"Don't be foolish. You can't even breed with her, Thane, unless you're willing to make her your equal. I will double the contract price, length, and whatever else you want. Name it, Thane."

I see Rhen suck in a breath when he doesn't back down. Raidon looks at Thane, but Thane doesn't acknowledge either of them. He just stares at the Alpha across from him. I feel his hand slowly cover mine and give it a gentle squeeze.

"My Omega is not for sale," Thane growls. Alpha Jake opens his mouth to say something, but Thane speaks over him.

"Ask again. I will tell you where you can shove our contracts and our treaty, Jake. Remember whose territory you're in. And remember who you are talking to," Thane says, his voice ice cold.

I swallow, waiting to see what he will say. I notice Rhen push his chair out a bit and Raidon shift in his chair before stretching his arm along the table and drumming his fingers beside Alpha Jake. Jake glances at Rhen and Raidon, when suddenly I feel Leon's hands slip over my shoulders. He squeezes them, making me glance up at him.

Their auras, and the testosterone in the room, are overwhelming. I feel Thane's thumb rub over the back of my hand, as if he's trying to soothe the instincts that tell me to bow at their damn feet. Which is becoming an actual possibility, if they don't drop their dangerous auras.

Jake laughs, putting his hands up in surrender. "Fine, fine. I don't mean to offend you, Thane. I didn't realize you were serious about this one," Jake says, though it's clear he is not happy about it.

"Now, shall we sign the contracts, or do you need me to escort you out?" Thane asks.

"I'll grab a pen, shall I?" Jake says, reaching for one from the cup in the center of the table.

"Leon, take Zara for a drink," Thane says, looking at him. I waste no time getting to my feet off Thane's lap. I take Leon's hand. Thane nods at us, and Jake watches us leave. I don't realize how shallow my breathing is until I step out of the damn room and feel a weight lift from my chest.

"Are you okay? He can be a dick, but he usually knows better than to challenge Thane," Leon says, steering me toward the kitchenette.

My hands shake as I grab a glass from the rack, filling it with water from the tap. I gulp the water down thirstily, needing the cool liquid to soothe the desert that sucked all the moisture from my mouth.

"Hey," Leon purrs, stepping closer and pressing his chest against my back.

"Geez, Zara, you're shaking," Leon murmurs, wrapping his arms around me, and continuing his purr. It isn't as potent as Thane's powerful Calling, but it helps calm my nerves as I lean into him.

Leon waits for me to calm down and feel more under control. The doors to the conference room open up, and Thane, Raidon, and Rhen step out with the Alpha. They seem all buddy-buddy again. As Alpha Jake passes the kitchenette, Leon's arms tighten around my waist, and I tense.

"I'll catch you later, Leon," Alpha Jake says, nodding to him before turning his eyes to me. I don't miss the odd glint to them that chills me to the bone.

"And I'm sure I'll see you again real soon, Zara," he says, drawing my name out longer than necessary.

"It was lovely to meet you," I tell him, my voice sounding robotic to my own ears. He says nothing, his eyes watching me. Thane claps a hand on his shoulder, steering him toward the elevator.

"Fuck, he is a dick," Leon growls against my neck as he buries his face in my hair. He didn't rat me out, but that does not make me feel at ease. No, it makes me even more worried for some reason.

CHAPTER
FIFTY-FOUR

~*H*arlow~

Raidon watches Leon and clears his throat awkwardly. At first, I don't understand, but then I hear Rhen arguing with Thane by the elevator. The worry I had about Jake is short-lived, knowing I now have to deal with a very angry Alpha.

"It's not her fault," Rhen growls, and Leon jumps away from me. Raidon peers down the hall toward the small lobby before his eyes dart to me nervously.

"She tried to leave, and she has no trouble controlling herself around us. She is bloody lucky she didn't send him into a rut!" Thane roars. I blink, and my stomach sinks. Is this because of Jake challenging him?

His fury is written all over his face when he suddenly appears in the doorway to the kitchenette. "If you pull that shit again, I will hand you over to the authorities," Thane snarls at me, and I take a step back. I swallow down the sickening feeling that is clogging my throat.

"Fucking Omegas! You and your stupid fucking hormones making you act like a—"

"Enough, Thane. Don't confuse the old shit with Harlow and Jake with what's happening now. Zara is fucking scared of him, not throwing herself at him," Raidon snaps, and his hand moves quickly to grip Thane's arm as he goes to step into the kitchenette. Instinctively, I step back from the fuming Alpha. Leon's chest brushes up against my back, and Thane glares daggers at him when his arm slips around my waist.

"Get back to work!" he growls at us before storming off. Yet, I'm stuck on what Raidon meant by that. This is the first time I met Jake, and I hate the man. He's responsible for killing my sister, so how could Thane possibly think I was throwing myself at him?

"He'll calm down. The Obsidian Pack Alpha always sets him off. Don't take it personally," Leon murmurs behind me before squeezing my arms and following after Raidon. Rhen sighs, wandering off also. They leave me alone in the kitchenette, more shaken than ever. Especially now, since at the end of the day, I'll have to go home with Thane like this. I chew my lip as I turn back to the coffee machine to stop it from quivering.

He just faulted me for something I have no control over. And yet, my stupid Omega instincts are telling me to follow after him and beg at his feet for his forgiveness.

One thing I am becoming aware of is that my instincts are becoming harder to ignore. Soon, my suppressants may not work at all, even if I had them.

I now know that Thane's serum is very much alive and active in my system. I'm acclimating to Thane and his pack, even if I don't want to. Their constant presence only proves how impossible it will be to continue hiding who I am from them. I need to consider the possibility of telling them the truth.

But what if it angers them? I need to leave anyway, and I won't have that chance if Thane kills me. But what if he forgives me for running two years ago and listens to my side of the story? What if I could stay? And I want to stay here. I could have a pack, something I never wanted but find myself suddenly hoping for. I want them, and it is becoming harder to ignore. I'm not sure if I can bring myself to leave, even though staying is becoming dangerous.

I finish making more coffee for everyone. Walking to each of their offices, I stop at Thane's and knock. My mug and his shake on the tiny tray. I can't stop the fear surrounding me. I'm not sure if I'm more scared about needing to leave or of wanting to stay. Maybe both. Maybe neither at all. All lines are officially blurred, and no path seems correct.

"Come in," I hear Thane call out, and I suck in a deep breath. My hands are sweating as I fight my instinct to beg at his feet and to run as far as I can from him. I slip inside. Thane is typing away at his laptop but sits back when I place his coffee cup beside him. He sighs, watching me. I turn to leave when his hand grips my wrist, making every muscle in my body tense.

He leans across, grabbing the tray from my hand and setting it down as he swivels in his chair, pulling me to stand between his legs. "I'm sorry, Zara. I didn't mean to take my anger out on you," he murmurs.

"It's fine," I tell him. What else can I say? He's made it perfectly clear the only reason I am here is because his mates seem to want me around. Thane sighs, letting my wrist go. I swiftly grab the tray and my coffee, heading for the door and away from him.

"I know you're not the same as Harlow," he says as I reach the door. I stop, if only because I'm scared he's realized that I *am* Harlow. I turn around to see if he has anything else to say.

"You're not her, I know that. It's just... Jake... We have a history revolving around Harlow and seeing him try to take you reminded me of when he did the same with her," he tells me, reaching for his mug. He sips his coffee, and I watch him, wondering what other information I can get from him. Maybe I can change his mind.

"You hate her because you think she killed your mother?" I ask.

He swallows, nods his head, and looks out the window.

"But you never found her. So, what if she didn't do it?"

"She did. I know she did," Thane says with unwavering certainty. I'm about to drop the subject, seeing I'm not going to get anywhere with this conversation, when the door opens. Raidon steps inside, holding a plastic zipper bag with some tubes in it and a needle.

"Leila dropped this off," Raidon says before smiling at me.

"Ah, finally. You might as well stay, Zara. I need you here for this anyway," Thane says, and I watch Raidon go over to the desk. He motions me to the chaise, and I sit down, dread pooling in my stomach. Thane unplugs his laptop and brings it over before sitting beside me.

"Raidon is going to take your blood so we can send it off to be analyzed, and you can help me fill out this paperwork to request a birth certificate, so we can register you with our pack," Thane says, logging into the council's online portal. My heart beats erratically when Raidon comes toward me with the needle.

"Should he be doing that? What about a proper doctor?" I worry.

"My mother used to be a pathologist. She taught me a few things, one of which is how to take blood," he chuckles, pulling on some gloves.

"What's your last name?" Thane asks. I blink, having been put on the spot. "And your real one this time, please," Thane clarifies.

"Perry," I lie; it's my grandmother's maiden name. I know he won't get a hit on Zara Perry."

"Date of birth and hospital?" he asks. I rattle off my actual date of birth and the hospital I was born at, thinking he won't be able to connect them with the wrong last name.

"I thought we had to wait until after we get the birth certificate before we could do the blood test," I tell them.

"My mom's handling it. My dad has a practice down on the main street, so we can do this here, and Mom and Dad will handle the rest," Raidon says.

I hiss when he jabs the needle in, and watch the vial fill with my blood. The scent of my fear perfumes the room at this revelation. I thought I could push this out a couple of weeks until we got the birth certificate, a week at the very least.

Raidon sniffs the air, subtly, but I notice. "What's wrong? You got some disease you didn't tell us about?" he chuckles.

"No, just worried what my levels will come back as," I lie. I'm worried about his father putting my blood up against the database and figuring out who I am.

"By the smell of you, your levels are very high. Not that it matters," Raidon says, and Thane growls beside me. Raidon shrugs at him, unperturbed.

"Because of Harlow?" I state.

"Yes, she got the last of my serum. I couldn't mate you even if I wanted to. I won't risk that," Thane states.

"Do you want kids?" Raidon asks abruptly. I swallow, glancing at Thane, but he doesn't react to Raidon's question. He doesn't look up at him or seem bothered in any way.

"I haven't really thought about children," I answer honestly.

"Well, just because Thane can't knot you doesn't mean we can't. Just something to think about," Raidon winks.

"Isn't that the point of the serum?" I ask.

"Yes, but I can't give you my serum. I don't have any left," Thane repeats.

"But the Alpha-of-Alphas is supposed to produce the first heir," I tell him.

"As I said, I can't. That doesn't mean they can't give you children, though," Thane says.

"And you would allow that?" I ask, a little shocked. In most Alpha Packs, only the primary Alpha produces children. In a regular pack, though, it isn't unheard of for the Omega to produce kids for the other pack members. Whoever the Omega mates with will determine what the child will be. Two Omegas mating will only produce Omegas, for example. Though finding a male Omega is rarer than finding a female one.

"Yes, of course. Our pack isn't like most Alpha Packs. I may be the primary Alpha, but I don't share those views, not anymore anyway," Thane says, staring up at Raidon. "I'd love any child my mates produce. They would still be my child."

I swallow nervously. They still want kids, even if I can't give Thane one? Well, I can. They just don't know that, and I'm not willing to test if there's enough of his serum in my system to try. In Alpha Packs, serum is used because the main Alpha grows in power and size when the other Alphas submit. Omegas are fragile, but sturdy enough to handle a regular Alpha. An Alpha-of-Alphas, on the other hand, has a knot that can kill an Omega without his serum. Many regular Alphas also give their serum to Omegas, to force a bond where there isn't one, or to hold more control over their Omega. It's barbaric, but it's how things have always been done.

But if Thane gave me his serum after already marking and bonding his mates, I would be stronger than all of them, except Thane, and a liability to the pack. Or so most Alpha-of-Alphas believe.

Omegas can mate with any pack member really, yet we are primarily desired by Alphas because only Omegas can produce an Alpha child and take an Alpha knot.

Alpha females, on the other hand, can't produce any children with another Alpha. Only an Omega can handle an Alpha's knot. Betas can mate with each other, and Alpha females can mate with Beta males. Those mating mostly produce more Betas, and sometimes, oddly, an Omega, but that is extremely rare.

Omegas can produce female Omegas with any partner. The entire thing is crazy and confusing. It's another reason I never gave much thought to children. I didn't want to risk having a girl and the chance she would inherit my DNA and not her father's.

Raidon places a cotton swab on my arm as he slips the needle out. "How long will that take?" I ask him.

"A couple of days," he shrugs.

"The request for your birth certificate has been submitted. It says it can take up to two weeks," Thane says, screenshoting the receipt and saving it to his desktop.

"So, about the children—" Raidon says, but Thane cuts him off.

"You're making her nervous. Let her get used to the idea of having a pack before we start harassing her for babies," Thane says, and Raidon nods.

"Sorry, I am getting ahead of myself."

"No, you're worried that I will change my mind, and you'll lose your chance to have kids," Thane says, closing his laptop and looking up at Raidon. "I'm not going to change my mind. I know how much you three want this," Thane tells him.

It sounds like he's still not fully on board with having an Omega. More like he's just doing it for them. Which makes my stomach sink, knowing it will cause a rift in their pack.

"We can talk about it more later," Thane says, dismissing us.

Great chat, I think, but I'm glad to have a chance to escape. Heading to my desk, I rummage through the drawer, spraying more de-scenter on before pulling the diary out when Raidon wanders over.

"What are you doing right now?" he asks, and I point to my computer.

"Do you want to come with me to drop this off? You can meet my parents," he says, holding up the baggie containing my vial of blood.

CHAPTER
FIFTY-FIVE

~H arlow~

I chew my lip, wondering if I'm allowed to leave when I'm not on my suppressants. But after speaking with Thane and apologizing for earlier, I feel a little more at ease. "How far is it?"

"Just down the road, and we can take the car. No one will catch your scent," he tells me. Rhen walks out of his office, and he stops to look over at us.

"Aren't you supposed to be working?" he asks, about to knock on Thane's door. Raidon holds up the bag he is holding.

Rhen's eyes dart to me, and he sighs. "She's not going anywhere smelling like that."

Raidon doesn't move to leave, and Rhen's eyes flick back to him. He raises an eyebrow at his mate.

"I said no! Zara, go wait in my office before this fool starts thinking it's a good idea to take you down Main Street smelling like sex on legs."

I peek up at Raidon, who is glaring at Rhen.

"Now, Zara," he growls.

244

I jump to my feet, only for Raidon to snake his arms around my waist and pull me toward him. He buries his face in my neck and whispers in my ear.

"Wait for him to leave, then come down the fire escape, meet me in the parking lot," he says, pecking my cheek.

I step away and raise an eyebrow at him. Rhen clears his throat.

"I said now, Zara," Rhen snaps, and I rush toward his office.

Geez, most Alphas paw over Omega pheromones, yet something must be wrong with mine because all I get is their anger. I huff, doing as I'm told while considering Raidon's proposal of sneaking off with him. I would much rather be with him than a brooding Rhen or murderous Thane. Even Leon is preferable, though he would slurp on me like his personal juice box.

Rhen doesn't leave the hall until after I hear Raidon leave. With a huff, I push open Rhen's office door and step inside, waiting by his door. I leave it cracked open and peek out, only to notice Leon smirking at me from his desk down the hall. He puts his head down and scribbles on a piece of paper before holding it up. In big, bold black letters, it reads:

I dare you!!

He drops his head, scribbling again. I peer down the hall toward Thane's office when Leon clears his throat, holding up another note.

Rhen loves a good chase.

I snicker, covering my mouth to muffle my laughter when he holds up the first note up again, his eyes sparkling with mischief. I try to mime for him to come with me, but he shakes his head. I glare at him before he taps his watch, telling me I'm running out of time. Glancing at Thane's door, I see it is still shut, and I kick off my heels, holding them in my hand before I take off toward the fire exit.

Just as I pull on the door open, I feel the heat of someone's chest against my back. He moved so silently that I didn't even hear him. I stiffen when I feel his breath sweep across my neck as he leans his face down.

"And where are you running off to?"

"There was a draft," I tell him, internally facepalming myself at my lame excuse.

"That's what happens when you open a door," Rhen purrs before gripping my hip and turning me around to face him. I notice Leon standing down the corridor, and I nearly snort when he holds up another paper note in big black letters.

I double dare you to run!

I roll my eyes. Is he so bored that he needs my death as entertainment? Rhen, however, mistakes the action as me rolling my eyes at him. He growls, gripping my face in his hands.

"Are you trying to sneak off with Raidon?"

"Just airing out my shoes in the draft," I tell him.

He doesn't find my words as amusing as I do. I notice Leon waving his arms, trying to get my attention. I can see the new note he waves at me. That man is trouble, and he is trying to get me to join in his silly little games.

Chicken

I am no chicken, and even if this is purely for Leon's entertainment, I decide to go against my better judgment. My blood sizzles in anticipation. Leon clears his throat behind Rhen, who turns to look at him. The moment his back is to me, I take off down the steps, hearing Rhen curse behind me.

Adrenaline pumps in my veins at the joy I get racing down the stairs. I finally understand what everyone means by the thrill of the chase. Though dangerous, and probably stupid, it makes my blood come alive, and I laugh, actually laugh, for the first time in ages.

I make it down seven flights before I feel his hand grip the back of my shirt. We hurtle toward the wall, and I shriek, closing my eyes as I trip over my own feet. A loud thud reaches my ears, and I hear the air expel from his lungs as he hits the hard surface. I remain unharmed, as he pivoted at the last second to take the brunt of the fall.

His grip tightens, and he growls furiously. "Are you insane, Zara?" he snarls at me.

I briefly wonder if I am, yet the adrenaline pumping through my veins makes me giggle, until I hear a growl from a few flights down.

Rhen's aura rushes out, and I hear rushed footsteps before the slamming of a door makes me jump, his hand around my waist the only thing stopping me from cowering under the weight of his aura.

"If they didn't get a whiff of you before, they certainly have now," Rhen growls, and I sniff the air, which is potent with my Omega scent.

I'm not given much time to be concerned before Rhen is moving back up the stairs. He is raging, and I suddenly don't want to go back up there, worried he will hand me over to Thane. Stupid Leon! He better own up to his participation in my misdoings, or he is going on a frozen blood bag diet.

When I don't move fast enough for Rhen, he growls, grabbing me and tossing me over his shoulder, and starts rushing up the steps toward our floor. The closer we get, the more certain I am he is about to dump me at Thane's feet and snitch. I push my hands into his back, trying to get him to put me down.

"Stop it. You're in enough trouble," Rhen snaps, but still, I struggle.

"It is Leon's fault, not mine. Blame him. He told me to do it."

"And you listened to him," Rhen snaps.

"Please, I'll be good," I tell him.

He huffs as if he thinks that's impossible for me. It kind of is. I'm always in trouble for something, and trouble tends to find me. Today, trouble came in the form of Leon and Alpha Jake, so third time's the charm.

I dig my elbows into his back and rest my chin on my hands. Rhen growls but sets me down after getting to our floor and closing the fire door.

I glance up at him to find his eyes a demonic black.

He smirks. "I won't tell Thane," he whispers, and I eye him suspiciously.

"My office now," he growls, pointing toward it, and I peer over my shoulder before sighing and stalking off toward it. I hear Rhen spray the de-scenter everywhere. I push the door open only to turn and close it, spotting Leon with a triumphant smile on his face. What is he up to?

FIFTY-SIX

~H arlow~

He's angry at me. I get it, but it's not like I control my scent. No matter how many times I spray myself or how many pills I take, for Rhen, it's not enough.

He's been on edge the entire day, and my little stunt just pushed him over, but at least he isn't handing me over to Thane. It's not a surprise when he pushes into his office and locks us inside. I wait for the scolding I'm sure I'm about to receive.

He smirks and walks past me. I watch him as he moves around his huge office.

Rhen shuts the blinds over the massive windows in his office and I groan. He locked us in, yet this seems a little too far, and something tells me that Thane won't be happy about his sudden need for privacy.

"Rhen, what are you doing?" I ask.

"It's not what I am doing, but what you will be doing," he purrs, his eyes darkening as he walks toward me.

I raise an eyebrow at him when he stops in front of me.

He places a hand on my shoulder and forces me to my knees,

249

nearly pressing his groin to my face. "Can you see what you do to me? You did this. You fix it," he snaps.

I shake my head and come up with the stupidest excuse I can think of, but still hope it will work. "Thane will catch us, and I'm not risking my job for your momentary pleasure," I tell him, looking at the massive bulge in his pants, the fabric strained tight over it.

"Is that the only reason you're saying no? You're scared to get caught sucking dick during work hours?"

"That's not what I said. Don't force words in my mouth."

"I won't force words into your mouth, but I will force my cock in it. Don't worry, I got it all covered." Rhen leans down to slide his hands in my armpits, pulling me back to my feet.

I almost trip when he pulls me toward his desk and shoves me underneath it, grinning at me as he sits in his massive office chair. "A good assistant can deal with any issue at the desk, under or on top of it. Work your magic, Omega."

I growl at him, pushing on his legs, trying to get out.

"Thane isn't the only one that can fire you, Zara. Just think about how lonely you'll be, locked in the Den by yourself every day, because you can't be trusted at home by yourself."

"Rhen!" I growl.

His eyes glisten back at me. He sighs. "I guess I'll just have to tell Thane you tried to run off? And he is in almost a good mood, too. Such a shame," Rhen purrs, using his hand to lift my chin. He brushes his thumb over my lips, tugging my bottom lip down.

"What's it going to be, Zara?" he asks.

"I better not get in trouble for this," I snap at him, looking to his straining pants.

My hands shake as I reach for his belt and slowly unbuckle it. I pull down the zipper and release his hard cock. I would rather die than admit this, but my mouth salivates at the view alone.

Slowly, I grip the base of his cock and bring it to my lips. I tease Rhen by rubbing the tip against my closed lips first. When I slowly part them and run my tongue over his tip, I can taste the pre-cum. I hold back a moan as I open my mouth and suck him in.

Rhen grips the edge of his desk and hisses under his breath. If we get caught, this is on him, and I'll make a point about that. Thane can't fire me for something his mate—and my boss—forced me to do. He certainly won't find out how much I'm enjoying it. I'll pretend I don't. Yet my aroused scent will probably give me away.

I bob my head and shove Rhen's length down my throat. My gag reflex makes me cringe, but I ignore the resistance and keep going. The sooner he's satisfied, the sooner I can escape his claws and get back to work.

His body tenses, and his cock twitches in my mouth. Though it's difficult, I smile around his girth, excited to be done with this bull-shit so I can slip back to my desk unnoticed.

Yet, just moments before I expect Rhen to fill my mouth, he pulls away from me as if I burned him. His gaze sears through me, and I wonder if I did it wrong. Having someone look at me like that stings, but I shake off the feeling and crawl out from under the desk and straighten my body.

Rhen got what he wanted; now, I can leave.

The moment I turn my back on him and take a step toward the door, Rhen's flush behind me. He slaps his hand over my mouth to keep me quiet and uses his stupid strength to bend me over his office desk.

"Do try to keep quiet," he chuckles, and his heady scent envelopes me. I moan, turning languid in his hands as his Calling slips out, enticing my senses and causing slick to drench the thin fabric of my thong.

Rhen keeps his one hand over my mouth as his other moves to grab the waistband of my slacks. He shoves them down my thighs.

He forces me against the desk with such strength I can't move, even if I wanted to. He slides his finger between my thong and pussy, gently tugging the tiny fabric to the side.

I can feel the tip of his cock dangerously close to my entrance.

Rhen gently kicks at my ankles, demanding I spread my legs further apart, and he presses his erection against my wet opening. In one brutal thrust, he sheaths himself deep inside me and my walls grip him instantly. His hand muffles the noise that tries to escape my lips, and I am suddenly very thankful for it.

"Fuck, you feel good," he groans, pulling all the way out before thrusting back in again. His thrusts are punishing, and I love every second. The thrill of being caught slivers in my veins. I push back against him, wanting more, and he laughs softly.

His fingers dig into my hip as he plows into me, my thighs slap the edge of his desk with each harsh thrust. His laptop slips off the edge and onto the floor when I hear the door handle jiggle. I push off the desk frantically as it begins to open. Rhen shoves me back down, leaning over me, his voice below my ear.

"You brought this on yourself. I want him to catch us," Rhen laughs, and my eyes widen as the door opens.

It's Thane. He folds his arms across his broad chest, but Rhen doesn't stop railing me into his desk, and I can't stop the moans muffled by his hand.

His gaze is intense as he leans against the door, watching. He doesn't take his eyes off me, and I feel the first tremors of my climax. My skin heats, and my walls clamp down on Rhen's thick length, when his eyes flick to Rhen.

"When you're done, we're leaving," Thane says before looking back at me. His eyes flash as I convulse. My eyes flutter closed as I come apart, gripping the edge of the desk just as I feel Rhen pull out suddenly. Moments later, I feel the splash of his warm cum spray over my lower back and ass. Opening my eyes Thane is gone and I sigh, relieved he isn't mad.

Rhen chuckles, grabbing some tissues off his desk and cleaning up the mess he made all over me, while I die of humiliation at being caught like this.

I hear Rhen fix his pants behind me, and I reach down, yanking mine up too.

"I think your little plan backfired. He didn't seem to mind at all," I tell Rhen, but he laughs, chucking the tissues into the bin.

"Oh, he is *pissed*. One thing to remember with Thane, little Omega, is that his silence, or any lack of communication really, is usually an indicator of how fucked you're gonna be when you get home," he laughs.

The smile on my face slips as I watch him walk out of his office.

"But it was your idea," I hiss at him.

"You shouldn't have run. You tempted me," he retorts, and I glare at his back, following him out. Leon waits by his office door, a smirk on his face.

"I want a front-row seat," Leon beams excitedly. Of course, he does. It was his idea to run, and apparently, me being punished is going to be prime entertainment.

"Don't think I don't know it was you who put her up to it, Leon. But don't worry, you'll get the best seat in the house: over my fucking lap," Thane calls out to him from the foyer. Despite being in trouble, I smirk. Serves Leon right!

FIFTY-SEVEN

~H arlow~

Raidon is waiting in the car when we reach the parking lot. He winks at me as I climb in. "Heard you got caught?" He smirks and I glare at him.

Rhen climbs in the front with Raidon. Thane slides into the back with me, and Leon sits on my other side.

"Why are we leaving early?" I ask, and Thane scoffs beside me.

"Are you seriously asking that?" he asks. "Your little stunt caused quite the stir. The whole building can smell you through the air-conditioning vents."

My cheeks flame at his words. I turn my attention to the front window. As we drive home, I wonder about how much trouble I'm in.

"Did your parents question you about the blood sample?" Thane asks Raidon, and he nods.

"Did you tell them?" Thane asks and Raidon sighs.

"They won't tell anyone," Raidon finally says.

"I'm not mad; I expected you to tell her. I know how excited your mother will be," Thane says, gripping his shoulder. Raidon visibly relaxes, but I only become more tense. The more people who know about me, the more people there are to be disappointed. I wonder if his parents would forgive me if they knew who I truly am.

"Mom asked if you're going to allow us to mate her?" Raidon chuckles. Thane sits back, leaning slightly on the door and watching me.

"His mother is sweet. You'll like her. She was best friends with my mother," Thane tells me, which makes me cringe. Great, she will definitely hate me if she believes lies about me killing her best friend.

"Yeah, Mom took the death of Thane's parents pretty badly. It's also why I didn't want to lie to her."

"I said it's fine, Raidon. Relax," Thane tells him.

"So, all of your parents are close?"

"Mostly for business purposes, except Elaine, Raidon's mother. She even tried to help us find Harlow."

"She did?" I ask nervously.

"Yeah, she was worried we wouldn't go through with it," Thane sighs.

"Go through with what?"

"Killing her. Elaine suggested that once we got a few kids out of Harlow, we should kill her. She wanted vengeance."

I gulp, wondering how the woman could hate someone so much when she only knows one side of the story.

"I just don't understand how you can be so certain that Harlow killed her."

"You're seriously defending that whore? She killed my mother, destroyed my family," Thane growls.

"You can't know that for certain though," I tell him.

"I can know for certain, and I do. My mother mind-linked to my fathers as her neck was slit. Her last words were, 'It's Harlow'. Harlow killed her and stole her car. Then she ran some poor, inno-cent man off the road and destroyed his family too. She's lucky the rogues got her because if they didn't, I would have made her death torturously slow," Thane growls.

"And your father?" I ask him.

"Fathers, I had two. Both of them killed themselves three weeks after her funeral. They weren't the same after the bond severed," Thane says peering out his window.

I look away from him, tears pricking my eyes at all the heartache I have caused, without actually being the one responsible.

But Thane's words make it abundantly clear that they can never find out who I really am. No way they would believe a single word that comes out of my mouth. Not when his mother's last word was my name, which just hammers an extra nail in my coffin.

When we finally get home, Raidon parks in the garage and shuts the roller door behind us. My mind is still trying to process everything I just learned and how I'm going to get myself out of this situation. It seems like running is still my only option.

I climb out of the car, and Leon smirks at me. I glance around to find Raidon and Rhen gone.

"Where did they go?" I ask, looking around to find the door leading into the house wide open.

"They bailed. They try to avoid Thane's punishments. They don't like being spanked; not that it ever stops Thane," Leon chuckles.

Spanking, as in like a child? Surely, he didn't mean it the way it came out.

"There will be no spanking today, Leon," Thane says, and I jump, having forgotten he was still waiting for us. I peer over at him, and he suddenly seems much more imposing. My eyes go to his huge-ass hands. Nope, I am not playing whatever fucking game is going on here.

I heard him say at the office that Leon would be spread across his lap, but I thought he was joking. Now, I see Thane differently. Who is this man? And why does Leon look excited? I sure as shit don't share the excitement that Leon is pretty much vibrating with.

Leon nudges me toward Thane, but I take a step back. Nope, I'll pass, thanks.

"Better to just take it and get it over with. You may even enjoy it." Leon whispers.

Is he insane? Nuh-uh, I am not having it. I shake my head, and Thane quirks an eyebrow at me.

"You run, and it will only be worse," Thane warns.

"Please run," Leon whispers behind me, laughing. "I dare you," he adds.

Thane looks like he is running out of patience. He clicks his tongue, and I wonder at my chances of escape. I'm not above shoving Leon in his path, just to give me a few extra seconds to get away.

There are two things I fear: Alphas and spiders. When it comes to facing either of those two things... sorry Leon, but I will throw your ass in the fire so fast.

After a few moments of our strange standoff, his patience wanes when I don't move, and he takes a step toward me. I stare at Thane. My eyes grow impossibly wide, and my bottom lip quivers. How can he think of such an outrageous thing?

I have no idea where this sudden wave of confidence comes from, but I know I need to stand up against his attempts to bully me into submission.

"And what if I don't want to? You don't own me. I never agreed to be a part of your weird pack punishments. You don't have the right to punish me for anything. Leon, yes, as much as I hate to admit it, you have power over him, but not me, Thane," I growl.

"Oh, this is getting good. Keep going. I wanna see him get really mad," Leon urges before shoving me toward Thane, who grips my arms before I can stumble into him.

"You do realize your little stunt back at the office ended with three of my employees being knocked out cold by security?" Thane growls in my face.

"Again, not my fault. Blame peer pressure," I tell him.

"I'll give you one chance to correct that answer, Zara. Just remember, most Alphas have their Omegas tucked away where the world can't see them. You don't strike me as the type who likes to sit at home, playing house. So, either you accept your punishment with Leon and keep your job, or you'll remain locked in your Den all day from now on," Thane tells me.

"Does that mean I'll get to sleep in?" I ask, and his canines slip out, making me gasp. At this point, I'm not sure what scares me more —his threat or the look on his face.

All this point, Leon steps aside, looking down at his feet in shame, as if he knows something I don't. Has Thane been doing these punishments for a while? I can only assume Leon doesn't bother running because he knows there is no escaping from Thane. I suppose I should act repentant too, since I'm just as guilty as Leon. Though I am sticking with the peer pressure story. What's one spanking if it means I get to keep my freedom? Without it, I would have no way of escaping once they learn who I am.

"Fine," I snarl, raising my voice a little just to prove a point. Thane can take all the pleasure he can get from this, but I will continue to show him how much I hate his idea of discipline, of holding up the order he creates.

Thane leads Leon and I up the stairs toward his room, a smirk playing on his lips. I roll my eyes at the ridiculousness of it all.

He opens the door to his room and shoves us both inside.

CHAPTER
FIFTY-EIGHT

~H arlow~

"You, over there," Thane orders me, pointing his finger at the massive bed in the middle of the room.

I glance at Leon. He gulps and nods, as if to tell me it's better to follow the commands and to not dare to talk back. Honestly, pissing off Thane is the last thing we need, given how much shit we are already in. So, I force down every instinct that tells me to defy the man, and I walk to the bed, fold my arms across my chest, and glare at him.

"Sit," Thane growls again, so I sit on the edge of the bed, while Leon stays standing at the door.

Does Leon plan on escaping as soon as Thane gets distracted, doing whatever he plans to do to me? Sweat breaks out on my forehead while my eyes dart between both men.

"Leon, on the chair," Thane orders, but this time, his voice is a little lighter, a little more caring and gentler, despite it still being a damn order. He is still tossing us around the room however he pleases.

Holding my breath, I watch Leon walk to the chair and sit down.

259

I expect a remark or something stupid from him, but he is so unusually quiet, I'm not sure what to think.

My eyes catch a movement to my right. I turn to watch Thane approach a massive dresser and pull open a drawer. The sound of metal on wood echoes off the bedroom walls, and I gulp at the mere thought of the torture devices Thane might keep inside.

He grabs something and lets out a quiet hum, turning to face Leon. My eyes instantly dart to him, and Leon grins for the first time since Thane announced the punishment we earned.

"Yes! Cuff me, Alpha," Leon whines with such amusement in his voice I know it has to be an attempt to get on Thane's nerves. Great, so much for doing everything we can to *not* piss Thane off even more. I just want this over with so I can plot out my next move and figure out where the heck I am going to go.

Once again, I expect a particular reaction for Thane. In this case, rage, growling, and possibly the use of extensive physical force, but, instead, Thane just chuckles.

He walks over to Leon, steps behind him, and cuffs his wrists behind the back of the chair. I watch how Thane leans into whisper something in Leon's ear, and his eyes instantly widen. The amusement fades from Leon's face as he shakes his head and mouths what appears to be 'Don't.'

"Too late," Thane hums as he walks around the chair. He goes as far as to cuff Leon's ankles to the chair, as if the cuffs behind his back aren't enough.

What on earth is he doing? And why did he order me to sit on the bed while Leon gets cuffed to a chair? It would only be fair for our punishments to be equal, but I guess Thane and equality don't mix here.

"I haven't forgotten about you, Zara," Thane muses, without so much as throwing a glance in my direction. I force down the lump in my throat and lick my lips, deciding it's best to stay quiet.

The sooner he starts his stupid punishment, the sooner we will be out of here. I can then forget about everything that happened and go hide in the Den.

Thane doesn't move from his position, crouched in front of Leon. I jump when I hear the sound of a zipper opening. There are some more odd metal sounds before Thane chuckles and stands up.

When Thane steps aside, I avert my gaze. Leon sits cuffed to the chair. His movements are restrained to only the bare minimum, and Thane looks more than pleased with his handiwork. And why wouldn't he, because as soon as I have a clear view, I can see Leon's cock is out of his pants, trapped inside some weird device.

"Now, it's your turn," Thane says, turning to me. He crosses his arms in front of his chest and watches me for a second; his eyes roaming over me.

I glance at Leon, possibly looking for some answers, but he just hangs his head, providing no help at all. "What are you planning to do to me?" I ask, still keeping an eye on Leon.

"Whatever I want. That's your punishment, Zara. Leon will sit there and watch me do whatever I want to you. Use your body however I please, but there is a catch." Thane moves closer to me, while a menacing grin spreads across his face.

"A catch?" I raise an eyebrow, glancing at Leon, who looks like he's in pain. My heart pounds against my ribcage as my eyes travel down to his cock, finally understanding what the metal device is for.

It's a cage, and the reason behind Leon's pain. It has trapped his growing erection. I know how they work, which makes me think Thane is speaking so openly just to torture Leon. The more aroused he gets, the less space he has in that cage.

At this point, I'm scared to even think of what might happen to Leon whenever Thane gets his paws on me, forcing him to watch an in-person, literal porn show.

"Your job's still at risk, too. If you cum, you're fired," Thane declares.

I watch as Thane strides closer. My heartbeat becomes louder with each step he takes, and I watch as his lips tug up at the corners

261

when he smiles. Why am I getting a funny feeling that I should have run?

He stops, just a few steps from the bed, and I gulp. I crawl up the bed, increasing the distance between us and looking for an opportunity to escape. Thane raises an eyebrow at me but says nothing. His eyes flicker black, dangerously, as if he is daring me to try it. His calm and cold demeanor sends a violent shiver up my spine, and I freeze.

Thane leans over the bed, his eyes on mine as his hand reaches out to wrap his fingers around my ankle. A shrill shriek escapes me as I am ripped toward the end of the bed with one hard tug. He steps back, letting me go, and I sit up. My eyes dart to Leon's before going to the door, calculating my chances.

"Strip. Before I do it for you, Zara," Thane says, and I frown. "One," Thane growls, and his hand twitches, as if he wants to tear the clothes off me.

I jump off the bed, quickly taking off my clothes piece by piece, until I stand before him in nothing but my bra and thong. I attempt to hide by wrapping my arms around my body, but with a single growl from Thane, I drop my arms at my sides, fisting my hands and gritting my teeth.

"Didn't I make myself clear, Omega? I said to strip, not model your underwear," Thane snaps at me. Why does Leon get to keep his clothes on?

Pressing my lips in a line, I give him my harshest glare and reach behind my back to unclasp my bra and drop it on the floor. Despite his blatant display of anger, I hear the slight groan he can't hold back as I slide my thumbs under the tiny strips of fabric and slowly slide the material down to my ankles.

Thane's eyes take in every inch of me standing before him, but my eyes look at Leon, pleading with him for a way out of this.

Thane slides a hand into his pocket, pulling out a pair of nipple clamps he must have retrieved from the drawer earlier. My eyes widen, and I shake my head, stepping back. The back of my knees hit the bed, leaving me nowhere to go.

"Don't move," he growls, stepping closer. I gasp and hold my breath when he brings his hand to my breast to capture my nipple between my fingers.

He plays with my nipple, then rounds it with the tip of his thumb. He grins sadistically as my nipple hardens under his touch. I nearly choke when he places the clamp at the base of my nipple, incredibly close to the areola. I suck in a sharp breath at the sting and clench my eyes shut at the painful sensation.

Repeating the process, he captures my other nipple in the second clamp, and I hiss as the pain spreads across my chest.

"Get on the bed: face down, ass up."

I freeze. He can't be serious.

"Thane, we get it. We're really sorry," Leon whines behind me. I stare up at Thane when he leans closer.

He traces his tongue along my neck and growls. "Bed, Zara. Now," he commands.

I have no choice but to do as he asks. I crawl onto the bed, but I pause when he speaks again.

"Spread your legs and turn your ass toward Leon; he earned the best view." As the words leave his lips, I glance over my shoulder, only to see Leon's furious gaze directed at Thane.

The only sound in the bedroom is our violent heartbeats and harsh breaths. Thane is calm as he walks back to the massive dresser and pulls open the second drawer to scan the contents inside.

The more time he takes rummaging, the louder my heartbeat gets.

Thane finally walks back to the bed, and he stops at the edge, only to look over his shoulder and wink at Leon. Leon glares at him. I have never seen Leon look so worked up and desperate.

I gulp when he tosses a set of cuffs, what looks like a butt plug, a vibrator, and a small bottle of lube on the bed beside my face.

"Change of plans. Lay on your back and spread your legs."

FIFTY-NINE

~L~ eon~

Thane is downright evil. I would be fine with another go at my ass, but what he's doing now is pure torture. The worst part is that he hasn't done shit yet, and I already feel like my balls are going to explode if he doesn't remove the damn cock cage soon.

Of all the things he could do to me, he had to go and choose the worst one.

It's cruel, waving a naked Omega before my eyes, and I can't get anywhere near her?

He's gotten his point across. I shouldn't have coaxed her into running from Rhen. I knew how potent her scent was, and the risks of encouraging such behavior could have turned really bad if Rhen hadn't caught her. Yet, no matter how many times I repeat that or beg for Thane to stop, I know he won't until he's decided he's done.

I try to shift in my seat to get more comfortable, but the pressure on my erection prevents me from making any sharp movements. I hate this shit, being denied what I want, and even more, watching Thane take what I want more than anything.

I let out a shaky breath as I watch Zara lie on her back and stare up at Thane. If hatred could burn someone, my mate would be up in flames right about now. His only response to the defiance burning in her eyes: a chuckle, full of mockery.

Thane grabs the leather cuffs and wraps them around Zara's wrists. He shifts a little and reaches for something. I squint my eyes, and my body instantly reacts when I notice another set of cuffs with chains attached to them. Those go on her ankles as Thane positions Zara before him—legs spread wide, hands cuffed to each ankle, restrained in the most vulnerable position.

My mouth salivates as Thane steps aside and takes her in. She's completely naked, spread so wide I could easily run over and shove my cock inside her with ease, if not for the damn cuffs holding me in place. The pain pulsating from my cock slowly moves to my head, pounding against my damn skull.

I lick my lips as Thane reaches for the butt plug and covers it with a generous amount of lube. "This will teach you both a lesson, and if it doesn't, I don't mind a repeat of this game we're playing. " Thane growls as he brings the plug right to her back hole and forces it inside her, without having enough decency to stretch her poor ass.

Zara's eyes widen. They look glossy, as if she's about to cry, but she holds back and bites her lip to keep in the scream, or moan, whichever it might have been. Fuck, now I want to know what it was!

"If you cum, you're fired, and you will spend the rest of your days trapped in the Den, Omega," Thane reminds Zara of the rules, and all I can do is try to give her an apologetic look. Man, she is going to hate me. I suddenly feel guilty about my part in this.

My eyes focus on the pink diamond poking out from her ass, and I can't stop wondering how good it would feel to shove my dick in there.

But of course, the thoughts are nothing but another form of torture. Thane knew what he was doing when he forced the cock cage on me.

He moves to the side of the bed and reaches for another of his toys. Finally, I get a full, glorious view of our sweet little Omega. Oh, how I want to fuck her and feed on her right now, with her trapped in that position.

Thane holds up some black device, and I frown at it until it starts vibrating. Holy shit, he's coming in with the big guns. There's no way Zara won't cum, which means she's losing her job in about ten minutes, and I'm moving to the Den to spend the rest of my days buried deep inside her. Yeah, I can live with this punishment.

I whimper as Thane brings the vibrator closer to Zara's exposed pussy, making him chuckle.

"You should've thought about the shit you do, before listening to Leon and running from Rhen," he says with so much anger dripping in his words. I realize now how stupid it was to encourage her run in a workplace full of ravenous Alphas.

I get it; I deserve this, but can't he just paint our asses black and blue and let us be? Surely we would learn from a punishment like that. Well, I wouldn't, but I bet Zara would.

I gulp as Zara's sharp intake of breath echoes off the walls. Thane presses the vibrator to her clit while rounding her entrance with a finger. My eyes focus on his hand, and I gulp again.

Zara's body shakes as he slowly pushes his finger inside her. The bare minimum, the very tip of it, before he slowly withdraws. Thane's playing with her senses, and speaking from experience, I know he's doing it on purpose—making someone cum by doing multiple things at the same time, even at such a slow pace, is easier than pounding someone into another galaxy.

I hold my breath as her aroused scent hits my nose, ten times more potent than her normal scent, and it was torturously strong before. I can't keep inhaling it because it's just another form of fucking torture, my body acting on instinct whenever I get a whiff of Omega arousal.

My mate is a tyrant, a heartless man who loves to watch me

suffer. Yet I know he must be struggling himself with how potent her arousal is.

A growl escapes my lips, and I close my eyes, unable to watch more, but Thane has another thing coming for me.

Zara has been quiet the whole time, but as the sound of vibration fades, it's replaced by her loud, violent moans.

He broke her; Thane actually broke her.

Bracing myself for whatever Thane has planned next, I force my eyes open and gasp at the view. If my cock was killing me before, now it's leading me straight to the grave. No, fuck it, it's digging the grave for me.

Thane's on his knees, his face buried between Zara's legs, and he's making the most shameless, loudest, and most fucking alluring sounds as he sucks and licks on Zara's heated flesh.

She's thrashing under him. Thane shoves his hands under her ass and grabs her, holding her to his mouth. He's eating her out like a starving animal, and I want to kiss his swollen lips for just a taste of her.

"Thane..." I can't stop the moan that escapes me, and my balls tighten at how desperate I sound.

He ignores me and dives deeper; judging by the sounds, he's thrusting his tongue inside Zara. Fuck, I want that too.

"I learned my lesson, I swear. No more games. Thane? Please! I learned my goddamn lesson," I whine as my voice breaks. My throat is dry, my heart is pounding violently, and the pain keeps coursing through my body. Worse, with each sound that leaves his lips, the cage digs in more.

Zara tries to get out of the cuffs; I see her muscles tense. She is so close to coming all over my mate's face. I'm surprised she was able to hold out this long.

Her moans and screams are burned in my memory as they become higher pitched. Fuck, she's so close. I want to shoot my load when she comes, but I can't because someone decided the best punishment for me would be orgasm denial with a damn show!

I brace myself for the moment this will end. Zara's juices cover Thane's face, and I can almost imagine the smug smile he'll have on his lips when he tells Zara she just lost her job.

However, literally seconds before she reaches climax, Thane pulls his face away from her dripping pussy and growls.

He gets back to his feet, wipes his lips using the bedsheet, and tosses it aside. My mate looks over his shoulder at me and gives me his most stern look. "If this doesn't teach you a lesson, just remember I won't go as easy on you next time."

And with that, Thane storms out of the room.

He leaves Zara and me behind, both of us still cuffed and begging for the release he denied us. I think this is the second stage of his punishment. And it is so fucking brutal! I can't tear my gaze from her. I groan, wondering how long he will leave us like this. Zara squirms but is unable to move much with how her knees are bent, hands locked to her ankles. If only she could close her damn legs, so I don't have to stare at her puffy, wet, pink lips.

I turn my attention to the door when I hear Thane telling Rhen and Raidon they aren't to touch us or remove our restraints.

"He can't leave us like this, right?" Zara asks, and I stare over at her, her chest is rising and falling harshly. At first, it takes a second to register her flushed face and heated skin; why Zara is suddenly panting and wriggling in discomfort.

"Fuck!" I curse, my dick hardening even more as I feel my knot stretch inside the cage. I am going to die. This is how I lose my cock, because I just realized that Thane has sent her into fucking heat!

~H arlow~

This is torture. Minutes tick by, then an hour. My hips hurt from the awkward position I find myself in. My shoulders and wrists ache, and it is getting swelteringly hot in here. I shift uncomfortably, and Leon groans.

"Zara, please, don't move. You're making it worse," he groans lewdly before releasing a savage growl.

"Can't you mind-link him?" Fuck, I would beg, plead, and kiss his fucking feet if he would just undo the restraints. I'm feeling claustrophobic, and panic is beginning to make my heart race.

"He is blocking the mind-link, and I think they left the house," Leon moans as I writhe, trying to turn slightly so I don't have to crane my neck to look over at him. He sighs when I manage to shift enough that he isn't given such an ungodly view of me.

"Did he turn the A/C off?" I ask breathlessly, sweat beading on my skin. I peer over at Leon when he doesn't answer. When I do, I find his eyes blood red, his fangs protruding, and he is breathing harshly.

"Your scent," he groans, and his face twists with savage hunger.

Heat pools low in my belly, spreading throughout my limbs, and slick saturates the bedding beneath me. I gasp.

"No, I just finished my heat!" I gasp in horror.

"You live in a house full of Alphas. Expect regular heats," Leon hisses, and my eyes go to the cage surrounding his manhood. My eyes bulge, and I feel lightheaded looking at it. Man, that's gotta hurt. The skin is so red it looks on the verge of bursting as it's strangled.

"Leon?" I murmur when he roars, kicking his leg out. To my horror, the chair leg snaps, and I could have sworn I hear his bones crack.

"I can't. I can't, Zara. Fuck, what was he thinking?"

"Can't what?" I ask in horror as the other cuff snaps at his thrashing.

"I will hurt you if I don't get out of here," Leon growls, the whites of his eyes turning red with his need to feed on me.

"What?"

"You smell so good!" He moans loudly, thrashing in his restraints. I watch his shoulder dislocate, and he snarls viciously when the cuffs still don't give. Fuck, the more he struggles to get free, the more my pheromones pollute the air.

His Alpha aura and pheromones drive me wild. Fear licks through my veins as he becomes enraged with his need to be free, but nothing he does is enough to break the restraints. I pray they don't give because if he gets out, with his bloodlust as it is, I am as good as dead.

"Try Raidon or Rhen," I plead with him as slick spills from me. I shut my eyes, trying to ignore the flaring heat that burns through me. My stomach cramps, pain tears through me, and all I want is to roll into the fetal position to ease it, but I can't move. As time slips by and darkness floods the room, I became lost to the heat, just as Leon becomes lost to his bloodlust.

~THANE~

"Something isn't right," I mutter, feeling Leon's discomfort. We've only been gone an hour, and he's never usually this distressed. I wouldn't normally leave him like that, but I figured they would be fine, if a bit uncomfortable, in each other's company.

We were not going to be gone long. We were called back to work after a fire alarm went off. A small fire was started in the loading docks, and we have to assess the damage.

"Fuck, I knew I should have left one of you there with them," I curse, spinning the car around. Luckily, we are only ten minutes away from the house, since Raidon had to stop by the post office.

"He'll be fine; slow down. The corners are making me feel sick," Raidon mumbles.

I'm going the speed limit, so his comments aren't warranted. I have this nagging suspicion something is wrong. I am accustomed to Leon's discomfort, but he has gone from uncomfortable to utter distress.

I'm cursing that I haven't marked Zara and made her pack yet, because then I would be able to feel her too and be able to better gauge the situation.

Driving back, we stop at the electronic gate. Rhen shifts uncomfortably, and I glance at him.

"No, something is wrong," Rhen confirms, and I peer at Raidon in the mirror, who is extremely pale.

No wonder he had been so grouchy in the car. He's mistaking Leon's discomfort for feeling sick.

"Raidon?" I ask him.

"Get to Leon," he rasps.

The gates finally open, and I drive straight into the garage, throwing the door open. I freeze the moment I step into the house, floored with the scent of her heat.

"Fuck," I curse, my eyes moving to the stairs.

"Why is she in heat so soon?" Rhen gasps, and my eyes widen, knowing Leon is wearing a cage.

"Why do you think? An Omega in a house with not just one fucking Alpha but four," Raidon snarls, taking the steps two at a time, racing to get to them. "Thane fooling around with her must have brought it on," Raidon growls. Rhen and I follow after him and he bursts through the door before I hear him gasp.

He moves quickly toward Leon, dropping to his knees in front him, working to release the cage that is strangling his cock. Leon thrashes, and I can see the blood pooling in his lap. Raidon is quick to remove the cage, while Rhen removes the cuffs. The moment he's free, Leon lunges at Raidon, sinking his teeth into his neck like a savage.

Rhen has to wrestle Leon off of Raidon. I stand there, stunned at the scene before me. Rhen's able to pull Leon off of Raidon, who then drags Leon out of the room before he can get to Zara.

"Deal with Zara while I help Raidon," Rhen growls, slamming into my shoulder as he moves to pass me, but I grip his arm to stop him.

"I'll help with Leon. I am of no use to Zara, Rhen. Not while she's like that," I snap at him, but he isn't hearing it.

"I'm not coming back in here until you mark her. If you had already, this never would have happened," Rhen says, glancing over his shoulder at her. Banging from downstairs has Rhen rushing out to help Raidon with our blood-crazed mate. I gulp, turning to see Zara writhing on the bed.

She is out of her mind in heat, unaware of her surroundings as the haze envelopes her. I crawl onto the bed, quickly removing the cuffs before pulling her into my arms and cradling her, but she isn't having it. She attacks me as soon as my skin touches hers, and my scent smothers her.

Turning in my arms, her claws slip from her fingers, slicing my shirt to tatters as she fights to reach my skin. Anything to ease her agony.

I wrap my arms around her waist. Her demonic, lust-crazed eyes glare back at me. Her pupils blow apart and retract with each wave of heat that rattles through her. Her legs wrap around my waist as I move to lean against the headboard, hoping Rhen or Raidon will come up soon to ease her pain.

My Calling slips out, and she moans, licking and nipping the skin at my neck while her hands paw at my pants to free my cock. "Zara, wait," I tell her, knowing I can't knot her, can't give her what she needs.

CHAPTER
SIXTY-ONE

~T hane~

My words fall on deaf ears, and I sigh, allowing her to do as she pleases until they return. Yet, the moment she frees me from my pants, she lifts her hips and slams down on me. I gasp, feeling my cock glide through her soaking wet folds and into her hot pussy. Her walls clamp tight around me, and she moans while I grip her hips.

I can't even remember the last time I fucked a woman. I know it was sometime before Harlow ruined us. Women are useless to me, and I prefer to watch anyways.

My head falls back against the headboard as she rocks her hips. Her lips return to my neck as she sucks and licks my skin, and I tangle my hand in her hair, bringing her lips to mine.

I plunge my tongue into her mouth, and she whines into mine, her tight walls squeezing my cock, making my need to pound into her tight pussy so much harder to resist.

My fingers grip her hair, and I tug her head back. My lips attack her neck and move to her chest. I run my tongue around her hardened nipple before sucking on it. Her breathing grows harsher, and she whines, not being able to move the way she wants with me holding her in place.

'Rhen?' I almost plead through the mind-link.

'Bloody busy right now,' he snarls, and I growl before gripping her hips and lifting her off me. I can't risk knotting her, not when it will most likely kill her. She snarls at me when I slam her down on her back, before flipping her onto her stomach.

My fingers dig into her hips as I pull her ass into the air before positioning myself between her legs. I shove inside her, feeling her stretch around my cock. She moans loudly, dropping her torso onto the bed. I withdraw slowly, watching my cock slide out of her before sinking deep inside her. Fuck, she feels good. So warm, so wet.

I slowly fuck her, waiting for one of them to get up here and take my place. I try to keep my head and not give in to instinct, which she is making difficult by continuing to push back against me. Her ass jiggles every time I thrust into her, spearing her with my cock.

Zara tugs at my thigh, silently begging me to fuck her harder, and I grit my teeth, knowing it isn't a good idea.

"Please," she whines, her walls slick and clenching tighter around me. I give in, slamming into her, wary of keeping my growing knot from breaching her entrance. Yet, as she climbs higher and higher, I begin to lose myself in the feel of her tight pussy gripping my cock. I feel my knot press against her, and she pushes back against it.

Her hot cunt stretches, wanting to take my knot, but I hold her hips tighter, making sure I don't hurt her. I feel her walls flutter, the rush of her heat making my thighs wet with her slick just as I feel my balls tighten. I know I'm close when suddenly she comes apart. I move to pull out of her and blow my load on her ass, but she rocks back and moans loudly. I spill myself inside her, and my blood runs cold, feeling my knot lock inside her.

"No!" I gasp.

I grip her hips, my claws slicing into her skin, and she moans loudly, rocking back against me as her heat abates. My eyes are locked onto her ass, which is flush against my pelvis, my knot locked tight inside her when she slumps forward in a haze, forcing me to follow her as she passes out.

The moment she does, my heart nearly stops, and the horror of what I've done crashes into me with the force of a truck.

"Zara?" I murmur, rolling and pulling her onto my lap. Her head rolls back onto my shoulder, and her eyes roll into the back of her head. I killed her.

I killed her!

"Rhen! Raidon!" I scream in a panic as I tap her face. "No, Zara. Zara!" I yell at her as I hear their pounding footsteps running up the stairs to get to us. I grip her face, turning it toward mine. Her eyes are still closed. I can feel warmth coating my thighs, but from our position, I can't tell if it's slick or her blood. My heart races in my chest when she doesn't respond.

The door bangs against the wall. Raidon and Rhen stop in their tracks, and their eyes meet mine.

"What have you done?" Rhen gasps.

"She moved as I went to pull out," I panic as Raidon climbs onto the bed. He grips her face, trying to pry her eyes open. Rhen stares at us in horror. I shake her arms while Raidon pulls her eyelids open again. My panic consumes all of us when she whimpers.

"Let me sleep," she whines.

Raidon's eyes go to mine before glancing between our legs, where I knotted her.

"She took your knot," Rhen murmurs, his lips parting in shock.

"How?" Raidon chokes, glancing back at Rhen as a sleepy Zara slaps his hand away.

I'm just relieved she is okay. I exhale, my heart rate slowing, and I can finally hear hers over mine, can finally see through my panic that her chest is slowly rising and falling. She wriggles, and I grip her hips, knowing if she tries to climb off me, my knot may still rip her apart.

"That's not possible," Rhen says as I tug the blanket over us. Zara falls back to sleep and snuggles against my chest, inhaling my scent as she awkwardly cranes her neck to bury her face into my neck.

"I don't understand how this is possible. Unless she was already serumed by another Alpha? She shouldn't be able to take you," Raidon says, looking just as confused as us.

"Her landlord said she was running from someone when she found her."

"Yeah, but who? We can't claim her if she's serumed to another Alpha, Thane," Rhen argues as I peer down at her. "We need to find out who she belongs to."

"No! I am not handing her back to whoever she was running from. She wouldn't run for no reason," Raidon growls, glaring at Rhen.

"If she is running from someone, the moment your mother uploads her DNA in the database, we'll know who it is," I tell him. "If she has serum in her system, it means she is registered."

"But to who?" Rhen asks.

I shrug, but something nags at me.

"Then what? We just hand her over?" Raidon asked incredulously. He's right. If she is running, she must have had a good reason. I brush her hair from her face.

"Fuck, when her blood comes back, her pack will be alerted. They will come for her," Rhen says, sitting on the edge of the bed and dropping his head in his hands. Sadness at the thought of losing her bleeds through the bond. Guilt floods me, knowing I got their hopes up for a chance for another Omega only to lose her too.

"We won't lose her," I whisper before sinking my teeth into her neck. My teeth slide through her skin and muscle, and she wriggles, but I hold her in place. My pack has lost enough. We aren't losing her too. I will pay the price for marking an Omega that isn't ours. Because they can't take her now that she is marked.

No one will.

CHAPTER
SIXTY-TWO

~H~ arlow~
Limbs wrap around limbs. It's hard to determine where one body starts and another ends. I'm tangled amongst the sheets and surrounded by potent Alpha scents. Every part of their skin that brushes mine is tingling and itching, as if their touch is trying to delve through the layers of my skin and override all rational sense.

I say rational sense, because suffocating under their potency seems to be something I am struggling with as I try to replay the events that have me waking up in bed with the four Alphas. The soft, steady heartbeat beneath my ear tells me I am laying on someone. That someone is Thane, his masculine scent invading my senses and making my mouth water.

Turning my head, I find Rhen beside us, his face so close. His lips mere inches from mine, where his head rests on Thane's shoulder. I sit up and straddle Thane's waist; the heavy arm draped across my lower back slides off. Peering over, I find Raidon. He rolls onto his back, and I spot Leon beside him.

Blinking, I yawn and stretch my arms above my head. I notice I'm naked, and Thane is naked underneath me. Rhen moves as I do, and I feel hands move along my thighs. I notice the stinging on the skin of my neck. Thane squeezes my thighs while my fingertips trace the mark, which prickles and sends a shiver up my spine as I touch it.

"Don't freak out, Zara," Thane murmurs, his eyes half hooded from sleep as he peeks up at me.

Don't freak out? How could he say that?

"You're ours now. That isn't something to fear," he mumbles as his hands move higher, tracing over my waist and ribs, to the sides of my breasts, his touch calming the frantic beat of my heart, but it does nothing to alleviate the panic in my mind. Every possible scenario, crisis, and disaster flits through my head, knowing the trouble I am in. I can never run now, never leave, because Thane will eventually track me down, no matter where I go. His mark on my neck will ensure that.

Trapped.

I feel trapped, and terror washes over me in waves as I become obsessed with the thoughts rattling around in my head, banging loudly and screaming at me about the danger I am in now.

Only, those thoughts are dismissed when I feel teeth sink into my neck, next to Thane's mark. The sharp sting jolts me out of my tumultuous thoughts and shoves me with blinding speed back to the present. I feel the warmth of Raidon press against my back, his teeth embedded deeply in my neck, marking me and tying me to him just as strongly.

Movement beside me catches my attention as Raidon pulls his teeth from my skin, and I watch Rhen lean in. Thane's fingers tangle in his hair as he dips his head between my thighs. His breath sweeps over my skin before his tongue rolls over the inside of my thigh. Pain slices through my skin as his canines mark my flesh.

A loud moan leaves my lips as heat and sparks rush to the apex of my thighs, making my skin vibrate as he marks me so close to my core. My head rolls back onto Raidon's shoulder, where he kneels behind me. He pulls my head back, and his lips brushed mine, before Leon's scent overwhelms me.

"You're mine now, Omega," he purrs as his lips trace a line down the other side of my throat, which remains bare. I expect him to mark me there, but his lips travel down to my chest before he sinks his teeth into the side of my breast, making me hiss. The sensitive skin there stings the most, and tears prick my eyes when he marks me.

Great, well, there goes wearing a damn bra until that heals. Rhen pulls his teeth from my inner thigh, and Leon pulls his from my breast before his tongue traces the blood trail that cascades down my ribs to my hip. I feel light-headed, yet something writhes and coils within me as their bonds slowly sink deep within my veins, embedding and tainting my soul with theirs.

I always thought it odd how Alpha Packs worked.

All of them have bitten me at some point, especially Leon. He sinks his teeth into me every chance he gets. However, not once did Rhen's or Raidon's bite marks remain, healing quickly afterward. But since Thane marked me, my skin remains raised and tender, scarring as each marking heals excruciatingly slowly.

Their marks will remain because their Alpha claimed me, which is one thing I always found fascinating. It shows the strength of a bonded pack Alpha, how his influence over his mates overrides everything, including mate bonds. A sort of power and control I could never fathom being responsible for.

Glancing at Thane, his eyes scan my flesh, admiring his mates' marks tainting my skin. His eyes flicker, and his lips tug at the corners to almost a smile.

"Welcome to the pack," Thane purrs, sitting up with me still in his lap, his arm wrapped around my waist. He pulls me closer, his lips demanding as he kisses me. His tongue traces across the seam of my lips before forcing its way into my mouth.

I sigh as the bond washes over me, giving in to him. Lips press to my shoulder, and hands grip my hips, making my eyes open. I pull away with a startled gasp as they touch me.

This is too much, too much all at once. I'm still trying to wrap my head around being marked, let alone jumping right into a fuck fest, which I can feel is their intention through the bond.

"Can I have a minute?" I ask, pulling away. It's overwhelming feeling them so clearly. I am struggling to differentiate between my feelings and theirs.

Thane growls, tapping my thigh, and everyone moves back from me.

"We won't hurt you, Zara," Thane says, and I blink at him.

This is a sham. Everything is a lie, and mate bonds shouldn't be based on a lie. I want to tell them. I open my mouth to tell them, but then the fear of Thane's deep-rooted anger resurfaces, and I close my mouth.

They will find out, and when they do, I fear their reaction. Thane's, I know, will not be pleasant.

"I need to shower," I whisper, climbing off him and over Leon. As I enter Thane's bathroom, I feel their curious gazes on my back. I shut the door before gripping the sink. What the hell have I done?

More importantly, what happens when they find out? Thane made his intentions for Harlow very clear, if they ever find her. Newsflash. They found her, and it is only a matter of time before they realize that.

Will they go ahead with their original plan to breed me and then kill me? Is that still an option now that they know me, or sort of know me? I cannot imagine hurting them, but would Thane still want the vengeance that blackens his heart when he learns the woman he is chasing is right under his nose and has been living in his house all this time?

A knock sounds at the door, and I jump, turning my gaze away from my reflection.

"Zara?" Rhen calls out.

"Yep."

"I thought you were showering?" he asks. The curiosity lacing his voice is apparent, and I quickly rush to turn the shower on before hearing him move away from the door. I let out a breath. Stepping into the shower, I linger far longer than necessary as I contemplate what will happen next and how things will play out.

SIXTY-THREE

~H arlow~

The next few days go by without a complaint. Everyone seems settled with the idea of Thane accepting me; well, everyone except me. No, worry gnaws at me every day. I wait for that dreaded email to come through, saying there are no records under the fake name I gave. Thankfully, Raidon's parent have been called away since his grandfather fell ill unexpectedly, and they haven't had a chance send the results of my blood test.

Raidon is beside himself with worry and has daily phone calls with his parents. It is strange seeing how close all of their families are.

Except for Thane.

Like me, he is on the outside looking in, though it's clear he adores his in-laws, including Leila, who is constantly harassing him about nieces and nephews. She isn't shy about her demands, even with me sitting right across from her as we all eat lunch in the conference room.

"Have you set up a nursery? What about a color scheme? I can help," Leila asks.

Thane sighs, setting his fork down and stretching his arms above his head before draping his arm across the back of Leon's chair.

"Leila, just stop. You know, we still have the old nursery that we set up for Harlow. Give Zara a chance to settle in before we start talking about babies."

I choke on my food hearing that, accidentally inhaling it as I gasp. Death by fried rice. I retch and heave, trying to suck in air when Rhen pats my back, and Raidon rushes over to me with a glass of water.

"You alright?" He worries as I gulp down the water. I nod my head before swallowing the food that just tried to kill me.

"Yep, went down the wrong pipe," I rasp out, and he lets out a breath, going back to his seat.

"Have you showed Zara? What did she think of it?" Leila continues talking about me as if I'm not here.

I shrink in my chair, glancing around to see Thane watching me.

"She'll see it when she's ready," Thane tells her.

When she begins to shoot out more questions, Leon growls, his hand smacking the table and causing Leila to jump.

"Leila, stop. Can't you see how uncomfortable you're making her?" Leon snaps. I am thankful he put a stop to her never-ending questions, only to be made more uncomfortable when their watchful gazes all suddenly snap to me.

Leila blushes, fixing her white blazer and doing up the button. "I should get back to work. Make sure you call me when you know how your grandfather is doing, Ray," she says, getting to her feet and gripping Raidon's shoulder as she passes. Her fingers give him a squeeze. My eyes lock on where her fingers touch him, and before I can stop myself, a feral snarl slips past my lips. Rhen drops his arm across my shoulders, tugging me to him.

I know it is irrational—she's their family—but she touched what's mine. I shake my head at my claim. When did I start seeing them as mine? The possessiveness I feel at her small gesture sends my blood boiling.

"Settle. Friend, not foe," Rhen whispers, kissing the side of my face, but I still want to tear her fingers off him and rip her damn hair out.

Leila looks at her hand and jerks it away, her eyes going wide and her lips parting. "Sorry, Zara—" she doesn't finish what she about to say and instead rushes out.

Thane quirks an eyebrow at me, smirking when my face flushes with heat at what I did.

"The bond is fresh still. It takes some getting used to," Thane murmurs. Raidon pushes his seat out before rising and walking over to me with a smug smile on his lips.

"My little Omega is getting her panties in a knot over me," he purrs, burying his face in my neck. I instantly relax in his embrace, his Calling slipping out and his hands wandering lower as he kisses up my jaw. I tilt my head, offering him more of my neck when Rhen clears his throat beside us.

"Raidon, we are at work. Can't it wait? We have deliveries coming," Rhen reminds him.

"Still plenty of time," Raidon retorts, pulling me up from my seat. I squeak when he shoves me against the table, and I hear movement behind me as someone clears the table just before Raidon all but tosses me on it.

"Raidon!" Rhen breathes out like a curse. Yet his hands are already reaching for my skirt, hoisting it up my hips.

"Don't snap at me, Rhen. You had her bent over a desk. Quit whining, or I won't share," Raidon growls at him as he rips my panties down. The lace gets caught in my heels.

I hear the heavy oak table groan under Leon's weight before his lips crash down on mine. His tongue invades my mouth hungrily, tasting every inch, while Raidon spreads my legs wide, pushing them up along my ribs. I tear my lips away from Leon, knowing the unsightly view Raidon has of me, before shoving my skirt down.

"Raidon, not here," I gasp. A quick fuck in one of their offices is one thing, but I know there are cameras in the conference room. My eyes dart to the one in the corner.

"Only we have access to these cameras," Rhen says, standing up.

"Hold her legs for me," Raidon purrs while gripping my hips and dragging me to the edge. Rhen grips my knee, and Leon slides off the table to grab the other. I cover my face from the view of all three of them staring between my legs as they spread me wide for him.

I feel his fingers brush over my lower lips, rubbing and smacking my pussy softly. "So pretty, so tight," Raidon purrs, sliding a finger inside me and corkscrewing it out. I moan, my walls squeezing around his index finger as he draws it in and out.

He plays with me. Teases me. My hands fall from my face to see Rhen and Leon's hot gazes watching as he fucks me with his fingers. His thumb brushes my clit. Endless moans spill from my lips as Raidon drops to his knees, his hot mouth covering me entirely while his tongue swirls and sucks on my clit. He slides his fingers from me. I am a lost mess of whines and moans, when I felt him press a finger against my back passage.

His tongue sucks harder as I feel it breach and force its way inside me. I buck at the odd sensation when lips suddenly crash down to swallow the noises coming from my mouth. Weight bears down on my left knee, opening me wider to Raidon's ravenous mouth and telling me the lips belong to Rhen.

His tongue tangles with mine, owning and claiming every part of my mouth, while Raidon adds another finger to my ass. I squirm, yet the feel of his tongue flicking and laving over my clit forces me to relax under the discomfort. I rock my hips as best I can with the way I'm held down, and Rhen breaks the kiss, leaving me panting. Rhen's fingers pull on my inner thigh, and Raidon lifts his head to watch as his fingers slip in and out.

Leon reaches over, prying my pussy lips apart before watching Rhen work his fingers deep inside my pussy. Leon groans, watching as both our mates play with me, when the ding of the elevator loudly rings out. I hear Thane's chair screech along the floor, and I jump in panic at the thought of being caught in such a precarious position.

Raidon's lips crash against mine as I try to sit up, the force sending me back against the table.

"Let Thane deal with it," he mumbles against my lips. His phone starts ringing in his pocket, just as Thane returns with a letter, which tells me the visitor was the lobby receptionist, dropping off the mail. As soon as Raidon's phone stops ringing, Leon's starts.

"It's your mother," he says, patting Raidon's shoulder. He sighs before releasing me to take the call.

"It might be about my grandfather. I'll be back in a minute," he says, taking his phone and walking off. I hastily pull my skirt down and climb off the table while I have the chance, turning to find Thane sitting back at the table, opening the letter he received.

Rhen walks around to see what Thane is looking at, while Leon takes advantage of having me all to himself, wrapping his arms around my waist while I frantically look for my panties.

"You might have to recheck the details," I hear Rhen murmur, just as I spot my underwear beneath the table. I scramble to retrieve them, pulling them on, only to look up to find Thane watching me.

"Everything alright?" I ask him. He opens his mouth to say something, but Raidon walks in, tossing his hands up when he notices I am no longer spread on the table.

"Really? I am gone for two minutes, and not one of you could keep her on the table," he growls.

"What was the call about?" Thane asks him, as he makes his way over to me.

"Mom is on her way to our house," he replies.

"Okay, well, I need to head home anyway and take care of this," Thane says, waving the envelope in his hand.

Thane gets up, and I quickly follow, knowing that means all of us are going home, though I'm nervous to be meeting Raidon's mother. Grabbing my bag, I retrieve my charger from the top drawer of my desk and spot the diary I stashed there. I haven't had a chance to shred it yet. Staring at it, I go to grab it when the elevator dings loudly.

"Zara," Rhen calls out to me. I quickly grab my charger, leaving the diary to deal with tomorrow. We drive home in silence. I can see something is bothering Thane—feel it through the bond we share.

"Zara?" Thane asks, reaching over to the glove compartment from the driver's side. He shuts it and passes me a document from inside. I take it, and my brows furrow as I look at the paper. "The details on that form, are they correct?" he asks. I notice it is a birth and death registry form. I glance over the form, chewing the inside of my cheek.

"Um, yep, looks correct," I state while my heart sputters frantically in my chest.

"They couldn't find your records," he says, pulling in through the electric gates.

"Might have to resend it," I tell him. His eyes dart to mine in the mirror before flicking away. He says nothing else, but the silence in the car tells me he doesn't believe a word I said. Or maybe I am reading too much into it.

CHAPTER
SIXTY-FOUR

~H~ arlow~

Once home, we all climb out of the car and head inside. Thane heads straight to his office upstairs. Raidon and Leon go to the kitchen, while Rhen stares at me as I slip my heels off just inside the door.

"Maybe go take a nap. I will wake you when Raidon's mother gets here." His words confuse me. It's almost as if he is trying to get rid of me.

"Is something wrong?" I ask, knowing that something definitely is.

"Thane is in an odd mood. Just let me speak with him—find out what is going on," he tells me.

That is a very vague answer, I think, but I decide not to argue. I head for the stairs. We've all been sleeping in Thane's room, so I intend to go there when he speaks up again.

"Maybe the Den. I need you to steer clear of Thane for a bit. Okay?"

"Why?" I ask.

"Because Thane detests liars, and he believes you are hiding something from him." I open my mouth to say something, but Rhen doesn't give me a chance.

"I'll handle it; it will be fine. Just go," he tells me, and I nod, moving up the corridor along the stairs. I feel like I am being put in the naughty corner, grounded like a child. As I pass the kitchen, Raidon and Leon wave at me as I reach for the basement door.

"Where are you going?" Raidon asks, grabbing a drink from the fridge.

"Rhen wants me in the Den," I tell him. I have a sinking feeling settling over me. There were two documents in that envelope, and Thane only handed me one.

Raidon and Leon look at each other, confused.

"We'll be down in a minute," Leon says, glancing toward the stairs. "I'll go find out what is going on first," he says, walking off.

With a nod, I head downstairs, yet I have a strange feeling I shouldn't go down here with each step I take. That fight-or-flight instinct kicks in, telling me something is seriously wrong.

Sitting in the Den, I snuggle beneath the blankets. After half an hour down here alone, I am struggling to contain my panic. My mind is going over all the scenarios of what may have angered Thane, while I sit replaying the day's events over and over, picking apart whether I might have done something wrong.

Eventually, sleep takes me, and I drift off, only to be woken by the sounds of a woman yelling. Opening my eyes, I blink up at the ceiling. The woman's voice grows louder, before it stops at the top of the stairs, making me sit up.

"Mom, calm down. What are you talking about?" Raidon yells, and I hear frantic footsteps.

"Where is the little harlot?" the woman snarls. At her words, my body instantly goes from groggy to alert.

"Elaine, enough! Stop and explain. What is going on?" I hear Thane bellow, his aura so deadly, I can feel it from all the way down here. Elaine's anger, however, is unwavering.

"Check for yourself. Her blood results came back. I want blood, Thane. I don't give a fuck if you marked her. She deserves death after what she did," the woman snarls.

My blood runs cold. I hear Raidon attempting to calm his mother, her voice growing more distant, and I eventually hear a car leave before hearing a thud that sounds like someone's fist hitting drywall.

"Thane?" Rhen asks.

I jump to my feet, looking for an escape, when I hear the door handle creak. I rush to the small storage area in the far corner. There is a small window I know I could squeeze out of if I can just reach it. It leads to the back lawn and gardens.

"Thane, what are you doing?" Rhen's panicked voice reaches my ears when the door bangs loudly against the wall.

His footsteps echo loudly on each step, and I know escape is useless, so I turn to face him head-on, hoping for the chance to explain. Moving out of my hiding spot, I cringe at his aura as he reaches the last step, his head turning from side to side, paperwork fisted in his hand.

"I can explain, if you would just—"

His head snaps in my direction as I step closer to him, touching his arm, which is a mistake. The back of his hand connects with my face, cutting off the rest of my sentence.

The sting of it burns my flesh, but before he can land another blow, Rhen tackles Thane. Leon quickly follows down the stairs. Thane and Rhen wrestle, and they fall into the pit. Leon reaches for me as Rhen is suddenly kicked and sent flying into the pit wall. Thane rises to his feet before tossing the paperwork at him, just as Raidon comes down the steps.

I glance at him, but his mood is just as wild as Thane's anger. Leon brushes my quickly bruising cheek with his hand while Thane climbs out of the pit. When he does, Leon puts himself in front of me. Rhen opens the document Thane tossed at him. He gasps, and I peer around Leon at Rhen, whose eyes dart between Thane and me.

"Can someone please tell me what is going on?" Leon asks, his hand on my hip, shoving me further behind him. Thane snarls, baring his canines at me, which have slipped free in his anger.

"Her name isn't Zara," Rhen says from inside the pit, where he is still looking over the documents.

"Okay, okay, she lied about her name. No big deal. That doesn't warrant violence or hitting her Thane!" Leon spits at him.

Thane's eyes go to mine as they fill with tears, his disappointment and rage bleeding through the bond loud and clear.

"Are you going to tell him, or do you want me to?" Thane growls, taking a step toward me. Leon side steps, blocking him.

"She is Harlow, Leon," Raidon speaks from the stairs, and Leon turns so quickly I almost miss the movement. He takes a step back from me as his shock comes through the bond.

His mouth opens and closes as he looks at me.

"Get her out of my house. Now! Before I fucking kill her," Thane growls.

"Wait, let me explain. I didn't kill your—" I stop when he shifts abruptly, his skin tearing as he lunges at me in his wolf form.

I stumble backward, falling on my ass as I scramble back on my hands and feet. He snaps his jaws at me, his claws making a terrible noise, like nails on a chalkboard, as they slice the ground. My back hits the wall, and I suck in a breath, his teeth inches from my face when I feel the mind-link open.

'You have one minute to get out of my fucking house before I kill you,' he snarls in my head while his powerful jaws snap at my face.

I nod my head, quickly glancing at the others who have fallen silent. Not one of them is going to let me explain. Thane steps back, his huge paws on the ground twice the size of my hands. Long claws, sharp as blades, flex on the ground, and I waste no time getting to my feet.

It's like the worst kind of walk-of-shame as I move past them, each averting their gaze while I make my way toward the stairs. As soon as I get to the first step, I take off running, like a dog with its tail tucked between its legs. My bare feet slap the ground, and I race for the front door. My hands grip the handle, and I toss it open, escaping into the dark of night.

SIXTY-FIVE

~R**hen~**

Thane storms off. I'm shocked that I didn't see it before. It makes so much sense now. Of course she wouldn't tell us who she was running from: it's us. All she heard from the moment we met is how much we hate her, how much she would suffer when we found her. All the secrets she kept are suddenly so clear. Everything is falling into place. I am stunned, and Thane is murderous. Climbing the stairs, I follow him upstairs.

It also explains Alpha Jake's bizarre reaction to her. Harlow was originally his. He bought her first.

"Thane," I call out behind him.

"She lied," is all he says before slamming the bedroom door in my face when I finally catch up to him.

"Thane, we can't just leave her to fend for herself! She's our mate!" I yell at him through the door. I hear him growl before the door is ripped open, and I am face to face with a snarling Thane.

"Then choose—her or me. I hate liars, you know that. And this! This isn't just some small fib; she killed my mother!" he roars.

I know better than to defend her. It will only make him think I'm taking sides and make things that much worse for her, yet I can't help it. Not while feeling what she feels.

All I know is what she feels at this moment goes beyond any pain I have ever felt. Is it despair? Sadness? Dread? Maybe all of those things, but it has my heart sinking into my stomach.

"Don't, Rhen! You defend her, then you've already chosen," Thane says. We stand off for a second before he finally speaks.

"You know where the door is. You want her, then go get her. But don't you dare come back here if you walk out that door," he snarls. He turns on his heel and slams the door in my face, just as Raidon and Leon come up the stairs and step into the hall. I glance back at them. Raidon says nothing while Leon looks between us both.

"You're kidding, right? He says he wants her gone, and that's it?" Leon asks.

I don't know how to respond. There is no way I can decide between them. I love Thane, but I also love Harlow.

Harlow.

It is so strange to think of her by that name, yet it fits. It's who she is.

Leon curses before leaving us standing in the hall. When I hear him take his keys from the hallstand, I wander toward the stairwell to see him open the door to the garage.

"Fuck!" I curse, chasing after him. I expect Raidon to follow, but as I looked up, he remains on the stairs, an indecipherable expression on his face.

"Go. I can't be near her right now. Just go, Rhen," he says, turning his back on me and walking off. Moments later, I hear his bedroom door shut, just as Leon starts up his car, making me snatch my jacket off the coat hook and rush out the door after him. Climbing into the passenger side, Leon opens the garage door before reversing out, scraping the side of Thane's car as he goes. I roll my eyes. As if we don't have enough problems.

Leon, unbothered by the damage he caused, spins the car around, racing toward the gates. When we reach them, we find her trying to find a way out. She turns, jumping to the side when the car lights reach her. Leon hits the buzzer, and the gates swing open. He slows down as we pull up to her and presses the button for the windows.

"Get in," I tell her. She glances at the back windows nervously, as if looking for Thane, before looking back up toward the house. "Get in the car, Harlow," I tell her.

"Why? Are you going to—" she doesn't finish, but we all know what she was going to say. Now that we know who she is, she doesn't trust us not to hurt her. She knows what Thane planned to do to her when we found her. Breed her, then kill her. Leon leans across me, peering out at her.

"We won't hurt you. And I won't let Thane hurt you," he tells her.

Harlow chews her lip, nervously glancing around as if calculating her chances of getting away if she runs.

Hesitantly, she steps toward the car and opens the back door before sliding into the seat. Leon fiddles with the heater, turning it on, while I lean forward to take off my jacket and give it to her. Her hands shake as she reaches for it, her eyes watching me as if I'm a snake that's about to strike. She pulls her arms inside it and clips her seatbelt. Leon drives into the city. The car is silent as I try to wrap my brain around what happened tonight.

"Where are you taking me?" I hear her ask softly. Turning my head, I see her peering out the window, watching the city lights zoom by.

"Finding a hotel," Leon answers her. It doesn't take long to find one.

"Wait here; I'll be back," he says, climbing out of the car and walking into reception. Harlow exhales, making me glance at her. She presses her head against the glass.

"Why did you do it?" I ask her.

296

"Do what? Lie? I thought that would be obvious," she says, and I see the way her eyes turn glassy with unshed tears. "You didn't want Harlow," she murmurs.

"No. I mean, why did you kill his mother? We would have looked after you. You didn't need to kill her," I tell her.

"I didn't kill her," she whispers.

"We saw you on the videotape."

"I don't know what you saw, but I didn't do it," she tells me.

"She told her mates it was you," I snap at her. How could we believe anything she has to say when she's been lying to us this whole time?

"I didn't kill her. Why would I? I barely knew her. What reason could I possibly have to kill her? Yet none of you would even give me a chance to explain, so why bother? You have all made up your minds about me already."

I'm about to demand an answer from her when Leon returns, climbing into the car. He tosses me a key before pulling around to the back of the hotel, looking for our room.

Once he parks the car, I climb out, before opening her door. "Get out," I tell her when she just stares up at me. When she doesn't move, I grab her arm, pulling her from the car and pushing her toward Leon, who catches her, not realizing how hard I nudged her forward. He growls at me, his fangs slipping from his gums and peeking out between his lips.

"If you're going to be a prick, why'd you come?" he snarls, leading her off toward the brown door with the key in his hand. He unlocks the door, flicking the lights on and stepping inside.

I need to check on Thane. Leon turns around when I don't follow and raises an eyebrow at me before sighing and tossing me his keys. I catch them and stare at them in my hand. I feel caught between my instincts. Two of my mates are hurting, and they both need me. Do I go back to my Alpha, or do I stay and keep my Omega safe? It's an impossible decision.

The instinct to keep her safe wins, though. I can check on Thane later, unless he decides to mind-linked me before then. So, I walk to the hotel room, step inside, and close the door.

CHAPTER
SIXTY-SIX

ONE WEEK LATER
~Harlow~

I've been stuck here for a week now. Rhen and Leon keep telling me Thane will calm down and come to his senses, yet no matter how many times I try to speak with him, he won't hear me out. He won't even give me a damn moment when he picks Rhen and Leon up for work each morning. I tried to explain to Rhen, but he refuses to believe me. He showed me video footage of the restaurant we went to, and I tried to explain that it was from before the accident happened, that it was when we left for lunch.

Yet her body was found in the garden on the other side of the restaurant, where she parked. It shows the car driving off, but most of the visual was blocked by a moving van, and you can't see that his mother was driving the car and not me. I can't explain it. If they had all the footage from the day, they would have seen who dumped her body there, because it certainly wasn't me. After that turned into a huge argument, I gave up trying to explain myself and trying to find a way to show them I'm not a murderer.

I honestly believe they just need someone to blame, and unfortunately for me, I am that person. Why would I kill a woman I had just met? I had no issues with her, so it made little sense that I would kill her just to escape them.

"Harlow?" Leon murmurs, gripping my shoulder where I lay on the bed.

"I am going to work. Do you need anything? I can grab whatever you need on my way back," he tells me. What I need is for them to believe me. Since that isn't happening, all he gets is silence.

Leon growls at me. "I could have left you. You do realize that don't you? Fuck, Harlow, just speak! It has been three days of nothing but your damn silence!" he snarls before turning on his heel and leaving.

Rolling over, I tug the blanket over my head and nestle beneath the covers. I have a feeling that Leon is only here so he doesn't lose his personal juice box. Rhen hardly speaks to me. For the first few days, when I tried to explain my side of the story to him, it would always turn into a screaming match, usually ending with him leaving. Raidon hasn't come to see me, and after hearing Rhen on the phone with him once, I didn't bother trying to reach out to him. He is as pissed off as Thane. Some part of me knows I can't remain here in this hotel room. One day, probably soon, Thane will order his mates back the house, and then what?

Partway through the day, I grow bored of daytime TV and decide to go see Bree. She will listen, or at least I hope she will. That is, if Talon will let me in after Leon told him what I had supposedly done.

Climbing out of bed, I pull on some jeans and a hoodie. I can't be bothered with a bra, so I skip it. I pull my hair into a messy bun and tug my hood up before slipping my feet into my sneakers. I leave the hotel with my key tucked in the back pocket of my jeans.

I have to walk because I don't have bus fare. I'm not even sure if Thane has paid me yet for the few weeks of work I did. Not that it matters. My handbag, wallet, and everything else are in his house, never to be seen again, probably.

Yet the walk does me some good, and the fresh air helps me clear my head. I didn't leave the hotel room all week, so all I could smell was Rhen and Leon. I reek of them.

It takes me a little over forty-five minutes to walk to the seedy strip club. Stepping inside, all I can smell is Omega pheromones, sex, and bodily fluids. Gosh, I did not miss this smell.

Walking around the dimly lit place, I move behind the bar and toward the back where the staff areas are. It doesn't take me long to find Bree. She's in back, getting ready to go on stage. She looks up when I enter, and a huge grin splits her face.

"Z! Please tell me you are here to work," she purrs at me. I wave to her and press my lips together in an awkward smile. She exhales loudly and sighs, patting the bench where she has her leg propped up, tying the laces for her boots up her legs.

"Talon told me what happened with your pack," she tells me.

"Where is Talon?" I ask noting that I haven't seen him.

"He's not here. You don't have to worry," she tells me, and I let out a breath of relief. "He's away for the whole week. He's opening a club in another city. I'm in charge while he's gone," she shrugs.

We chit-chat for a bit before she has to go on stage. I watch her as she works, and when she comes off stage, I follow her out back while she yells at the girls who are dawdling and not where they're supposed to be. They rush off, leaving us alone. I explain my version of events to Bree.

"And they won't listen," she clicks her tongue, annoyed. "Stupid, typical Alpha men! You can't tell them shit!" she snarls before pursing her lips. "So, what are you going to do?" she asks, and I shrug.

"I was going to leave, but I have no money, and nowhere to go," I tell her. She thinks for a moment as she gets into her next outfit.

"Are you looking for work?" she asks, and I sigh.

"I suppose I am. I am clearly fired as their assistant. But what about Talon?"

"He'll be gone all week. Though we will have to drench you in

301

pheromones. With that mark on your neck, you reek of them, but we can smother their scents."

"I can't work nights, though. I don't want them knowing and giving them an actual reason to hate me."

"That's fine, I can move shifts around. Can you be here around nine in the mornings for this week?"

I nod my head, knowing they leave at 8 a.m. each morning. It will be tight, but doable.

"What about Talon?" I ask again.

"I will handle Talon when he gets back," she assures me.

"Okay, great," I tell her, and she smiles before giving me a hug and checking her phone. She digs through her bag before grabbing her wallet and slipping me twenty dollars.

"Catch a cab back. They knock off soon, and you won't make it back in time to shower before they get back," she says, showing me the time on her phone, and I gasp.

"Shit!"

"A cab should be waiting out front. I had Mila call one for you ten minutes ago. Go. I'll see you tomorrow," she says, and I nod before pausing.

"Uh, where will I be working?" I ask her.

"Behind the bar, don't worry," she tells me, and I sigh in relief before rushing out to find the cab.

~ L eon~

I am pissed! Thane hired a new assistant, and she starts tomorrow. The thought of anyone but Harlow sitting at that desk irritates me.

"Thane, this doesn't feel right, having another female here. Harlow will be able to smell her on us," Rhen tries to explain to him.

I have a feeling that is exactly his intention. He is beyond pissed that we are staying with her, and he's trying to drive a wedge between us. Having a new assistant, and a female one at that, will only cause problems for us with Harlow. Omegas are possessive, sometimes even more so than Alphas.

"I don't care. We need an assistant," Thane says.

"Then let Harlow work here or get Leila to!" I snarl at him. Thane says nothing. He just ignores me and walks off. I curse, shaking my head.

When Thane drops us back at the hotel after work, guilt gnaws at me as I step into the room, which is ridiculous, because I've done nothing to feel guilty about. When I walk in, I'm shocked that she isn't in bed, but in the shower. She hadn't moved out of the small

Den she's created in days. Yet, today the bed is made, and she isn't in it.

Rhen's brows furrow worriedly, as do mine. We both peer over to the bathroom door where we can hear the shower running. It cuts off, and she emerges in nothing but a towel, looking delicious. She jumps, startled, not having heard us come in before her usual blank expression settles across her features.

Well, that hasn't changed then. She clearly isn't talking to us still. Rhen sighs, falling onto the made bed. He sniffs the pillows and his face scrunches up. I know what he's upset about. They don't smell like her anymore. It feels wrong in here. And who opened the damn windows? I move, slamming both of them shut.

Harlow moves about the room getting her pajamas on, not saying a word before she climbs into bed beside Rhen, who rolls and moves to encase her in his arms. She doesn't fight him or try to wiggle out of his grasp. As much as she may hate us, we know she still craves her Alphas. She needs us, just like we need her. Rhen melts against her back, burying his face in her wet hair.

I wait for him to break the news to her about the new assistant, but he doesn't, so we fall into the same routine we've had every night. Silence, TV, eating, and then bed.

Climbing in beside her, I tug the blankets back before tugging her closer. She sighs, offering me her neck, just like she does every night. I sink my teeth in, and she moans before clamping her mouth shut, not wanting me to know the effect my bite has on her.

I feed on her for a few seconds before pulling away. Her blood tastes different tonight, stronger. Licking my lips, I brush the pad of my thumb over the bite mark, trying to figure out what is different about it. I suck the blood drops from my thumb, swishing it around in my mouth.

"What is it?" Rhen asks, looking at me over her shoulder.

"Nothing. She just tastes a little different."

"Maybe she needs vitamins?" he offers, and I shrug, unsure, but I will let Raidon know. She's been under the weather the last couple of days, but there's nothing to indicate she's getting sick. It could also just be because of stress. Thane's blood always tastes different when he's angry or stressed.

~HARLOW~

The next morning, I get up as soon as they leave and haul ass to get dressed before racing to the other side of town for work. The moment I step inside, Bree yanks me toward the back before giving me a change of clothes. I slip on the slutty looking outfit while she covers the marks on my neck and douses me with so much spray-on pheromones it makes me gag. She does a sniff test and gives me the thumbs up.

I work behind the bar all day. Today is actually on the busy side, maybe because of the construction going on across the street, but I make almost $150 in tips. So at least I can catch a cab to work for the rest of the week and still have some money to stash away.

"Hopefully, that construction lasts a while. It might get this place out of the red with all their workers spending their lunch breaks here," Bree laughs, waving a wad of cash in my face. I chuckle, making and pouring drinks. By the time my shift ends, I am exhausted.

My feet throb, and my lower back aches as I climb into the cab. The fake pheromones are making me feel queasy the whole ride home. So queasy, I chuck the money at the driver and rush out of the car to spew in the garden out front of the hotel. Shame washes over me as people stare, but I don't want to throw up in the man's cab.

When I regain myself, I wipe my mouth with the back of my hand. Big mistake, as it is covered in pheromones, making me gag. I run for my room. Jamming the key in the door before rushing to shower. The smell is terrible. I shower quickly, knowing I still have to take my clothes downstairs to wash so they don't smell like pheromones by the time the guys get back.

I open all the windows and air the place out. I make sure to wash every bit of makeup off my face. Once finished, I take my clothes to the small dry cleaner attached to the hotel. I hand the clothes to the girl behind the counter and give her my room number. She scrunches her face up at the smell of them but doesn't comment.

Great, she probably thinks I'm a hooker. Once back in my room, I find a place to stash the cash I made today, leaving only a twenty in the bottom of my shoe for the cab tomorrow morning. I really need to get my handbag and wallet back so I can keep them on me. It feels weird stuffing my tips into my bra all damn day.

I mind-link Leon and ask if he can pick them up for me, but he says he is already on his way here. I groan. He asks if I want or need anything, but I don't bother replying, instead, just curl up in bed. My belly rumbles hungrily, and I reach for the phone, ordering room service for myself and ordering them the usual meals they seemed to get every night.

Sitting back, I wait for them to arrive. Only when they do, instinct has me sniffing the air as the breeze from the open windows waft their scents to me. They smell wrong, and before I can stop myself, I launch myself off the bed at them. My legs wrap around Rhen, who curses as he catches me, stumbling back out the door and into Leon.

They both hit the concrete, and as embarrassing as it is, I can't seem to stop as I search for the source of the scent on them. My claws slip out, tearing the buttons on Rhen's jacket and popping the buttons on his shirt. I bury my nose in the flesh of his chest, sniffing to see what he did, but the smell is only on his clothes, not him. A feral, crazed growl leaves me when I realize it's the scent of another Omega on them.

Tears burn my eyes as Rhen tries to soothe me, his hands in my hair, uncaring that he's lying on the dirty ground. My hands reach for Leon. I need to check that he didn't touch her; I need to know. My

306

bond screams and wails. My heart feels like it is going to tear out of my chest. When an arm wraps around my waist to drag me off them, my bond reacts irrationally. I want to kill her; kill the woman whose scent is on them. Only seconds pass as I thrash in my captor's arms, while Leon and Rhen get back to their feet.

Raidon's scent smashes into me, and he purrs. The same sickly sweet Omega scent covers his clothes too.

"Shh, I know. I know, Harlow. We never touched her," he murmurs.

I bury my face in his neck as he turns me in his arms. He turns back to the room, and as he does, I spot Thane standing beside his car, his arms folded across his chest.

Did he stay just to watch my reaction to them? Is this some sick game to him? He's trying to hurt me, and that startling realization hits me like a slap in the face. How far will he take this? I struggle in Raidon's grip, wanting to be put down. Anger courses through me that he would do this, and that they would let him. Raidon sets me on my feet in the hotel room as rage engulfs me.

"Get out!" I snarl at them.

They stop, looking at me. "I said, GET OUT!" I scream, turning breathless. They glance at me warily, and only then do I realize my claws are out, and so are my canines. Blistering hot anger courses through me. I can't bear to even look at them.

"Harlow," Leon murmurs.

"Get the fuck out!" I scream, pointing at the door. They look at each other before quickly leaving, and I follow, slamming the door behind them, along with all the windows.

"Harlow?" I hear Raidon whisper on the other side of the door, but I don't answer—instead, I fall into a heap on the floor as the bond pulses through me, broken and screaming out for them.

They eventually leave. I hear them argue with Thane in the parking lot. It's clear this is his doing, but they went along with it. I feel betrayed, sickened that I am so replaceable.

CHAPTER
SIXTY-EIGHT

~ **H**arlow~

Later that night, my bond nags and screams at me until I finally contact Leon, needing him to come over. It is 1 a.m., and I'm still awake. My body feels wired, feral. But Leon doesn't come. Instead, it's Raidon who knocks on my door. I stare at him as he stands in the doorway. He doesn't smell of the strange Omega anymore, which I am thankful for. I don't think my bond could handle smelling her again tonight. We stand there awkwardly. Today is the first time I've seen him since Thane kicked me out.

"Thane wouldn't let Leon or Rhen come, so..." he shrugs as if he's some sort of offering to replace them. I say nothing, just step aside, allowing him to enter. He looks at the torn sheets on the bed and sighs. My mini Den is ruined, destroyed, and so is the mattress.

"I will have the hotel replace the mattress tomorrow, and linens," Raidon tells me as he climbs into the ruined Den I made. His presence soothes my aching bond as the room becomes flooded with his scent.

When sleep does take me, it is only because his scent invades my every sense as I lay on him, but his movements wake me early in the morning, and so does the knock on the door. I roll off him as he climbs out of bed, covered in goose feathers from the torn-apart comforter.

The simple motion of me rolling off him has me racing for the bathroom. I barely make it to the toilet in time. I heave and retch as I lose the contents of my stomach, which thankfully isn't much. I couldn't bring myself to eat any food last night, not after smelling that Omega's scent on them.

Fingers brush my neck as someone grabs my hair, tugging it back away from my face.

"See, I told you something is up with her," comes Leon's voice.

"Probably just the crap from yesterday. She was quite distressed when I got here last night," Raidon says.

"He never should have hired her! I don't even want to go in the building!" Leon growls behind me, and my eyes sting with tears. When I am done, I smack Raidon's hands away, and he turns on the shower while I strip out of my clothes.

"I'll take her blood just to be sure," Raidon says. I roll my eyes, stepping under the spray. I know exactly what this is. It is my damn bond that they crushed and pulverized!

"Don't you have to get to work?" I snap at Leon when he remains by the bathroom door, watching me.

"We won't take another Omega, Harlow. You don't need to worry about that," Leon tells me.

"So, she has a pack then?" I ask him, peering over my shoulder at him. He groans, resting his head on the door frame.

"She's a rotation Omega," I choke, emotion threatening to suffocate me. "He hired a rotation, Omega?" I whimper. The thought terrifies me.

Rotation Omegas usually chose it as a career. It pays well, and they get passed around. Sure, some Omegas are forced into the rotation when they break the law or don't register, like I did, but a lot like the lifestyle it offers. And knowing this stings even more because without a pack, Thane only has to click his fingers, and she will be on her knees for him.

"Just go, Leon," I tell him, pressing my face under the water as a horrid sinking feeling settles in the pit of my gut. Leon sighs, and I hear him walk off. Tears stream down my cheeks, hidden by the water from the showerhead. When I hear Raidon come into the bathroom, I shut the water off and reach for my towel.

Raidon points to the spa bath, and I shake my head. "Harlow, please don't make me order you," he says.

"First a new Omega, and now you're going to order me around just to insult me more?" I snarl at him. He grits his teeth and points to the edge of the bath. I roll my eyes.

"I just want to be sure. Leon said your blood has been tainted lately, likely due to stress," he says as he grabs my arm, pushing me back to sit.

"So what if it is? I highly doubt there is much that can be done about it!" I snap at him.

"No, but it might help us convince Thane to let you come home," Raidon retorts, gripping my arm before plunging the needle into it. I hiss and jerk my arm back, but his grip is like a vice as he fills his stupid vials.

"Don't you want to come home?" he asks. I scoff.

"What, so I can smell your new assistant every night? I'll pass, thanks."

Raidon mutters under his breath and curses before placing a cotton swab on my arm. He then turns and walks out of my room. When I am sure they are really gone, I get ready for work and head out. It irritates me that Thane has them working with another Omega—especially while I am working behind the damn bar making sure the men don't come too close. I could never betray them like that, and here he is, flaunting it in my face!

A growl leaves me. Fuck them then! Bree's always said that working the floor pays more, and if it means getting out of here faster, I will take her up on it. They can have their stupid Omega! Thane has pushed me too far this time.

Once again, I make good tips today, and I speak to Bree about moving to the floor, but she doesn't think it's a good idea.

"Z!" she calls out to me, using my fake name as I'm about to leave. I wander back over to her, and she motions for me to follow her as she slips into the back.

"I have a private show on Friday night for some big names. I was going to ask Bianca, but if you really want to make money, good money and fast, you can cover it."

"What about Bianca?"

"I haven't asked her yet. So, if you want to do it with me..." She pauses, waiting for my response.

"How much, and what do I have to do?"

"Enough to get you out of this city." She chews her lip nervously, glancing out the doors. "It's in the function room," she whispers. We aren't supposed to say what goes on up there, and I've never asked, though I have a good idea what sorts of shows go on in there.

"Wait, it's an orgy?"

"Not quite, but yes. These clients, though, have asked for a particular show," she says, chewing her nails.

"What sort of show?" I ask.

"They want two girls in the glory hole boxes. They also want to film it."

"Wait, you have a glory hole up there?" I ask, a little shocked.

"Forget I asked," she says, waving me off. My brows crease. She said it will get me out of the city, so that means it has to pay well. And I won't even have to look at them.

"How many and how much?" I ask her as she turns for the door.

"Fifteen are booked, but that doesn't mean they will all join in," she says, and I swallow. That is so many dicks.

"And they won't see us at all?"

"No. From the waist up, we will be completely covered by the box and black cloth. If at any time you want out, I can have Bianca on standby."

"And how much does this pay?"

"10k. So, five each, for four hours,"

"Wait, you earn 10k for those upstairs shows?"

"Sometimes more, sometimes less. Depends on who the clients are. We charge according to whatever their fetishes and kinks are. They are also all STI screened two days before and have to use protection."

"Fuck! I'm in the wrong business! Who would have thought I can make that much by strapping a mattress to my back?" I chuckle. Bree laughs.

"And now you know why I do it. Also, Talon doesn't take a cut from the shows upstairs. They are my shows. He makes his money from the bar up there. So, you in?"

"That will definitely go a long way to getting me out of here."

"I have another on Saturday, if you can escape your captors," she tells me. I know it will be hard enough to come up with an excuse if I come back late on Friday. Saturday, they will be all over me, demanding to know where I was.

"We'll see about Saturday. But Friday, I'm in," I tell her, and she smiles.

"Sweet! Now let's go celebrate," she says, looping her arm through mine.

"Don't you have to work?" I ask her.

"Nope. I have tonight off. Shelley is covering for me, so let's go out. My treat," she tells me, and I giggle. *Why the fuck not?* I think. It isn't like Thane gives a fuck about me. He is intent on trying to hurt me.

"You know they will find me eventually?" I tell her.

"So what? They kicked you out; they can't expect you to not work. And besides, you only work behind the bar," she says. "Well, until Friday anyway. And they shouldn't have hired a whore to work for them!" she growls, hailing a cab. "Let's head back to my place. I have some clothes you can borrow, and we can go to Craze to celebrate," she says, smacking my ass as a cab pulls up. I laugh and slide across the seat when she opens the door.

CHAPTER
SIXTY-NINE

~T hane~

Sarah wanders into my office without knocking. I glare at her, but she just smiles sweetly and places a mug on my desk. I am mentally cursing myself for hiring the girl. She is too handsy, always trying to touch us, always talking. I can't stand her! I hired her out of spite because I am furious. And now I am stuck with her. She steps closer to my desk, and I turn my head to look at her.

"What?" I snap at her. She flinches, but plasters that sickly sweet smile on her face, which has me internally shuddering with revulsion. She doesn't even bother with suppressants. It's like she is hoping to send one of us into a rut. She doesn't realize that we already have an Omega, and we don't want another one. Shit, I don't even want the one I have, so she stands no chance in hell of getting with my pack.

"Do you need anything else?" she purrs.

"Yes, for you to get the fuck out of my office!" I snarl at her. She pales as my aura smashes against her, and she runs out. I glare at the mug she left on my desk before turning my attention back to

314

my laptop, before Raidon rushes into my office, making me look up.

He has a furious look on his face. "She has got to go! I swear if she tries touching me again, I will break her fucking fingers!" he snaps, falling into the chair across from me.

I lean back in my chair, knowing he's right. The girl is driving us insane, and not in the way that Harlow did. No, this bitch is on the prowl for a wealthy pack. That much is clear, with the way she all but throws herself at us.

My mates are furious, and so am I, at my own stupidity. I wanted to hurt Harlow, and I knew her smelling another Omega on them would drive her insane, cause her anguish. But now, this Omega is upsetting my mates. They despise her and want her gone.

"Thane, either she goes, or I will fucking quit!" Raidon snaps at me.

"Quit?" I ask him. Does he not realize he owns part of the company? He can't just fucking quit. When I took over this place, I made us all equal partners. I knew nothing about the business, and I needed their help. I never wanted to be trapped in an office all day, and I barely knew anything about what my fathers did here until I inherited it.

"Yes, I will fucking quit! I don't want another Omega prancing around here! And she doesn't even fucking work! I swear she stands by our damn doors waiting to see if our mugs are empty," he growls angrily.

"I'll speak with her," I tell him.

"No. You will fire her. Or you will have another scandal on your hands when I fucking kill her, and she goes missing!" Raidon snaps angrily before rising to his feet.

"Where are you going?" I ask, not wanting him to leave, knowing that bimbo will try to come back in here.

"Back to *my* Omega!" he snaps at me while digging his keys out of his pocket.

"What about the meeting we have?"

315

"Handle it yourself," he says, storming out of my office. I shake my head when I hear him call out to Leon.

"Leon, we are leaving!" he yells out. I hear his office door open; Leon is all too eager to leave. The moment they're gone, Rhen rushes into my office. He locks the door behind him, his laptop in his hand. As soon as he sits at my desk, we hear the door handle twist, and he growls menacingly.

"Vile woman!" he sneers when we hear her heels clicking on the floor as she wanders off.

We hide out in my office until our upcoming meeting with Jake, but he cancels at the last minute. He says he can't make it. That something came up, and he has to return home. Which is fine by me because I want out of this building and away from my damn 'assistant'.

However, as we pack everything up to leave, the mind-link opens up. I know they went home because they had mind-linked earlier to let me know a package I was waiting for had arrived.

'What's up?' I ask.

'Have you seen or heard from Harlow?' Leon asks, and I feel Raidon force the link open and join the conversation.

'What do you mean?' Rhen asks.

'We're at the hotel, but she isn't here. We searched the entire damn building!' he snaps. Rhen jumps to his feet in a panic.

'Maybe she went for a walk,' I tell them as I look out the window. It is just turning dark outside.

'We have been looking for her for the past hour, Thane. Since we got here.'

'An hour! And you are only just now mind-linking!' Rhen yells at them. I growl and get to my feet, knowing damn well they will annoy the fuck out of me until I track her down.

'We are on our way,' I tell them, cutting off the link. We leave and I tell Sarah to head home. Her shift finished an hour ago. I know why she lingers, but she doesn't stand a chance in hell with any of us.

We meet up with the others at the hotel and search every nook and cranny of the place yet find no trace of her. She feels perfectly fine through the bond. Happy even, which pisses me off. She is excited and happy about something, while her mates are in a fucking panic.

We go to Talon's club, but she isn't there, before trying her old apartment. I have no idea where else she might be. She has no money or anywhere else to go. We tried Bree and Talon's place, but no one is home. We try calling Talon, and when he can't get a hold of Bree, we figure Harlow is likely out with her somewhere.

It's 10 p.m. by the time Talon calls back. He finally figured out where Bree is, and we head straight to the club he tells us she is at. Through the bond, we can feel she is fucking drunk, which only angers me more because she is putting herself at risk going out without us in this city. When we arrive, we see it is one of Bree's friend's clubs, which explains how she got Harlow in without ID.

Stepping into the place, I groan when I see Sarah. Of course, she has to be at the same fucking club our mate is at. Raidon shoves past her and into the club, searching for our mate. Rhen nods upstairs and moves past me, heading for the stairs. I try to evade my assistant, but she beelines straight for me.

"Are you here to see me?" she purrs, brushing her fingers across my white button-down shirt.

"Definitely not! Now fuck off!" I snap at her. Her cheeks turn red at my harshness. Stepping further inside, all I can smell is pheromones, mingling scents, and liquor. I make my way around the place. Bodies gyrate against each other, and the strobing lights annoy my eyes, when the mind-link opens up.

'Over there,' Rhen says.

I look up at him to see him pointing behind me, where some booths are. Turning around, I spot Harlow in the back with Bree, both of them laughing hysterically while Bree gives her a lap dance.

CHAPTER
SEVENTY

~ **T**hane~

Bree stumbles, also drunk, and Harlow grasps her wrists before she can fall onto the table. Both of them erupt in fits of giggles, along with the other girls in the booth. They must be Bree's friends because other than Bree, Harlow has none. Probably because she is a fucking liar.

I climb the few steps leading up to the booth. A furious growl tears out of me, and they all go quiet. Bree jumps in fright, and Harlow has the gall to roll her eyes at me.

"And that will be the fun police, here to drag me away!" she slurs, leaning heavily against the girl beside her. I reach out to grab her wrist, but she growls at me, jerking her arm back. I glance around at the other girls, who all stare at her with concern.

"She's fine, Thane. I will make sure she gets home okay," Bree says. I shake my head.

"Harlow, get up!" I snap at her. She giggles, and Rhen comes up behind me.

"Bree!" he spits through gritted teeth.

My eyes run the length of Harlow. She might as well have been naked for all the coverage her clothes give her. Rhen, also noticing her lack of clothing, reaches down and grabs her wrist, pulling her out of the booth.

She smacks into his chest as she stumbles forward.

"Why are you dressed like that?" I snarl at her.

"Why do you fucking care?" she retorts.

I growl at her tone. Rhen tugs his jacket off, trying to drape it over her, but she flings it off.

"I am not leaving," she declares.

"Yes, you fucking are! I will drag you out of here kicking and fucking screaming if need be," I tell her, gripping her arm when she tries to tug her way out of Rhen's grip.

"Hey, come on, Thane. No need to be rough with her," Bree tells me, touching my arm. I shake her off and glare at her.

"Shut up, Briana! Just because Talon lets you do whatever the fuck you want doesn't mean I will put up with this sort of behavior!"

"Talon is not my Alpha. Or my mate!" Bree retorts.

"But I am hers! Now sit the fuck down and mind your own damn business. I know you talked her into this stupid shit. No way would she have come out on her own!" I yell at her when Harlow smacks my chest.

"Hey! Don't talk to her like that!" she says, swaying on her feet.

I push her toward Rhen, who grabs her, moving her toward the exit. Raidon spots us, looking relieved, and he makes his way toward us. Rhen struggles with steering Harlow outside, mostly because she doesn't want to leave. As we finally reach the doors, I groan when Sarah's scent hits me.

Rhen stops abruptly, and I almost run into his back.

"That scent!" I hear Harlow shout just as Sarah comes racing over, waving her arms excitedly.

"Fuck!" Rhen curses, just as Harlow registers that this is the same scent she has smelled on her mates for the past few days. The savage noise that leaves her has everyone around us backing up, including Sarah, who stares at her, horrified, when Harlow suddenly lunges.

I shove past Rhen, my arms locking around Harlow's waist as her claws narrowly miss Sarah's face. Sarah shrieks, and Raidon shoves her away.

Harlow turns feral in my arms, and everyone around us scatters while I try to keep a hold of her. Sarah tucks tail and runs, just realizing why we've shown no interest in her advances at work.

Because we already have an Omega.

Great! This scene will be plastered all over the papers tomorrow. Harlow claws and kicks at me as I toss her over my shoulder. The bouncers at the doors are quick to open them, relieved they won't have to deal with an Omega fight. Stepping outside, the fresh air blasts my face. I can feel Raidon's anger burning behind me. Rhen's too. Leon stands by the car, pushing off the trunk when he sees Harlow's thrashing body over my shoulder.

"I hate you! I fucking hate you!" Harlow yells at me. Her fists smash my back and she kicks me between the legs. I grunt and freeze, momentarily losing my vision. I fight the urge to choke on my damn balls, which now feel like they are in my throat. I grip her legs tighter. But she goes stiff as a board, straightening up, and her fists smack the top of my head.

"Put me down!" she snarls, hitting me wherever she can. When that doesn't work, I adjust my grip on her, and she goes limp in my arms, slipping out of them and crashing to the ground at my feet.

"Harlow, stop it! You are causing a fucking scene," I snap at her.

"You brought your fucking whore with you!" she screams at me, tears streaking down her face in anger.

I grab her, but she turns to dead weight in my arms. "Stop it! Or I will go back in there, drag her out, and mark her right here in front of you! Is that what you fucking want?" I scream at her while trying to grab her. She freezes at my words, and the hurt that smashes into me through the bond makes me want to take them back when she looks up at me.

I'm not expecting the hand she whips at me. Her claws rake

across my face as she slaps me, and I can see my blood spray across her face.

"Go claim your fucking whore then!" she yells at me before getting to her feet.

Rhen glares at me. Are they seriously not going to help me with her? It angers me more that they would watch her lose her shit at me and do nothing to help. She is causing a fucking scene! This is bad for all of us.

I can feel them all glaring at me as she goes to stalk off. I reach for her, wrapping my arm around her waist. She thrashes before tossing her head back. It connects with my nose, and I hear the sickening crack. Blood spurts out, forcing me to drop her. I growl, grabbing for her again, and shoving her against the car door. Raidon growls at me. I glare at him.

"Stand down!" I snap at them when he goes to grab me, along with Rhen. He freezes under my command. They all do. Except Harlow, who continues to thrash in my grip.

"Stop!" I scream in her face. She fights it, but eventually complies as the command washes over her. She glares daggers at me. I'm about to order her into the car, when she spits in my face.

I grit my teeth. If she were a man, I would have pummeled her for that. Instead, I growl, my grip on her tightening as I open the door and shove her in the back seat. She kicks the door open when I try to close it, and her heel comes off when I try again. She growls as I shut it. I wipe her spit off my face, when the door flies open and her heel smashes me in the side of my face.

"I hate you! You fucking asshole! I hope you get fucked up the ass with a pineapple, you Alphahole!" she drunkenly screams at me, trying to get out of the car. I grab her arms, shoving her back in. My knee is pressing between her legs as I push her further in, pinning her to the seat while my mates growl at me, wanting to pull me off her but unable to move while still under my command.

"Get off me!" she screams, thrashing and kicking.

"Keep fighting me, Harlow, and I'll pull up that fucking, non-existing dress and spank your ass in front of everyone out here! Now stop, unless you want your bare ass across the front page of every damn newspaper by morning."

"Fuck you!" she sneers at me.

"Submit," I warn her.

"No!" she snarls, glaring at me.

"Submit!" I scream the order in her face, sick of her stupid little games. She wants to act like a damn animal? I will treat her like one! She whimpers, and tears fill her eyes as she tries to fight it, before finally submitting and bearing her neck to me.

The moment she does, I sink my canines into her neck. She screams, the sound deafening. She will get no pleasure from my bite, just pain, to show her who is in charge. I hear our mates' whimpers behind me when I use our bond to knock her out. They want to kill me as I force all my anger into the mark, making it as painful as possible. She will think twice about crossing me now.

CHAPTER
SEVENTY-ONE

~R hen~

Anger courses through me as I am forced to watch him make her submit. He never does that to us, and I feel her pain vibrate through the bond, the betrayal she feels. Thane climbs out of the car, wiping his mouth with the back of his hand.

"Get in the car. We're going home," he snaps, yet we all remain where we are. I can't believe he just did that. It was cruel, and he knows it. Yet, he feels no remorse for his actions. Almost as if he enjoyed hurting her. Like some sick form of vengeance for his mother.

"I said get in the car," he snarls at us.

Leon whimpers as the command rolls over us, his feet moving toward the car. Both mine and Raidon's hands whip out, stopping him. Thane raises an eyebrow at our challenge. He can make us submit, but if he does, we will never forgive him.

"I had no choice. Look at how many people are watching with their fucking phones out," he snaps at us. We had drawn a crowd, and this will be splashed over every paper tomorrow. The headlines will no doubt read about how harshly Thane treated an Omega. It

323

doesn't look good, but she wasn't in control of her actions. He knows how territorial Omegas are, and he reeks of Sarah. What did he expect?

"Get in the—" his words cut off when her irritating, nasally voice reaches my ears. He drops the command as Sarah rushes across the road, her heels clicking furiously.

"Alpha! Alpha!" she calls out. I turn, about to tell her to fuck off, but we are indeed surrounded by many onlookers and are in enough hot water already.

"What, Sarah?" Thane asks as she slows to a stop beside him. She bats her fake lashes at him, and I can feel his hatred toward her through the bond.

"I know you are having trouble with your Omega. And I wonder, maybe you're looking for a replacement? She doesn't seem to be very submissive."

Is this whore for real right now? I am astonished at how desperate she is coming across. Gold-digging whore! She knows we have an Omega. Now I kind of wish Thane let Harlow at the bitch. She steps closer, brushing her hands down his chest. Raidon growls at her.

"We will talk about this tomorrow at work," he tells her, glancing around at the people watching.

"No, Sarah, you are—" I say, before being cut off.

"We will discuss it at work tomorrow," Thane growls.

I was about to tell her that she's fired and not welcome near us or Harlow. How dare she? To think that we would just toss our Omega aside for her. I grit my teeth while she paws at him, disgusted, not just with her but with Thane for not immediately putting her in her place. Fuck what the media says!

With a growl, I climb into the car. I grab Harlow, dragging her limp body out. Thane growls, and Raidon rushes toward Leon's car, opening the door.

"Leon, now!" I order, and he rushes after us. Raidon climbs in the back of the car, and I pass her to him before jumping in the driver's side.

"What are you doing?" Thane snarls.

"If you are willing to entertain the idea of her, then sleep by yourself," I snap at him before slamming the door shut just as Leon slides into the passenger seat. Thane's anger burns through the bond, but I don't care. I tear out of there and head back to the hotel.

When we arrive back at the hotel, I open the back door so Raidon can climb out with her. He carries her to the room. I open the door as she starts to come to. The moment she does, she throws up all over him. Raidon curses, looking up at the ceiling.

"I'll get the shower going," Leon says, rushing into the bathroom.

"Sorry," Harlow mumbles, almost incoherently. "I don't usually drink," she slurs.

"I can tell. It is fine. Go back to sleep," Raidon tells her, letting his Calling slip out, lulling her to sleep with its calming effect. Raidon walks into the bathroom and sits on the edge of the tub. I help him to peel off her dress and strip her bare, while Leon tries to clean up the mess she made of Raidon's shirt.

Once she's naked, I strip my own clothes off before taking her, so Raidon can undress. He definitely needs a shower now. I step into the shower with her, sitting on the recess while Raidon grabs the removable shower head and starts rinsing his chest.

"So gross," he says, quickly washing.

"She didn't mean it," Leon is quick to defend.

"I know. It doesn't make it any less gross, though," Raidon tells him before grabbing the soap and rinsing her with the showerhead. We wash her quickly, and Leon grabs towels as we take turns holding her while we get changed and try to dry her off. We give up on dressing her and just place her in bed naked.

Leon moves to shower himself, closing the door behind him. I climb in bed, laying behind her with Raidon on her other side.

"What now?" Raidon asks.

"We have a meeting in the morning, but I don't care about that. We need to fire Sarah; I don't want Thane making things worse by keeping her around."

Raidon nods his head before rolling into her.

"I also need to speak to my mother, so I can get Harlow's test results," he tells me, and I nod before reaching behind me and flicking off the lamp on my side of the bed, leaving only Raidon's on. When Leon gets out of the shower, I can feel his burning hunger. He needs blood, but as he peers down at her sleeping form between us, he shakes his head.

"Leon?" Raidon asks, tilting his head to the side. We all know now that he feeds on her. She will always be his go-to.

"I can wait," he says, but instead of climbing into bed with us, he moves toward the couch. I know he doesn't want to risk feeding on her while she sleeps. Not that he hasn't before, but I can feel after everything with Thane tonight, Leon doesn't want to take anything from her without her consent.

"If you get uncomfortable, you have us, Leon," I remind him, and he nods, grabbing the spare blanket and pillow, before climbing onto the couch farthest away from her.

CHAPTER
SEVENTY-TWO

~H arlow~

I awake to the sound of one of their phones ringing loudly. I have a wicked hangover, and the room's bright lights burn my eyes as I squint up at the ceiling. My eyes widen, and I sit up abruptly, half in a panic that I'll find myself locked in the Den. Relief washes over me when I find myself back at the hotel.

"Yeah, we know. We are on our way," I hear Rhen tell presumably Thane. Raidon comes out of the bathroom, trying to fix his tie.

"Here," I tell him, tossing my legs over the side of the bed, ignoring the nausea that bubbles in my empty stomach and has me wanting to run to the bathroom.

Raidon wanders over to me, yanking the tie off, and I stand on my tippy toes to quickly fix it for him while his hands move to my hips.

"How are you feeling?" he asks.

"Fine," I tell him, though my neck stings. Tears try to brim at the memory of the woman's scent all over them and then seeing her. I know it is foolish with what I am planning to do on Friday, yet all the same it still hurts.

327

Thane has made it clear he doesn't want me, and he has overall rank when it comes to decisions in the pack. I know it. They know it. Waiting for him to come around is foolish. He won't even give me the time of day to explain. And as much as they claim to be on my side, I can still feel that they don't believe me. I feel their distrust of me, so it is pointless.

"We'll be back tonight; don't leave the hotel, please," Raidon whispers before pressing his lips to my forehead. He steps away, grabbing his phone from the charger and wallet off the small stand by the door. Rhen quickly pecks my cheek before rushing out the door.

"Where is Leon?"

"Leon left early. He's struggling with his bloodlust," Raidon tells me. Why didn't he feed on me, then? Is he angry about last night?

"He could have fed," I begin to say.

"I have to go; we're late," Raidon says before rushing out and leaving me staring at the door. It takes all of two seconds after they leave for that empty feeling in my stomach to change to a rising feeling in my throat, and I run for the bathroom to throw up. I am still puking when I hear the hotel phone start ringing. I groan, wiping my mouth on the hand towel before retrieving it and moving back toward the bathroom to shower and brush my teeth.

"Hello," I all but groan into the phone.

"Thank goodness, can you fill in for Tammy today? She can't come in," Bree says, not sounding the slightest bit sick.

Thane never paid me for the few weeks of work I did, and I am desperate for cash. I hate living off them, yet at the moment, that can't be helped. I know they will pitch a fit if they find out I am working back at Talon's though.

"Yes, but you will have to pay for the cab. And I need to shower first," I tell her.

"Deal, thank you. You're really saving my ass," she says.

I chuckle, shaking my head before hanging up and turning the shower on. I still feel like shit even after I hop out and rummage around for anything half decent to wear, even though I will borrow one of the uniforms when I get there. I doubt my baggy sweats and hoodie will earn me much in tips.

Climbing in the cab, I find Bree had in fact, called and paid ahead, which saves me having to run in and raid the register to pay for the fare. I wonder where the money in my bra from yesterday went, when I remember I left it at Bree's house.

When I climb out of the cab at the strip club, I glance around and tug my hood up over my head. I am usually not here this late. I hate the idea that I might be seen in case it gets back to Thane and my mates.

Most mornings, people are too distracted with their commute. Afternoons are the same, that or parents doing school runs. Yet at this hour, it is mainly shoppers taking their sweet ass time as they leisurely walk around, taking everything in.

Yet after last night, and catching a glimpse of the morning paper by the lobby doors, I know that my face is a lot more recognizable than it used to be. I'm splashed across every paper, and the scene we caused is the talk of the city this morning, so I am kind of thankful for the masks we always wear. Well, those of us who want our identity kept secret, anyway.

Moving toward the doors, I hear someone clear their throat as I grip the door handle. My eyes move to the side when I see Alpha Jake step out from the alley on the side of the strip joint. My heart rate quickens at seeing the man responsible for killing my sister.

"Harlow," he says, stepping closer, and I yank the door open.

"Harlow, wait, just hear me out. It isn't what you think. I want to help you," Alpha Jake says, and I scoff. His actions say otherwise.

"Help me? You killed my sister."

"No, I didn't. Zara is the reason I am here," he tells me.

Does he think I am an idiot? I know he killed her. I know exactly how she died.

"Bullshit," I snarl.

"I can explain. I had to say that. I—"

329

I step inside, ignoring him. It makes me nervous that he is here after seeing him in the office the other week. Why is he still in town? A shiver runs up my spine. I'm not worried about him snitching about me working at Talon's because then he would have to admit that he went looking for me. So I force him from my mind, and I head back to the staff area so I can change.

When I come out, I find him sitting at the bar, and my stomach drops.

CHAPTER
SEVENTY-THREE

~Harlow~

Instead of going to my regular station, I make my way up the stairs to the VIP section to find Bree working behind the bar upstairs. She smiles and waves me over to her, and I quickly rush toward her and what little safety there is behind the bar.

"Thanks for coming in," she says before looking downstairs toward the lower bar.

"That man down there came in twenty minutes before you did," she tells me, nodding toward Jake and glancing down at him nervously.

"He knows your name."

I swallow and nod.

"As Harlow," she whispers. Tal and Bree know my real identity now, yet the fact he figured out where I work and came here frightens me.

"Apparently, he was here last night, asking about you," Bree tells me.

Now that worries me. I don't offer her an explanation. Though it makes me curious as to why he is here.

"His name is Jake. He's the Alpha responsible for killing my sister. She took my place in his pack," I tell her. Saying that out loud makes the sickly feeling in my stomach worse, remembering how angry he was when he found out he had the wrong Omega.

"Stay up here today; I'll have Shane stay in case he gives you a hard time," Bree tells me, giving my arm a squeeze before going downstairs. She is due on stage in twenty minutes. I hate the idea of being here by myself, but know it can't be helped. Besides, Shane will step in if he tries anything.

I set to work, trying to ignore Alpha Jake the best I can, yet he remains most of the day. When I think he is finally getting up to leave, relief fills me, but it is only temporary. Instead, he comes to the top bar, where I am. Shane, the security guard, watches him closely and never leaves my side. But his presence is becoming harder and harder to ignore.

"Are you going to ignore me all day," Jake asks.

"Yep, I have nothing to say to you," I tell him while sliding the drink he ordered over to him. He sighs.

"Does Thane know you are working here?" he asks, and my hands stop what they are doing as I wipe the counter down.

"Chill, I won't tell him. That isn't why I am here," he tells me, and I return to my cleaning.

"So why are you here?" I snap at him.

"Are you happy with your mates, Harlow?"

I glance at him. Do I look happy? I could be at work with them, but instead, I'm sneaking around behind their backs, trying to find a way out of this city that isn't going to have me eating out of dumpsters and sleeping in alleyways.

Jake moves closer and leans over the bar before whispering. "Zara sent me," he says, and I grit my teeth.

"You're lying. Your pack killed her," I snap at him, and he leans back, looking toward where Shane stands watching him. Yet as long as he doesn't try to grab me, he will remain where he is.

"No, we realized as soon as she was brought to us that she hadn't bloomed. We aren't monsters, despite what the media says about my pack."

"You knew and forced her anyway?" I ask, glaring at him. Jake shakes his head.

"Once an Omega is bought, marked, and mated, a pack can't take another; Zara bloomed the next day," Jake tells me, looking around. "Think about what I am saying, Harlow," he whispers, unbuttoning his shirt. He jerks the collar aside, revealing his neck.

"We waited, would have waited forever if need be. She begged us to save you. Said that you promised each other to never be separated. The only way for a pack to have two Omegas is if one is dead," he tells me.

"We gave her my serum when she bloomed. I tried to buy you for her. When I found out Thane used his last serum on you, I convinced her to let you stay with him. He is a good man, and I knew you would be safe with him. But then you killed his mother and went on the run. We have spent the last two years searching for you, hoping we would find you before he could get his hands on you," he tells me.

"You're lying. Packs can have more than one Omega. And even if what you're saying is true, how did you get away with faking her death?"

Jake sighs.

"Why would I lie, Harlow? As for your other question, I can't tell you here. Too many ears. But ask your mates. The laws changed three weeks before Zara came to us. They made it stricter. Once marked and mated, that is the only Omega for the pack. No new ones, and those that do take another are heavily penalized."

"So, Thane can't take another Omega?" I ask him.

"Not unless he wants to pay over a million dollars in fines. Not that he can't afford it, but why risk it when you have his last serum running in your veins," Jake tells me, buttoning up his shirt.

"Omegas are becoming rarer. It is also why the council is so quick to chuck Omegas into rotation these days, trying to bring population numbers up. One thing goes wrong, and an Omega is forced into the rotation—parking ticket, arrears in rent—the council has become desperate. I wouldn't have been able to bid on you had they known Zara was alive."

"You could just be saying all this. Those marks could be from anyone in your pack," I tell him.

"I could be, but when I saw you, saw how frightened you were, I stuck around. I found out you worked here. I knew once Thane figured out who you are, he would want your head."

"Then prove she's alive, call her," I tell him, knowing I would recognize her voice anywhere.

Jake shakes his head. "No, we just got her to a good place. I am not getting her hopes up only for you to decide not to come. So again, Harlow, do you want my help in getting out of here?" he asks.

How can I trust him? For all I know, he could be the one who killed Thane's mother and set me up. He could whisk me away only for me to find out my sister is indeed dead.

"What do you mean about her not being in a good place?" I ask him.

"Our pack has lost a lot. I am not willing to lose my mate or this baby by destressing her," he tells me.

My sister is pregnant? That makes no sense. She's dead. I saw the autopsy report.

"Then how am I supposed to believe you if you won't let me speak to her?" I tell him.

He slides a folded piece of paper over to me. "My number. I am staying in town until my meeting on Friday with Thane. Decide before then. I have to leave on Friday to get back to my family," he says, standing up and sliding his stool under the bar.

"Did you have anything to do with Thane's mother's death?" I ask. His brows pinch.

"No, you killed her. Didn't you?" he asks, seemingly genuinely perplexed. I shake my head.

"But Thane thinks you did?"

"He won't let me explain. They have some shitty grainy footage of me leaving a restaurant with his mother before she died. But I didn't do it. We were run off the road and attacked after that. She told me to run."

"Can you prove this?" he asks. I shake my head, knowing I can't. No one else was on the road besides the people that tried to capture me.

"Have you told Thane this?" he asks.

"I tried; he wouldn't listen," I admit.

"I'll look into it. But remember, Harlow, Friday. Decide by then or I will leave without you," he says before leaving.

I am so confused. He was acting very differently when I saw him at the office a couple weeks ago. Like two completely different people, and I don't know which version of him to trust. If he is right about the laws changing around Omega purchases, that is also more motive to try to deceive me.

When my shift ends, I quickly change back into my clothes. I'm about to leave when Bree hands me a plastic bag.

"Your shoes and clothes from the other night," she tells me, and I curse. I left the clothes and shoes I borrowed from her at the hotel.

"Thanks, I will return yours tomorrow when I come in," I tell her before bidding her goodbye, catching a cab back to the hotel, and doing my normal after-work ritual of ridding myself of the scents from work before my mates arrive.

CHAPTER
SEVENTY-FOUR

~R~aidon~

We've waited for Thane to fire Sarah all day, and it is almost over. I swear it's almost as if he is punishing us for going against him last night. Hearing my door handle twist, I look up and glare at the door, hoping it isn't Sarah. Relief floods me when I see it is just Rhen, and my body visibly relaxes. Leaning back in my chair, I fold my arms across my chest.

"Have you heard from your mother about Harlow's blood test yet? They should have come back by now," Rhen asks. I sigh, reaching for my phone and calling my mother.

"I will ask her," I tell him, dialing her number. "Has Thane fired her yet?" I ask as I hit the call button.

"No, but I will before the end of the day if he doesn't," Rhen tells me.

The phone rings twice before she answers.

"What's wrong, son? You can't wait five minutes to speak to me," she says, and my brows furrow.

"I am calling about Harlow's blood tests," I tell her.

"Well, we can chat soon; I am just about to step into the elevator. I got those glazed donuts you like, and some for Sarah. She is such a lovely girl," Mom tells me, and I press my lips in a line; that bitch even got her hooks into my mother.

"When did you speak to Sarah?" I ask her.

"Earlier, I called the office when you didn't answer. She seems nice, so I thought I would come to meet her. She said you are considering taking her as your Omega," she tells me, and I see Rhen's hands fist at his sides as he eavesdrops.

"No, actually, Rhen just fired her," I tell her and look at Rhen, pointing to the door. He gladly obliges, storming out in a fury that she would dare make such a claim. And to my mother of all people!

"Fired her? I only spoke to her an hour ago," she says, and I growl, annoyed.

"We have an Omega already, mother."

"Nonsense, you can't keep that murderous little whore; I won't accept her, Raidon."

Rhen returns, popping his head in the door and mouthing to me, 'Where is she?'

I shrug. She was in the lobby, last I saw.

"Good thing you don't need to. She is our mate, not yours," I tell her when I hear a loud bang from Leon's office. I stand, trying to look out the door.

"Mom, I need to go; I will see you when you come up."

She tries to say something to me, but I hang up, too concerned over the commotion. I can hear Rhen losing his mind. Stepping around my desk, I move toward the door before seeing Thane rip his door open across from mine. I just hope Rhen doesn't kill her.

Stepping into the hall, though, I find Rhen has a hold of her arm, and she is bleeding. Rhen snarls, and he shoves her toward Thane as she whimpers, her face turning red with embarrassment. Yet I can't pay attention to what is going on, more focused on Leon's door, where they had just come out.

"Fuck off! She is not to set foot in this building again!" Rhen yells at Thane who grabs her arms before she stumbles into him. He looks her over while I step past them, heading toward Leon's door.

"What did you do?" Thane growls at her, his voice growing distant as he walks off somewhere with her. Stepping into Leon's office, I find him stiff as a board, sitting in his chair. His face has blood on it, but I can tell he is holding his breath, as if he is afraid to move.

"I can't," he growls, and my eyes widen when I realize she tried to make him feed on her. I turn to rush back to the kitchenette, but Rhen already has a wet cloth in his hand as he comes behind me. I snatch it before rushing over to him; his entire body is tense. A bloody handprint is on the side of his face and over his lips.

I growl, scrubbing it off, yet the moment I do, he snarls and lunges at me. His teeth sink into my neck, making me grunt at the force he uses to bite me, not only using his fangs but his canines too. Thane bursts into the room as my ass slams against the desk. As Leon tears into my neck, Rhen moves toward me, but I shake my head. Leon needs to feed. He has been holding off, waiting for Harlow to give him permission. That woman tried to use his own instincts against him. His tongue laps at my neck.

"Where is she?" Rhen demands, turning on Thane.

"Gone, what happened?" he asks, and I toss the bloody cloth at him.

"Sarah happened," I snarl as Leon sinks his teeth into me again, higher up my neck this time as he tries to rid himself of the urge for Omega blood. I curse, wanting to kill her. Thane sniffs the cloth and growls.

"This is your fault. We told you to get rid of her," Rhen snaps at him just as I hear the elevator door sound down the corridor. Thane looks over his shoulder and back at us.

"Did he... he didn't—"

"No! But he was stiff as a plank when I walked in. She cut her hand open and was practically in his lap while he was frozen, fighting his damn urges to feed on her, Thane!" Rhen yells at him just as I see my mother step into the corridor. She wanders over to us before noticing Leon feeding on me like a damn savage. She quickly averts her gaze.

"I'll just go find Sarah, shall I, while you, ah..." She doesn't finish, walking off, not wanting to witness such an intimate act between mates. To my mother, this would be just as horrifying as the time she walked in on me jerking off when I was a teenager. Neither of us ever mention it, but once eye contact was made, it was too late. I can laugh now about it, although it was horrifying at the time.

"You won't find her. She's gone. Though, Ma, you can help me clean out her desk," Rhen tells her before shoving past Thane, who is watching Leon with concern. Mom nods, talking to Rhen as they make their way to her desk. I rub my hands up his sides, starting to feel a little lightheaded.

Thane, feeling I can't take much more through the bond, comes over to us, presses his chest against Leon's back, and purrs at him. The Calling doesn't have the same effect on us as it does Harlow, yet it entices Leon enough to pull his teeth from my neck and seek out our Alpha. Leon turns toward Thane, who is already undoing his top three buttons. Leon impatiently paws at him, his hunger nowhere near abated. It won't be until he feeds on Harlow. We just need to get him calm enough to walk him out of the building without attacking anyone.

"Go see your mother; I will stay with Leon," Thane tells me, and I grab a tissue off his desk, dabbing at my neck and my now ruined shirt. Closing the door behind me, I see my mother pouting as she helps dump the contents of the desk into a box.

"She seemed so nice on the phone; I can't believe she would do such a thing," my mother says. Rhen sighs, and I know he is only holding his tongue because she is my mother.

Moving toward the desk, Rhen slides the donut box over to me.

"Eat before you pass out," he orders, and I roll my eyes. Mom is watching me closely. She tosses the contents of the top drawer into the box with a sigh before coming over to me as I rummage through the donut box. She pressed a hand to my clammy face.

"Oh, you look a little pale, son. Eat up."

I roll my eyes at her concerned tone, only for her to pinch my face between her fingers.

"Don't roll your eyes at me, son. I will—"

"What, Ma? Throw a hip out trying to catch me to smack me," I laugh, and she slaps my chest and clicks her tongue.

"Harlow's blood tests?" I ask, biting into the donut.

"Yes, yes, I will get to it."

"You haven't done them yet?" Rhen asks, and she sighs.

"I will get to it when I get back to the clinic tomorrow."

"Please, you've had all week. Tomorrow is Friday, Mom!"

"Fine, fine, I will have the results for you tomorrow. I promise," she adds, and I huff annoyed while shaking my head. "So, Sarah?"

"Will never be our Omega," I tell her. Rhen wanders off, and my mother sighs, knowing she is one step from being kicked out with the tension up here at the moment.

"Well, I guess I will head home. Do you want me to drop this in the bins or to Sarah?"

"Sarah, it will save us having to. Thane said she is apparently waiting for her belongings in the lobby downstairs with security."

Rhen retrieves her handbag dumping it into the box of fuzzy pink crap she stocked her desk with. I shake my head, and Rhen passes the box to my mother.

"Fine, I will give this to her as I leave," she tells me, and I lean down, pecking her cheek, and so does Rhen. He presses the elevator button for her, while I make my way back to Leon's office to check on him and Thane.

AN HOUR LATER

"I want to grab dinner on the way home," Rhen tells me. I am too preoccupied with thoughts about Harlow, though. She felt off all afternoon, almost anxious.

"What?" I ask Rhen, not catching what he said.

"I asked what you want to get for dinner," he says, shaking his head.

"Anything. Tell Thane to pick it up, I want to get back to the hotel," I tell him, and he nods his head. Leon is quiet in the back. Thane is following in the car behind us. I am anxious to see his reaction to Harlow. He wanted to take Leon home with him, but he refused, so Thane insisted on staying with us until he is sure Leon is okay.

I'm worried about how Harlow will react to being near him after the other night. I see Thane turn off in the side mirror, and I know Rhen must have mind-linked him when my phone starts ringing. I pull it from my pocket and groan when I see it is my mother, but I answer it anyway.

"Hey, Ma."

"I am just letting you know I gave Sarah the box, but she said the book on the top isn't hers. I think it belongs to the other one," my mother says, not even hiding her disgust for Harlow from her voice.

"Should I bin it?" she asks.

"What book?" I ask.

"I don't know. It looks like some diary or notebook; rubbish," she says.

"No, drop it back to the office tomorrow when you bring the blood test results," I tell her, adding the extra reminder.

My mother sighs. "How about I stop over tomorrow night after I finish at bingo with the girls? I will drop it off with Thane. I don't want to see her again by going to that damn hotel," she snaps at me.

"Fine, but Mom, I want those blood results by the time I finish work tomorrow," I tell her before saying goodbye and hanging up. I rest my head back and exhale. Her hate toward my mate is starting to irritate me.

SEVENTY-FIVE

~ H arlow~
I feel like absolute shit. I think I have food poisoning from the salad that Bree gave me for lunch. Or maybe it's from nerves after seeing Jake. I have no idea what his intentions are, yet after everything, I highly doubt they are anything good. Hearing the door open, I glance at it from where I lie huddled beneath the blanket. The moment they step in, I snarl, tucking my face beneath the blankets. They reek of her, and I refuse to give Thane the satisfaction of seeing me give over to instinct and scent them; he won't catch me off guard again.

"Shower!" I snarl at them when I feel one of them touch the blanket, about to pull it back. Rhen bristles and wanders off. Seconds later, I hear the shower turn on and their soft voices.

Shuddering at the sickly scent wafting out with the steam, I burrow deeper beneath the blanket, hoping to hide from its sickly perfume. I hear the door open again and then the window.

"Damn, it reeks in here," I hear Thane's angry voice, and I freeze beneath the blanket. He is right. It stinks of his bitch assistant. Now I regret washing the scents from work off. If I had known, I would have left my work clothes on just to spite him, so he knows how it feels.

I don't bother sticking my head out from beneath the blanket. I wait for him to leave, only for him to wander into the bathroom, which has me sitting up, just as Leon walks out with a towel wrapped low on his hips.

"Better?" he asks while coming over to me. He raises an eyebrow at me when I say nothing.

I roll my eyes but lean forward, sniffing him, and can only smell our mates and the scent of vanilla and honey soap. I nod when he cups my face in his hand.

"Are you okay? You look ill," he asks.

"Yeah, think I have food poisoning," I murmur, glancing at the bathroom door when Rhen, too, wanders out. I watch as they get changed into boxer shorts, and Rhen rummages through some containers I think Thane brought in with him. He hands me one but the thought of eating almost sends me running for the bathroom. Instead, I nestle back under the blankets as he climbs in bed and sits beside me.

My eyes flick to the bathroom door as Raidon comes out, and I look up at Rhen.

"Why is Thane here?"

"Because my mates are," Thane answers, also stepping out of the bathroom, and Leon tosses him a pair of Rhen's shorts to slip on.

"Why don't you stay at Sarah's?" I growl at him.

"She was fired today," he says but doesn't deny she is an option. My stomach sinks, knowing he is only here because they are. It is a stupid notion, but it still stings.

For the most part, Thane spends the night glaring at me, and I spend the night pretending not to notice when Leon climbs over Rhen, forces himself between us, and pulls me on top of him.

It is getting harder to be here with every second that passes, as I watch them across the room from me. I was able to get my jealousy under control when they finally stopped touching her and pulling her around like a damn yoyo. Raidon and Rhen are asleep, and I watch Leon climb off the bed I'm on. I growl at him. He ignores me, climbing over Rhen and squeezing between Harlow and Raidon. He rolls onto his back, pulling Harlow on top of him, and I watch as she sighs.

"If I make you sick, it isn't my fault," she tells him. She has been sick most of the night, but Leon is itching to get his fangs into her. She sweeps her hair over her shoulder and offers him her neck. She hisses as his teeth puncture her skin, before the pain turns to ecstasy and she moans softly.

I move uncomfortably, turning my gaze back to the TV. I try to ignore them, when I hear her hiss again, making me look over to see he bit her again. She smacks his shoulders, trying to push off him yet his grip only tightens.

"Leon, stop," I snap at him, and he groans, her hand reaching for Rhen as she squeezes his shoulder.

"Leon, enough!" I snap at him. He is crazed by his blood lust, and I grit my teeth when her hand feebly clutches at Rhen, her nails scratching down his chest. I see his eyes flutter as Leon's fingers tangle in her hair, and she makes a choking noise which has me jumping out of bed.

I smack Rhen hard in the chest as I reach over him to grab her, and he jumps. His eyes fly open, looking at me alarmed as I catch Harlow around the waist. Her legs kicking and hands clawing at Leon, trying to get him to stop. Rhen rolls, grabbing his face.

"Let her go!" I command him.

He does so reluctantly, as I grab her off him. She sways, leaning into me when I set her feet on the ground. Rhen looks murderous as he glares at our mate. Harlow squirms in my arms, coming back to her senses as she clutches her neck. I shove her toward my bed while Rhen wrangles Leon under control, waking Raidon, who wraps his arms around Leon. He fights for a few seconds before snapping out of it and realizing he isn't getting out of Raidon's grip.

Rhen sits up and looks at Harlow before waving her to come to him, and she moves toward him, but I turn, shoving her back toward my bed.

"She can sleep with me," I snap at him, pissed off that he didn't wake to her panic. Neither of them did.

"No, I am fine, now," Harlow says, but I climb on the bed as she tries to hop off it for a second time.

"Lay down. You stay here!" I order her. My command washes over her, making her entire body tense, before she is forced to submit and crashes back onto the bed.

"Stop ordering her around, Thane. If she doesn't want to sleep with you, she doesn't have to," Rhen snaps as I drop the command.

"And how many times has that happened," I snarl at him, pointing to Leon, who I can feel is wracked with guilt.

"It hasn't. We are just tired. It's hard sleeping here," Rhen defends. "Come here, Harlow," Rhen tells her, and she goes to sit up when I drop my arm over her waist, tugging her back and tossing my leg over hers.

"You remain here," I tell her. She glares at the ceiling for a second before rolling to face away from me. I sigh, tugging her closer. I hear Rhen curse behind me, but I ignore him.

They aren't the only ones with trouble sleeping. I haven't slept in days, and it is because they spend every night here with her, instead of at home with me.

SEVENTY-SIX

~H arlow~

I wake up early to Thane climbing out of bed. I snatch the blanket, tugging it over my face as he gets ready for work. I want to steal a couple more hours' sleep before I have to get to work for the private gig. Yet as I listen to them getting ready, Jake's words from yesterday nag at me. All night, I waited for Thane to leave so I could ask them; that didn't happen. I have no choice but to ask now, because Jake is leaving today. I'm still pondering whether or not to go with him, yet at the same time, the thought of leaving makes that sickly feeling in the pit of my stomach worse.

Rolling over, I see Raidon climb out of bed with a groan before he slaps Leon's ass hard, making him jump.

"Wake up. We gotta get to work," Raidon snaps at him.

Thane wanders into the bathroom, and I know now is my only chance to see if Jake is telling the truth about the council laws changing.

"Can I ask you a question about the council?" I ask Rhen just when Thane wanders out. I roll my eyes and let out a breath.

"What did you want to know?" Rhen says as he buttons up his shirt.

"Nothing, it doesn't matter," I tell him, and Thane looks over at me.

"What do you want to know, Harlow? You aren't going into the rotation if that's what you want to ask him," Thane snaps at me.

I blink at him because that is definitely not what I was going to ask. Yet his words nag me.

"What if I already put my name down?" I spit back at him. All that earns me is a growl from the lot of them.

"You better fucking not have!" Thane yells at me, and I shrug.

His anger is loud and clear as it courses through the bond.

"Not like I'm pack, remember? I'm only thinking of my future, you know, since it won't be with you!" I snarl, yet my bravado wears off pretty quickly when he crosses the room in a rage.

"Did you put your name on a rotation list or not?" he says, grabbing my arm.

"And if I did?" I ask while glaring at him. He curses, shoving me back.

"She didn't. She is just trying to piss me off," Thane says, turning back to finish getting ready. Rhen exhales and runs a hand through his hair before reaching for his jacket.

"What do you want to know about the council?" Rhen asks.

"I heard some of the hotel workers yesterday talking about how the council had changed the laws about packs owning Omegas. That they are only allowed one now," I lie. No way am I telling them about Jake tracking me down, or where I was when he did.

"They said the laws changed just before your pack bought me," I tell them. For some reason, saying that out loud puts a sour taste in my mouth. They bought me. As if I was merely a belonging, a possession. A fucking Alpha's possession.

"Yes, that is correct," Rhen says, looking at Thane, who doesn't seem to be the least bit happy that Rhen answered my question.

"So, if you took Sarah, what would happen?"

"Nothing, I would have to pay a fine," Thane tells me, as if the fine is just an inconvenience, not an actual issue. Great.

"But we aren't getting another Omega!" Raidon snaps, glaring at Thane.

"Anything else?" Rhen asks me. I shake my head and lay back down, watching as they finish getting ready for work while thinking about what Jake said.

"Did you know Jake was the other bidder?" I ask them, suddenly curious.

"Yes, but you had already received my last serum," Thane snaps.

"You could have given them a new serum," I tell him.

"And have an Omega that ranks the same as me within the pack?" He laughs and shakes his head.

"Why not? Is everything about control with you, Thane?" I retort.

"I am Alpha, not some Omega. You have Alpha blood in your veins, and I am not giving you Alpha-of-Alpha blood. You would outrank our mates and match me. I am not fucking stupid enough to hand my pack over to a murderer," he replies, snatching his jacket up from off the back of the chair.

"I never killed—"

"I don't want to hear more lies, Harlow. Unless you are going to tell me what really happened, I will not hear it," he says.

"I have been trying to tell you what happened. You won't fucking listen!" I yell at him.

"We have it on video!" he screams at me. "Footage doesn't lie."

"No, apparently only I do. You could always command the fucking answer out of me, but you won't on the off-chance you're wrong and you punished and blamed me all these years for no fucking reason!" I yell at him.

He growls but says nothing; instead, storming out of the place and slamming the door. Leon, Rhen, and Raidon stare at the door. Thane's fury is palpable, bleeding into us all through the bond. I open my mouth to say something, only to snap it shut when Rhen holds up a hand.

"You just had to press his buttons, Harlow. When are you going to learn being a brat will get you nowhere with him?"

Stunned, I just blink at his words. I know it's Thane's anger making him say this, but to be told to just submit and be quiet after being called a liar grinds my gears. So, they don't want me to lie, but I can't speak the truth either.

"We will never get you back home at this rate if you can't learn to watch what you say!" Rhen snaps at me before stalking out the door. Raidon exhales and walks over to me, pecking my forehead but saying nothing, and Leon quickly pecks my cheek before rushing after them.

I stare at the door after it closes.

They will never believe me.

No matter what I say, they are never going to believe me— instead, choosing to believe some bullshit footage that only shows we came out of a restaurant together.

By the time I crawl out of bed and start pulling my clothes on, it's lunchtime. Our earlier argument just reiterates the fact that I am making the right choice by leaving. After I finish work tonight, I am catching the first bus out of here.

I could leave with Jake, but I don't trust him either. What if it is a trap? I want proof that my sister is alive before I throw my life away and blindly follow him. For now, I just need to get the fuck out of this city. I can figure out the rest later.

Grabbing one of their backpacks, I stuff as much of my stuff into it as I can, only to curse that I still haven't gotten my handbag back. Sighing, I know I will have to figure something else out because asking for it back will just make them suspicious, especially after I asked about the council and then got into an argument with everyone this morning.

When I finish, I call a cab. Nerves start setting in about what I am about to do. Every second that ticks by as I wait for the cab has nausea building, and bile rises up my throat. The trip there doesn't help. When I walk inside, I stop in my tracks when I see Talon is back early.

Bree tries to wave me off, shooing me, but it's too late. He spins around and spots me.

"What are you doing here? Does Leon know you're here?" he asks. I swallow, looking at Bree nervously.

"I need to show you something," she says, tugging on his arm.

"Yep, just wait a second, I want to know why Harlow is here," he tells her, shaking her hand off and walking toward me.

"I asked her to come in. We're short staffed, and Leon gave her permission," Bree blurts out. Talon stops, glancing between the two of us. I nod in agreement, but Talon seems confused.

"Now, the cash register, I can't get it to open," Bree tells him, tugging him behind the bar. He sighs, glancing at it before bending down to fix it, and Bree points to the back room while Talon is still distracted. I rush back, hoping to escape to the functions section before he sees me. I grab my clothes and toss my bag in the locker before racing upstairs to get ready.

CHAPTER
SEVENTY-SEVEN

~ T hane~

Alpha Jake keeps looking at his phone throughout the meeting. He seems somewhat distracted, and I end up cutting the meeting short. He is getting on my nerves.

"We can do this another time. You are clearly distracted," I tell him getting up from my seat.

"Sorry, I have something going on, but yes, we can go over the last of the details over the phone," he tells me, and I nod. I want to leave early today anyway. I want to see if I can convince my mates to come home, or even just one of them. I can't handle being in that damn house by myself. The quiet is driving me insane.

I walk Alpha Jake to the elevator when he pauses at Harlow's old desk.

"What about your Omega? Why isn't she in today?" he asks, and I growl, not liking him speaking of her.

"Did you know who she is?" I ask him. He was the other bidder, and from what I heard from Harlow, he knew her twin sister. That is, if she was telling the truth.

"No. What you mean?" he says.

I shake my head and motion for him to leave. "Safe travels," I tell him.

He looks like he wants to say something, but I am already walking back to my office. On my way there, I hear my desk phone ring. Pushing my office door open, I move quickly to grab it before it rings out. Picking it up, I see it is Elaine.

"Hey, Elaine," I answer the call.

"Well, finally, some good comes out of that wench," Elaine tells me, and my brows furrow at her words.

"Pardon?"

"Harlow, some good did come from her, and now you can be done with her."

"Elaine, I am not taking Sarah as an Omega," I tell her.

"Oh, I know that you boys are too stubborn for that. I am talking about Harlow. She's pregnant, Thane. I've got her test results in my hand. She is pregnant. So, you can get your pup—or fingers crossed she's pregnant with more than one—then we can kill her. Problem solved: breed her and bury her," Elaine tells me.

"Harlow is pregnant?" I ask her.

"Yes, did you not hear me? Is it a bad line?" she asks, mistaking my silence for a bad connection. "Hello?" she says after a few seconds.

"Okay," I tell her.

"Okay. Thane, you need to get her home before she runs off and uses that baby against you. That is why I called you. We have already lost so much because of her. And I refuse to lose a grandchild too. At least some good has come out of this mess," she says, and I swallow.

I hardly hear anything else she says after that. I hang up just as Rhen and Leon wander into my office, also wanting to leave early today.

"What's wrong with you?" Leon asks, stealing my bottle of Coke off my desk. Opening it, he takes a sip of it.

"Harlow is pregnant," I tell them, a little shocked by the information. Leon chokes on his next sip.

"She's pregnant?" Rhen asks.

"Elaine just called me," I tell them just as Raidon comes in. He stops, glancing around at us, feeling all our shock.

"So, is someone going to speak?" Raidon asks, peering at us.

"Harlow is pregnant," Leon blurts out, yet despite this good news, they watch me warily, as if nervous about how I'll react to this information.

~HARLOW~

I feel like throwing up. I glance at the clock as the time gets closer. I am on the verge of a panic attack in the small room attached to the functions room as the security helps set up the boxes we are expected to lay in.

I shake my hands and pace the small room, trying to encourage myself. It is just a job, yet I feel sickened by what I am about to do. I'm not like Bree. This isn't a business transaction to me. This is my body; I can't detach from it like she can.

Hearing voices as the function room fills with people, I glance around nervously for Bree before peering through the black curtain that separates us from the men on the other side. The door opens, and Bree rushes in. She thanks the security staff, who assure us they will be on the other side of the curtain to make sure they don't try to hurt us in any way. Hearing that makes the pit in my stomach open up more.

"Breathe, Harlow. They won't hurt us, and Shane is on the other side. It'll be fun. Just relax!" she says, rubbing my arms before slipping her clothes off, leaving her in just a bra, panties, and heels.

Bree is about to climb onto the table and slide her bottom half through when the door opens, and Talon walks in, his head down as he peers at his phone.

"We are three girls shor—" his words cut off abruptly when he lifts his head and sees me. His eyes run the length of me before he pins Bree with a glare.

"No! Are you fucking insane, Bree? Thane will kill me," Talon says, grabbing my arm. Bree rushes to my side and gives him a shove.

"She is a grown adult and can make her own decisions, Tal," Bree snaps at him.

"She has mates. I don't even like that you are doing this shit, but you insist. I would rather get rid of these shows altogether."

"And what, Tal? Make me a fucking housewife?" she snaps at him.

"Yes, I don't like you working the floors either. We've talked about this!" he snarls at her, and I am completely forgotten as they start to argue.

"Wake up, Talon! You don't want me. I'm not an Omega; I can't carry your children. I am not going to commit to you only to be tossed aside."

"I am not one of those Alphas, Bree. I don't want kids! I have told you this!" he snarls before reaching for me. He jerks me toward him, and Bree grabs my other arm.

"Let her go. Thane doesn't give a shit what she does, Talon. She doesn't even live with them after he kicked her out! What does that say about her being their mate?" she snarls.

"He kicked you out? I know you fought, but Leon told me they are talking to him and will sort it all out," Talon says, looking confused.

"See, she doesn't belong to him."

"I don't like this. No, she still bears their mark, Bree!"

"You don't have to like it. And with some de-scenter, they won't even be able to tell," Bree is quick to defend, tossing the can I just used at him. Talon grits his teeth and storms out, slamming the door.

Bree squeezes my arm. "He won't say anything," Bree tells me, waving him off.

Bree climbs up onto the table using a small stool, she waves for me to do the same, and I chew my lip, having serious second thoughts about doing this. The room on the other side is full of voices, and I hear security explaining the rules, what they can and can't do to us, and the repercussions if they tried, when I hear a familiar voice.

I have no idea why, but it has my brows scrunching as I try to place where I've heard the voice before. I listen to the men's banter and chatter. I shake my head, changing my mind when Bree climbs off the table and grips my arms.

"It's just sex. Do you want to leave the city or not?" she asks, looking me dead in the face.

"I do; I just don't think this is the way for me to do it," I tell her. I regret not taking Alpha Jake's offer. I still have his phone number. Maybe I can call him. I hear the familiar voice again. I peer toward the curtain.

"It's five thousand dollars. That will get you out of the city and set you up until you find a job," she tells me.

Yeah, but it still won't last long, and I'm not sure I can go through with it.

"Maybe Tammy," I suggest when the deep voice has my head turning toward the curtain. I step forward when she grabs my arm.

"I need to know. If you can't, I'll get Tammy. You have ten minutes, so choose now. Are you in or not?" she asks, and I swallow, feeling guilty that I wasted her time.

"I'm sorry, Bree. I can't do it."

She drops her head and sighs.

"It's okay, I'll send for Tammy," she says, running her fingers through her hair. She tugs the curtain back slightly and peers out at Shane, yet makes sure to keep herself hidden from the men on the other side.

"Can you ask Tammy to swap places with Z?"

He nods, walking off when she closes the curtain.

"Who are they?" I ask her nervously.

"Some Alpha Pack," she says dismissively, when I hear that voice again. It has me pinching the side of the curtain to look out. Peeking out, I see men drinking and moving around when the one directly in front of the curtain steps aside a little more, letting me look past his body at the others, and I gasp. Mr. Black?

I take a step back, letting the curtain close.

"Z?" Bree asks, knowing better than to use my name when a flimsy curtain is all that separates us from them. I shake my head.

"I need to go," I tell her, spinning on my heel and ripping the door open. I rush out, only for a set of hands to grip my arms tightly. A feral growl tears out of him, as he jerks me to him.

"When Talon called me, I thought he was fucking lying," he snaps at me.

I gulp, looking up at Thane.

CHAPTER
SEVENTY-EIGHT

~**H**arlow~

I wrestle out of Thane's grip.

"I didn't do anything, and as you can see, I'm leaving!" I screech. Thane looks me up and down, disgusted at my work attire.

"Oh really, then why did Talon call to tell me you were about to get fucked in a damn glory hole? All you've ever done is try to whore yourself out!"

I am shocked he dared to call me a whore. I was a virgin when I met them. My mouth still hangs open at his accusation.

My initial shock wears off, now replaced with seething anger. I snarl at Thane. "I wouldn't even be here if I didn't need the money to support myself. It's not like you paid me for all the work I did. Nor did you have the decency to bring my purse to the hotel. You don't fucking want me. None of you do! You won't fucking believe me or let me speak. All you want is to breed me and then kill me for something I didn't do!"

He listens to my outburst with an unreadable expression on his face. He reaches for me, but I pull away.

"Why don't you just go and find your fucking skank whore of a secretary and leave me alone? Cut your losses, Thane. I will never allow you to treat me like some broodmare, then put me out for slaughter after you get what you want from me!" I snarl at him.

Thane is initially taken aback before he growls at me. "News flash, Harlow! You're already pregnant. And your death can't come soon enough for me! I've had enough of your nonsense!"

I blink at him in shock. Did he say I'm pregnant?

"You'd only need money for one thing, and that is to run away. But not with my child, you won't."

No! I can't be pregnant. He has to be lying. I am totally blindsided, although it would explain why I have felt like shit lately. There is no way I am going to let him take me and take my baby.

Thane lunges at me, trying to grab me and haul me out of here. My claws extend as I swipe at him to keep him back, grazing his chest through his shirt. "Harlow!" Thane grits out.

I bolt for the stairs, but not fast enough as Thane rips me back by my shirt. "Get off of me, you son of a bitch!" I say while thrashing in his grip, not caring about the attention I am drawing.

"Enough, Harlow! Submit!" he snarls, forcing his command over me and making me freeze on the spot.

I am motionless under his command. Tears stream down my cheeks, unable to fight it. How could I be cursed to endure such sadistic control? Being born an Omega is not a blessing; it is a curse.

A curse that killed my parents, a curse that took my sister from me, and now a curse that will end my life after he takes my baby from me. All for something I didn't do. I should have died that night along with my parents; if I had, none of this would have happened.

Thane steers me down the stairs; Talon is at the bottom, holding my backpack. I reach for it, only for Thane to snatch it out of my grip.

"You won't be needing this with where you will be staying until our pup is born," Thane threatens. Talon looks away guiltily. Thane steers me into the main floor to find everyone staring in our direction. Thane's grip on my arm is painful as he marches me toward the front doors.

Stepping outside, Rhen is standing beside the car on the curb. He glances at me briefly before pressing his lips in a line. His burning anger and disgust smash into me, and I wither and recoil inside as I feel it through the bond. He opens the back door as Thane shoves me toward it, and Rhen grips my arm as I stumble toward him.

"I wasn't going to—" I try to tell Rhen.

"I don't want to hear it," he says, stuffing me inside the car and slamming the door shut. I cringe at the loud bang as they both climb in the front of the car. The wheels spin and screech before Thane takes off, sending me backward in my seat before I scramble for the seatbelt.

Dread pools in my stomach as we get closer to the packhouse. I try to speak to them, try to explain. It all falls on deaf ears. They never even acknowledge my words. They speak over me, as if they can't hear me. Yet their fury is loud and clear through the bond.

If only I had marked them, maybe they would be able to feel the extent of what I say, maybe they would see. Instead, they get glimmers but nothing else, not like the way I can feel them since they marked me. And I don't like what I feel radiating through the bond from all of them.

As Thane pulls up to the enormous gates in front of the mansion, I reach for the door handle. Thane's growl in the front seat causes me to drop my hand as I meet his gaze in the mirror. Time slows, as if lengthening the torture. He drives up the long driveway, and my heart races in my chest as he pulls up out front. Still, they say nothing to me.

"Leon?" I ask them as hope starts dwindling. Once inside, I won't be leaving alive, and I suddenly find adrenaline pumping through me as I toss the door open, only to be ripped backward, having forgotten to take my seat belt off. My claws slip-free in my panic, shredding through the belt that has a stranglehold on me, and I take off across the manicured lawns toward the front gates.

I get about twenty meters before Thane catches me. His arms wrap around my torso as he pulls me back against his chest. I thrash, kicking and screaming. I will not go to my death easily. So, I scream, hoping one of the neighbors on this long-ass street will hear me.

"Stop it, Harlow. You brought this on yourself," Thane snarls in my ear. I scream in frustration and thrash harder, but it's pointless, and before I know it, we're inside the mansion, and he heads toward the Den.

"No, please, Thane. I wasn't going to do it!" I scream as I kick and drag my feet as the door comes into view.

"I wasn't, please! I wasn't going to go through with it! Bree was getting Tammy!" I scream. Thane snarls, dragging me through the house.

"Command me! I can prove it, please!" I scream when Raidon, hearing the commotion, steps out into the hall from the kitchen.

Thane stops, and I look at Raidon helplessly.

"You weren't going to go through with it?" Raidon asks, and I shake my head.

"She is lying," Thane snarls.

"Command her," Raidon snaps at him.

"It could hurt the baby," Leon says, stepping out behind him.

"Not while she's still this early," Raidon tells him, and I know that must be true because Thane commanded me at the club, and I know he wouldn't risk his baby.

"You were going to back out?" Raidon asks me, and I nod, pleading with him to believe me.

Thane growls, spinning me around to face him, and he grips my face in his hand.

His command and aura wash over me, and his arm around my waist is the only thing keeping me upright as I grit my teeth through my body's spasms. His grip on my face is bordering on painful as he speaks.

"You will answer truthfully," he orders, and I nod, tears brimming in my eyes.

"Were you going to participate in Bree's gig?"

"No!" I breathe out in relief as the answer peels off my tongue easily, and they can see I wasn't going to do it. I hear Raidon exhale behind me, yet Thane doesn't drop his order or command.

"Were you going to run?" he asks, and my entire body tenses as I fight the urge to answer. Wait, that isn't supposed to be the question.

"Were you going to run?" he asks slowly, pressing his aura harder on me. I whimper, not wanting to answer.

"Yes!" I breathe out through gritted teeth.

"How, if you had no money?" he asks, and I realize he's trying to see if I was planning on doing anything else at the club. I would have preferred that answer over the one I didn't consciously know I was going to make.

"I was going to ask Alpha Jake." The moment the words leave my lips, my heart nearly stops. Consciously, I planned to consider it, yet subconsciously my mind is apparently already made up, based on the words that spill out of my mouth.

His command drops. "Fucking whore," he snarls, his fingers digging into my face.

"No, wait. Alpha Jake said he could—" My words die off as his command rolls over me painfully as he shoves the full weight of it on me.

"I don't want to hear any more of your lies. You won't speak unless spoken to; I am done hearing your voice," Thane snarls. I open my mouth to speak, yet nothing comes out. He made me mute!

Tears prick my eyes as he spins me around and shoves me toward the Den door. I move toward Raidon, but he takes a step back from me and points to the Den door. My eyes widen in horror. They aren't going to help me. Are they going to let him lock me down there?

When I don't move toward the door, Thane grips my arm roughly, jerking me toward it before ripping the door open. He stomps down the steps, dragging me behind him before stopping at the bottom and shoving me into the vast underground room. The only windows down here are slightly over a foot wide and maybe a little taller, but they are too high for me to reach. There's no natural light, no escape but the door we just came through.

"Make yourself comfortable. You will be spending the next four months down here," he snaps before turning on his heel and heading up the steps. I want to ask what he plans to do after the four months. I know the answer, but I need to hear him say it. Surely, he won't rip my baby from my arms and kill me? He can't be so cruel.

I chase after him climbing the steps two at a time. As he opens the door and I reach out for the handle, he slams it in my face and clicks the lock in place. I bang on the door, screaming out silently since I can't speak.

I bang on the door for hours before giving up. It is clear I'm not going anywhere. Trudging down the steps, I fall into the Den, knowing there is nothing down here to aid in my escape. Yet I won't stop trying, and Thane better hope I don't get out of here, because if I do, I am coming for him first.

CHAPTER
SEVENTY-NINE

~L~ **eon~**
I stare at the door for about twenty minutes as she bangs on it. Thane simply walked away after ordering us not to let her out. Hours had passed, and still, she bangs and hits the door. However, her banging is getting softer, almost as if she is running out of energy.

Sitting at the table at dinner, no one says anything. I have mixed feelings. Thane proved she was going to run off with another Alpha. Yet she wasn't going to go through with the glory hole thingy Talon warned us about. But why did it feel so wrong, despite knowing she was going to run, taking our baby with her?

"Leon, eat," Thane growls as I push my food around the plate.

Has he fed her yet? I wonder. My appetite is completely gone, my mind is consumed with my mate, locked in the Den below our feet. Dinner is awfully silent and tense, while Rhen's and Thane's fury is palpable. It courses through their veins like hot lava and bleeds into Raidon and me, twisting our thoughts and feelings about the matter at hand, yet no amount of anger I feel toward her makes the guilt lessen.

"I have to help Ma move next week, don't forget," Raidon suddenly tells Thane. Thane nods, waving him off.

"I know. We can help if you want?" Thane asks him before taking a bite of his food. Raidon shakes his head.

"No. Dad will be there to help. I'll be fine," he tells Thane, who nods. They talk amongst themselves while they eat. I don't join in. I have nothing to say. I feel strangely numb, like an outsider looking in. I am on autopilot. Raidon gives me a few worried looks and kicks me under the table several times, reminding me to eat.

Yet my mind is elsewhere. It's with Harlow in the Den. The look of betrayal she gave me when I didn't help her won't leave my head. She stared at me as if I was her lifeline, and then I killed her by saying nothing in her defense.

Once we finish eating, I move to the kitchen to help Rhen do the dishes. We have a dishwasher, but Thane complains about how they should be cleaned before placing them in the dishwasher. I never understood it.

My eyes keep going to the door across the kitchen; the basement door leading to the Den. The banging had stopped about an hour ago, and only her silence followed.

I place each washed dish in the dishwasher, my eyes constantly going to the door until Rhen clears his throat.

"She was leaving us, Leon. What choice did he have?" Rhen reminds me. I nod my head.

"We need to face it. She may be our mate now, but we clearly underestimated her cruelty. I know you feel guilty, but think about it, Leon. Had she left, what would she have done with our baby?" he asks, and I try to think.

I truly believe she didn't know she's pregnant. But now he asked that question, and it is all I can think about.

She was going to run off with Jake. No pack would raise another Alpha's baby. She would have had to abort the pregnancy. Or if she kept it, would she have used the baby as blackmail if we tried to get her back?

"See, don't feel guilty. She did it to herself," Rhen tells me, giving me a nudge with his elbow. Once we finish, we switch all the lights off and head upstairs to bed. Except I don't go to Thane's room like we all usually do.

Instead, I go to mine; I don't want to be with my mates if I can't be with all of them, and that includes Harlow. Despite everything she did, I still love her, even when I know I shouldn't.

Hearing the door creak open, I lift my head to see Raidon step into the room. He strips his shirt off as he makes his way toward the bed.

"Why are you in here?" he asks, climbing over me to the wall side and slipping under the blanket. I say nothing, letting him manhandle me as he tucks me beside him. "Leon..."

I shake my head. I know he is about to give me the same lecture Rhen did earlier. I know she will run if they let her out. But Thane could command her not to leave the house. He doesn't have to lock her down there. As much as I love Elaine, I know she is a big part of the problem, pestering Thane about what she thinks we should do with Harlow.

CHAPTER
EIGHTY

ONE WEEK LATER
~Harlow~

I have been down here for a week now, and I am going stir-crazy. There is no TV down here, no window low enough for me to look out of, only the bed and the bathroom, plus a few storage boxes at the far back. I rummaged through them and only managed to find some paperwork and a red pen, along with an old lamp shade.

On day two, I tried the windows, but I couldn't get them to unlock. I thought about smashing them but knew they would hear, and I'm not sure punching one is a good idea. I would probably only end up hurting myself. So instead, I do what I do every day, shower and sleep.

I eat whenever Thane or the housekeeper opens the door and sets food on the top step. I tried waiting by the door a couple of times, but the mealtimes are so random that I would end up with a sore back and have to leave the steps, only to miss the brief chance I had. It makes me wonder if there is a hidden camera on the stairs I can't see.

Sometime later, I would guess around lunchtime, I hear the door open before my food is set on the step and Thane's scent wafts to me. My belly rumbles hungrily, and I force myself up before stopping by the documents I have been using to doodle on. Glancing at the steps, I wonder if he is in the kitchen still. Retrieving the red pen that is running out of ink, I scribbled on a piece of paper.

Can I have a TV?

I glance at my handwriting before climbing the steps to retrieve the sandwich left there. It is the same thing every day. I am getting sick of eating ham and tomato sandwiches for lunch. Sick of eating soup and bread for dinner. Mostly I hate the oatmeal I get every morning that I always tip down the toilet. I can't stand the smell of it.

Climbing the steps, I look at the gap at the bottom of the door and slide the paper through, pinched between my fingers. I wiggle it, hoping someone is in the kitchen and sees it. A few seconds later, it is plucked from my fingers, and I gasp excitedly that someone is here. A few seconds later, it slides back under the door.

"No!" Thane snaps at me from the other side of the door, and my stomach sinks. It is so quiet down here, so lonely. Fighting back the tears, I use the pen to write something else.

A book?

I slide the paper under the door again, and it doesn't take long before it is plucked from my fingers. I get no answer this time. Instead, I get the front page of the daily newspaper pushed under the door. I stare at it. Emotion chokes me, that he would deny me something so minuscule. What does it matter if I read? Yet I have one page of a newspaper that is mostly taken up by a black and white photo.

I try to peer under the door's gap, thinking maybe the rest just didn't fit through, but all I see is the tiles that lead into the kitchen. With a sigh, I grab my sandwich and walk back down the stairs with my half a page of reading material.

He could have at least given me the comic section, or maybe a horoscope page. Instead, I get some crap about a new development that is being built somewhere on the other side of the city. The page ends before I can find out the juicy details of where exactly. Not that it matters, it isn't like I will ever get to see it.

As the day passes, I slip deeper into my head, deeper into the depression that comes with it. The door opening and footsteps on the stairs make me shoot upright from inside the Den.

Thane walks down the stairs with a tray in his hand. I stand, hoping to convince him to let me come upstairs. The moment I move to climb out of the Den, he commands me.

"Remain where you are until I leave," he orders as he sets the tray down on the tiny table that is attached to the floor. I know because I tried to move it closer to a window. The command washes over me, making every muscle tense, freezing me on the spot.

Once he sets the tray down, I hear more footsteps on the stairs. I glance up to see Rhen glaring at me while carrying down a load of laundry. He sets it on the counter beside the washing machine and loads it in. Neither of them say anything to me, which bugs me. A conversation other than the bizarre inner monologue running in my head would be nice.

Once they have loaded the washing machine, they both leave, and I feel his command go with them. I find, when I make my way over to the tray; that it has two books on it.

I pick both up, looking at them. Is he just being cruel? Is he taunting me, knowing it would be pointless for me to read these. They are both about pregnancy: what to expect after the baby is born. But by Thane's claims, I will never get to hold my baby, so what's the point, if not to taunt me?

Setting them down, I look in the bowl. My soup is almost cold, but I begrudgingly mop every bit up with the piece of bread. When I am done, I once again shower.

I hope they run out of hot water upstairs with all my showering, and their water bill gets ridiculously high. Fuck him. Once I hop out though, I am again bored with nothing to do. I move toward the small table and pick up the books, glancing over them.

As I read over the back of one of the books, the washing machine does its little jingle, telling me the load is finished. I suppose it's something to do. Boredom will be the death of me if I don't die by Thane's hand first.

So, I take the washing out and dump it in the dryer. Maybe if I help, he will get me different books, or maybe give me the TV I asked for. Even prisoners are allowed a TV in jail. It's not like I asked for anything too extravagant.

CHAPTER
EIGHTY-ONE

TWO WEEKS LATER
~Harlow~

Thane and Rhen come down at dinner time every other day to toss their laundry in the washing machine. Thane always commands me to not move until they both leave. Other than that one sentence, I am granted nothing by way of conversation. I am beginning to forget what my own voice sounds like.

Yet every two days, I get to dry and fold it. It's incredible how such a silly task can become the highlight of my day. It is something to cure the boredom, if only momentarily.

Today, when Thane comes back down to retrieve the laundry, I peer over the side of my Den. I don't bother moving, knowing he will command me to remain still if I do. It seems pointless and is just unnecessary pain.

He moves toward the basket of folded clothes tucking it under his arm. Only, when he turns around, he doesn't head for the stairs. He stops at the edge of the Den.

I stare at him, wondering what he wants, when he reaches into his jacket pocket. He tosses something on the cushioned floor. I stare at it, not daring to move toward it in case it is some sort of trick.

"Rhen linked it to his card," is all he says before he walks back up the stairs. I only move to retrieve the device when I hear the door shut and lock in place—a Kindle. I stare at the device, and tears prick my eyes. I am crying over a stupid e-reader, and I can't even tell if they are happy or sad tears. I am crying for something so stupid. So basic. It isn't a TV, but it is something. I always loved reading, but I could never really afford books, and they are a bitch to carry while on the run.

~Raidon~

Leon needs blood. He has gone three weeks with only feeding on us, and his hunger is burning out of control. I already checked with my mother, who said while not ideal, it won't hurt our baby to feed on Harlow, though it would weaken her physically. Were-babies aren't like human babies. They are more durable, but the mother isn't.

Since she is carrying an Alpha baby, the pregnancy will be even more draining on her, the baby growing far bigger than other weres in the short period. Werewolf pregnancies only last 16 weeks, and Harlow should be roughly six weeks along now. Any day now, she will begin to show.

"Who is the extra plate for?" Thane asks, pointing to the dinner plate on the counter. This is why I insisted on cooking tonight. Thane rarely lets anyone in the kitchen to cook dinner. He likes cooking. So, I am not shocked that he was instantly suspicious when I asked to do it.

"It's for Harlow."

Thane taps the bowl he just prepared, full of minestrone soup. I keep trying to tell him she needs more than that, but for some reason, he is using food as a punishment, since he can't punish her the way he does us.

"I am taking Leon down there. He needs blood," I tell him.

"No! What if he loses control and kills her?"

"What if he does lose control, Thane, and goes down there while we're sleeping and kills her?" I argue. She isn't human. She has more blood pumping in her systems than they do. Plus, my mother would never risk her grandchild if she thought it might kill Harlow or the baby for Leon to feed. Thane thinks for a second before he sighs.

"And your mother said it's okay?"

I nod. He just can't feed off her too long. And Harlow will feel weak and dizzy for a little bit.

Thane presses his lips in a line. "Once a week, and no more than that, Leon," Thane tells him.

Leon nods. It is like watching someone go through withdrawal. For a week, he's okay with just our blood, but any longer and he starts to get antsy. By now he's gotten irritable, erratic, and constantly needs to feed on us.

"I mean it, Leon, you can't be feeding on her every day like you were before," Thane warns him.

But I have another question that no one has addressed yet. What are we going to do with Leon if Thane kills her? And the baby? A baby needs its mother. And I honestly don't believe I could rip it from her arms.

"Go, before I change my mind," Thane snaps at us. I snatch the plate of food off the counter and head for the Den.

Walking down the steps, the room is awfully silent, depressingly so, but damn, is her scent is potent after being locked in here for weeks. Leon growls behind me. As I get halfway down the stairs, I find her sitting amongst the cushions with the Kindle Rhen gave her in her hands. She lifts her head before her eyes widen as she gets to her feet. Only when she does, do I feel Thane's oppressive aura directly behind me.

"Remain where you are," he orders her. I glance over my shoulder to glare at him as he follows us down the steps. I was hoping to ask her if she's okay, to speak with her, just to hear her voice again. With Thane behind me though, I know that won't be happening.

She watches us approach. Thane takes the plate from me, setting it on the table along with the bowl of soup. If he is giving her a choice, surely, she will pick the steak and vegetables over the same soup he feeds her every damn night.

When Leon jumps into the Den, what little excitement she had dies as she instantly recognizes why we came down here. If I could, I would sleep down here, but lately Thane's punishments have been brutal whenever we attempt to sneak down or try to speak with her.

He even commanded us not to use our mind-link to connect with her. Rhen hardly comes out of his room, barely speaks to us. He just sits in his room stewing in his anger and sadness. He stopped coming to work a week ago, and the place is barely holding together without him. Only since he's been gone did I realize he runs that place more than Thane does.

She opens her mouth, but no sound comes out. Realizing she can't even beg, her shoulders drop as she falls on her butt. Leon tries to speak to her, to coax her to look at him, but she refuses, just offers him her neck and stares at the bathroom door.

She knows we're here to use her, not free her. And that makes my stomach sink. Leon stares at her for a few seconds before he rises to his feet. I look at him and watch as he climbs out of the Den.

"Leon?" I ask him, but he shakes his head, climbing the stairs two at a time.

"I'm not feeding on her when she doesn't want me to," he snaps at us before I hear the door slam.

Harlow stares after him, but it's Thane that breaks the silence.

"Next time you won't refuse him unless you want me to hire a fucking Omega feeder for him," Thane snarls at her before storming out. A whimper escapes her, and even I think that is a low blow. Playing on her instincts.

"Shh, I made you dinner," I tell her, hoping she will reply. She can speak if spoken to. She can say yes and no. Maybe not hold an actual conversation, but she can answer. She offers me silence before rolling over and laying on her side.

CHAPTER
EIGHTY-TWO

FOUR WEEKS LATER
~Harlow~

I am finally showing, though I suspect I should be much larger than I am now. I don't bother to get up when I hear the door open as someone sets my food on the top step. I haven't seen anyone other than Thane for a few days now. I know they all had a huge fight, ending with Thane smashing the place up when he refused to let them down here.

I also heard the housekeeper talking to the gardener while I sat on the step the next day, eating my lunch. She asked him if they should call Thane to let him know Rhen packed up a bag and left the house.

And I haven't heard from or seen him since. The house is awfully quiet, and I hear Raidon arguing on the phone with who I think is his mother. He tells her she needs to stop calling Thane and that she is making things worse. Raidon and Thane got into a huge fight, which resulted in him leaving, but I think he came back because Thane refused to let Leon leave, saying he's too dangerous since he isn't feeding. He refuses the Omega feeder and refuses to feed on me.

However, when Raidon returned, they only fought more, and when Thane came down that night to do the washing, he had a split lip and a bruised cheek, which makes me wonder what condition Raidon was in.

But this morning I heard Rhen's voice when he returned; I have yet to lay eyes on him. Not that I care to. I don't care about much anymore at all. I ignore the stink of the porridge and toast on the steps. My appetite is entirely gone, and I am too exhausted to climb the stairs.

When lunchtime comes around, I hear Thane curse before swapping the trays over. I remember opening my eyes at the noise before closing them again. Nothing entices me out of bed. I couldn't care less. What is the point of waking, if only to stare at the ceiling all day?

The Kindle keeps glitching because there is hardly any wifi reception down here, so I quickly gave up on it. I read both baby books back to front and am sure I can recite each page word for word if I tried because I read them so much.

The lights turning on, however many hours later, have me yawning and squinting. I am about to go turn them off when I hear footsteps. Sitting up, I see Thane coming down the stairs. I wonder if it is laundry day, but I think it is tomorrow.

"You have slept all day," he says, stopping at the side of the pitted Den.

I say nothing. What else could I possibly be doing? Sure, I could go for a short stroll to the stairs and back. Yeah, I'll pass on that.

"You should eat. Maybe read. You can't spend your entire day asleep; you haven't even drunk anything today," he says.

My brows furrow, and I peer over my shoulder at him. He points at the busted light under the stairs.

"That isn't a light; I can see you down here. Now get up. You need to eat or fix your Den." he says.

And what use would that be? After reading those baby books, I know Omegas are supposed to go through some bizarre nesting stage where they will destroy every part of their Den only to rebuild it. Well, I, for one, can't be bothered.

I snuggle further under the blanket and bury my head under a pillow. Thane growls and wanders back upstairs. I go back to sleep. I hear him set dinner on the step. Still, I remain in bed, even when he returns to pick up the untouched plate.

The following day, I wake to hands touching me. I jolt to find Leon staring at me, his hands on my belly. I must have been in a deep sleep because I didn't hear him come in. I can see Thane doing laundry behind him.

Seeing it is only Leon, and I knowing he won't hurt me, I roll back onto my side. His hands are warm as he rubs the sides of my growing belly, sparks rushing across my skin. The tiniest of movements prod at his hands, making him giddy beside me as he tries to feel for it again.

"Does it feel strange?" Leon asks me. I shrug, kind of used to it now, though it felt odd at the beginning. I am trying not to get too attached. The baby is never going to be mine.

"Thane, come and feel," Leon says, stopping abruptly as he instantly regrets the words. He glances down at me, obviously realizing I do not want Thane's hands on me.

"Never mind, sorry," Leon whispers.

"Come on, Leon. You saw her, and I am done here."

"Maybe she can come up for a while?" Leon asks, but I shove his hand off me. I already know the answer, so why would he ask?

"Leon, now."

Leon's eyes darken, turning a deep crimson red as his fangs protrude and his face twists in anger while he kneels beside me.

"This is bullshit, Thane. You don't get to decide for all of us," Leon spits at him.

"Yes, I do. That is why I am Alpha. Now get out before I make you," Thane snaps at him.

I swallow, recognizing that deadly tone in his voice. He means every word. Not wanting to see Leon hurt, I roll over and away from him.

"Rhen's right. You don't deserve to be Alpha—not anymore," Leon snarls as he gets up and climbs out of the Den. He stomps up the steps. I feel Thane's deadly aura and know Leon is in for it when Thane gets up there. However, I pay no attention, tuning out my surroundings as I go back to sleep.

The sound of the washing machine wakes me a short time later, and his scent, before the sparks rush over my skin. I think it is Leon with him who is touching me, yet when I open my eyes, it is Thane hovering over me.

His hand is on my belly. "You need to eat, if not for you, then for this baby," he tells me before sighing. I can tell he wants to feel the same movement Leon felt earlier, but he is touching the wrong spot. His brows pinch together. Rolling my eyes, I grab his hand, and he freezes as I move it to the right place and press down on his hand.

He chuffs. "You need to eat, Harlow. Don't punish this baby for your mistakes," he says. I ignore him, reaching for my pillow. Thane growls and rises to his feet.

"You have an ultrasound next week," he tells me. I turn my head to look at him. That means I get to leave this place.

"Eat, please. I'll make you whatever you want," Thane says before climbing out of my Den. He climbs the stairs as the wheels turn in my head over the ways I can work this to my advantage. I am mostly excited for fresh air and light, real light. He leaves and shuts the door. I wonder if he means what he said about me being able to pick my own food. Testing that theory, I climb up, searching for my pen. I have to tear a piece of the cardboard box off to write on.

I scribble on it; I have been craving pancakes and Allen's candy snakes. And that pasta thing he made once, but I don't know what it is called. So, I write pasta spirals with the white sauce. Climbing the stairs, I stuff it under the door before I hear someone pick it up.

I try to peer under the gap, wondering if I will get anything off the list. I know better than to get my hopes up. It's probably just a trick to make me get up. Sniffing myself, I realize how terrible I smell, so I wander back down the stairs and head to the shower. I wash my hair and it takes me half an hour before I get all the tangles out.

Hearing the door open, I step out of the bathroom in my towel to see Thane carrying a tray down. Sniffing the air, my mouth waters. He sets the tray on the table before turning to pull the stuff out of the dryer.

Before I realize it, I follow my nose to find everything I asked for on the tray. I inhale my food, not even caring that I am eating pancakes and pasta simultaneously. To me, it tastes good. Better than the crap he's been making me eat. Thane raises an eyebrow at me and goes to grab the basket off the table as I finish. When his hand moves toward my empty plate, I snatch the bag of suckers off the tray before he takes them.

"I was going to leave them; I'm not taking them from you," he says at the savage snarl that I don't expect to escape from my lips. I clutch my suckers to my chest, intending to savor and ration them, in case he doesn't give me any more. I've had a wicked sweet tooth lately, and I never get anything sweet, other than the horrible green apples he recently added to my breakfasts. Although they are more sour than sweet.

I take my suckers, hiding them in my Den, but not before taking a blue one from the bag. Covered in sauce and pancake syrup, I nestle back under my blankets, naked. I bite the snake's head and sigh. For once, the cravings will not drive me mad all night.

CHAPTER
EIGHTY-THREE

ONE WEEK LATER
~Harlow~

My life is nothing but repetition, except for this week, when I have the ultrasound. The doctor came here to the Den. That was my breaking point, when I lost all hope that Thane is ever going to come to his senses and let me out of here.

He told me about the ultrasound last week. I was so excited to be leaving the Den; I was almost bouncing on my feet as I waited by the stairs for him to come get me. Only when the door opened did I realize he was bringing the ultrasound to me.

The doctor uses a portable device, and I try to tune out what he says to Thane. I no longer care. This is not my baby; I am merely its incubator. He's made that perfectly clear.

"Have you booked her in for regular midwife appointments?" the doctor asks him. I pretend not to listen, staring at the screen full of moving limbs. A stupid smile on my face as I watch my growing bump from a new perspective. One that makes the movements inside of me so much more real.

"No, she will be birthing at home; Raidon's parents will help with the delivery," Thane tells him, and my head turns to look at him.

He expects me to give birth in the Den? With a woman who has made it very clear she wants me dead as soon as the baby is born? What about pain relief? What if something goes wrong?

"Oh, well, she is in competent hands then. Do you want to know the gender?" he asks Thane, who nods his head. The doctor moves the device around, pressing harder and making me want to pee, before he declares, "It's a girl!"

The doctor is beaming happily. Thane huffs, but I don't miss the ghost of a smile on his lips. I am surprised at his excitement. Most Alphas want boys to carry on their name.

"Okay, you have her birth plan sorted, but what about afterward? Harlow will need a six-week check-up after delivery. Or will Elaine handle that too?'

"We are unsure as of yet. If not, the rotation facility may handle it," Thane tells him. The doctor's brows furrow in confusion, and my head turns to stare at Thane in horror.

"Mr. Keller?" he asks, glancing down at the mark on my neck. It doesn't go unnoticed that the doctor never once addresses me. This is typical with Omegas; the doctors always speak to their Alpha, not them. This is hierarchy at its finest.

"Once the baby is born, we will be rejecting her, and she can either go into rotation or face the consequences of her actions," Thane says, looking at me pointedly. I don't know which option is worse—death or being forced into rotation.

"Her actions?" the doctor asks, glancing down at me suddenly, as if I am some crazed criminal.

"That is none of your concern, Doc. Pack business, and I am free to do as I please with my Omega," Thane says, while I just blink at how insensitive he is being. I am the mother of his child, and those are the only two options he is offering me? I shake the thoughts away, my arms wrapping instinctively around my belly.

I listened to them argue and fight all week. Rhen and Thane fight constantly now.

I spend the vast majority of the day asleep. I wake up around lunchtime to the sound of the door opening. When I see it's just a sandwich and fruit, I turn away, not bothering to climb the steps.

Thane is no longer forcing me to eat the same thing every day. Raidon, I know, convinced him that I need more than what he was feeding me. I need a larger variety of foods. Yet I can't be bothered with climbing the stairs to eat the bland, tasteless crap he serves me today. I will lose my mind if I have to eat one more damn apple. Any fruit other than apples, but I am sick of apples. I return to my Den and drift back to sleep.

Later that afternoon, I wander over to a window. I drag a chair over and try to peek out. I try in vain to open it, but it doesn't budge. With one last heave, I growl, becoming angry, and I punch it. To my astonishment, the glass cracks. I stare at my bleeding hand for a second before looking at the fractured window. Adrenaline pumps through me at the thought of escape, and I punch it again. I don't even feel when it cuts into my hand, but I do feel the breeze outside as the glass continues to break.

Now I just need to find a way to climb up high enough to squeeze through it. It will be a tight fit, extremely tight with how large my belly has gotten, and I hope I don't get stuck. I probably won't escape unscathed, but my freedom is right on the other side of this busted window.

Looking around, I grab whatever I can to get myself as high as possible. Breaking the window is one thing, but I don't have the strength to lift myself up and through it. With blood dripping everywhere, I stack cushions and boxes on top of the chair. I get that little bit closer until finally, I dare to climb up. I am still shocked that I broke it!

I have been trying to smash, break, and open it for weeks. Nothing I did worked. Yet, in a moment of pure frustration, I did it.

Maybe the window felt sorry for me and my pathetic attempts from earlier.

Trying to balance on the stack of crap I piled on the chair, I have to turn my head sideways to fit it through the tight gap. Gripping the sides of the window frame, I pull myself through. The glass digs into my hands as I try to heave my body through the small opening. I hiss in pain as glass shards, still stuck in the frame, slice through my back. As I hang from the window, my head, arms, and chest outside in the cool afternoon breeze, I discover another issue: how do I get my stomach through? My skin is tight, and my belly is bulging.

Kicking my legs, I manage to twist on my side and grip the top of the tiny window frame. Glass tears through my sides and hips as I force myself through the window. Once I'm out, I peer down at my body to ensure I didn't cut anything vital.

I'm free!

My skin is slippery as I brush my hands over my legs and hips to get rid of any remaining glass. My skin is slick with the warmth of my blood. Yet my belly is unscathed. Glancing around, I can hear the gardener mowing the lawn on the other side of the house.

I can't run down the long driveway; it's too exposed and I would be spotted easily. In my state, someone will definitely call the authorities, who would only drag me back here.

So instead, I step out past the wall and peek around the corner, only to stop dead in my tracks. Thane is standing in front of me, looking extremely angry with his arms folded across this chest. I pivot to run in the opposite direction, only to find Rhen walking up from the other side of the mansion, with Raidon close behind him.

I was so sure they were at work.

"Harlow," Leon breathes, coming up behind Thane. His disappointment is loud and clear through the bond. But what did he expect me to do? What are the chances of finally breaking a window the moment they are due home?

I couldn't have waited. They would have noticed the broken window, which makes me wonder if Thane was watching me through the camera the whole time. Thane waves for me to come to him. I shake my head. He growls as I give a wistful glance to the forest on the edge of their property.

"Think about it, Harlow. You can't speak unless asked a question. You have no money, no place to go, and no way to get there even if you did," Thane tells me. Tears burn my eyes at his words, knowing he's right.

"I should make you go back in the same way you got out," Thane tells me. I press my lips in a line glancing over my shoulder at the broken window. There's shattered glass all over.

"So, what will it be?" Thane asks.

Instead of answering, I turn back to the window. Rhen's shriek of panic and Thane's fear rattle through the bond as I move toward the window. Going in will be a lot worse than crawling out. Hands grab my hips as I bend down, but I'm not going for the window frame.

No, I want the massive shard of glass I saw. My fingers wrap around it just as I am yanked backward by Thane. I struggle in his grip as he snarls, turning me around. Aiming for his chest, I stab him.

I stare at the glass protruding from him in shock as blood begins to soak his shirt.

CHAPTER
EIGHTY-FOUR

~**H**arlow~

The glass slices my hand, making it difficult to grip and aim where I stab him. I miss his shoulder and embed it a little below his collarbone.

Thane grunts, and my eyes go wide, seeing what I did. I can't believe I stabbed him. Thane's grip on me tightens as he looks at the glass protruding from him. I wanted to stab him, but I still can't believe I actually had the guts to do it. To hurt another person.

The anger I felt instantly dissipates with the horror of what I did. Thane growls furiously, and the entire front of his shirt turns bright red as he yanks the glass out. His face twists in fury and his canines protrude frighteningly fast.

I hear a menacing growl off to the side of me. Before I can turn to see who made the savage sound, I catch a glimpse of Leon as he blurs past me and tackles Thane to the ground. Leon punches him, making Thane's head snap back with the force. I can tell through the bond that Thane is startled by the sudden attack.

I am startled.

Attacking your Alpha is suicide. I think that the only reason

386

Thane takes such disrespect is because they are mates, with a fully forged bond.

Yet being mates doesn't stop Leon from raining blow after blow down on Thane. Raidon and Rhen stand by, shocked by Leon's actions, before they finally react. Leon's fangs protrude from his mouth, and he rips Thane's head to the side before tearing into his neck. Thane's attempts to throw him off grow weaker and weaker until eventually he falls slack. His command over me drops abruptly, making me wonder if he's dead or if he's just weakened enough for his hold to break.

Time seems to stand still. I see Thane's eyelids flutter with one last feeble attempt to push Leon off. He lays there limply. Did Leon just kill Thane? Yet, by the steady beat of his heart, I know he is still alive. Leon sits back on his heels and wipes his hand across his mouth, smearing blood all over his face. Seconds later someone grabs my arm, but the feral snarl that leaves Leon's lips has them jerking away from me. Glancing over my shoulder, I see it is Rhen.

"Let her go," Leon said, his voice ice cold, and it chills me to the bone.

"Leon?" Raidon speaks, his voice barely a whisper. "What have you done?" he asks, looking down at Thane.

"I can't watch him treat her like this anymore," Leon tells him before reaching into his pocket and fishing out a set of keys.

"Go!" Leon says, tossing them to me. I catch them, staring at his car keys. My heart is beating rapidly in my chest. What am I supposed to do with these?

"I... I can't drive," I stutter out. Leon tilts his head to the side to look at me before looking at Rhen and back at me.

"You can't drive?" Leon asks.

"Well, no shit, she ran a car off the road when she tried to escape last time," Rhen growls behind me, making me jump away from him.

Raidon looks between us all, but my eyes stay on Thane, who is passed out on the grass, bleeding profusely.

"She can't be here when he wakes up," Leon says, looking down at Thane, confirming my earlier thoughts that he will be alright.

The tension and fear are loud and clear through the bond. I can't decide, however, if they are afraid for themselves or me. We all know there will be hell to pay when Thane wakes up.

Rhen grabs my arm. "We haven't got much time," he says, shoving me toward the house.

"Rhen!" Leon snaps at him, rising to his feet. I glance at him and realize he is willing to fight all of his mates for me, if needed. Rhen stops and looks over at him.

"What are you doing?" Leon asks as Raidon moves closer to Rhen, his eyes calculating as he looks Rhen over. I swallow, knowing if they attack each other, I will be caught in the middle. Instinctively, my hands move to protect my belly as I try to step away from them.

"Getting her out of here," Rhen tells him.

"Wherever you take her, he will find her. He will order you to tell him," Raidon says.

"Which is why I am dropping her in the city," Rhen tells him before looking back down at me.

"We can't come with you, Harlow. We've been his mates for too long. Our bond is fully forged, and it will lead him straight to you," he tells me.

I nod, but that doesn't stop the sick feeling in my stomach at the thought of being on my own.

"We haven't got much time," Raidon says, rushing ahead of us. Rhen leads me toward the garage door, and I see they must have just pulled up as I made my escape. The doors are still open, and Rhen pushes me toward the house. My steps falter, and I come to a stop.

"You can't leave half-naked and covered in blood." I shake my head, knowing the prison this place is. "We aren't Thane," Rhen whispers behind me, nudging me forward.

Hesitantly, I step inside to find Raidon ripping through the linen closet. Rhen runs up the stairs. Raidon drops a bag on the ground before tossing me some clothes and adding more to the bag. I slip off the ruined clothes I'm wearing.

Leon rushes past me in a blur as I stand in the hallway. He returns moments later with a wet cloth and de-scenter. He scrubs off the blood with the cloth. The de-scenter stings the slowly healing cuts that cover my body.

"Taxi will be here in five minutes," Rhen says before dropping a heap of cash he retrieved from somewhere in the bag. Raidon nods and zips it up.

"If you run out," Raidon says, pulling his wallet from his back pocket. He pulls a card out and hands it to me, "withdraw what you can and get the hell out of wherever you are. Thane will be watching our cards."

"I don't know the Pin," I tell him.

"It's your birthday, your real birthday, not the one from your shitty fake ID," Rhen says behind me. "We all use the same pin," he says.

"I need someone's phone," I tell them, knowing they will have Alpha Jake's phone number. It is the only place I can think to go, knowing Tal's or Bree's will be the first place Thane will look for me.

"Make sure to toss it when you're done with it," Rhen growls. I have a feeling he knows why I want his phone, but he hands it over anyway. Thane will hesitate before stepping into another Alpha's territory. That would cause issues, and there are sanctions in place. Unless approved by the pack Alpha, it is forbidden.

Thane may be the boss here, but he doesn't own Clairview City. That is Jake's territory, and at the moment, the only place I would consider safe, despite my condition. I just hope he is genuine about what he said, because I am not letting him hurt my baby.

"Get rid of the phone, quickly. Take whatever numbers you need and get rid of it," Rhen tells me.

Hearing the intercom for the front gate, we all look to the door. Leon hits the buzzer to let the taxi in. Raidon grabs my bag and moves toward the front door. My heart beats faster, knowing I'm getting out of here. The thought of being free is just as scary as remaining.

It is incredible how a person has the ability to be comfortable in their misery, and leaving here for the unknown scares me more than Thane. Yet I'm not going to lie down and die or let him rip my daughter from me, so I suck in a breath and move toward the door.

Raidon opens the trunk and tosses the bag in. I move toward the back door, and Leon opens it. The driver, although startled, says nothing when Leon grabs me before I can climb in. His lips crash against mine.

"Take care of our daughter," he whispers when he pulls back. "When we can, we will come for you. When it's safe."

"Find a way to contact us so we know you're okay," Raidon tells me.

"But Thane—"

"We will handle Thane. Until then, it isn't safe for you here," Rhen tells me. I chew my lip before hopping into the car. Rhen shuts the door, and the driver pulls away.

"Where to, Ma'am?"

"The train station," I answer him, pulling Rhen's phone out and unlocking it with my birthdate. I scroll through the contacts, pulling up Alpha Jake's number. My hands shake as I hit the call button and lift the phone to my ear. The phone rings a few times before finally, he answers.

"Rhen?" Jake asks. It sounds like he is somewhere loud, with lots of noises in the background.

"No, Alpha Jake, it's Harlow," I tell him. My heartbeat picks up, and I feel sick to my stomach at what I am about to do.

"Harlow?" he says in a hushed tone.

"I need your help," I tell him.

"Where are you?" he asks, and I let out a breath.

CHAPTER
EIGHTY-FIVE

~**H**arlow~

Alpha Jake tells me to catch a train. He will pick me up at the Clairview City station because it would take hours for him to drive here. He offers to make the drive, but when I explain why I can't wait, he agrees that the train is the better option.

I sit with my bag clutched tightly in my lap, the strap over one shoulder. I'm in the very last carriage, where the security guard is. He watches me curiously but says nothing about me being here.

My eyes sting from exhaustion, but fear keeps me awake and alert. Each stop the train makes has me staring out the window, worried Thane will be there to retrieve me and drag me back to the Den. After an hour, I relax slightly.

The security guard clears his throat, and I snap my eyes open. I hadn't even realized I had closed them. In his hand, he holds a wrapped sandwich, offering it to me.

"Eat. You look pale," he says, his eyes roaming over my face and down my arms. I thank him and take it.

His eyes dart to my hands, where there's still blood beneath my fingernails. His aura slips out, and only then do I realize he's an Alpha. It makes me suddenly nervous, but he moves back to his side of the carriage and sits down before eating his own dinner.

I look at the egg sandwich wrapped in clear film. The carton looks untampered with, so I open it. My stomach growls hungrily. I polish it off in four bites, which makes the security guard chuckle. My face heats with embarrassment, but he shakes his head and rises to his feet before handing me the other half of his. I shake my head.

"Take it. I can get more from the other carriage," he tells me, and I thank him. He sits back down. He gets up at each stop to watch the passengers. He wanders off a few times to check tickets before returning and retaking his seat. I groan, wondering how many stops before I get there.

"You can sleep; I won't let anyone near you," the security guard tells me. I chew my lip. He's been kind so far, and not at all creepy. But he's still an Alpha, and I am an Omega.

Yet as the train slowly continues, my eyes grow heavy. I fight to remain awake when I feel something soft placed over me. My eyes fly open to find the security guard placing his jacket over me and glancing at my ticket.

"I will wake you up before your stop," he says with a nod and sets my ticket back in the side pocket of my bag. I watch him move back to his seat. "Sorry, instinct to protect. You're an Omega. Your descenter isn't working because you're—" He points at my belly.

Those instincts are clearly dead in Thane. Just the thought of him twists my stomach and makes my heart race, but sleep takes me moments later, suddenly feeling a little reassured.

"Ma'am?" his deep voice says, shaking my shoulder. I jump glancing around in panic.

"Sorry, didn't mean to startle you, your stop is next," he says, pointing toward the window, and I see we are pulling into another station. I nod and check to make sure I have everything.

Minutes later we pull up at Clairview City Station. I step off the train, nervously looking for Alpha Jake when I am suddenly surrounded by three huge men. I turn to run back to the train when I hear Jake's voice.

"Don't be frightened, Harlow, it's just my mates." One of the men steps aside and I spot him. I step away from the dark-haired man with a crooked lip from a scar running through it.

When I first saw the men, I instantly assumed I had fallen into a trap. Yet none of them touch me. In fact they are very careful not to, which is odd because the platform is crowded and there isn't much room. Instead, they just crowd around Jake and I as we exit the platform and walk out to the parking lot.

"Was the train okay?" Jake asks. It feels strange trying to make small talk with someone I don't know. We stop beside two black SUVs. The three men climb in one while Alpha Jake opens the trunk on the other. I take my bag from my shoulder, feeling a little nervous about getting in the car with him. Yet when I pass him the bag, he jerks his hand back when my fingers accidentally touch his.

The bag falls and hits the ground. He quickly bends down to retrieve it, giving me an apologetic smile, and motions me toward the car. I shake off his strange behavior. Yet when he gets in the car and grabs hand sanitizer from the glove compartment, I wonder if maybe he has a cleanliness issue.

"Sorry. Omegas. Well, you know," he says, and my brows scrunch together. He starts the car and pulls out, the other following close behind as we make our way out of the city.

"So, how many mates have you got?" I ask nervously.

"Eight," he says simply, but I am horrified. Eight mates! I shake the thought away. I would die if I had eight Thanes in my life. One is plenty.

I get nervous the further we get from the city. As we turn down a dirt road, his phone rings through the car's Bluetooth. Jake holds a finger to his lips and points to the screen on the dash. The name 'Bub' pops up on his display. He answers it by pressing a button on his steering wheel. My world suddenly stops at the sound of the voice on the other end. A voice I would recognize anywhere. A voice I had been wanting to hear for over two years.

"What's up, Love," Jake answers.

"Where are you?" she demands.

"Almost home, I have a surprise for you," Jake tells her.

"What sort of surprise? Ooh, is it a trifle?"

Jake laughs at the question.

"Something better," he replies

"What is better than trifle?" she asks. "Now I want one! Why did you mention trifle?" she demands, sounding very much like a pouting Omega.

"I will send Travis back to get you trifle."

"Wait, Travis is with you? Have you seen Donnie and Sam?" she asks.

"They're behind me, but if I don't get off the phone, I can't let them know to turn around and get your trifle."

"A Malteser one," she says.

"Yes, okay, a Malteser one. I will see you soon," he tells her.

"Don't forget the trifle," she tells him before hanging up. I blink at the screen before seeing the lights flash on the car behind as they turn around, heading back into the city.

"She fucking loves anything with chocolate," Jake laughs, and I stare at him.

"You weren't lying? She really is alive?" I gasp. I can't believe it. All this time I thought she was dead.

"I would not lie to you. Everything I told you is the truth," Alpha Jake tells me as we pull up to an extravagant mansion, lit up like a Christmas tree.

"But the other Omegas? The ones you bought before me?"

"They were members of my former pack, one I stepped down from. I gave that pack to my brother before creating my Alpha Pack. Those Omegas got themselves in trouble and were forced into rotation, then auctioned. I brought them back to the city, changed their identities, and returned them to their families. Packs are family, even after you leave one," Jake tells me.

"Then why buy an Omega if you already had some here?"

"Same reason any Alpha-of-Alphas does: I needed to find one with strong enough genes to take my knot," he says.

"So, they aren't dead?"

"What? No! You shouldn't believe everything you see in the media. Alpha Packs are always painted poorly. Especially those like mine and Thane's. We are constantly in the news, and rarely for anything good," Jake tells me as he pulls up front.

I suddenly understand why he freaked out when I touched him, and why the others didn't get too close. Not because they are grossed out by me, but out of respect for Zara, knowing it would send her crazy if they came home stinking of another Omega.

Despite that, it doesn't stop the feral snarl that leaves her as he steps through the door in front of me. I hear a struggle, and Jake rushes toward her, ripping off his jacket, which would smell like me after being in the car together.

Another man comes down the stairs opposite the foyer. He stares at me as I step inside. I turn to find Zara savagely tearing at Jake's clothes as she scents him.

"Calm down, it's your surprise," Jake tells her, when her hand suddenly whips out to slap him. A man on the sofa beside her chuckles as Jake rubs his jaw.

"You dare come here smelling of some whore!" she roars at him, and I hear Jake sigh loudly.

"That whore is your sister," Jake tells her, stepping aside and motioning toward me. She blinks.

"Harlow!" she whispers. Her eyes turn glassy as her lip quivers. She moves to stand. Jake and the two men on the sofa move to help her. I see why; she is massively pregnant, and she looks frail as hell.

"Steady, Love," the man beside her says. I can hear the panic in his voice, and I move toward her quickly, so she won't try to come to me. Her fingers reach out for me, and I clutch them when she breaks down, turning to a sobbing mess as she falls back onto the sofa.

"It's really you. You're really here. I thought you were dead," she breathes. I smile sadly, tears streaming down my face at the sight of her. She is the same as I remember, but so, so different. I help her sit down.

"You're pregnant," I gasp.

Her eyes go to my rounded belly, which is nothing compared to the size of hers.

"And so are you. You have a pack?" she asks, staring at my belly in confusion before looking at Jake.

My mind is reeling. I have so many questions, and I can tell she does too.

CHAPTER
EIGHTY-SIX

~ R**hen~**

We had to sedate Thane. She hadn't even left the driveway by the time he came to. Raidon tackled him as he chased after her. If she was still here, I know he would have killed her. In his rage, he had completely forgotten that she is pregnant with our child.

"I can feel him waking up," Raidon groans as we watch him stir on the bed. Leon sits beside him, his blood boiling; I can feel it through the bond. His temper hasn't dampened in the slightest, which is worrisome given his hunger. I don't trust him not to take another bite of Thane.

We don't bother cuffing him or tying him to the bed. He can order us to remove them, so it would be pointless. Our only chance is to reason with him. Getting up, I pull the blanket back to check if his chest has healed. Thankfully the wound is completely closed now. All that remains from Harlow's attack is a faint scar.

When I go to tug it back up, his hand moves with a speed that makes me jump as he grips my wrist. Raidon growls at him as his claws slip free from his fingertips, grazing my skin.

"Where is she?" Thane snarls, ignoring him. He sits up, leaning against the headboard before glaring at Leon. "You nearly fucking drained me," he snarls, baring his canines at him.

"And you were going to hurt her," Leon retorts with venom in his cold tone. Thane swallows, and he lets me go.

"You sent her back to the hotel?" Thane asks. I glance at Raidon nervously, but it is Leon who answers him.

"We have no idea where she went. We let her go."

"You what?" he snarls, tossing the blanket back and jumping to his feet. Raidon shoves me aside and steps in front of him, standing toe to toe with him. My heart beats fast at the clear challenge.

"You dare challenge me," Thane says as his entire body trembles in rage.

"I should have weeks ago," Raidon tells him.

"Stand down!" Thane tells him.

"Make me."

Thane growls and pushes him aside, only for Raidon to grab him and slam him against the wall. Leon gets up, standing on the bed as Raidon holds him there. We all know who would win if Thane decides to take the challenge. Thane is our Alpha for a reason.

He was the strongest of us before we submitted to him, and now that he has our blood in his veins and has marked us, he is far more than just an Alpha. The man is lethal. Raidon knows this, but he doesn't seem to care when it comes to Harlow. Thane, recognizing how much he would have to hurt Raidon to make him submit, relaxes in his hold.

"I am not your enemy; I am your fucking mate," Thane snaps at him. I watch as Raidon leans closer, so their chests are almost touching.

"And so is she," he snarls before shoving off him.

Raidon steps back from him, but not too far. Thane could pass him easily if he wanted to.

"So, we just let her go? Let her run with our daughter?" he says before cursing under his breath.

"She wouldn't have to run if you could control that damn temper of yours," I tell him.

"Temper? She killed my mother!"

"I don't think she did. You have a lot of enemies, Thane, and it was no secret that your mother was leaving to pick up our Omega. It was plastered on the front page of every newspaper that we were caught bidding in the Omega Auctions," Leon tells him. He had a point about that. It was plastered everywhere, but no one knew whether or not we won the Auction.

"You need to bring her back. Now!" Thane roars.

"We can't. We don't know where she went," Leon says slowly, emphasizing every word. Yet I have a vague idea of where she might be.

"Fuck! You know she won't come back, right?" he says, kicking the chair beside him. It flies across the room and into the dresser, narrowly missing Raidon.

"Calm down. She will come back," I tell him, and he scoffs. "She will. We marked her. The bond will pull her back here, but if you can't control yourself, she will only run again," I tell him.

"As if I would give her a third chance to run from me again," he snaps, and Raidon growls at him.

"When it comes to Harlow, that is no longer your decision," Leon says, jumping off the bed.

"Excuse me?"

"You fucked everything up. You are the reason she tried to run."

"And you let her!" Thane screams at him.

"Because she is not a piece of fucking property to be owned!"

"Well, she sure fucking cost me enough!" Thane yells, and Raidon punches him. His head whips to the side at the force. I move quickly, knowing Thane will come up swinging. I'm right, his fist stopping just shy of my face as I force myself between them.

"Everyone needs to calm down," I say.

"No. He needs to leave before I fucking kill him," Thane growls in warning, and I swallow. Raidon's heat seeps into my back before he storms off.

"Where are you going?" Leon asks him.

"To my parents'," Raidon replies, slamming the bedroom door behind him.

I rub my temples at the mess our lives have become. Leon clicks his tongue, making me look over at him.

"If you want Raidon gone, then I'm going too," Leon tells him. Thane growls, but doesn't stop him.

"Those idiots want to believe her lies," Thane snarls, and I press my lips in a line.

"Even if she did do it, Thane, would you really kill the mother of our child? Or put her in rotation?" I ask him. His answer is quick, and I can feel he means every word.

"Yes. She doesn't deserve to be a mother after killing mine," he tells me. My eyebrows raise before I nod.

"I was hoping for a different answer, but you are truly blinded by hate for something we aren't even sure she did," I tell him.

"We have video evidence!"

"From grainy footage where we can't even make out their faces. Even you said it was strange that there was no footage of them exiting the parking lot."

"It's her car, the plates matched on the traffic cam."

I shake my head. There is so much that doesn't make sense about that day. Why did it take so long for someone to notice Hana's body in the parking lot? And the tire marks where the car was found line up with it being run off the road, not Harlow running someone over. Yet every report had the same conclusion: Harlow's guilt.

The authorities refused to let us get involved. We hired a private investigator to look into it, and while he said things didn't add up, he couldn't find anything to prove Harlow did or didn't do it. All evidence pointed to Harlow, yet why would she kill Thane's mother? She could have just taken the keys and run. Hana probably would have let her. She was non-confrontational by nature; she would have just let her go and then called us.

I just can't picture Harlow cutting Hana's throat so badly that her head barely remained attached to her body. Harlow looked so shocked when she stabbed Thane. She looked horrified at what she had done.

"I can't believe you are questioning me on this when all evidence shows she did it," Thane hisses at me before clutching his hair in frustration.

"You want someone to blame. You need justice for her death, but that doesn't mean it was Harlow. Think, Thane. She was willing to let you command her to ask about it. Now, why would she agree to that if she is guilty?"

"Because she knows I wouldn't. She knows I hate commanding you."

"Yet you had no issue commanding her down in the Den or at work. She had every reason to assume you would do it, Thane," I tell him, turning on my heel and moving toward the door.

"Rhen? Wait! You're not leaving too, are you?"

"We'll be at Elaine's. She needs help unpacking anyway. She hasn't gotten much done."

"But you're coming back here?" he asks, sounding almost desperate.

"Not while you can't see past your fear of being wrong."

"Being wrong?"

"Yes, Thane. Being wrong. That's why you didn't command her. Because if she's innocent, all that anger you harbor for her will turn to guilt knowing the one person you've hated for all these years is the one person you should love," I tell him before walking out, leaving him on his own.

CHAPTER
EIGHTY-SEVEN

~**H**arlow~
I wished for this day for so long. To wake up from the nightmare where she no longer exists.

My other half.

A bond between sisters is sacred, but as twins, we are one and the same. Identical yet individual. We are more than blood. We are two halves of a whole.

For years, I thought she was dead; I grieved her, missed her, and wished more than anything to trade places with her, believing all this time that she was dead because I was too scared, too weak, to go with the pack that I was originally sold to.

She sacrificed herself for me, and that is a guilt no sibling wants to live with. I thought that I had lost the other half of my soul. That's what she is. But she was here all along.

"How are you here?" I murmur, unwilling to let her go just in case she vanishes, and I wake up in the Den to find this is all a dream —that my mind has finally broken and conjured all this just so I won't be alone anymore.

Zara looks at Jake. "They knew I hadn't bloomed, and they

waited. Our scores were the same, Harlow," she tells me when I hear a soft crying noise, making me look up at the ceiling.

"I will get him."

"You already have a baby? I have a niece or nephew?" I ask her, watching the man move off the couch and toward the door.

"Yes, a nephew. His name is Mason. He is one year old," she says, looking down at her belly. She lets go of my hands to protectively cradle her large bump.

"Would have had two by now, but our daughter was stillborn," she murmurs, looking at Jake as if in apology.

"It wasn't your fault."

"We all know it is," she whispers, her eyes turning glassy. "I should have listened," she murmurs, and he crouches next to her.

"I shouldn't have told you; I knew you would have wanted to come with us," he tells her before leaning down and pressing his lips to her belly. Confusion washes over me as I listen to them.

"She would be almost two; I named her after you," Zara tells me, sniffling. I can hear the agony in her voice. "She was so beautiful. Perfect," Zara says, and I swallow as she stares off into space. Now I understood why Jake didn't want to mention anything to her when he saw me at Tal's.

She is different from who I remember, broken in ways I can't imagine. I would have added to that torment had I not come back with him. I wonder if I would have been the same had Thane managed to take my daughter from me. It's why so many Omegas on the rotation are a little unhinged. It's also why there are strict laws prohibiting Alphas from keeping mothers away from their children.

They have visitation rights and are allowed to remain with their child for the first year, kind of as a way to wean them off of them. It's also why there are limits on how long an Omega can remain in rotation, how many offspring an Omega can produce while in rotation, and why so many end up in psych wards or heavily medicated after leaving rotation.

It is also why so many turn into Omega feeders. They use the high from a vampire bite as a drug, a way of self-medicating. To think that would have probably been my future had I not escaped.

Hearing the door open behind me, the three men from the train station walk in. I turn to watch as they filter into the room, rushing over to her.

"What's wrong, Love?" the tall, dark-haired one asks, cupping her face. She doesn't react, just stares off vacantly as if she looking straight through him. He brushes his thumbs down her face, and she appears to snap out of whatever trance she is in. She shakes her head.

"Travis!" she breathes, patting his face, and he leans down, kissing her forehead.

"That's right, love, I'm right here," he tells her. My heart breaks for her. To see her so changed from the bubbly girl that was my sister.

"Sam's got you something," he tells her, and a blonde man behind me holds up a bag, watching her worriedly.

"Trifle?" she asks, her mood instantly lifting.

The man who left to tend to their son returns. "I got him back down. He wanted his plushie," he tells her, climbing back on the oversized couch and laying behind her. He tugs her back to lean against him.

"I'll go get you a bowl and spoon," Jake tells her before he clears his throat.

I glance at him, and he motions for me to follow. With a quick nod, I tell my sister I will be back before following him through the massive house. Everything is ridiculously white. I thought Thane was a clean freak, yet he has nothing on my sister and her mates.

I follow him to a huge kitchen, Sam following behind me. He sets the bag on the island countertop and moves toward the cupboards, retrieving bowls and setting them down on the counter.

"My sister, she's different," I tell him. Sam stares at me, but Jake nods his head.

"Yes, she hasn't been the same since the accident," Jake tells me.

"What accident?" I ask him.

"We got a lead about six months after you went missing, just outside Thane's territory. We went searching for you. Zara demanded to come."

My brows furrow as I try to remember where I was. I had stayed in a town just outside the city for a few months to lay low. "Ryde?" I ask him, and he nods.

"Yes, anyway, we tracked you to the edge of town, but Zara was sure she could smell your scent by the river nearby. It was around the time there were all those storms. As she approached the river's edge, the ground gave way, and she fell in. She was washed down the rapids and got banged up pretty badly. By the time we reached her, she had washed onto the bank. She was full-term. She survived, but our daughter didn't."

"And she blames herself for that?" I ask him.

"We asked her to wait here, told her we would search for you. She insisted on coming," Sam tells me, dishing out the chocolate trifle into two bowls. He slides one across to me, making sure not to touch me in any way.

"It was an accident. After that, we didn't tell her whenever we got a new lead. Zara also hasn't left the house since. She has terrible anxiety and agoraphobia," Jake tells me, and I chew my lip.

"She's gotten worse, since falling pregnant with the twins, identical girls this time," Jake tells me.

I follow my sister's mates back to the living room, having already forgotten the way. She holds out her hands for the bowl Sam brings her. I sit on the floor as Jake and Sam climb on the lounge with everyone else. She may be my sister, but I know better than to get too close to her mates or to make myself comfortable in another Omegas house. We are territorial by nature, and even though she knows it's me, I don't want to cause her any distress.

Zara has so many questions, asking where I've been and what I've been up to. What my mates are like. I can't bring myself to tell her any of the bad things, instead giving her vague answers, not wanting to upset her in any way. But her eyes trail over the cuts that still cover my skin, despite having almost fully healed. She doesn't push for more information, seeing I am uncomfortable answering.

After being here a few hours, though, and watching how her mates are with her, it makes my bond tug and yearn for my mates. I ask where I can sleep, sadness bleeding into me that I will never have the same relationship she has with her mates. I excuse myself and Jake shows me to a guest room on the opposite side of the house.

"I'm sorry, we have to put you over here. She sleepwalks sometimes, and she isn't lucid when she does. If she picked up your scent, it might overwhelm her, and we don't want her to attack you," Jake tells me. I nod my head in understanding. There is too much risk, given I am an Omega in another Omega's house, but the stillness on this side of the house is even quieter than the Den back home.

I borrow some of Zara's clothes and take a shower. Staring down at my bump as I wash with the citrus-smelling soap, I feel lonelier now than I even did in the Den. Especially after seeing how doting my sister's mates are with her. They treat her like a precious gem, showing her such love, while mine can barely look at me. It stings. Climbing in the huge soft bed, I feel cold, and the scents are all wrong. I struggle to fall asleep in this unfamiliar place.

CHAPTER
EIGHTY-EIGHT

FOUR DAYS LATER
~Harlow~

I thought after coming here and finding my sister that the rest would be easy. That I would find my place here after a day or two, but I miss my Den, even though I despised being held prisoner in it. It was driving me insane, yet being here is much of the same. I have no place, not here, not even with my sister.

Zara was my home for so long, and I thought I would find that home again with her. But that isn't the case. It is far from the relationship that I once found such safety in.

Now I have no home, and the home I crave is a toxic one. What my instincts are telling me to go back to is bad for me; yet still I crave that familiarity. Sitting here, watching my sister with her mates, getting the support and love she always craved and wanted within a pack, makes me feel even more lonely. I'm like the third wheel, or ninth in this case.

Eight mates, I am still trying to wrap my head around the fact she has so many. Yet at this point, I would take any one of mine, even

Thane's overbearing ass, just to feel like I have someone, anyone. This is not my home, and she is no longer my safe place.

It's so far from the reality we once shared that all I can see is the distance between us, how far removed we are from each other now. We're twins, connected in the most sacred and pure of ways, but she's different now that she's suffered a great loss. She is no longer the girl I remember, and neither am I.

Gone are the two girls, once joined at the hip. Polar opposites, yet one and the same. I'm Harlow again, an identity I just got back, but I'm not sure who that is anymore. And Zara is traumatized, stuck in the loss of her daughter—stuck in a past I can't relate to because I wasn't there for her when she needed me.

I don't know how to bring her back from the brink, just as she doesn't know how to bring me back from the coldness that is taking me over. We have become identical strangers. Our wants and needs changed over these last couple of years. I've realized that I learned to live without her, learned to be on my own, and only now do I truly realize how alone I am.

No one in my corner, no one to watch my back, and I suddenly find myself walking a path I never expected. A path that we don't share, but isn't solely mine either, and I now recognize the trauma that it causes me.

She left a bad place and found a home. I left a bad place and found loneliness, emptiness. Zara carries children that will grow up feeling safe and loved, with support and stability. The child I carry will have only me. I get no support, and once again, I find myself in that familiar, helpless place of having only myself to rely on.

I let myself believe, if only for a brief moment, that I had found a home. Even when I was locked in that dreaded Den. That place was miserable, but I had found comfort in my misery. It was mine, but I had lost that too.

I'm starting from scratch again, when I never really had scratch to begin with. Back down the rabbit hole I go. I keep trying to crawl my way out, but I can't seem to recreate any sense of home. And that clarity smashes into me when Jake comes to sit with me on the huge verandah of the home that I will never have a place in.

"I made you hot chocolate," he says, passing me the mug and handing me the blanket draped over his arm.

"Thanks," I tell him, accepting the warmth the hot chocolate offers, while making sure not to touch him. I feel contagious, like I've been infected with a plague. Everyone is so careful to keep their distance. I am so touch-starved that I suddenly miss the pack that I never wanted in the first place, and who never wanted me. They are the one thing that was mine, yet I was denied that too.

"We're worried about Zara," Jake finally says after a few moments of stretched silence. I nod my head, knowing this was coming.

I know me being here is disrupting her. Having her so close disrupts me too. Omegas aren't meant to be sister wives, which is funny to me, given we are sisters, yet my presence makes her uneasy. Just like Sarah being around my mates made me uneasy.

Zara sleepwalked into my room the other night. My scent was in the kitchen, and it sent her on the hunt. She almost attacked me before she regained her senses. Before she recognized who I am to her. But for those few tense seconds when she entered my room, I feared for my life. Because there is no way I could hurt her, not even to defend myself. Not when I just got her back.

"I'll find somewhere in town to stay," I tell him, looking out at the rolling hills that surround the place. It's a slice of heaven out here, yet not even heaven would have me in this wide space.

Jake nods. His hand reaches out for mine before he pulls it back. I smile at him knowing it must be hard having two Omegas under one roof.

"We have a guest house at the back of the property if you'd prefer that. It's close enough that you can come over to see her whenever you like. We usually only use it when Zara puts one of us in the doghouse," Jake chuckles.

I nod my head, and he rises to his feet. "Zara is making breakfast.

Although, I should warn you, she can't cook for shit. Just smile and bear it, but don't insult her. She thinks she is a master chef, and rarely cooks," he laughs.

"Thanks, I will come in in a few minutes," I tell him, and he goes to walk off, before pausing. He reaches into his pocket and hands me his phone. "Rhen called. Your mates are worried about you, Harlow. You should give them a call and let them know you're okay."

"But Thane—"

"Thane won't get past my borders without me knowing. You can call them, Harlow."

"But if he comes here," I panic, worried about my sister's state of mind.

"You can't avoid them forever, and honestly, I'm surprised Thane hasn't come here already—I know he watches his mates' phones. Rhen, Raidon, and Leon have been blowing mine up trying to reach you."

"You're not worried about Thane?" I ask him. Jake shrugs.

"Yes and no. Yes, because I have his Omega, and I know what I would do if someone took mine. And no, because I know he won't hurt you, not while you're carrying his child. Thane has always wanted children, he just didn't know it," he tells me.

"You used to be close to Thane?" I ask him. He sighs.

"We have a strained relationship. Hana, his mother, was my godmother, Thane and I grew up around each other. We were always competitive. We never had a brotherly relationship. But Hana, I loved that woman as if she was my second mother."

"But how does that prove he wants children?"

"Because it was Hana that bought you from the auction. Thane didn't bid on you; it was his mother. He didn't know about it until after he won. Hana played with his money, and she was the one that sent in his serum," he laughs.

"That's why she picked me up?"

"Yes, same reason I sent my mother to get Zara. It's better that way. Omegas are flighty and sometimes need a reassuring face, and who better than another Omega? Someone who's been in their place."

"Hana was in a facility?" I ask him and he nods.

"Yes, with my mother and Elaine. They grew up in that place together," Jake tells me and my brows furrow. "When I found out Zara took your place, she told me what happened. We faked her death, hoping to bring you here and help you find a pack. But when I found out Thane was the winner, I knew you would be in safe hands; that Hana would look after you. But then she was killed, and you went missing." Jake sighs and runs his fingers through his dark hair.

"My pack helped with the investigations, but we got nowhere, almost like some big cover up."

"But Mr. Black gave your money back?" I asked him and he nodded. I feel kind of guilty, since I had suspected the Obsidian Pack for years, I just had no proof. He must read the thought on my face because he chuckles.

"You thought we were behind it?" he says, shaking his head. "We gave the money to Omega Aid—Thane's mother was a humanitarian, in a sense. Hana tried to have the rotations banned. The money I got back for Zara went to her charity to help Omegas get back on their feet once pulled from rotation. Thane is building a sanctuary in his mother's honor. That was always her dream. He just bought the land for it recently. I saw something in the paper about it a couple weeks ago, saying that he finally purchased the land and received the council approval for the go ahead."

My brows furrow, remembering the newspaper article he gave me on a new development. I never did find out what it was for. I didn't see his name in the part of the article I read, but it makes me wonder if it's the same development.

"And you thought I was guilty of killing her," I tell him, and he shrugs but nods his head.

"Yes and no. Some things didn't add up for me, or Thane. He was so blinded by his anger he put a bounty on you when he couldn't locate you." Now that surprises me, although it isn't overly shocking either.

"You contain his last serum, his last chance for the grandchild his mother always wanted. His mother pestered him constantly for an Omega, for you. Thane gave her his serum to shut her up. Hana told my mother it was like pulling teeth from him, but that she was going to show him what it means to have a complete pack. A real one, with an Omega that will love him and his mates, once he claimed them and they submitted to him."

"But you said *he* wanted kids?" That doesn't sound like he wanted any to me. Jake nods his head.

"He just didn't know he did, until he saw how happy his mother was and how happy his pack was. They officially submitted to Thane after he won the bid. They knew once Hana placed the winning bid that they could officially become a pack. After Tara, she—"

"Tara?"

"Yes, my half-sister. She's my father's first child. Her mother was a rotation Omega. She took all of Thane's serum, but she was on birth control. I tried to tell Thane not to take her as his Omega, that she only wanted his money after my family disowned her, yet he loved her, or thought he did. Rhen refused to submit while Tara was around. I think he knew something was off about her. Thane believed once she got pregnant that Rhen would come around to her.

"Tara took nearly everything from Thane. Rhen is the one who pointed out the money was going missing."

My stomach drops, learning that I wasn't meant to be theirs. They originally intended to take Jake's sister. It also makes me wonder where she is, and I find myself asking.

"Is Tara—"

Jake waves me off. "You don't need to worry about Tara; she's dead. She got herself mixed up in some underworld issues with the vamps. She became one of their feeders, and well, we know how personal feeders end up," he tells me, and I swallow.

"Thane caught her cheating, then discovered she had been

stealing money from his fathers' business. Thane confronted her, and she ran off with her pimp. They lost nearly everything, but they didn't notice at first. She was their assistant. That's how it all started, Thane felt obligated to help her, since Hana was my godmother. She then weaseled her way in by letting Leon feed on her," he tells me, and I wonder if that was how his blood addiction started.

"Leon became addicted to her Omega blood. It fucked him up pretty badly, and he ended up in rehab after she died. It is also why Thane and I have a very unhealthy business relationship. I think he thinks I blame him, but I know my sister. That's why I tried to warn him," Jake tells me with a heavy sigh.

"Call your mates, Harlow," he tells me pointing to the phone. "If Thane comes, and you don't want to go, we'll deal with it when the situation arises," he tells me before wandering back into the house and leaving me with more questions than answers.

CHAPTER
EIGHTY-NINE

~T hane~

Every morning, I awake to find myself in the Den, savoring the last remnants of her scent. I spent the past four days living alone, working alone, and just being on my own. None of them will take my calls, but I do, however, notice numerous calls going to Alpha Jake's phone. I can feel their anxiety, how much they crave her and miss her. I feel the same way.

I pushed them too far, and I pushed her to leave us. Yet, locked in my depression, I can't bring myself to face them. Feeling their disappointment in me crushes the parts I had refused let break for so long. Or so I thought, because now I realize that they were already broken —some façade of which I thought was whole. I am just kidding myself, hiding behind my guilt, behind my anger. My mother will be cursing my name for what I've done. I know I should have gone with her to get Harlow; I shouldn't have let her go on her own. It is a mistake I will have to live with for the rest of my life.

Climbing the stairs from the Den, I move toward the kitchen island where I left my phone, hoping by some miracle that they called, or that I will find a message saying she returned to us. We've already lost so much. This time it isn't someone else that took from my mates—it's me, and that's the guilt that guts me the most.

I sigh, seeing no messages or missed calls. I dial Raidon's number, but the phone rings out. Setting my phone down, I fill the electric kettle and move to start it when a message arrives from him.

Raidon: *She is safe.*

Just three words, but the relief they cause me is immense.

You spoke with her? I send in return.

This is the first contact I've had with any of them. I don't want to risk calling and have him not answer.

Raidon: *Yes, but you need to leave her alone, Thane. I know you are watching our calls, and I know you know where she is.*

Me: *Come home. Tell her to call me.*

Raidon: *It's not home without her there.*

His reply angers me, and I set the phone down, knowing better than to reply while angry. Raidon is hot-headed. It's why we clash the most. I will get nowhere with him by arguing. But he is right, I know she is with Jake. I also know, as much as we don't get along, Jake knows better than to hurt her.

Our families are all connected, even if we don't see eye to eye, and there are some boundaries he will push; like when he was pestering me about Harlow at work. But ultimately, he knows better than to cross me. Alphas are competitive by nature. He does it for the challenge, but we both know who would win if we were to ever actually fight. He may have more mates than me, which technically should make him stronger, but I am one thing he isn't. I am Alpha-of-Alpha born. My mother was not just my fathers' mate, but their equal. My mates' submission only enhances that ten-fold.

I'm making my coffee when my phone suddenly vibrates, and I glance at it before reaching for it.

Raidon: *She wants to come home, but she is too scared to.*

I stare at the screen, pondering what to reply. Every time I think of Harlow, that blistering anger returns. All I see is her drenched in my mother's blood. I think of Tara, and the way she manipulated us until we were too blind to see what she took from us. I never loved Tara, even though I thought I did. I fell in love with Zara, only to learn she was really Harlow. She's a liar, just like Tara. She manipulated us into believing she was someone else, and I want to punish her for it. Instead, I ended up punishing all of us.

Me: *Then tell her to come home.*

Raidon: *And what is she coming home to, Thane? She thinks you want to kill her or that you'll put her in rotation.*

I sigh, now regretting the words I told her. Not even I would be cruel enough to go through with killing her. Nor would I subject my mates, or myself, to a broken mate bond by rejecting her. I also wouldn't deprive my own daughter of a mother. I need her to fear me, because her fear somehow makes my anger for her seem reasonable.

A minute or so passes when my phone vibrates again. This time it's an image. It's of Harlow and her twin. The caption attached reads: *Her sister is alive, Jake faked her death.*

My brows furrow in confusion as I think back on everything I know. How is her sister alive? And why would Jake lie about it? It would explain why he never joined the auctions again. I had not once seen his name on the monthly listings. I assumed he found an Omega within his city, or one on rotation, but that must be why he was pestering me about Harlow. He tried to cover his scent, but I now remember the underlying hint of an Omega on him. That's why it angered me so much when he asked about her. That and her obvious fear of him.

Raidon: *That is why he wanted her, Thane. Not for himself, but for her sister, his mate.*

Me: *You believe him?*

Raidon: *I believe our mate. She is safe, but she wants to come home. I'm not going to get her if you're just going to lock her in the Den or plan on hurting her after our daughter is born.*

I swallow, trying to wrap my head around this new piece of information. It does explain Jake's unrelenting help after my mother died. I thought it was for his mother, but now I question those intentions.

Raidon: *Thane, are you going to give me an answer? What will you do if she comes back?*

Me: *I don't know.*

I answer honestly, knowing he will feel any deception. I don't know. Without her, my pack will fall apart. Without her, I will go fucking insane with constant worry. Will she even come back? I know I would drag her back kicking and screaming if needed, but they would hate me more for it.

Getting dressed, I move about the house, ignoring my housekeeper vacuuming before grabbing my keys off the dresser. Picking them up, I spot the old photo of my parents. Guilt gnaws at me, seeing their once happy faces. Guilt for letting her go alone that day.

The longer I stare, the more I feel her eyes scolding me. I feel the disapproval I know she would have over this situation. Growling, I stalk out of my room, intent to go to Elaine's and speak with them. Their nervous energy and unease bite at me as I drive down the street. I need to see them, speak with them, and convince them to come home. Driving across town, I'm distracted as I head toward them.

I'm so distracted that I don't realize I am leaving the city until I see the sign saying so. Cursing, I pull over on the side of the road. I'm about to make a U-turn and head back, but that tugging feeling inside me and the longing from the bond have me gripping the steering wheel. My knuckles press tightly beneath my skin. Before I realize what is happening, or if I can stop it, I have a panic attack.

I feel like I am dying. That my heart will stop at any second. Sweat beads and rolls down my neck. My phone starts ringing. I can feel my mates' panic bleeding into me, reinforcing my own, solidifying it in place. I find myself frozen, staring at the screen's dash with their names popping up. I am losing my damn mind, losing myself in grief, anger, and guilt.

Never in my life have I suffered a panic attack, but my life is so chaotic right now, I'm not too surprised. The very seams I have been trying to hold together toss me blindly into the new experience. Names keep popping up as Raidon, Leon, and Elaine try calling me. I know they can feel it and know it is a foreign feeling for them from me. My hands are locked on the steering wheel as I try to break through the adrenaline pumping through my veins. I can hear them in my head, trying to talk to me. I hear the mind-link open. I am muted, stunned, and embarrassed by what is happening. I feel weak, and just as it feels like it is easing, another surge rushes through me.

The Bluetooth speaker starts ringing again; a private number pops up while they keep telling me to answer their calls, telling me to pick up and calm down. With great force, my finger slides over the button on the steering wheel.

"Thane?"

Silence

"You're scaring everyone, please speak."

The moment I hear her voice I break. The panic attack lifts and is replaced with grief for what I lost. I lost the family I created. I hurt her, and yet here she is, calling me despite her fear. Whether it is because she cares or because they asked her to, I don't care. I'm just relieved and destroyed at the same time hearing her voice.

"You're okay, Thane. I'm right here," she tells me as I press my head against the steering wheel. I suck in a huge lung-full of air, feeling as if my lungs had compressed.

"Breathe, Thane, it will pass. Just listen to my voice, and breathe," she says.

I nod, focusing on her voice while I cry stupidly into my steering wheel. I feel ridiculous—I didn't even cry at my parents' funerals. I didn't cry when Tara turned up dead. I never cry. I always saw it as weakness.

Yet here I am, crying over Harlow leaving us, crying over the shame I feel knowing I let my mother down; crying over the woman I want to protect more than anything, but who I hurt beyond belief all because I am too stubborn to see what is right in front of my face. She isn't capable of hurting anyone. I blamed her so I didn't have to blame myself. Rhen was right. I blamed her because I needed to believe I didn't waste the past couple years hating the woman I now love.

CHAPTER
NINETY

~ **T** hane~

Harlow hangs up the moment she hears Rhen's voice outside my car. I'm still parked on the side of the road when they find me. Rhen says nothing as he peers down at me, and I rest my head back on the head rest.

"You got her to call me," I breathe and I close my eyes.

"No, but she was on the phone with Leon when we felt you freak out."

So she called on her own accord, not because they asked her to? I swallow and nod my head.

"You're not driving like this—climb over to the passenger seat," Rhen says, pushing on my arm to make me move. Sighing, I relent and do as he tells me, quickly moving to the other seat as he climbs into the car.

"Are we going home?" I ask him.

"Is that where you want me to drop you?" he asks, and I turn my head to look at him.

"Are you all coming home?" I ask him and he purses his lips but says nothing.

"I want to go wherever you are all going," I tell him. He nods once, and we follow Raidon back to his parents' new place.

The Hamptons-looking home is vast, and it's everything Elaine has always wanted. It is also out of the city and surrounded by forest. Rhen pulls into the garage and shuts the car off before climbing out. Elaine stands by the door, staring at the cars as she worries her lip between her teeth. I find no comfort here, even surrounded by my mates. When I don't climb out of the car, Raidon opens my door, looking at me expectantly.

"Come on, Mom made lunch," he tells me. I nod once before he steps aside. I follow him through the house. With neutral tones and high ceilings, it resembles a show home. I know Elaine is very house proud, she always has been.

"Are you staying the night dear?" she asks me as I step into the huge gallery-style kitchen that overlooks the living room with its open floor plan and sweeping polished floors.

I look at Raidon. It's his mother's house, not mine, and I'm not sure I am welcome despite her asking. I take a seat on the couch. Leon comes in moments later and watches me closely as he moves toward the living area. I want to feel anger at him for draining me, for knocking me out, yet I feel nothing but numb, desensitized to the anger I felt before.

He stops in front of me, as if asking for my forgiveness. It is me who should be asking for theirs. When he doesn't move to sit, I reach for him, gripping his wrist and tugging him down next to me. He sighs, leaning against me. I can feel his burning hunger, the need to feed from his Alpha. As strong as it is for Harlow.

"Yes, Ma, he's staying the night," Raidon answers. I don't realize how much I am hoping he would say yes until the words spill from his lips. Elaine smiles fondly at her son. We've always been close, and after a little while, I find myself relaxing in her new home.

THE NIGHT IS LONG AS MY MATES SETTLE INTO THE ROUTINE THEY'VE HAD FOR the past few days here. Raidon's father goes to bed early. The local hospital is understaffed right now, and he is called in to assist on early morning rounds.

Elaine sits on the armchair across from us going through boxes of paperwork she needs to sort out. Rhen is beside her, going over her finances on his laptop. She hands him a folder and he accepts it, flicking through the pages for something he needs for her taxes. I let them be, turning my attention back to the TV. Rhen packs up his laptop, having finished whatever it is she asked of him. I watch as he stretches and yawns.

"It's finished, I just need to send it in tomorrow," he tells her before rising to his feet. He leans down, pecking her cheek. "I'm going to head to bed," he tells her, and she nods, going back to her task.

Leon and Raidon are quick to follow after him. Leon stops behind Elaine, looking at me expectantly. I sigh. I am much too wired for sleep right now, but I know he is asking for me to join them.

"I think I will do the same," I tell Elaine, getting to my feet as she pulls out some journal. She looks it over with a confused expression. I lean down pecking her cheek as she opens it.

"Night, son," she tells me, picking up whatever fell from between its pages and landing on the floor by her feet.

I follow Raidon and the others to a room upstairs. They had pushed two queen beds together. I feel awkward, almost as if waiting for permission to rest with them. Yet as they climb into bed, I find myself following, and within moments of my head hitting the pillow, my eyes close as their familiar scents surround me. Feeling the bed dip, I go to roll when I feel the sharp pierce of Leon's fangs as they sink deeply into my neck.

Turning my head so he has better access, my fingers find their way into his hair. As I caress his scalp, his tongue laps hungrily at me, enticing a moan from my lips as I pull him on top of me. His hard cock digs into my stomach as he moves against me before pulling his fangs from my neck. My blood dribbles down from his lips as he pulls back, his tongue poking out to lick it up as I hold him in place.

Raidon groans beside Rhen, feeling Leon's sudden arousal and mine as I relish his weight atop me, the feel of him in my arms as he peers down at me. Gripping the back of his neck, I draw him closer, and he groans as his lips move against mine, just as demanding as his fangs were embedded in my neck. My tongue sweeps across his lips, and they part, granting me access as I tug at his boxers.

Unfortunately, before I can revel in the desire coursing through me, the door bursts open and the light is flicked on. Leon lurches to the side as Elaine's scent wafts to us. I sit up rubbing my eyes against the sudden brightness.

"Geez, Mom, knock next time," Raidon growls at her as he, too, sits up. Startled, I peer toward the door where Elaine stands, white as a ghost. Alarm courses through me seeing her so frightened and I toss the blanket back.

"Mom?" Raidon asks her as Rhen groans at the lights.

"I made a mistake," she whispers, and my brows scrunch together in confusion. Her skin is clammy as she steps into our room. The journal I saw her with in the living room is clutched in her hand. She grips it so tightly that her knuckles are pressed white beneath her skin.

"Mom?" Raidon asks, but it is me she moves toward.

"I'm sorry. Oh god, I am so sorry," she pleads as tears begin to steadily stream down her face.

"Sorry for what?" I ask her, completely confused by whatever could have her so spooked. The look on her face is one of immense grief and fear, as broken as the one she wore when she learned of my mother's death. Elaine hands me the journal.

"She didn't do it. She didn't kill Hana," she murmurs, before her legs give out from under her. Her knees hit the floor hard, and Raidon rushes to her side, gripping her under her arms and hauling her to her feet.

"What are you talking about?" he demands as I flick open the journal, wondering what she's talking about. The first page is chock full of old photos: a photo of Harlow and Zara, photos of them with their parents. Yet it is the next page that has me startled beyond comprehension.

It is a drawing of my mother, so precise, so exact, it is as if I am staring at her in real life.

"Harlow, son. She didn't do it; she didn't do it," Elaine sobs into her son's shoulder just as the door bursts open again and his father comes running in, searching for his distraught mate.

"Oh, she'll never forgive me for what I have done," Elaine wails as I flick through the pages to find a drawing of the car Harlow supposedly ran off the road. I start reading, the words on the page telling a different story from the one I know.

My mother told her to run.

Most shocking of all is one of Harlow's drawings—it's of the lead investigator on the case, and the label above his head reads 'murderer'. I stare down at her neat handwriting, the wheels turning in my head as I finally see everything from Harlow's perspective, so different from the story I was originally told.

From the way she describes my mother, it is clear she felt safe in her presence, not at all threatened. I learn so much from the journal. Tales of her fight. She speaks of her shame, and the guilt she feels for her sister. Her fear as she learned of my mother's passing, worried they still hunt her, as they did through the forest after running them off the road. She lay inside a hollowed log for three days, too scared to move, covering her scent in thick mud.

Everything proving her innocence lies within these pages, along with everything we didn't know, and the pictures she drew of the men she has feared since that day. My heart races as I turn each page, before I look up to see Elaine's frightened face.

She flinches as I stand, as if afraid I would strike her for her part in blaming Harlow. The book falls to the bed, lost from my grip as I rush toward the bathroom.

I barely make it to the toilet as I purge the contents of my stomach, sickened by my actions. Sickened at what I have done to a woman just as innocent as she always claimed to be. My stomach twists at the deep pit forming, and I realize just how truly I have fucked up. The evidence is right there. Now I have no excuse for the things I have done. No way of making it up to her or correcting the wrongs I have made.

All I can think is what have I done? What have I done to the woman I love? She will never forgive me, but I will surely try to make it up to her, if she will have me.

CHAPTER
NINETY-ONE

THREE DAYS LATER
~Harlow~

I speak with my mates daily. All except Thane, and I refuse to speak about him. They appear to accept that. Besides the day he had that panic attack, for whatever reason, I haven't spoken to him. Although, he has tried to speak to me. I ignore his messages, not ready to delve into the arguments I am sure will come from that.

It helps with the loneliness of being in this guest house by myself, however, this place still doesn't feel like home, and I know it never will. No matter how much I try to settle in here, the longer I stay, the more unsettled I become.

I hear the phone I recently bought start ringing. I get up from the small sofa I am reading on. Walking over to it, I notice it is a private number.

Pressing answer, I put the phone to my ear, only to see movement out the small window in the kitchen. Jake is walking down the hedge-lined path that leads from the mansion toward the guest house.

"Hello?" I murmur into the phone, turning toward the door to unlock it for Jake. I flick the lock on the screen door and push it open for him. Thane's voice on the other end of the line makes me jump.

"I didn't think you would answer," he says, and I immediately hang up, heart racing in my chest at the sound of his voice. The phone immediately starts ringing again as Jake steps into the small kitchen.

"Hey, Jake," I tell him, glancing at the phone screen. He seems nervous as he scratches the back of his neck. I wonder if my staying at the guest house is still making Zara antsy.

"I need to head into town, and I need to take my mates with me in case things get messy. Can you sit with Zara until we get back?" he asks, and I smile. I was about to head up there to see her anyway. I am excited to finally be able to spend time with her, just us. She is never alone. She always has one of her mates with her, and the realization that none of them will be staying behind for her suddenly worries me.

"Is everything alright?" I ask him.

"It will be. I'll sort it out," he tells me, not offering anything more than that.

"Okay, I will just grab my charger. My phone is nearly dead," I tell him, and he nods, waiting by the door for me.

I follow him along the path back to the main house. Upon entering, I find Zara's mates in loose fitting clothes, as if they are expecting to shift. That makes me even more nervous. Mainly because I know whatever is going on must be serious if all of them are going. Zara is asleep on the couch, completely unaware of what is going on. Yet the moment I enter the room, she picks up on my scent and her eyes fly open.

She smiles sleepily. "Sis, you came up?" she says, yawning before rubbing her eyes. When she opens them, she stares at her mates, who are getting ready to leave.

"Where are all of you going?" she asks them. Her eyes suddenly glaze over, and I know she is mind-linking one or all of them. Sam hands Mason to me, who is eating a toffee apple.

"Aunty Haha," he squeals, and I kiss his sticky cheek. My name is too much of a mouthful for him, so I am now called Aunty Haha. I find his nickname adorable. He offers me some of his toffee apple, and I take a bite of the sticky goodness, making exaggerated chomping noises. I make my way over to Zara, whose eyes flick to me nervously.

After everyone leaves, Zara puts on Mason's favorite movie. I tell her I will make popcorn after he keeps complaining that he needs it. Zara's feet are ridiculously swollen, and she looks like she is in pain. Ligament pain from her huge belly is making her uncomfortable and even the prenatal belly belt isn't offering her much relief. Walking into the kitchen, I put the popcorn in the microwave and wait, listening to the popping noises as the paper bag expands. I am only gone for a few minutes when I hear Zara's blood curdling scream as she shouts out for Mason.

The sound makes my heart lurch in my chest, as I race out to find that Zara is no longer in the living room.

"Zara?" I scream out, looking for her while rushing through the place, only to find her at the back of the house. She is in a full-blown panic attack standing by the glass sliding doors that lead onto the patio, trying to breathe and scream out for her son.

"Zara?" I stutter, but she can't even speak, just keeps pointing out the door as she tries to breathe. I peer out to find that Mason has walked out back to his small sandbox, completely oblivious to his mother freaking out behind him.

"It's fine, I will get him," I tell her, stepping out and wandering over to him. I pick him up, and he giggles. I nearly throw my back when he starts kicking out his legs.

"He's fine, Zara, see. Perfectly fine," I tell her as she clutches her chest. Her breathing slows as she peers warily out the door, one hand clutching her belly. She is as pale as a ghost. Her eyes glaze over and I know one of her mates must be mind-linking her after feeling her terror.

Mason continues to kick, wanting to go back to his sandbox,

and I set him down. Zara whimpers, making my eyes dart to her. I know she is afraid to leave the house, I just didn't think it was this extreme. What if no one was here, and the house caught on fire or Mason escaped her? It worries me how bad her mental health is. It is heartbreaking to see and sad to know she never leaves this place.

"I'm right here," I tell her before grabbing one of the patio chairs and placing it inside the door. "Sit. I won't let anything happen to him," I tell her, wanting her to sit down. Picking up Mason is one thing, I don't think I would have enough strength to lift her if she fainted.

I sit out back, watching Mason, and Zara sits just inside the door watching us. "You never come outside?" I ask her, and she shakes her head.

"Why?" I ask her, but I don't think even she truly knows what scares her. Her hands smooth over her giant belly, and she looks at her son guiltily.

"I... I can't," is all she says.

"What about the patio?" I ask her, and she shakes her head, looking like she may run at the mere thought.

"Do you miss it?"

"It's not safe," she says, and I look at her son, who for the past half an hour has been trying to get her to come look at his sandcastle.

"What if I hold your hand?" I ask her. Still she refuses.

"Mommy," Mason calls pointing at his castle. Zara cranes her neck to look, but he is too far for her to see.

"Pass me your phone. I will take a photo," I tell her, and she stands to retrieve it from her back pocket. As she hands the phone to me, I grip her hands and hold her there. Her eyes widen, and she shakes her head.

"Harlow, I can't," she rushes out. Still, I don't let her hands go.

"Yes, you can," I tell her, but she is still stuck in her own head. Mason calls for her, excited to see his mother standing by the door.

"Just a few seconds," I tell her. She closes her eyes and shakes her head, her fingers digging into my wrists.

"Do you trust me?" I ask her.

"Always," she whispers.

"Then keep your eyes closed," I tell her, and I see her swallow.

"Remember when we went to the theme park?" I ask her, and her lips tug up at the corners.

"Yes, Mom didn't want to get on the rollercoaster," she laughs, and I take a step back. Her lips part, but her feet slide across and over the small lip of the door frame.

"But we couldn't get on it without an adult," I chuckle. "And Dad refused. He was more chicken than she was. He wouldn't let go of the railing when she tried to force him to go with us." She laughs, and I take another step.

"I still remember his squeal when Mom tried to pry his fingers off the railing," Zara laughs. I glance over my shoulder at Mason.

"So Mom went, and she screamed the entire way," I laugh, remembering her ear piercing screams between us, and her death grip on our hands to the point that I thought my fingers would never work again. The way she prayed to some god about not dying and confessing her love for him, if only he would let her survive.

"She threw up on Dad when she got off. She was so green, and Dad had to walk around with no shirt on for the rest of the day," Zara laughs. "Dad was so sunburned."

I chuckle, remembering that day as if it were yesterday—a day not long before we lost them.

"Yeah, then she got back on it again with us at the end of the day," I tell her, and she smiles.

"I miss them," Zara says. I nod my head and give her hands a squeeze as we inch closer to the sandbox.

"Do you ever wonder why we survived and they didn't?" she asks.

"Every day," I whisper, and she nods.

"Me too."

"They would have loved Mason," I tell her.

"And Little Low," Zara says. She shudders as the breeze rushes over her skin and she tenses. We are still a few yards away, but she is outside. "I can't, Harlow."

"You are already here," I tell her, and her eyes pop open, darting to mine. "And just look at how excited Mason is," I tell her. Her lip quivers as her eyes dart past me to her son.

Mason moves closer before rushing toward her and grasping her legs. I let her go as she brushes her fingers through his hair. I retrieve the chair from inside the door and bring it over. She may not move any further from where she is, but this is something. She left the house. No matter how small a step that is, she at least took it.

I wait with Zara until Sam returns home. The shock on his face when he sees her sitting on the back patio watching Mason makes me giggle. He looks stunned before shaking himself. He doesn't make a big deal out of it, for which I am glad, instead coming over to peck her cheek. I get up from my seat, offering it to him, before retrieving my phone from inside. I need to lie down and don't feel like being a third wheel.

Walking back down the pathway to the guest house, I am excited to sit down. The moment I enter, I instantly fall onto the couch, only to groan as my phone starts ringing. I pull it from my back pocket, seeing the private number cut across the screen, just as the door opens and Jake steps inside.

"I'm sorry, Harlow, I couldn't stop him from passing the border. I did ask him to wait, and Raidon came with him."

My stomach sinks as the phone continues to vibrate in my hand. I sit up.

"Pardon?" I ask. Jake sighs and glances back at the front door.

"Thane is here. It's why we went into the city. I thought you had been talking with your mates? He says otherwise," he asks, and I swallow guiltily.

"I have. I've just been ignoring Thane," I admit, breathing out.

The phone rings again. Holding it up, I glance at it before pressing my lips in a line and answering it.

"Please, don't hang up," Thane's voice says on the other end.

"You need to leave, Thane," I tell him. Hurt pangs through the bond, but fuck him. He hurt me too, and I am not going to feel bad for not wanting to see him.

Jake points toward the main house, and I nod, knowing he just came down here to warn me.

"Harlow, I am not leaving. I did not drive all this way only to leave without seeing you," Thane tells me. I stare at Jake, who is waiting for me to tell him to leave. "Just pull over. She's gone silent," I hear Thane tell Raidon. I growl, annoyed.

"I'm in the guest house out back," I tell Thane, hanging up on him.

"Wait," I call out to Jake. He stops and looks at me. "You're not going to make me go back with him, are you?"

"No, of course not. Say the word, Harlow, and I will get the council here. Worst case scenario, we have tranquilizers to sedate him, and Raidon will take him back home. You aren't alone here. Sam is already on the roof with his gun ready. Thane knows all this, so scream and he will find a dart in his ass. Sam won't miss. That I can assure you," Jake tells me.

I follow Jake to the door where he points to the roof of the main house, and I find Sam up top. He waves to me, and I nod once to him, only to see Zara's other mates wandering around this side of the property, which they usually don't do.

"Fine," I breathe. I feel a little safer, knowing they are loitering. And it will be good to see Raidon. Walking back inside, I grab my jacket. Since the sun started going down, the temperature has dropped significantly. A shudder runs up my spine as I hear their car pull around to the side of the guest house.

Fear courses through me, wondering if Thane will come barging in and drag me out, kicking and screaming. Yet Thane doesn't even enter. Raidon is the one to open the door, making me spin to face him. All fear leaves as his scent wafts to me. My bond tugs painfully at his presence, and my feet move of their own accord as my body smashes into his.

"Ah, I missed you," Raidon growls as he grabs me. My legs lock around his waist, and my nose buries in his neck, devouring his scent —a scent that I find intoxicating and soothing. His fingers tangle in my hair as he kisses the side of my face, yet I can feel the tension in him, that underlying worry he feels for Thane. Raidon chuckles, his hands caressing up the sides of my bulging stomach.

"You look good. Better," he murmurs, and I realize I'm crushing my bump against him. I drop my legs to stand. Embarrassment floods me at how I threw myself at him.

"Rhen and Leon?" I ask.

"At home, this was kind of a spontaneous idea. One minute I was driving to work with Thane, when he suddenly pulls onto the highway, saying he wants to see you," he tells me, scratching the back of his neck.

"I know you don't want to see him, but he won't hurt you. Jake's mates will shoot him the moment he moves; Thane agreed to those conditions."

"I'm not going back," I tell him, and Raidon purses his lips before he sighs.

"Just hear him out."

"I have done nothing but listen and hear him out. It's me he doesn't hear, Raidon," I tell him, stepping away from him.

"He'll listen this time."

I shake my head. "He isn't the only one that didn't listen to me. None of you did."

"We didn't keep you prisoner though," Raidon says.

"But not one of you stopped him from doing it either," I snap at him.

"Just—he won't leave, Harlow. I am not asking you to forgive him, but he won't leave unless you go out there. He'll damn well camp outside your door."

"Then tell him to pitch a fucking tent and happy camping," I tell Raidon, turning back to the kitchen.

"I'm not really the camping type," Thane says, making me spin around. So does Raidon, to find Thane standing inside the door with his hands in pockets.

CHAPTER
NINETY-TWO

~ **H**arlow~

My heart sputters frantically in my chest. My eyes instantly search for another exit, yet find none. Thane pulls his hands from his pockets, holding them up in surrender.

"I won't hurt you," he says, and I can feel the guilt emanating from him, loud and clear. I won't let it sway me. He felt guilt when he had me locked down in that Den, but it didn't stop him from doing it. I am not foolish enough to go running back there on some false promise of him having a change of heart. He still believes I killed his mother; still believes I ran from them. And I did stab him. Surely, he hasn't forgiven that.

"Just hear me out. I can't make things right if you don't let me speak," he tries to reason, but I am far from reasonable right now.

"No!" I tell him. My voice is more of a savage growl, warning him to back off. Even I am shocked by the ferociousness of it. I am not going back to that Den, and I will die before I allow him to take our daughter from me.

"I get that you're angry—"

My eyebrow raises at his words. Anger does not describe the feeling I hold for this man.

"I never wanted this life. I never wanted to be used as an object for someone else's pleasure or as a broodmare to create heirs for Alphas. Certainly did not want to have my voice taken away or my choices; did not want to be commanded to do things against my will or be constantly called a whore just because I was born an Omega, which is outside of my control. I was treated worse than an abused dog for weeks!" I spit at him.

My words taste like venom on my tongue. Fury, like never before, wraps around my limbs, and I have to fight the urge to shift, knowing it will hurt our child. Raidon glances at me nervously as fur spreads across my arms, and I shut my eyes, trying to control my anger. Shifting is dangerous right now.

"Harlow, you need to calm down," Thane says.

My eyes snap open, my vision changing as my anger rises; my canines slip free, jabbing into my bottom lip as I try to anchor myself and not give in to the urge to rip him apart, an instinct so unnatural and purely driven by my anger for him. But if he thinks I will roll over and be his little bitch, he is very mistaken.

"Calm down? I should calm down? I was held prisoner and deprived of basic human rights! Then you threatened to have my daughter taken from me, only to be left with the choice of death or being whored out in rotation.

"I will not go back to endure that again. I would rather die fighting, to ensure my daughter never has to go through the hell you all put me through!" I scream at him, pointing an accusing finger at him, only to realize my nails have turned to claws.

Raidon steps closer. I snarl at him when his Calling slips out. I will not be sedated, especially not by them. Raidon backs closer to Thane, and I don't miss how Jake's mates step closer to the guest house outside the windows.

"We know you didn't do it, Harlow. I know you didn't kill my mother," Thane tells me.

"What do you want, a pat on the back? Forgiveness? You won't get that from me, not after what you did. I told you I was innocent, and still, you refused to believe me," I tell him. Raidon hesitantly steps closer, and my eyes dart to him.

"Don't!" I warn him when he reaches for me. *Calm down, pull yourself together,* I think, trying to calm the blistering hot rage coursing through me.

"I'm glad you all finally realized that I've been telling the truth this whole time. Although, it is a little too late to repair the damage done."

"It's not too late, Harlow. We can fix this," Thane says moving toward me when a growl comes from outside. He freezes, growling back at them.

"I never want to see any of you, ever again. There is nothing further to discuss, so leave. Don't ever come looking for me or *my* daughter ever again. Your next visit might not be so welcoming," I tell them. Raidon swallows, glancing at Thane while I glare at him.

"Harlow, you don't mean that," Raidon says, and I turn my face to look at him.

"I am not letting you take my daughter. How do I know this isn't some ploy? Just for you to take her from me as soon as she's born?" I ask him.

"It's not," Thane says. My eyes move back to him as he steps further inside.

"I'll scream. Sam won't miss," I warn him.

"I am not here to hurt you or to drag you back. I want you to come back, willingly and on your own terms," he says.

"My terms are 'get the fuck out'. I am not going anywhere with you. You'll just command me to do whatever you want ," I tell him, taking a step back. "So, leave," I swallow, hearing my words resonate back at me, knowing he could just order me. Jake and his mates will be none the wiser if I suddenly volunteer to go back with them. My heart races faster.

"Thane, let's just go," Raidon says, stepping in front of him.

Thane watches me for a second, and I suddenly find myself caught, like a deer in headlights, waiting to see what he will do. Thane glances over his shoulder to where Zara's mates are now on the path in front of the guest house, before looking back at me.

"I'll give you my serum," he says finally.

"I already have your serum."

"My new serum, Harlow. I won't be able to command you. We will be equal," he says, pushing his hand into his pocket. He pulls out a vial, holding it up to show me. The silver and red liquid swirling through it glistens.

"I can't take that while pregnant. And, how do I know it isn't one of theirs?"

"It's not. It is my blood and my venom," he says, holding it out to me. "Take it. You'll be able to tell as soon as you open it," he says. I hesitantly step forward before snatching it and stepping back.

I unscrew the cap and sniff it, finding Thane's potent scent. Not just his scent, but all of their scents mixed with his, proving this is his new serum, one that would make me equal to him. I look at Raidon, who is watching me, and I can feel his shock at what Thane is giving me.

"I can ask my mother—" Raidon says before I cut him off.

"Your mother's not coming anywhere near me," I tell him. He swallows, but nods. She's just as bad as Thane. Maybe even worse because she's an Omega and should have some empathy for other Omegas.

"Come home," Thane says, but I shake my head.

"You have the vial. Use it. It won't hurt you or our daughter; it will just strengthen you and her. I already checked," Thane says.

"I'm not coming home," I say.

"Then at least come back to the city. You can choose where you stay. Fuck, I will give you the house and stay at a hotel until you trust me." He's almost begging at this point

"No, I don't trust you," I tell him.

"How do you expect me to earn it back if you don't give me a chance," Thane argues.

"You want me to trust you? Then leave, and let me choose if I want to come back. I am not getting in that car with you," I tell him, not trusting him not to lock me in the trunk and force me back into the Den.

"Then go back with Raidon; I will find my own way back," Thane says, looking at Raidon.

"I can take him home," Jake says behind Thane, who glances at him and nods. "You take that, and he has no power over you," Jake tells me, nodding to the vial in my hand. I stare at it.

"He won't be able to command me, but it doesn't stop him from hurting me, Jake."

Jake sighs and nods his head.

"I'll give you whatever you want; just come home," Thane tells me.

"Will you void the Omega contract?" I ask him. Thane swallows, folding his arms across his chest. "This stops me from being commanded, but by council law, you'll still own me. I'll have no say if you decide to take my daughter and chuck me in rotation."

"If I void the contract, you're fair game for any Alpha, Harlow. I can't do that; it would put you at too much risk," Thane tells me. I shake my head; I would rather take my chances.

"Pick one of them then. I won't void the contract I have with the Omega Sanctuary or the council, but I can change the ownership title over," Thane says, and my eyes dart to his. "Pick one, Harlow. I am not leaving unless you come back to the city," Thane says, and Jake growls at him.

"I won't force her, so stand down, Jake. Sam might not miss, but I can kill you long before he takes his shot," Thane warns him confidently, without even glancing at the Alpha at his back.

"Harlow, please," Raidon whispers.

"I'm not leaving until the contract title is changed," I say.

"I can do it online. Jake just needs to lend me a computer."

My eyes darted to Jake, who nods his head, confirming what he says is true.

"Fine. Sign me over to Leon," I tell him. Thane nods. I don't miss the pang of hurt from Raidon at my not choosing him. Leon is the only one who believed me, and he attacked Thane for me while Rhen and Raidon would have let him drag me back to the Den.

"Pack your bags then," Thane says, turning toward Jake, who steps aside.

"I'm not leaving until I see the title change," I call out to him. Thane stops and nods once.

"Anything else?" he asks. I think for a second.

"Yeah, I'm taking your room. You get the fucking Den," I tell him. He presses his lips in a line but nods once before following Jake.

NINETY-THREE

~H~ arlow~

Thane hands me the new title before we leave, proving it is in Leon's name. Jake also called and double checked for me, to make sure the title change fee is paid and the transfer went through. I am solely relying on Leon to not fuck me over now, and that kind of scares of me.

I feel bad about making Jake drive hours away from Zara when she is so far along. So, when it comes time to leave, I suck it up and let Thane ride back with us. Staring out the window, I watch the scenery go by. A small part of me is relieved to be going back. Their scents alone calm the deep void I feel after being separated from them. Another part of me is intent on making them pay for what they did, so I don't speak to them the entire drive back, no matter how much they try to engage me in conversation.

I know I couldn't stay with Zara and her mates any longer. It would have only caused more stress. I hate that the mate bond has such a strong pull on our instincts; that it makes me depressed without them. Loving and hating someone—what a confusing clusterfuck this is.

I must have dozed off along the way, getting some actual sleep for the first time in what feels like forever. Someone opens the door that I am leaning on, waking me up. Their hands catch me as I topple out of the car. My eyes fly open as sparks rush over me for a few seconds before I turn and kick blindly. My heart is racing in my chest, and I am pretty sure I pull something twisting around so quickly.

"Fuck!" Rhen groans, dropping to his knees as I clutch my chest in panic. The snarl that leaves me echoes through the garage as I slide back across the seat to find Raidon helping him up. Movement out of the corner of my eye has my head turning as Thane walks around the front of the car.

"Leave her, just back off," Thane tells them when Raidon moves to placate me with his Calling. Their Calling doesn't hold the same effect it once did; I see it for what it is. Drugging and addictive, a sedative I don't want, no matter how quickly it will soothe me. I would rather have panic and pain, which means I am still fighting, keeping the tether of my will in my grasp.

"We won't touch you; we are just letting you know we are home," Thane says from beside the door. He makes no move toward me.

"Where is Leon?"

"He'll be here soon, he went to get dinner," Rhen coughs rubbing his manhood that I just kicked.

"I'll wait for him here," I tell them, not willing to move from my spot if he isn't here.

"Harlow, it is freezing out here," Thane tells me.

"I said I will wait for Leon, now get away from me," I tell him.

"Fine, I'm going," he tells me, turning on his heel and walking through the door leading to the foyer.

"You lot as well," I snap at them when Rhen and Raidon linger.

"Can we get your bags from the trunk at least?" Rhen asks. I peer out the back window before quickly nodding. Once they are gone, I reach for my handbag, snatching it up and rummaging through it for the vial. I haven't taken it yet. I could, and I think Thane believes that I have, but it will make our daughter just as strong, and dealing with that when she becomes a teenager could be a disaster. Finding it, I slip it inside my bra.

Plus, if Thane does try to command me, call me stupid, but I want to know. If I take the serum, I will be at his level. I won't feel the command. I need to know I can trust him. One command, and I am out of here and never coming back.

Twenty minutes pass before Leon finally arrives, the garage door lifting as he pulls in beside Thane's car. He rushes past, and I can feel the excitement bubbling in him, knowing I am back.

"Leon?" I murmur as he reaches the door. He freezes, his entire body going tense before he turns around. A silly grin splits onto my face. Gosh how I missed him. The bag of Chinese food in his hand is forgotten, as he drops it. Moving with his hybrid speed, he crushes me in a hug as gently as possible.

"Finally," he groans into my hair, and I wrap my legs around his waist as he presses me against the car door.

"Did they do anything? I wanted to come, but they had already left. We can stay at the hotel, or maybe we can go—"

I cut him off, pressing my lips against his and tugging him closer. He only takes seconds to get over his shock before kissing me back, his hands trailing down my sides as he caresses the sides of my belly and hips.

"I guess I am cooking then," Thane says, making us pull apart. Leon growls at him ,and Thane raises an eyebrow before he looks at me.

"What do you want for dinner?" he asks.

"I will cook for myself. I am not eating anything you make," I snap at him, and he stares up at the ceiling. I know he hates having anyone else in the kitchen, but I wouldn't put it past him to put something in my food, and I sure as shit am not eating porridge or whatever he decides to make. He may say I have a choice, but choices are always limited with Thane.

"Very well," he says, walking off. Leon turns his face back to me, a smirk on his lips.

"So, what are you cooking? He rarely lets anyone cook," Leon tells me.

"I can make two-minute noodles, or the potatoes you make, like gravy?" I ask him. Shit, I should have thought this through. I can't cook for shit. There was no need at the sanctuary, and noodle cups were pretty much all I could afford after I left.

"Sounds interesting. Can't say I've eaten two-minute noodles before. Are you sure you don't want him to cook?" Leon asks, trying to not hurt my feelings.

Unlike Zara, I'm fully aware I can't cook. My kitchen skills involve coffee, microwave food, and sometimes unburned meat, but when that happens, it's pretty much raw. I can't win.

"Nope, I am cooking or boiling water," I tell him.

"I don't think we even have noodles, but we can check," he tells me, gripping my ass and hoisting me higher, as he moves inside.

"I can walk. I know I'm heavy."

"Hybrid, and I want to hold you, so shh," he hisses at me, and I roll my eyes at him.

THERE ARE NO TWO-MINUTE NOODLES. I AM TRYING TO WORK OUT measurements for a recipe I found online. It is one of those four ingredient recipes, which is a lie. Since when aren't condiments an ingredient?

"Are you sure it says to add that much salt?" Leon asks. I look at the recipe again while clutching the spoon and salt over the pot. That glance makes the bag of salt tip and pour into the pot in a heap. I gasp, tossing it aside before dropping my spoon inside the pot.

I am making some strange version of pumpkin soup that I can't pronounce. Why not call it what it is: pumpkin soup. That's all it seems to contain. It looks nice, though it smells a little funky.

"I can order pizza?" Leon offers as I stir the pot. Man, I would hate to be the one to wash all these dishes.

"I just spent all that time peeling that thing and working over this ridiculous stove, you're eating it," I snap at him, becoming flustered as I fish for the spoon, before giving up.

"I'm sure it will be tasty," Leon lies, and I narrow my eyes at him.

"You know I can feel you right? I can tell you're lying," I say to him, pointing a finger at him.

"I will love it because you made it," he tells me, and I shake my head before turning back to stir.

"Okay, I think I need to put cream in it," I tell Leon. He hops off the counter to fetch it for me, and I pour in the amount of cream that the recipe asks for. Whatever this is, it does not look like pumpkin soup, and why is it so lumpy?

"Argh, it's sticking to the bottom," I tell Leon while using the ladle to try to break up the chunks of pumpkin, only to find the spoon I dropped in earlier.

"Are you sure you aren't supposed to pour some of the water out?" Leon asks, peering into the pot.

"It'll do, I'm hungry," I tell him, retrieving some bowls. I'm about to dish it out as Rhen and Raidon walk into the kitchen.

"Thane is out there, on the verge of tears over being kicked out of his kitchen," Raidon chuckles before he stops.

"Nope, he will definitely cry when he sees the state of his kitchen," Rhen says, looking at the mess.

"What are you making?" Raidon asks as I pour the lumpy soup into the bowls. It looks nothing like the picture at all.

I push the bowl toward him, and he smiles awkwardly. "Looks interesting," Raidon comments, but he accepts it with an awkward smile.

"I should probably take Thane's out for him. He will die if he sees the kitchen in this state," Rhen tells me before snatching his bowl off the counter and moving toward the dining room.

"That was quick," I hear Thane say.

Grabbing a spoon, I scoop up some of my soup. I obliterate every taste bud with that one spoonful. It sprays out like a fountain, coating Leon, who's leaning against the counter and has yet to take a bite.

"So much salt," I choke racing to the sink and putting my mouth under the faucet, gulping the water down.

"I'll order pizza," Leon winks at me. I grab my bowl, dumping the contents into the sink before wandering to the dining room when I hear the whispers. Popping my head around the corner I see Rhen sniffing his bowl. No fucking way would I eat even another spoonful of that oversalted shit. I should have let Thane cook.

"Eat it. She made it; you'll eat it. I don't care if she served you dog food, you're eating it," Thane hisses at them. I duck back around the corner, trying to stifle my giggles. Leon raises an eyebrow at me, and he shows me the pizza options.

"Should I tell them you're ordering Pizza?"

"Nah, let them suffer," he says, and I elbow him. "Suffer deliciously," he quickly adds, and I roll my eyes.

"You didn't try it."

"Pretty sure I did when you spat it all over me," he says, placing his phone down after ordering. He helps me clean up the kitchen, my stomach rumbling. Curiosity gets the better of him, and he decides to try some from the pot as I stack the dishwasher. He blanches, and I look at him, watching him swallow down my shame as if he is swallowing a golf ball.

"It is an acquired taste," he heaves. "And I don't think the pumpkin was cooked long enough; it's still hard," he adds as he retches into the sink.

I am halfway through rinsing the pots when the doorbell rings.

"I'll get it," Leon sings out, rushing toward the door just as Thane wanders out of the dining room. I move aside, watching as he rinses his bowl before stacking it in the dishwasher. Rhen follows not long after him; sweat coats his brow, and he looks a little green when Leon returns with pizza.

446

Rhen blinks at him. "What is that?" Rhen growls at him.

"Dinner," Leon says. I press my lips in a line to prevent a smile, before rushing off after Leon to the living room.

"Dining room," Thane calls out.

"Nope," I reply, not wanting to sit at the table with them. Raidon groans as he and Rhen follow us out. I can hear Thane cursing about us eating in the living room and not at a table.

Leon and I share a pizza. The others don't touch it.

"Are you going to eat?" I ask them, eyeballing the garlic bread before snatching it off the coffee table.

"I am oddly overfull," Rhen says.

"My stomach can't handle anymore. I'm full," Raidon says, groaning and turning onto his side when Thane comes out. I can feel his anger over the mess on the coffee table, but he doesn't say anything. Instead, he sits on the couch beside Rhen to watch the movie I put on.

CHAPTER
NINETY-FOUR

~ **T**hane~

Harlow refuses to be alone with us without Leon. It doesn't matter where he goes; she even follows after him for the few seconds it takes him to drop the pizza boxes in the bin. I try not to let it get to me, try to remind myself that she feels safest with him, but it doesn't help my jealousy or that of our mates as we watch her with him.

Yet none of us say anything to her about it. We just let her be. No matter how much it kills me watching them, I don't push her. By the time the movie ends, she's fallen asleep on top of Leon. He goes to move, not realizing she's passed out, so engrossed in the movie that I can't even remember the name of. I am too absorbed in the fact that she is here that I spend the entire time watching her, while festering in my jealousy.

Raidon, however, moves before I can and grips Leon's shoulder as he goes to stand. He points to Harlow, making Leon look down at her head in his lap.

"Wake her and take her with you. She will freak out if she wakes up and you're gone," I tell him.

448

"I want to shower. I am covered in her soup; it's sticky," he whispers, tugging on his shirt that is splattered in orange gunk.

Yeah, that was not an enjoyable meal. I can't wait until she forgives us, if she ever does, because I am never letting her cook again. Her cooking is atrocious. Steaming hot garbage would have been preferable. Who the heck uses water in pumpkin soup and then doesn't drain that starchy water out? The mere thought of it has my stomach turning.

Raidon nearly vomited, and that man gags on nothing, not even dick, so that says something. Leon carefully slips out from under her. "I'll be quick," he murmurs. Rhen growls at him, knowing his idea of quick is completely different from ours.

"Leon!" Rhen snaps at him in a hushed voice.

"I'll be five minutes," he hisses back at him.

Raidon and Rhen look at me. I roll my eyes at them, knowing they want me to leave in case she does wake up, just to lessen the damage.

"I will go clean or something," I tell them, too wired to go down to the Den to sleep. Getting up, I move to the kitchen and grab a cloth.

I already cleaned the kitchen but figure a second go-over will ensure the stench of burned food and other residue is gone. Leon saying he will be five minutes is a hit and miss.

He has a tendency to forget the concept of time, so we all know his idea of five minutes and an actual five minutes are two separate things. It is also why we always tell him he has appointments an hour before they start. Giving him the correct time guarantees he will be late, tell him it's an hour before, and he may just show up on time.

Raidon comes into the kitchen about ten minutes later, muttering about Leon taking his damn time, and Rhen wanders in too.

"Where are you sleeping?" Rhen yawns.

"Where she told me to—the Den," I tell them, and Raidon bristles.

"Yeah, I didn't think you would go through with that," Raidon says.

"I'll manage," I tell him, not wanting to admit I have been sleeping down there anyway, unable to bear not having her scent around. Although not a speck of it lingers down there anymore.

"Leon?" we all hear from the living room. All of our heads snap in her direction, and I drop the hand towel on the counter before wandering down the hall to let her know he is showering, when she rushes out of the room. Harlow stops in her tracks when she spots me.

"He's showering, he'll be back down soon," I tell her, and she nods her head. Her eyes dart to the staircase when Rhen and Raidon come out of the kitchen behind me. I listen to her heart rate pick up, and I curse them. Her heart was beating fast when it was just me, now it's worse. I see every muscle in her body tense, and I know she is about to run for the stairs.

In the blink of an eye, she's off. I reach for her, seeing the panic on her face. I curse, knowing it is because I am standing near the basement door. She runs for the steps, missing the bottom one as I go to grab her, only to trip on the second. My heart damn near stops in my chest as I watch her throw her hands out to brace herself.

My hand fists the back of her shirt, pulling her back before she hits the stairs. Harlow screams the most blood curdling scream I have ever heard—the sound visceral—making my stomach sink wondering if I hurt her.

"You're—Argh!"

She bites my arm as it wraps around her chest, holding her steady, before she tosses her head back, catching me on the chin. I shake my head as pain ricochets along my jaw, and my arm tightens around her chest, above her breasts, when something hits the floor at my feet.

"Shh, stop. I am not going to hurt you," I tell her before flooding her with my Calling. Raidon leans down, picking up whatever fell. It is the vial of my serum. He holds it up, and I take it from him as his eyes dart back to Rhen. She hasn't taken it. Why didn't she take it?

She melts against me, leaning back as she is forced to surrender to my Calling. Pounding footsteps sound on the floor above, and Leon comes rushing out in a panic, sliding into the wall and nearly down the stairs. I pocket the vial and sigh, feeling his blatant fear through the bond.

My other hand smooths over her belly. I rub it before scooping her legs out from under her. I tuck her to my chest and walk up the steps to Leon's room. Leon glares at me but says nothing as he opens his door.

"I swear, Thane, I will fucking kill you if you hurt her," he growls at me, and I glare at him.

"She tripped, I grabbed her, and she freaked out," I tell him, setting her on the bed. The moment my Calling releases her, she snaps out of her daze and shuffles away from me. I fish the vial out of my pocket and hold it out to her. Her eyes widen as she feels her bra, which must have been where she had it.

She stares at me before leaning forward hesitantly.

"Take it; it's yours," I tell her, and she quickly snatches it before moving closer to the wall.

"Goodnight, Harlow," I tell her before walking out of the room and back down the stairs. The bond has me wanting to run back to her and beg for forgiveness at her feet. I shake off the urge, knowing I would probably just scare her more, and I walk down to the Den.

CHAPTER
NINETY-FIVE

ONE WEEK LATER
~Harlow~

Leon and I return home from an ultrasound and are walking through the door when his phone starts ringing. He answers it as I walk into the house, only to find that Thane is home and sitting at the counter reading a newspaper. He sets it down as I make my way to the fridge, and I can hear Leon arguing with whoever is on the phone, still in the foyer.

"How did your ultrasound go?" Thane asks.

I glance at him over my shoulder. We hardly speak, and I prefer it that way. It is easier to just stay away from him than deal with his moodiness.

"Harlow?" he says, and I continue to ignore him, grabbing a bottle of water and moving toward the foyer to find out what has Leon so upset. As I pass Thane, however, he reaches out and grips my wrist, stopping me. I jerk my hand from his grip and glare at him.

"Can you answer me, please? All you do is ignore me," Thane sighs, wiping a hand down his face before scratching the back of his

452

neck. "You can't just ignore me. You are pregnant with our child. We have to at least co-parent."

"Our daughter has three other fathers. I don't have to do shit with you," I tell him. I'm about to turn away when he stops me again, making me growl at him. I was locked in that damn Den for a month, and he expects me to just forget it. Without even a fucking apology?

"Fine. Just go," he sighs as Leon walks in. He grabs a bottle of Coke from the fridge.

"Everything alright?" Thane asks him.

"No, I need to go see Talon. He is having issues with one of his vendors."

"I can go," Thane says, standing up, but Leon shakes his head.

"No, stay. I will deal with it. Watch Harlow for me," Leon says, and I sputter.

"Why can't I come?" I ask, not wanting to be stuck at home with Thane.

"Because his vendor is a vampire, so neither of you are getting anywhere near him," Leon replies.

"Well, why can't Thane go?" I ask, pointing at Thane.

"Nope, his blood is just as addictive as yours. I'll handle it," Leon says, pecking my cheek and walking off.

"Leon!" I shriek in panic, rushing after him.

"Harlow, enough! It isn't safe. Thane's your mate too. He won't do anything. He hasn't, has he?" Leon asks. I look at Thane beside me and swallow nervously. It will be the first time I am left alone with him since coming home.

"I'll call Rhen and tell him to head home, okay?" Leon says, cupping my face in his hands. He presses his lips against mine, and I sigh.

"No, I'll be fine. Just go," I tell him, and he looks at Thane who nods to him before he turns on his heel and leaves.

Dread fills my stomach as I turn to find Thane watching me. He says nothing as I wander into the living room and flick the TV on. I am watching the midday drama when he walks out and sits on the couch across from me with his newspaper. I try my best to ignore him, but his presence has me on edge. Although, I am curious as to why he is home so early.

"How come you aren't at work?" I ask him. He briefly lifts his head to glance at me.

"Because I wanted to be here when you got home from your ultrasound, so I can find out what is happening with your pregnancy and our daughter," he says simply, and I roll my eyes.

"She is fine. I'm sure Leon would have told you later. You didn't have to come home early," I tell him.

"No, he wouldn't have. None of them tell me anything regarding you."

I scoff. He sets the paper down, looking at me.

"Our mates barely speak to me, Harlow, and they won't until you start."

Shaking my head, I turn my attention back to the TV. "I have nothing to say to you. Nothing nice anyway,"

"Your anger I can handle. Your silence is driving me insane," he mutters, opening his newspaper.

"Wow, it must be so damn hard not having your mates speak to you. Sucks, doesn't it? Try being mute, too; that will really drive you crazy. Silence is one thing, but being mute? Having your voice stolen from you for so long that you forget what it even sounds like. Eventually, you start believing you never had one in the first place," I tell him. Saying the words out loud makes them truly sink in. For both of us.

Thane says nothing, but I can feel his gaze as he watches me—feel the guilt writhing through him. We sit in awkward silence for what feels like an eternity, when he finally speaks.

"Harlow... I... I know..."

Turning my head, I look at him, watching him struggle with whatever he is trying to say, when he stops for a second. "I know what—"

"No, you don't know. You don't know because you grew up with the privilege of being born an Alpha. You always had a voice, and when I finally found mine, you took it, proving it was never really mine to begin with," I tell him.

"You think because I am an Alpha, I had it easy? I have had responsibility shoved on my damn shoulders from the moment I could walk," he snaps at me.

"And what responsibility is that, Thane? The pressure of knowing you will have everything handed to you on a silver platter, because of your DNA. That you will be able to pick and choose every aspect of your life, deciding which Omega you will destroy, so you can raise the next Alpha asshole?" I scoff.

"I have spent every damn second of my life training and being brought up in my parents' image. Raised with the responsibility of knowing I will be the one everyone turns to, to protect them, keep them safe. I thought you killed my mother. What did you expect me to do, Harlow? Just forgive you and move on?"

"Yes. Because I didn't fucking do it!"

"And you lied to us, all of us!" he screams at me.

"I lied because from the moment I met you, all I heard was how much you fucking hate Omegas! How much you wanted to kill the woman you thought killed your mother! Was I supposed to add that to my fucking resume? 'Assumed killer of Mrs. Keller!' I lied because I had no other choice, and you proved that because the moment you found out, you locked me in the Den without letting me explain," I retort.

Thane tosses his newspaper on the coffee table "You should have come to us instead of running for two years!"

"I was fucking scared! I was barely eighteen, Thane, barely a fucking adult. I watched someone get murdered. I thought my sister was dead because she joined a pack and couldn't take the knot, and I was worried I would end up exactly like her. I didn't want to be an Omega. I hated what I am, and for two years I was convinced I killed my own sister because she took my place. She took my place because I was terrified of being a pack Omega, only to be told that she was dead and I was being shipped off as a damn breeder to a pack I didn't fucking know!" I scream at him.

"You should have come to us. You could have called or gone back to the sanctuary or—" He clutches his hair in frustration. "I know you must have been scared; it's why I sent my mother to get you. We didn't want to scare you."

"Your mother is the one who bid on me."

Thane lifts his head and looks at me, shocked.

"You didn't want me to begin with. You wanted Tara."

Thane blinks at me.

"Who told you that? Did Jake say that?" he asks, and I look away. "I never loved Tara. Tara, she was—"

"You don't love me either. How could you? You don't know me. I was just a purchase, like buying a damn car."

"We would have taken care of you, grown to love you, Harlow, and you us."

"See now, that's the difference, Thane. I would have been forced to love you, forced to mate you, accept you. That choice was never mine; it was always yours."

"It wasn't mine either! You said it yourself, my mother bid on you. I wasn't shopping for a fucking Omega. But it is my responsibility to keep my pack together, to keep the city in check. All that was expected of you is that you stand by us. Nothing more and nothing less. Spit out some kids, and that's it," he snaps, and I blink at him.

"So simple, right?" I ask him, folding my arms across my chest and shaking my head.

"No. That is not... That came out wrong," he shakes his head and growls. "We would have looked after you."

"I didn't need looking after. I needed freedom. I wanted a life outside of the one expected of me!"

"But you're an Omega!" he screams.

"Exactly! And not by choice, by blood. You think growing up and being told you will run a city, a pack, is hard?"

Thane looks at me, folding his arms across his chest. "All that is expected of you is to lie on your back! Do that, and you get every-thing else handed to you," Thane snaps.

"Really? You want to compare the differences, Thane? Is that what you want?"

He tosses his arms up in the air. "Fine, you want to play this game, go for it!" he says.

We are so far off from the original topic now—his apology—I might as well toss it out the window. He wants to play 'who had it worse'? Fine. Let's fucking play then. I press my lips in a line, furious; so furious, my hands begin shaking as I stifle the urge to shift. I can't believe he thinks that all that is expected of Omegas is to lay there and spit kids out.

"Well?" Thane asks expectantly.

"Your mother was an Omega," I tell him.

"Obviously!" he growls.

"Do you even know what Omegas are taught?" I ask him.

"Well, obviously not. I went to an all-Alpha school."

"Private school," I tell him.

"And so did you. That is what the sanctuaries are for. Parents are given a choice to either use the public schools, home school, or the private sanctuaries. We had it the same on that front," Thane tells me, and I laugh.

"No, we did not. I spent my childhood on the run with my parents, Thane. My mother didn't want us to have the same upbringing she did. Zara and I were lucky to live somewhere for more than a month before the authorities came for us. We were prac-tically raised in my parents' car."

"And that was her choice," he says.

I shake my head, not because he is wrong, but because he thought she had a choice.

"Yes, it was. Zara and I hated her for it. We wanted to live some-where where we didn't have to run, where we could grow up and make friends, where we could have our own rooms, belongings, a life."

"You can't blame me for your upbringing," Thane says. I shake my head, holding up my hand.

"I'm not done, and I am not blaming you, but your way of thinking is how every Alpha thinks. Zara and I hated our parents, until we figured out why they did it. We were tossed into the sanctuary right after they died; became wards of the state. And the first thing they teach us is how to please an Alpha. On our first day there, we weren't taught math or science. We are taught how to pleasure an Alpha," I tell him.

"Sex education. Everyone is taught that," Thane says, and I chuckle.

"We thought it was a sex education class too. Turns out, every class was like that. How to sit, how to speak when with an Alpha, how to obey, even how to suck dick. Normal classes ended at the age of twelve. No more art, no more English, or whatever the fuck you were taught. It is all about how to pleasure an Alpha. Taught about the serums. Told how we will die if we can't take their knot. Taught the laws surrounding our ownership. Taught how we aren't people, we are belongings. That's what they teach you in the sanctuary."

Thane opens his mouth, no doubt to dispute what I said, but I cut him off.

"Then we are given a choice: rotation or pack life. Those are the two choices we are given. That's it. Now imagine growing up hating your parents for running, only to learn that they were running because it was the only chance we had for a normal life. Omegas are raised to be used and abused. Nothing more and nothing less. Expected to obey, look pretty, and open our damn legs and accept any dick that is forced on us. Sure, they tell us it will be a lavish lifestyle, and we won't have to work unless we choose rotation; told that we will be adored by our packs, if we choose one or if we are sold to one. But all I saw was that my future depended on how well I could fuck!"

Thane appears to think for a second, his brows pinch together before he leans back to look at me. "My mother never told me that."

"Why would she? She was raised to obey too—raised to be an Alpha's whore," I tell him, getting to my feet.

"Harlow," Thane says as I leave. I am over this argument already.

Stopping, I stare at the ceiling for a second. Digging into my back pocket, I pull out the ultrasound picture and hand it to him. Thane takes it, brushing his thumb over the image.

"Your mother told me you were a good man. That you would look after me," I tell him and he looks up at me. "For our daughter's sake, I hope that's true. Because if she is born Omega, I hope you see more than dollar signs over her head. I hope you value her more than you do me; value her enough to look past her DNA. If she is born Omega, her fate is in your hands, just like mine is," I tell him, walking out of the living room and up the stairs.

CHAPTER
NINETY-SIX

~Harlow~

Once I am back in Leon's room, I shut the door. I don't intend to speak with Thane again until he pulls his head out of his ass. Yet, in true Thane form, unwilling to be on the tail end of a losing argument, he busts the door down within minutes of me climbing into bed.

A squeak leaves me as the door bangs against the dresser, making the mirror on top rattle.

"You don't get to yell and scream at me and then run from me." He is furious, but I can tell through the bond that his anger isn't directed at me. As he moves closer to the bed, I shuffle upright, knowing all too well how unpredictable his mood swings are.

"I'm not going to hurt you. For fuck's sake, Harlow, stop flinching. I have never beaten you."

"No, you only locked me in a damn Den and ordered me around and used your damn aura on me," I snap at him. My hand slips to the nightstand, where I keep the wolfsbane spray Rhen gave me. My fingers wrap around the can, my finger on the trigger.

"I can't take what I did back, but you can stop throwing it in my face every damn chance you get," he growls. His eyes turn onyx and his canines protrude. My eyes widen in horror as flashbacks of him chasing and charging at me flood the forefront of my mind. Thane reaches for me, and I shriek, squeezing the trigger, only for the nozzle to be facing the wrong way, accidentally drenching and blinding myself.

I choke, gasping for air as I inhale it. My eyes and skin burn as if I have been doused in acid, and I drop the can and claw at my face.

"Fuck!" I hear Thane swear as I blindly reach for the blanket, needing to remove the substance burning me. Hands move under my legs and ass as I flail and cough on the wolfsbane.

"Don't swallow it," Thane panics. I feel cold water blast me from the ensuite's shower. My feet slip on the floor, yet his arm under my belly holds me steady.

"Hang on," Thane says, scrubbing my face with soap while I spit out torrents of water so I don't swallow any. The soap makes my eyes burn even more. I can hear the mind-link open. Thane is trying to reply to them, yet all I can focus on is the burning of my skin.

Eventually, the pain eases. I blink, my vision returning, and I stare at the black tiled wall. Blood coats the floor from the spray eating away at my skin. Something is forced against my lips. I choke as his metallic-tasting blood floods my mouth.

"Drink. It's my blood," Thane urges. I grab his wrist, swallowing it down. His blood doesn't work as quickly as Leon's, but I can feel my skin heal slowly the more I drink it.

"Did you swallow any?" Thane asks, and I shake my head, pulling away from his bleeding wrist. I hate that I can't shift. Everything takes longer to heal without it.

"Geez, Harlow. I'm not going to hurt you," Thane says before sticking his hand inside my shirt. I grip his wrist, my nails digging in; he hisses and growls behind me as his hand slips into my bra.

He steals the serum that I always keep on me, and I snatch it off him. "I'm not taking it. Use it, Harlow," he whispers, and I peer up at him over my shoulder. Thane adjusts the shower temperature, turning the heat up.

"I'm pregnant, Thane; it will affect our daughter."

"Our daughter has four fathers and a stubborn-ass mother to keep her in line. Use it. She will be born Alpha. It will enhance my DNA in your system and override yours, ensuring she won't be Omega," Thane tells me, and I look at the vial. "There is no way in this world I would let our daughter be sold off, even if she does choose that life," Thane growls.

"Omegas are rare, Thane. We are almost extinct."

"Fuck the rest of the world; I don't care about them. I only care about you and our daughter," he tells me.

"It changes nothing, though. The entire Omega system is wrong. That's my point, not that I hate being Omega. Well, I do. But I see why we are necessary to Alphas."

"Well, what do you want then? I can't win with you. You wanted space; I gave you that. You wanted me to sign you over to Leon. I did that. I sleep in the Den because you told me to! I don't know how else to make up for what I did up to you!" he growls.

"You could apologize! Let's start with that!" I snap at him.

"I did apologize!"

"No, you acknowledged you were wrong. Big difference."

"It's the same thing," he says, and I turn around to face him.

"Are you being serious right now?" I ask him.

Thane blinks at me before reaching for my shirt and peeling it off while I scramble to try to keep it. Thane tosses it out the shower door, ignoring me, slapping my hands away as he undoes my bra and the button on my jeans.

"Thane!" I snap at him as he undoes the zipper.

"I'm helping you," he retorts, jerking his hands away. I growl at him, removing my own damn pants while he rids himself of his shirt.

"Fine. I am sorry," he says like a sulking child being forced to apologize to a sibling.

I press my lips in a line and shake my head. "Just get out!" I tell him, reaching for the controls to turn the heat up more.

CHAPTER
NINETY-SEVEN

~H arlow~

"I apologized, didn't I? You said apologize. What else do you want me to do, get on my damn hands and knees and beg you to forgive me?"

"Well, that wouldn't hurt," I snap back at him sarcastically, and he suddenly drops to his knees. I blink at him as he stares at my huge belly. Any lower, and he will disappear under it, just like my damn vagina, which I haven't seen in two weeks.

Thane stares at my stomach and the stretch marks that now lace my skin. As if seeing how huge I am now really makes him see exactly what my body contains. Ten little fingers, ten little toes, and one beating heart that he helped make. His feelings through the bond tell me he wants to touch it, feel her move. His apology is long forgotten, mesmerized as he watches my belly ripple as she moves inside me.

His hands move to my hips before running up and across my belly. He rests his hands on the sides of my belly, and her movements stop for a second before it feels like she rolls, my belly moving in a wave beneath his hands, and he smiles, glancing up at me.

Thane leans forward on his knees, pressing his lips against my belly before resting his ear against it. He exhales, and I brush my fingers through his hair. He turns his face into my palm, kissing it.

"Don't cut me out of her life, Harlow," Thane whispers.

"I was never going to cut you from her life, only mine."

"I don't want to be cut from yours either."

"Then prove to me you are worth keeping in it. I am sick and tired of living up to everyone else's expectations, when no one bothers to try to live up to mine," I tell him, and he looks up at me.

"And what do you expect of us?"

"I expect you to listen, to stand behind me because the only damn thing that ever has is my shadow. And I am tired of running; I am tired of fighting to be heard. I want to be seen as more than just an Omega. I expect you to let me be Harlow, expect you to let me make my own decisions. That is all I expect of you."

"You want to make all the decisions?" he asks, and I sigh before shaking my head.

"Not all. I just want to be included in them, especially when they affect me. I am sick of being told to sit and obey, to be seen and not heard. You own this city. You have the power to change things, not just for me, but for her," I tell him, running my hands over my belly.

"We are not objects; we bleed and hurt like everyone else. But we are taught to never show our pain because we are taught to expect it. I don't want her to grow up knowing her worth is dependent on her Omega score. I want our daughter to grow up with a voice, and I want her fathers in her corner when she uses it because that's where I'll be."

"She won't have to worry about that. You have the serum."

"And if she is born Alpha, Thane? Then what? Problem solved? She will grow up with the same mindset you have, that Omegas are beneath her. That I am beneath her," I tell him.

"I don't understand what it is you're asking of me?"

"I don't want to be your Omega, Thane. I also don't want to be an Alpha. No titles. I want family, everyone equal, everyone heard,

465

everyone loved. I want this city to be safe for her no matter her status."

"You want me to change the laws everyone has lived by since forever?"

"No, you can change them in this city, but in the rest of the world that will take time. Make this city a safe haven for Omegas. You have the power to do that. You're the ranking Alpha here; you have a say in what laws are made because you help make them."

"What's the point of changing the laws here if they won't change everywhere else, Harlow? It will just cause an uproar."

"Exactly! We'd be setting an example. A foundation for change. That is what your mother wanted. I have spent the last few weeks reading up on everything your mother did, and you know what she lacked? Her Alphas. Omegas are seen as property, yet your fathers never fought for their so-called property when she took on the councils; when she tried to open the very same facility that you are building in her honor."

"No, she was equal to them. They gave her their serum."

"Equal only in the sense that she couldn't be commanded by them. That is all the serum does. If she was really their equal, she wouldn't have needed that serum because they would never have attempted to command her in the first place. My guess is the reason they gave her the serum was the same reason you gave me yours. Because they fucked up and needed to earn her trust. And if that is the case, then it is the same reason why I haven't taken it; I shouldn't have to. I want to be equal to you because you see me as equal, not on the false pretense of being equal under a serum I shouldn't need if you loved me."

"That's why you haven't taken it, not just because of our daughter?" he asks.

"I need to know I can trust you. The serum stops you from commanding me. It doesn't stop you from controlling me, though. There is nothing stopping you from dragging me back down to that

Den; the only difference would be you couldn't command me down there. You'd have to drag me."

"So that's all you want?"

"Yes. And I want the begging and pleading you offered. I am enjoying seeing you on your knees. You may beg for my forgiveness now." I laugh when Thane raises an eyebrow at me.

"I've never had to beg before," he mumbles.

"Well, it will be a humbling experience for you then, so hop to it; I'm waiting," I chuckle, smiling down at him.

"I feel like I am getting the short stick here. I'm the only one being forced to do anything. If I am going to humiliate myself, I want to know what I am going to get out of it," he says, rubbing my thighs.

"A family. If you keep your word," I tell him.

"And if I don't keep my word?"

"Then you better get used to being on your knees because you'll have a lot of begging to do."

Thane laughs and kisses my belly.

CHAPTER
NINETY-EIGHT

~ R hen~
"Thane, let me help, at least; I'm not that bad at cooking," I hear Harlow tell Thane as I walk into the foyer. Raidon gives me a look, hearing them. They aren't arguing, and they are in the same room together without being at each other's throats. Walking into the hall, I hear Thane huff. He has this pained look on his face.

"Harlow, please let me do it. You can watch."

Oh, god, please say yes, I think to myself. That woman could burn water.

"My cooking isn't that terrible, and you..."

Thane raises an eyebrow at her. I stifle my laugh as I watch them quietly. Raidon and I had raced here the moment we felt her pain, but seeing them now, Thane is taking care of her, and they seem to be getting along.

"You ate the spaghetti I made," she huffs. He grabs her hips, setting her on the countertop.

"A+ for effort, but you can't cook to save your life. I can't stand eating your cooking anymore. I don't think my stomach can take it. But if you insist, I will suffer in silence until it kills me," he laughs.

"Well, it wouldn't be suffering in silence now that you told me," she says, shoving him away.

Raidon comes up behind me, and they finally realize we are watching them. Harlow's face lights up.

"Tell him, Rhen, my cooking isn't as horrid as he is making it out to be. You liked it, right?"

I look between her and Thane, not wanting to hurt her feelings, before nudging Raidon to answer for me.

"Yeah, I like it; I don't know what he is talking about," Raidon says.

"Right, Rhen?" Raidon smiles at me, waiting for my answer as Harlow's eyes narrow, looking at me expectantly.

"Well, is it that bad?" she asks, wanting the majority ruling to say she can cook, but I want to live and not die from food poisoning.

"Well, you'll never be a chef, but it's edible," I tell her. She purses her lips, and Thane rubs his hands up her thighs.

"See?" he says.

Hearing the door, I look back to see Leon wander in. He stops in his tracks as he spots Harlow and Thane in the kitchen, Thane standing between her legs. I can feel his shock through the bond, but it is also clearly splashed across his face as Leon stares at them openly.

'Stop staring, don't ruin it,' Raidon growls through the mind-link.

I step into the kitchen, and Thane moves aside as I lean down and peck her lips. "Let Thane cook," I tell her. She sighs and reluctantly nods her head. I can see she doesn't completely trust him but is giving him the benefit of the doubt.

"Fine," she says, hopping off the counter when Leon wraps his arms around her. He tugs her against him, whispering something in her ear that makes her arousal scent the air before he rushes her off to make her shower with him.

"Leon!" Raidon scolds, feeling his hunger.

"I'm fine," he tells Raidon. Leon has not fed on her once since she came home. He refuses and has been drinking from blood bags, which is beginning to get on all our nerves because it causes his scent to change for a few hours afterward.

"Go with them. He doesn't feel right," Thane nods to Raidon, who saunters off after them. Thane grabs some pots and pans out from the cabinet.

"Leon had to bail Talon out again," I tell Thane, who nods his head.

"I figured as much by his mood."

I wait for Thane to blow up. He is sick of the trouble Talon causes Leon. We all are, but he is family. However, Thane's usual tyrant mood at such matters doesn't come as expected.

Instead, he starts getting ingredients out.

"What are you making?" I ask him, stepping behind him and wrapping my arms around his waist. I drop my chin on his shoulder. I have missed this, missed my mate, but he had to learn she is our mate too, and we won't accept how he treated her if he isn't willing to learn from his mistakes.

We all groveled, begged, and earned her forgiveness over the past few days, but what he did is inexcusable, just as it is inexcusable that we let it go on for so long.

"Lasagna."

I nod and kiss the side of his neck as he pulls the meat from the packet. I press him against the counter. His hands hit the countertop.

"Rhen, I'm cooking," he snaps at me, and I chuckle at his grumpy ass. Some things never change with him. I nudge my hips against him, and he smacks my thigh.

"I have nipple clamps upstairs with your name on them," he warns me, but I grip his hips, spinning him around. He growls at me until I press my lips against his. His growl turns to a purr, and he grips the back of my neck, deepening the kiss, biting my lip, and making me moan.

"Don't tease me. Don't ruin my good mood," he growls at me, letting me go.

"Maybe I am not teasing," I tell him.

"You should, be because I need to cook. Now go harass the others and get out of my kitchen," he snaps at me, reaching for the kitchen towel. I chuckle, turning away from him when he flicks it, making me jump at the sting of the towel snapping against my ass.

"I'm going, I'm going," I tell him, walking off. Finally, things are getting to some form of normal. Walking upstairs, I move toward the main bathroom, where I can hear their voices. Pushing the door open, I find Harlow watching them shower as she sits on the vanity wrapped in a towel, her hair dampened and droplets of water running down her shoulders.

CHAPTER
NINETY-NINE

~R hen~

"You're not hopping in with them?" I ask her, retrieving a towel from the cupboard under the sink.

"My scent overwhelmed him," she says, and I look at Leon worriedly. He has been off since he arrived home, and if Raidon is in there with him, something must have gone down for her to be sitting at the sink looking upset.

"I don't get why he doesn't just feed off me," Harlow mumbles. He could, werewolves have more blood than humans, but still Leon would rather not risk it.

"Because he has gone cold turkey. He will struggle to stop," I tell her, shucking her under the chin before unbuttoning my shirt. Raidon hops out so I can take his place, and I don't miss how she licks her lips or the scent of her arousal as she watches him grab a towel, securing it around his waist.

"Don't look at me like that. You know I want you," he says to her.

Her hormones have been all over the place lately, and she even attacked Leon while he was asleep the other night. Yet none of us are willing to touch her, afraid of hurting her, or worse, afraid of her

472

trying to mark us. We know it will be upsetting for her when she realizes she can't.

Leon can't touch her at the moment. Sex and bloodlust go hand in hand, and without Thane, he doesn't trust himself. Raidon is worried about hurting her, and I don't want to have the awkward conversation that her mark won't stick until she accepts Thane. We know she wants to mark us. We can tell by the way she scents us, her instincts to claim us growing stronger the longer she is around us. She wants us to be hers as much as she is ours. However, none of us want her to feel pressured into marking Thane just so she can mark us.

I can see our lack of contact is starting to bother her, though. Harlow growls, slipping off the counter and walking out. Raidon sighs, watching after her.

"She wants to mark us," I tell them.

"Yeah, and I won't be the one to break it to her that it won't work unless she marks Thane first," Raidon tells me.

"Well, they seemed to be getting along today," I tell him, unbuttoning my pants and slipping them off. Stepping into the shower, though, I wonder how much longer we can avoid that conversation. She will have to mark him if she wants to mark us, and I can tell she isn't anywhere near there yet with Thane.

I step under the shower's spray when the mind-link opens up, and Thane's angry voice slips into my head.

'Is there a reason Low looks upset?' he asks, and I sigh as Raidon answers him.

Fuck! Looks like that conversation will be happening sooner rather than later, I think to myself, knowing that it won't play out well. Everyone knows that in Alpha Packs, the most dominant Alpha is the head. One thing they don't teach in the schools though, and that most Alpha Packs don't advertise, is that to mark any member of the pack, you must first mark the Alpha.

Just like Thane had to mark her before any of us could, she needs to mark him before she can mark any of us. It's the same with severing the bond. The Alpha is the key, and that makes it the greatest weakness of all Alpha Packs. If the Alpha dies, all of our bonds break, which often causes the people themselves to break. It is a form of control no one wants to talk about. All of us are linked to Thane. He hurts, we hurt, he breaks, we all break. His word is law, and his life is our life. Broken bonds don't last without the Alpha.

If something happened to one of us, we would survive it as long as we have our Alpha, but if something happened to Thane, it would kill all of us—not physically, but you just don't survive that sort of pain. We all submitted to him, gave him his power in a sense, and made him the strongest, although he already was the strongest of us. If something happened to him, we would never gain that power back, because it dies with him. Without him, we would be regular werewolves, despite our DNA.

And Harlow is an Omega. Once she marks Thane, if he dies, she will die with him, and that is something none of us are ready to tell her. Once she marks him, there is no way out for her. Only Thane would be able to break their bond, and we all know he will never let her go. She has to come to the decision by herself, without our influence, just as we all had to come to that decision ourselves.

Harlow isn't completely helpless, however. Once the bond has been completed, Thane will always choose and protect her over all of us. Our lives depend on him and his will depend on hers. If she breaks, Thane breaks. If she dies, Thane will die too. Without her, his instincts will go crazy, and so will he. It's what happened to Thane's fathers after Hana died, which is why they ended up killing themselves.

It is also why most Alpha Packs chose rotation wolves. Omegas have always been seen as weak, and marking one would give rival packs an easy target. A pack is only as strong as its weakest link. She will become ours, and she will be the biggest weapon our enemies can use against us.

'*Where is she?*' I hear Raidon ask Thane as I rinse my hair out.

'*The living room. I will check her in a minute,*' Thane answers him.

Opening my eyes, I find Leon staring at the door. "What's wrong?" I ask him

"She thinks I rejected her."

"She is hormonal," I tell him.

"Yeah, but you should have seen the look on her face," he says, rinsing the soap off and stepping out.

"She'll be fine; Thane will speak with her," I tell him.

"Yeah, well, hopefully she gets them in check before dinner," Raidon says, and I had completely forgotten. Fuck!

"Why by dinner time?" Leon asks as I shut the water off.

"Mom and Dad are coming over for dinner," Raidon says.

"Fuck! Maybe Thane should have let her cook," Leon says, and Raidon shoots a look at him.

"She wants to apologize."

"Yeah, but if she upsets Harlow, I won't hold my tongue. I love Mom, but I love Harlow more," Leon warns him. Great, that's all we need: a ravenous hybrid, a hormonal pregnant Omega, a raging Thane, and in-laws.

Yep, this will be the dinner from hell.

CHAPTER
ONE HUNDRED

~H~ arlow~

My stupid hormones are rampant. I know I am being over-sensitive and slightly irrational at Leon's rejection and how Raidon ripped me out of the shower when Leon growled at me. Yet my bond craves them, and none of them will touch me. It is driving me crazy, and I am sure it is driving Raidon, Rhen, and especially Leon crazy, considering I sleep in his room.

After getting dressed in cotton shorts and a tank top, I make my way back downstairs with a towel wrapped around my head. Whatever Thane is cooking smells delicious. I wander into the kitchen to find him frying ground beef and what smells like herbs. I grab a bottle of water out of the fridge.

"That was quick," Thane states, and I shrug, wandering off. "Harlow?"

I don't bother answering. Instead, I keep walking into the living room; I grab the remote and flick the TV on before settling into my spot on the couch while trying to ignore the urge to either cry or touch myself.

These stupid hormones have me all over the place. Shouldn't I be all glowy and lively? How come I get the short stick on pregnancy? Some part of me knows this because while I was away with Zara, my bond craved them. Now I'm finally back here, yet they still deny me. The irrational part of me thinks they are doing it to me because I look like a stretched-out beached whale, and they are repulsed by me.

I am ten minutes into a show when Thane calls out to me from the kitchen. At first, I ignore him, but when he sings out again, I roll my eyes. Shutting the TV off, I move to the edge of the couch and force myself up. Wandering into the kitchen, I find Thane placing dinner in the oven.

"What's wrong?" I ask him.

"I was going to ask you that," he says, setting the kitchen towel on the counter.

"Seriously, you made me come all the way in here for nothing?" I groan, about to turn away from him when his hands grab me, landing on my hips before sliding beneath the tank top I'm wearing. With just his touch, my bond reacts, having been deprived by all of them. A moan escapes my lips, much to my embarrassment. My eyes widen, and I go to jerk away from him when he starts to purr, the sound vibrating from his chest against my back.

"You can always ask, Harlow."

"Believe me, I have. They won't fucking touch me," I snap at him angrily.

"Because they're scared of hurting you," he tells me before leaning down. His breath sweeps over my neck as he flicks my hair over one shoulder, his hand on my hip tugging me closer.

"I have no such qualms," he purrs, running his nose along the column of my neck. My eyes flutter shut, my hormones wreaking havoc as his arm wraps around me, his hand squeezing my breast while the other sneaks into my pants to cup my pussy. The pressure of his hand alone has me pushing back against him, wanting—no, needing—his touch when he snaps me out of my lust-filled craze.

"I will need you to ask, though, Low. I will not be blamed for any regret you might feel afterward," he tells me before his lips move to his mark on my neck. He kisses it and waits for me to speak while my face flames. A few hours ago, we were at each other's throats. And now, what am I supposed to do? Ask him for sex to put me out of my misery. Like I am asking him to service a damn car?

He purrs, the sound deep as his Calling washes over me, and I press back against him. I should be mad, I should want to kick his balls out through his ass for using it on me, but I find no bitter feelings about it.

"I still need your permission, love."

I nod my head, and he growls, nipping at my neck, making a breathy moan escape me.

"Words or I will stop."

"Yes, just don't stop." I swear if he stops, I will kick him in the balls for giving me—hmm, what is the female equivalent to blue balls? Blue flaps? Blue clit? That doesn't sound right. I shake the weird thought away as his fingers suddenly move, caressing against me, teasing and toying with me.

My hips move against his hand before his fingers slide into me. His fingers push in as deep as the angle will allow. He slides them out before sliding them back in and curling them. I lean against him, losing myself to the feel of his fingers, his chest vibrating against my back as he Calls to me.

"More," I breathe, hips rocking against his hand. My hand feebly grabs his wrist, needing more. The sensation has warmth pooling in my belly and my inner walls grip his fingers hard.

Thane growls, sliding his fingers from me, and the feral growl that leaves me has him dipping his head and nipping my neck and mark.

"Patience," he purrs. Gripping my hips and spinning me to face him, he backs me up against the counter, and I grip his arm in question.

He grabs my face and kisses me. I melt against his lips as his tongue invades my mouth, my hands releasing his arm, so I can brace them around his neck. Thane clears the counter with a swipe of his hand, not breaking the kiss and knocking everything into the sink before he grips my hips. He lifts me onto the counter. My heart races in my chest.

Thane presses between my legs, running his fingertips over my cheek to grip my jaw, bringing his face down to mine. He brushes his lips over mine, once, twice, and then dives into a kiss that sends the world spinning around me. His hand drifts from my jaw, down to my neck, over my arm, to my hip, then back up to my side, where it stops on my breast. He pulls away, just as breathless as I am, and I read the question in his eyes. He waits for permission, yet I am too far gone, craving his touch as I reach for him.

Thane smiles as he slowly bends down toward me. His lips brush gently against mine. His fingers untie the drawstring on my shorts before gripping the waistband. Placing my hands on the counter, I lift my hips as he pulls them down and off. My shorts are on the ground the next second, and he is back to standing between my legs, his cock pressing against my core.

He runs his lips over my neck, and I tremble under his touch, a sigh escaping me as he sucks my skin hard, leaving marks along it before gripping the hem of my tank top. In one swift movement, he removes it before his mouth is back on my body. His lips run down toward the top of my breasts. I moan at the amazing sensation as he sucks and nips at my hardened nipple, his touch sending electricity everywhere as my skin buzzes and the bond thrums with anticipation.

His lips come back to my neck, kissing and sucking it, making me moan lightly. His hand moves up, a small smile curving at the corners of his mouth before he kisses me again, just once. He pulls away, looking down to watch as his hand drifts slowly up my naked breast, stopping every inch or so to massage softly. Time stops, and I hold my breath.

My skin becomes warm under his touch. I stare up at his face, watching his expression change as his hand gets closer to my nipple. When his fingers finally inch their way up to my perky nipple, he lightly grazes his thumb over it. It instantly peaks. I moan in immense pleasure. Thane groans when he sees it, turning his face back to mine. The fire that has grown in his eyes burns into me, and I know I am done for. I know I would toss everything out the window just to keep his hands on my body.

He kisses me again, his tongue tangling with mine as his hand returns to my face, brushing my hair over my shoulder. He steps back, unbuttoning his shirt. His eyes sweep over my body, another low groan escaping from his beautiful lips, and desire courses through me, his gaze making me hyper aware of how much I crave this gentle side of him.

He steps closer, moving to stand in front of me. His lips meet my already bruised neck from the marks he left there. He kisses. I sigh. He licks. I moan. He sucks, and I shiver. He nibbles, and I gasp. I get chills when he groans.

Thane then stands straight, looking at me, watching his hand move over my swollen belly. I find no repulsion in his gaze, only desire. He runs his fingers over my pussy. It is already wet with slick, embarrassingly so.

Looking at me with a smirk, I can tell he is enjoying the reaction my body and bond are having to his touch. It makes me blush, only to cry out when he grips my hips, dragging me to the edge of the counter before resuming his teasing, only this time, he starts rubbing my clit and I moan in pleasure.

Thane circles my clit, adding some pressure to his fingers. My moans grow louder, and my heartbeat rises. But in the next second, he pauses.

"Thane, please," I moan and beg. If he leaves me like this, I will skin his dick alive and fry it for his dinner. Yet he doesn't move—motherfucker will eat his own sausage if he pisses me off. His eyes run the length of me, drinking me in. I am about to explode in rage that he would rile me up, only to stop.

He growls softly, his eyes flickering to onyx. I am naked, and he is mostly silent until a purr escapes me, reacting to the growling sound he makes. He stands in front of me and admires me for a moment more, following every curve, drinking in every nervous movement I make as I wait to see what he will do next. His gaze drinks me in, moving from my boobs, my belly, my hips, and my already wet pussy. My cheeks heat under his gaze. I'm almost tempted to jump off the counter and make a run for it, knowing any second my instinct to pounce is about to embarrass me.

Before I get that chance, Thane drops to his knees, grips my hips, and buries his face between my thighs, his mouth covering me. His tongue flicks against my clit, his hands pushing my legs higher and forcing me to lean back onto my elbows.

His tongue swirls and tastes, and I lose myself to the sensation, my hips moving against his hot mouth.

I arch my back as I feel the pleasure start to overwhelm me. At that moment, he grabs my hips, plunging his tongue inside me. The sudden shock makes me scream out in bliss. I feel my pussy convulsing, my inner walls pulsating as I cum hard.

My eyes roll, and I let my body shudder helplessly as I ride out the waves. Thane stands, and my hands instantly reach for him, wanting him to bury his cock inside me.

I frantically tug at his belt, and he chuckles. His hand tangles in my hair as he draws me closer. I rid him of his belt, leaning forward, my mouth licking and nipping at his flesh as I reach my hand inside his pants. My fingers wrap around his hard cock when I suddenly hear voices, making both of us freeze. There is a woman's voice I've heard before and a man's voice that I do not recognize. Raidon's frantic voice also reaches my ears.

"No, stay out here!" he calls, but it is too late. My head turns, and I make eye contact with the woman. Her eyes widen, and her face turns crimson before she spins on her heel, clamping her hand over the strange man's eyes, just as a shriek leaves my lips. I don't know who is more mortified, me or her. Thane grabs me off the counter, shoving me behind him and hiding my exposed body from the people who entered.

"Get out!" Thane's voice booms. I peek around him to see Raidon hurrying them down the hall.

"Raidon, a word," Thane snarls. The venom in his voice has goosebumps lacing my skin. The people disappear, and I hear them move into the living room when Raidon comes back, looking like a frightened mouse.

"What the fuck are they doing here?" Thane demands, his aura flaring out, making my legs go weak under the pressure. His hands grab me, realizing how close I am to him, and his aura instantly drops as he clutches me to his side.

"She invited herself," Raidon replies. "She wasn't supposed to get here so soon," he adds, and I look up at Thane.

"And you didn't think to fucking tell me," Thane snaps.

"I was going to, but you were distracted," he offers, and my face flames. I want to know who they are. That woman's voice is familiar, and her scent reminds me of Raidon's, only weaker.

"Get rid of them. I will not have her fuck everything up. You should have said no," Thane snaps at him, and Raidon sighs, "I can't believe you would be so stupid to agree to such a thing right now," Thane tells him, letting me go.

"I didn't. I told you she invited herself. I was going to tell you."

"Who are they?" I ask, peeking out from behind Thane. Raidon looks at the ceiling, not wanting to respond.

"Answer her. This is your fuck up, so you can be the one to tell her," Thane growls at him, reaching for my shirt and handing it to me. I yank it on and hear Raidon make a noise like he is clearing his throat.

"She came to apologize. She wants to make it up to you."

My brows scrunch together, and Thane kneels, helping me slide my shorts up my legs while I grip his shoulder.

"They're my parents, Harlow," Raidon says as Leon wanders in behind him.

"Rhen is keeping them distracted," Leon says, his eyes darting to me.

She's the woman who wanted me dead. Who told Thane to breed and kill me? My stomach sinks, and my fear perfumes the room.

"I'll get rid of them," Raidon offers, seeing the distress on my face. Thane nods, though I can see Raidon doesn't enjoy the thought of telling his mother no.

"It's fine. Just keep her away from me," I tell him, and he stops.

"Raidon will make them leave, Love. You don't have to see her," Thane tells me, and Leon nods before glaring at Raidon.

"It's fine. I will have to deal with her one day, right?" I ask, looking up at Thane. He leans down, pressing his lips to my head.

"If at any point you want them gone, say the word, and I will make them leave," he tells me before looking at Raidon. "And you, I will deal with later."

Raidon nods his head before wandering back to greet his parents.

I hope I'm not making a huge mistake by seeing her tonight...

Also by Jessica Hall

MY OTHER KINDLE BOOKS

Fated Series
Fated To The Alpha
Fated To The Beta
Cursed To The Alpha
Blessed To The Luna
Her Desired Alphas
Their Desired Luna

Darkness Series
Tempting Darkness
Tasting Darkness
Taming Darkness

Savage Series
Sinful Mates
Sadistic Mates
Sinister mates

Sinister Series

Surviving My Mates

Surrendering To My Mates

Forbidden Love Series

Fated To Them

Fated To Her

Fighting My Demons

Amazon.com: Jessica Hall: books, biography, latest update

AUTHORS I RECCOMEND

AUTHORS SUPPORT AUTHORS

Check out my personal recommendations.

Jane Knight

Want books with an immersive story that sucks you in until you're left wanting more? Queen of spice Jane has got you covered with her mix of paranormal and contemporary romance stories. She's a master of heat, but not all of her characters are nice. They're dark and controlling and not afraid to take their mates over their knees for a good spanking that will leave you just as shaken as the leading ladies. Or if you'd prefer the daddy-dom type, she writes those too just so they can tell you that you are a good girl before growling in your ear.

Her writing is dark and erotic. Her reverse harems will leave you craving more and the kinks will have you wondering if you'll call the safe word or keep going for that happily ever after.

https://www.facebook.com/JaneKnightWrites

Amazon.com: Jane Knight: books, biography, latest update

Club Savage Series
Savage Mates
Savage Hunt
Savage Love
Savage Daughter

Dragon Series
Her Dominant Dragon
Her Trapped Dragon

Moonlight Muse

Looking for a storyline that will have you on the edge of your seat? The spice levels are high, with a plot that will keep you flipping to the next page and ready for book two. You won't be disappointed with Moonlight Muse. Her women are sassy, and her men are possessive alpha-holes with high tensions and tons of steam. She'll draw you into her taboo tales, breaking your heart before she gives you the much deserved Happily Ever After. Dark and twisted, she'll keep you guessing as she pleasurably tortures you with her words, making you ready for the installment.

Amazon.com: Moonlight Muse: books, biography, latest update

The Alpha Series

Her Forbidden Alpha

Her Coldhearted Alpha

Her Destined Alpha

Magic of Kaeladia Series

My Alpha's Betrayal

My Alpha's Retribution

Made in the USA
Coppell, TX
07 December 2023

25528140R00291